THE ROSE OF YORK: LOVE & WAR

The Rose of York

LOVE & WAR

Sandra Worth

END TABLE BOOKS

First edition 2003
Second edition 2006

ISBN 0-9751264-0-7
ISBN-13 978-0-9751264-0-0

This is a work of fiction based on real people and real
events. Details that cannot be historically verified are
the product of the author's imagination.

END TABLE BOOKS
Yarnell, Arizona, USA
Castlemaine, Victoria, Australia

web
www.endtablebooks.com

email
inquiries@endtablebooks.com

Cover image
Lamia by John William Waterhouse
Oil on canvas, 1905

Printed in the United States of America

10 9 8 7 6 5 4

What Reviewers are saying about
THE ROSE OF YORK: LOVE & WAR

"I enjoyed it enormously, partly because I learned so much about life lived in those times—so perilous, so painful, so changeable from moment to moment. I also met in your book a Richard III radically different from the one I have known all these years in Shakespeare's play. It was exciting to get a completely different view of him..." – *Dennis Huston, Ph.D., Rice University Professor of English Literature and 1989 Carnegie Mellon Professor of the Year*

"Expounding an historical epic of honor and love during the time of the Wars of the Roses, *The Rose of York: Love & War* is both dramatic and evocative in its portrayal of struggling souls making the best choices they can in an unjust world. A deftly written, reader engaging, thoroughly entertaining and enthusiastically recommended historical novel that documents its author as a gifted literary talent." – *Small Press BookWatch, Midwest Book Review*

"Sandra Worth has crafted an historical fiction novel that is a true 'classic.' This reader avidly awaits the second novel in The Rose of York series, *CROWN OF DESTINY,* to see what becomes of this hero, Richard '...the flower of men, To serve as model for the mighty world.'" – *Viviane Crystal, Member Reviewers International Organization*

"Worth has done meticulous research... Though conversations and some incidents must of necessity be invented, she makes them seem so real that one agrees this must have been what they said, the way things happened." – *Ricardian Register, Quarterly Publication of the Richard III Society, Inc., Vol. XXIII, No. 2*

"This powerful book, impeccably written, with its tender love story and brilliant analysis of Richard III's legacy, convinced me that Shakespeare completely misjudged this remarkable king who reformed the jury system. Not since *ATLAS SHRUGGED* have I been so deeply moved." – *the honorable Ramona John, Texas author and judge*

"Fascinating." – *Anthony Cheetham, author of* The Life and Times of Richard III

"A beautifully written novel, etched by a masterful storyteller." – *Wendy J. Dunn, author of DEAR HEART, HOW LIKE YOU THIS? Winner of the Arizona Book Publishing Association 2003 Glyph Award for Best Fiction – Adult*

"Love & War is an extraordinary epic... Through Ms. Worth's clean, polished prose, a window is opened (of which the sights and sounds are magnificent) and from it flow the voices of the anguished and the proud, the glorious and the damned, the just and the unjust. Perhaps the highest compliment I can pay Ms. Worth, however, is my keen desire to learn more about Richard III, his perils and triumphs, sorrows, and regrets. This first book in Ms. Worth's Rose of York series, in fact, deserves a wealth of accolades for its very ambitious nature, and its balanced exploration of Richard, Duke of Gloucester, before he became king of a troubled kingdom." – *C.L. Jeffries, Heartstrings, romanticfiction.tripod.reviews.com*

"Great writing coupled with an amazing story propelled this book into the Perfect 10 category." – *Jani Brooks, romancereviewstoday.com*

"Sandra Worth has an extraordinary achievement in her characterization of Richard. Reading it, I had the feeling of a living being whose mind I can touch... *The Rose of York: Love & War* deservedly won the Authorlink Grand Prize in manuscript form." – *Joy Calderwood, theindependentreviewsite.org*

"The reader will feel, as I did, that surely they can put the book down after the next chapter ends—but that won't be the case. They'll become so entrenched in the drama that time will catch them unawares." Overall rating: Five Hearts – *theromancestudio.com*

"This account of war, political intrigue, reversals of fortune, difficult choices, and death is interlaced with the romantic love story of Richard (Plantagenet) and Anne Neville, daughter of Warwick the Kingmaker. Sandra Worth presents these historical figures in a compelling and believable manner. This is one historical novel that will keep you entranced until the very end. Then you won't be able to wait for the second book." Guide Rating: Five Stars – *About.com*

The Rose of York: Love & War is the winner of eight awards and prizes in Florida, Georgia, Texas and Arizona, including the Arizona Book Publishing Association's 2005 GLYPH AWARD for Best Fiction – General.

More and current information is available
at the author's web site: **www.sandraworth.com**

FOREWORD

by Roxane C. Murph

The Wars of the Roses, the fifteenth century dynastic conflict between the houses of Lancaster and York for the crown of England, had its origin in 1399. In that year, John of Gaunt's eldest son, Henry of Bolingbroke, who had been exiled by his cousin Richard II, returned to England with an army. Claiming that he had returned only to reclaim his inheritance, he gained the support of many of the English against the unpopular king and his hated favorites, and he succeeded in seizing the throne, and eventually had Richard murdered. The former king's heir apparent, the young Roger Mortimer, was thus deprived of his rights, and for more than fifty years the Lancastrians, in the persons of Henry IV, Henry V, and Henry VI, held the throne in relative peace.

The reign of Henry VI, who suffered frequent bouts of madness, became markedly more troubled after his marriage to Marguerite d'Anjou. She dominated both king and court, and was bitterly opposed to the Duke of York, Mortimer's heir, who had a better claim to the throne than Henry. In the 1450s, when the enmity of the queen and her favorites began to pose real danger to the Yorkists, the duke, in company with his cousin the earl of Warwick, rebelled, and in October, 1460, after five years of sometimes-open hostilities, York laid claim to the throne. In December of that year he was killed at the Battle of Wakefield, and his eldest son was successful in claiming the throne as Edward IV.

Virtually all the figures of the period, both major and minor, have attracted the interest of historians and writers of fiction, but none so much as Richard III, the last Plantagenet king. He has aroused the greatest passions, both for and against him. Beginning with Sir Thomas More, through the Tudor chronicles of Hall, Holinshed, and others, Richard III was portrayed as a murderous, deformed monster who clawed his way to the throne over the bodies of Henry VI and his son, his own brothers, and his two nephews. The most vivid of all these portraits came from Shakespeare, whose depiction of the king stamped itself on the consciousness of all future generations.

This view, however, did not go unchallenged. In the seventeenth century, George Buck and William Cornwallis published defenses of Richard III, as did Horace Walpole in the eighteenth century. In the nineteenth century, Sharon Turner, John Heneage Jesse, Caroline Halstead, and others also come to Richard's defense, but the most spirited challenge to the so-called Tudor myth came in the twentieth century, with both historians and writers of fiction joining the fray. Probably the most influential of the king's defenders were historian Paul Murray Kendal, whose *Richard the Third* and other books on the Yorkist period viewed him in a sympathetic light, and Josephine Tey, whose novel *The Daughter of Time* vigorously challenged the traditional view. The Richard III Society, founded in England in 1924 to educate people about the king's life and times, now has chapters in many countries, and has been responsible for much of the increased interest in the subject.

As interest in Richard III has grown, so has the number of books written about him, both fiction and nonfiction. Although some historians, such as Alison Weir and Desmond Seward, cling to the old stereotype, most historians have generally taken a more balanced view, but the greatest change can be seen in the many novels written by his partisans. Although some novels still portray him as Shakespeare's monster, the great majority of those written in the past thirty or forty years are much more sympathetic, portraying Richard as a human being who lived through troubled times, showing great courage, devotion, and occasional faulty judgment, while attempting, usually successfully, to live up to his motto, *Loyaulte me lie*, Loyalty binds me. *Love & War*, the first novel in *The Rose of York* trilogy, is a worthy addition to this growing body of work.

Roxane C. Murph is an independent researcher and freelance writer in fifteenth century English history and the Wars of the Roses. A former Chairman of the U.S. Richard III Society, she is the author of The Wars of the Roses in Fiction: An Annotated Bibliography, 1440-1994, *Greenwood Press, Westport, Conn., 1995, and* Richard III: The Making of a Legend, *Scarecrow Press, Metuchen, N.J., 1977, reprinted 1984.*

In a tumultuous era marked by peril and intrigue, reversals of fortune and violent death, the passions of a few rule the destiny of England and change the course of history...

Richard: Alone in a dangerous world, he is an orphan who has known exile, loss, tragedy, and betrayal. When at last he finds love, his loyalty is first challenged by war, then by the ambitions of a scheming queen. Time and again he must choose between those he loves until—in the end—he is left no choice at all.

Edward: A golden warrior-king, reckless, wanton, he can have any woman he wants, but he wants the only one he can't have. When he marries her secretly and makes her his queen, he dooms himself and all whom he loves.

Bess: Edward's detested and ambitious queen. Gilt-haired, cunning, and vindictive, she has a heart as dark as her face is fair.

George: Richard's brother. Handsome, charming, and consumed with hatred and greed, he will do anything it takes to get everything he wants.

Warwick the Kingmaker: Richard's famed cousin, maker and destroyer of kings. More powerful and richer than King Edward himself, he attracts the jealousy of the queen and seals his fate.

Anne: The Kingmaker's beautiful daughter. She is Richard's only love, his light, his life...

John: The Kingmaker's brother. Valiant and honourable, he is Richard's beloved kinsman and Edward's truest subject, but when the queen whispers in the king's ear, he is forced to confront what no man should have to face.

The Houses of York, Lancaster and Neville, 1399 to 1465

EDWARD III

Black Prince

RICHARD II

Lionel, Duke of Clarence

Anne Mortimer === *m* === Richard, Earl of Cambridge

Richard, Duke of York

Edmund*, Duke of York

Ralf Neville, Earl of Westmoreland === *m* === Joan Beaufort

Cecily Neville === *m* === Richard, Duke of York

John of Gaunt*, Duke of Lancaster

HENRY IV

HENRY V

HENRY VI === *m* === Marguerite d'Anjou

Thomas, Duke of Gloucester

Henry Stafford, Duke of Buckingham

Richard, Earl of Salisbury

Richard Neville, Earl of Warwick

Isabelle   Anne

John Neville, Lord Montagu

issue

George Neville, Archbishop of York

Thomas Neville

Anne, Duchess of Exeter

EDWARD IV

Edmund, Earl of Rutland

Elizabeth (Liza), D. of Suffolk

Margaret, D. of Burgundy

George, D. of Clarence

Richard, D. of Gloucester

Edouard, Prince of Wales

* For simplification of this chart, John and Edmund are shown as if they have traded birth order. Broken lines denote a missing generation.

ACKNOWLEDGEMENTS

First and foremost, my thanks go to my publisher who accepted this book in August 2003 and, undaunted by the Herculean task of a three-month turnaround necessitated by the unusual circumstances of this book, made the impossible happen in November. I also extend heartfelt appreciation to those special people—many of them strangers—who went out of their way to help turn a false start into a good outcome. They know who they are. No acknowledgement would be complete without thanks to members of the Richard III Society for their support and friendship, particularly Dale Summers, Myrna Smith, and Roxane Murph who wrote the foreword of this book at short notice, as well as P.W. Hammond who granted me an interview in London, and the Yorkshire branch of the Society, which includes John Audsley, the late Anne-Denise Worsnop, and Moira Habberjam who, eight years ago, welcomed a complete stranger from the U.S. into her home to tour the Ricardian North. I also wish to thank the ever-helpful staff of the British Library and the Manuscripts Room, as well as the staff of the university libraries of Berkeley, Boston College, Harvard, Houston, Rice, Stanford, Texas and Toronto. Others who contributed in a significant way to this effort are my agent Irene Kraas, my family (especially my lovely daughter Erica Harris who helped in so many ways), and my friend Dr. Dolores Drysdale, who for years insisted I could write. This book owes an enormous debt to my friends Hazel Bankston, Professor Dagobert Brito, author Beth Clegg, author Wendy Dunn, Ann Elliott, Florence Graving, the hon. Judge Ramona John, Garretta Lamore, Dick Lemmon, Dr. Barbara Low, Nicole de Roumefort, Linda Shuler, Dale Summers, Mary Tilley, Beatrice Villiger, Susan Winston, and Wendy Zollo, all of whom have stood by me with unfailing encouragement and support throughout its long birthing.

Live pure, speak true, right wrong, follow the King—
Else, wherefore born?

—*Idylls of the King*, Alfred, Lord Tennyson

For the whole earth is the sepulchre of famous men;
and their story is not graven only on stone
over their native land,
but lives on far away without visible symbol,
woven into the stuff of other men's lives.

—Thucydides

PROLOGUE

Caen Castle, 1470

"I won't!" Anne cried. "I won't wed him, Mother!"

"What's this?" demanded a harsh voice behind her.

Anne whirled around. Her father stood at the threshold of her bedchamber.

"She says she'll not wed Prince Edouard, my lord husband. I can't make her see reason…"

Warwick's expression hardened. He entered with long, angry strides, stopping in front of her. "Are you mad, girl? Do you not comprehend? I have arranged a marriage for you with a *prince*. A future king!"

"I wish no marriage, my lord father," entreated Anne. "I don't love him. I love Richard."

"What has love to do with marriage?" he thundered. "King Edward married for love; 'tis the reason we are here! Had he done his duty, we would not have been exiled, deprived of all we hold dear. I see now that we've indulged you, you insolent little fool. God's blood, but you shall marry. You shall do your duty!"

"I wish to be a nun, Father. Let me take the veil, dear Father…"

"A nun? *A nun?* You choose to be a nun instead of a queen, you unworthy wretch?" He took a threatening step towards her.

Anne gathered her shift around her and backed away. "I'll not wed! I don't love him!"

"You shall be Queen of England one day! Are you not proud? Do you not count yourself blessed?" Warwick blustered, reddening. A vein throbbed in his temple. "Is this our thanks?"

"Father, I beseech you on my knees!" pleaded Anne. "Don't make me do this."

"You will do it, or by God, I'll have no more to do with you!"

"Let me take the veil," she sobbed. "I pray you, Father…"

"You'll do as I say or I'll throw you into the streets, you disobedient wench!" He stepped forward, raising his hand to strike her. Anne shrank against the wall, trembling. She didn't know this glowering, fuming stranger. The father she'd known could never have hit her. She shielded her face, braced herself for the blow.

The Countess threw herself between them. "Nay, my lord! Let it lie. She'll come to her senses, I promise you. She's a good child. She'll do what she must. She'll wed him."

"She will indeed, or I'll turn her out," he raged. "You can beg, die, hang, starve in the streets, for on my soul, you'll not see my face again! I'll have nothing to do with you. I have given my word to King Louis, and I'll not go back on it. By God, you shall marry Edouard!"

CHAPTER ONE

"Turn, Fortune, turn thy wheel…"

The messenger tore through the night. The desolate, snowy streets of London posed little danger in the comforting dark, but at Tower Bridge he reined in his nervous mount. Torches flared along the bridge, casting lurid shadows on the traitors' heads lining the poles. They leered at him with mocking grins as snowflakes melted into their empty eye-sockets and rotting flesh, pervading the eerie night with menace. He calmed his horse and braced himself. Cautiously, he trotted past the chilling sight, averting his face from the light. The sound of lapping water drew his attention to the inky river below where a boat was bearing a prisoner to the Tower. The man's chains glittered a warning as he passed beneath the bridge and the water-gate screeched open to receive him. The messenger wondered if it was someone he knew, and shuddered.

Once over the bridge and safe again in the shadows of the night, he spurred his mount. Minutes later, at a stately stone mansion on the Thames, he gave the password and gained hasty entry. Racing up the steps, he was surprised to find himself face to face, not with the captain he'd come to seek, but with the Commander of the Yorkist army who was said to be fighting in the Midlands, the mighty lord known to all England as *Kingmaker*. He fell to his knees and delivered his fearful tidings.

The Kingmaker paled. Barking orders, he grabbed his cloak and made for his horse, his retinue in hot pursuit. Together they galloped along the deserted streets and drew up before a gabled home set behind a wall.

"Who goes there?" demanded a guard.

"*The Kingmaker*, Richard Neville, Earl of Warwick."

"Password?"

"White Rose Vanquishes Red."

"Enter!" The gate was thrust open.

The small courtyard filled with the shouts of men and the neighing of horses. Two young faces, one blond, one dark, appeared at the window above the entry, noses pressed against the glass. The boys' eyes widened when they saw the Kingmaker. He entered the house, and the faces disappeared from the window.

~*~

"It's Cousin Warwick, Dickon!" exclaimed the older boy.

Richard choked back a cry. Their cousin, Richard Neville, Earl of Warwick, had fled London months ago. If the Lancastrians caught him, he'd lose his head. No doubt he'd be chopped into pieces first, as traitors always were unless their sentences were commuted. *She* would never commute Warwick's sentence. *She* was England's Queen, the savage Marguerite d'Anjou, and she was very angry with their cousin Warwick, maybe because he had called her the *Bitch of Anjou*. He wasn't sure what a bitch was, but Nurse had scolded him when he'd asked and told him he must never use the word himself.

"Isn't London dangerous for him?" he asked breathlessly. "Father said that London's for Queen Marguerite—even if she is away in the North. Do you think Cousin Warwick lost the battle, George?"

"Worse than that, Dickon, or he wouldn't have come himself," his brother replied.

Richard took tight hold of George's hand as they cracked the door open. With his ten-year-old brother leading the way, he stole along the corridor that was decorated with greenery for Yuletide, tip-toeing carefully on the creaky floor. Voices drifted up from the hall downstairs: a man's nasal tone, sounding alarmed, insistent; and a woman's softer cadence, anxious and pleading. His mother? But that wasn't possible! His mother was a Neville, proud and fearless—she never raised her voice, never

17

implored anyone for anything. She gave commands calmly, like the queen she would be when his father won the throne from Marguerite's husband, mad Henry of Lancaster.

They halted at the staircase. The man's voice had risen in volume and grown heated.

"No one would do such a thing, I assure you—'tis preposterous. They are only six and ten. My gracious aunt Cecily, even this wretched queen wouldn't harm such young children!" A pause. "In any case, I came only to bring you the news, sore tidings though they be. Now time grows short and I myself must leave with all haste."

"You cannot go without them!"

"I must. They'll slow us down."

"You didn't see Marguerite at Ludlow—she's capable of anything! In God's name, has she not proven it to you with this dreadful deed? Oh, my beloved lord husband... my sweet Edmund..." Her voice broke.

Richard and George exchanged glances. What could have happened? They descended the steps. Richard gasped and grabbed the pillar for support. He had never seen his mother this way. Not even at Ludlow when they'd been captured by Queen Marguerite's troops. She stood in the centre of the torch-lit room, surrounded by Warwick's men, clinging to his velvet doublet. Her blue eyes held a wild expression and her golden hair hung dishevelled around her shoulders.

"You must take them, fair nephew. You *must.* They may be babes, but they're brave—they'll ride hard. They won't slow you down, I swear it! They'll die unless you take them with you. She'll murder them as she did their father and Edmund at York."

Now Richard and George understood the awful truth. Richard let out a wail. George ran down the stairs. "Let me at her!" he yelled. "I'll burn her at the stake, the stinking witch. I'll rip her entrails out. Let me at her. I'll send her to Hell!"

For a moment, everyone stared at them. Then George, kicking furiously, was restrained by Warwick's henchmen. Eyes turned to little Richard on the staircase, gripping the pillar mutely with both hands, ashen pale and vibrating like a plucked harp string.

"Richard," said his mother softly.

From somewhere in the shadows, his nurse materialised. She sank down on the step beside him and gathered him to her. "Come, my sweet little lord... Come, my dear one..."

Richard didn't hear. He didn't feel her arms around him. He felt only the cold, and the fear, and the only thought he had was that he mustn't cry. Nurse had said that men didn't cry, and he knew his father had expected him to be a man.

"*Ludlow*," Cecily breathed. "That's how he was at Ludlow." She turned desperate eyes on her nephew. "You weren't at Ludlow, nephew. What Marguerite did there was Devil's work. And what she has done at York has changed the world forever." She lowered herself to her knees, clasped her hands together and looked up at him beseechingly. "I humble myself to you, my Lord of Warwick."

A shocked gasp went around the room to see England's true queen kneel at Warwick's feet. Even Warwick seemed stunned. He stared at her a long moment. Then he gave a tense nod.

"Make haste, then. We've no time to lose. She's closing in on London even as we speak."

~*~

Richard stood in the courtyard, unable to stop his teeth from chattering. He didn't know what was happening. Men were shouting, running to and fro, bringing horses from the stables and swords from the armoury. Torches flared in the blackness, and the courtyard smelled of smoke and manure. Some of the horses were frightened, too, for they neighed wildly and reared up on their haunches.

Richard shivered. He was so cold. He felt Galahad's soft head nuzzle him from behind, as if to tell him it would be all right. All at once strong arms lifted him up high in the air and dropped him roughly into the saddle. He wanted to cry.

"What's the matter with you?" Warwick's harsh voice pierced his consciousness. "Be a man, you snivelling coward!" Galahad's reins were forced into his hands.

Richard didn't want to be a coward. He wanted to be like his brothers, brave and bold and strong. Especially his oldest brother, Edward, to whom Galahad belonged. He bit back his tears.

"Can you ride like a man, or must we carry you like a babe?" demanded his cousin.

"I can ride," Richard managed, hugging Galahad's belly closer with his trembling knees and forcing himself to meet his cousin's eyes. Galahad was his friend. Galahad would help him ride. A groom hastily adjusted the stirrups and placed his feet into them.

"But I need my lute," Richard said, trying not to whimper. "I can't ride without my lute." He chewed his lip to make it stop quivering.

"God's Blood, someone get him his damned lute!" Warwick yelled.

His nurse disappeared into the amber light flowing through the open doorway and ran out with his instrument. One of Warwick's men strapped it tightly to his saddle.

"*There!*" said Warwick, and gave Galahad a smack. on the rump.

Galahad leapt forward.

~*~

My father is dead.

Panic gripped Richard anew, sending his heart pounding with terror. He bent low in the saddle and spurred Galahad with desperate urgency. The black night reverberated with the thunder of fleeing horse hoofs, all pounding the same message: His father was dead. His brother, Edmund, too. Now *they* were coming for him.

It isn't fair, he thought, choking back a sob. *They* were the ones who had stolen the throne. *They* were the ones killing people and burning the land. His father was the rightful heir to the crown, not Henry of Lancaster! His father would have set things right. But his father was dead, and his brother Edmund slain as he made for Sanctuary. The Lancastrians had won.

It isn't fair!

The frigid December wind whistled past, drying his tears, stinging his cheeks, whipping his hair. He could feel Galahad's lathered belly burning and heaving for breath. Richard bent low in the saddle to make it easier on him and caught a wave of spume in his eyes. Poor Galahad. He released the pressure of his spurs on his flank and pulled on the bit to ease their pace. The road glistened in the light snow. They twisted around a corner and galloped between two dark hedgerows. He thought of his mother and gave a shiver. He wore no hat or gloves and his ear lobes were numb, his knuckles raw, near frozen. But it wasn't the cold that chilled him. It was his mother's loss of composure. He didn't really understand the struggles between York and Lancaster for the throne of England, but he knew that the way his father had died had changed the rules.

"Make haste, Dickon," Warwick shouted, his voice ringing out of the darkness ahead. "*She's* not far behind, I warrant."

Richard didn't want to hurt Galahad by digging in his spurs, but it wouldn't be good for Galahad, either, if the Queen caught him. Nurse had said that the queen would chop him up and feed him to her hounds because he was a Yorkist horse.

Galahad plunged ahead. Richard whipped his head around to steal a terrified glance behind him. There was no sign of the queen, only a sea of bobbing torches and his cousin's bodyguard of eighty strong in their jackets of Neville scarlet bearing Warwick's badge of the Bear and Ragged Staff, their taut faces illuminated in the flames, their breath frosting the night.

Only when he was neck-to-neck with George did Richard dare slow Galahad again. He always felt better with George. George had all the answers and knew no fear.

"Will we make it, George?" Richard rasped, nearly choking on splatters of frozen mud kicked up by the horse's galloping hoofs.

"To Sandwich, aye…"

"And Burgundy?"

"Depends," George panted, "on our cousin Warwick."

CHAPTER TWO

"Descending thro' the dismal night—a night
In which the bounds of Heaven and earth were lost…"

The storm struck without warning.

In the bow below the high deck and still higher forecastle of Warwick's *Grace a Dieu*, where he and George had been ordered to stay, Richard huddled between a chest nailed to the floor and a barrel of wine lashed to the wall. No one had told him, but he knew with sudden clarity, that dragons lived in the sea, and they'd all risen at once, thousands of them, to churn the waters up from the depths and drown the sky. He clutched the iron latch tight and dug his fingernails into his palm to keep himself from screaming. His stomach heaved one way and his head another, and terror pumped his heart so hard it banged in his chest like a wild bird caged. Nor did it help that the air was foul and smelled of tar, sewage and sweat. He wanted to retch. He wanted Nurse to hold him and comfort him. He wanted to shriek and kick the walls as Galahad was doing in his corner stall nearby, and like the other horses at the stern of the vessel. But if he did, George would never let him hear the end of it. He held his breath and bit down until his teeth hurt. How he admired George! Even storms and dragons couldn't frighten him. He had tied himself to the port railing with a strong hemp rope, which let him move around without danger of being swept overboard, so that he could watch the churning sea. Gripping a timber post, he peered out through slits in the gilded trelliswork that decorated the bowsprit on the port and starboard sides.

"Holy Saint Michael and the Angels!" cried George, throwing Richard a glance as he cowered in the shadow of the lantern that swayed from a beam in the ceiling. "The seas are white, Dickon—*white!* White as the milk Nurse makes us drink." Even in the dim light, Richard could see the wonder in his eyes. He couldn't be sure, but he didn't think a white sea was a good sign. Seas were not supposed to be white.

"Are we going to sink, George?"

"The *Grace a Dieu* can't sink, you dullard! Look at all the decks it has, and all the carvings."

"Really?"

"Dickon, don't you know anything? Cousin Warwick never takes half measures. This is the best ship in the world—and the biggest. A hundred feet long, for Christ sake, with three masts instead of two, and sides five feet thick, and sails of the most costly Genoa linen gold can…"

A great wave cut George off. Water crashed over the poop with the sound of a cannon shot and the main mast almost drove into the sea. Barrels and ballast down in the hold slammed into one another and everything not secured above the hatches—barrels, ropes, pulleys, canvas, and chests—was swept overboard. Galahad tried to escape, shrieking and snorting, rearing and plunging against the chest board of his stall. Water spouted down through the floor planks of the bowsprit above Richard's head like dozens of fountains. He sputtered for breath and dug deeper between the barrel and the coffer. Men were shouting, slipping and sliding, saved from the sea only by the ropes tied around their waists. Slowly, the ship righted itself.

"All hands on deck!" shouted Warwick, his voice faint above the roar of the water. "Shorten topsail! Lower the main yard! Haul up buntlines!" He stood on the poop, leaning against the wind, his cloak flapping in the squall.

As men at the clew lines battled to drop the thundering canvas to the yards, one wrestled with the rope ladder, fighting for every step. The sudden tempest had given them no time to prepare the ship, and now the wind battered the sails with ear-shattering force, threatening to shred the sails of Neville scarlet. Every man's gaze, like Richard's own, was fixed on the man climbing the ladder. Up, up he went, the small unsteady figure, inching his way along the weaving ratlines like an ant on a too-slender reed.

He lost his foothold. A gasp went around the ship. For an agonising moment he dangled by one hand. Then he plunged to his death with a bone-chilling scream. His body thudded on the deck.

A silence fell that even the storm seemed to respect, for the winds quieted and the ship steadied. A second man appeared on the ratlines. With the same heart-stopping anguish, Richard and the ship's crew watched his every laboured move. Smiles eased their taut faces when he reached the topsail, but as he struggled with a stay, a corner of the canvas came loose and struck his chest. He lost his balance, then fell headlong into the black void, his shriek of terror reverberating in the night.

Another wave submerged the ship. The stern rose with a queer lurch and the bow plunged into a chasm, sending men sprawling. Richard saw the white sea looming above them high as a castle wall, then the tip curled like some monstrous tongue and hung there as if to savour the taste before devouring them. It broke over the ship. A hideous groan rumbled through the vessel and it shuddered. The mizzenmast crashed down.

Warwick's frantic orders to the helmsman drifted through

the roar. "Helm hard a' port! More hands! He cannot put up the helm!"

No one answered his call. "It's no use!" someone cried. "We're going to die!" Voices rose in prayer. "God the Father of all mercies…"

Warwick ran down the poop ladder, grabbed a kneeling man by his collar and pulled him from the rail to which he clung. "Is that what you want? To die?" he shouted. "By the fiend, you will, unless you do as I say!" He flung him back, grasped another by a fistful of shirt. "You have a wife and children, Summers. They'll starve without you! Do you not care?" He thrust him aside and seized the next. Richard's heart gave a twist. The lanky fair-haired boy reminded him of his dead brother, Edmund. "And you, Bankston, what about that bonnie lass you claim to love? Is she not worth living for?" He looked around at the eyes fixed on him. "Where's your courage, you gutless milksops? Do you see me wailing and sobbing? We've survived worse! Follow my orders and live! Each man to his place. We haven't failed until we give up."

"But two are dead!" a mate cried. "Unless we shorten sail, we'll sink, sure as fish swim!"

"I'll not ask you to do what I won't do myself!" yelled Warwick, tearing off his cloak.

Before men could stop him, he was climbing the ratlines. The wind whipped him. He lost his footing once, but he recovered. Lightning flashed, thunder shook the skies, and still he climbed. Some crossed themselves and said prayers while clutching rope lines and cables; others stood hugging the rails, slack-jawed with awe as he undid the stays, first one, then another. He gathered up the wildly beating scarlet canvas and furled it tightly together.

It was done.

A mad cheer went up. The men ran to their stations; buckets were passed down into the hold, filled, brought up, and emptied.

Another struggling line of men tripped and stumbled as they secured the rope, staggering across the rolling deck, but now smiles lit their gaunt, hollow-eyed faces.

Richard left his wedge, crawled to Galahad, and received a welcoming whinny for his troubles. Now that the ship had eased its savage lurching and it was steadier below, Galahad's belly wasn't heaving as much. Richard reached between the wood fencing of the stall and stroked his neck.

"We're going to be all right, Galahad," he whispered, scratching the white blaze around his forehead that gave him a look of wonderment before moving to one of his honey brown ears in the way Galahad loved. "You don't have to be afraid anymore. Cousin Warwick has saved us." Galahad batted long gold eyelashes and nuzzled him. Richard could smell the steamy warmth of his body. He rested his head on Galahad's cheek, remembering the many times he'd stolen into the castle stables seeking his friend's companionship during the civil war between his father and the wicked queen. He was glad now to give Galahad back some of the comfort Galahad had so often given him. "You're a brave horse," Richard said, "and if Edward wins the throne, I promise I'll have his archbishop bless you."

"What good will that do?" demanded George, who had sat down to rest now that the great excitement was over.

Richard flushed. He had forgotten to keep his voice down. "He'll be a better horse. And he'll get into Heaven when he dies." He hoped that was a good reason. The truth was, he didn't really have one. He just thought it would be nice for Galahad to be blessed by an archbishop.

"You witless dunce, a horse can't…"

The seas broke over the ship again and the vessel gave a violent roll. Frantic with fright, Galahad reared. He kicked at the wood of his stall. A sharp snapping sound ripped through the small cabin as it cracked. He charged again and it gave way. He bolted out. The long leather strap that leashed him to a timber post yanked him back momentarily, but he reared again and the strap unravelled. He plunged out across the gangway onto the main deck.

"No, Galahad!" Richard screamed, running after him. "Come back, come back!"

With all his might, Richard jumped for the leather strap dragging behind Galahad. He landed on the gangplank with a bruising thump, caught the end of it, and pulled hard to slow Galahad, but he might as well have been a plume in the wind, for Galahad, oblivious, dragged him out onto the deck.

A gigantic wall of water crashed over the ship. Galahad lost his footing, went sliding across the deck, shrieking fiercely, and Richard followed, clinging to his strap, screaming *Galahad!* but his cries were blown from his lips by the wind that bore Galahad's shrieks to him. He felt its icy blast in his face, the sting of the water like hot stones against his flesh, then water gushed into his nose, knocking the breath from his lungs and sweeping him away. He surfaced once, caught sight of the foaming sea, and knew he was going overboard. As he headed at breakneck speed for the side, something slammed into him. The stunning pain in his body forced his fists open and Galahad's strap slipped out of his hand. It was something solid, curving, with a waist like an hourglass. He closed his arms around it and clung for his life as the ship pitched again.

The water receded and he saw that it was the capstan that had broken his fall. There was no sign of Galahad. The icy water lashed at him, loosening his grip as the ship heaved. He stared at the white-streaked seas yawning below, and screamed, loud and long. The ship rolled again, threatening to shake him into the depths, and he would have been swept away in the next wave, had it not been for Warwick.

Warwick was descending the ratlines when Galahad burst from below. He saw what was happening, understood there was only a slim chance to save Richard from certain death, and knew that if he took that chance, it might well cost him his own life. In the span of a single falling grain of sand, he made his decision. He grabbed the end of a dangling rope, swung from the ratlines to the capstan, reached down and snatched Richard up by the arm. The ship rolled again and the rope swung out over the sea. With the great lantern on the ship's stern burning fiercely in the darkness, they hung over the surging waves while the wind whipped at them and the rain hammered. Then the ship rolled back on another wave and they moved over the planking of the aftercastle. Hands reached up, seized them, and pulled them down.

As if Galahad's life had appeased the dragons of the sea, the storm then subsided and the ship steadied. Warwick himself carried Richard below into the cabin and made sure he was secure.

"That was a damn foolhardy thing you did, Dickon," he said, not unkindly.

Richard bowed his head so Warwick wouldn't see how his lip trembled. For, all at once, he felt overcome with grief and despair. His father and Edmund were gone. Now, Galahad, too. He would never hear his whinny of greeting again; never feel his warm breath on his cheek. A choking sensation tightened his throat. He wanted to cry, but he didn't. He had to be strong, as his father would have wished.

"May I play my lute?" he asked, not looking up lest brave Warwick should see the cowardly tears in his eyes.

Warwick snapped back the heavy brass locks on the coffer behind him, opened the lid, and took out the lute.

"The men would like that," Warwick said.

Hugging his lute to his breast, Richard strummed the chords, sending a soft ripple of song into the harsh night, for Galahad.

~*~

Bruges was an alien place. Richard wanted to go home more than he'd ever wanted anything in his life. Sometimes the longing was so acute, it churned in his stomach like a hunk of sour cheese. He felt guilty. He didn't mean to be ungrateful. A rich English merchant with ink-stained fingers by the name of William Caxton had taken them into his home, and Duke Philip the Good of Burgundy had shown them around his palace, which was filled with wondrous marvels. George had enjoyed it greatly, but a bare castle in England would have made Richard happier. He was lonely in Bruges. He missed his sister Meg, and Nurse, and his mother, but most of all, his brother Edward, who had stayed behind to fight Henry of Lancaster's fearful queen, Marguerite. He didn't think he could bear it if Edward died, too.

Richard pushed his Latin assignment away, leaned his chin on his arm, and gazed out the window. Snow was falling, and along the canals that ran through the city by the score, people were rushing by, bent against the wind. He yearned for the curving Thames, which was wide, and blue, and lined with shiny pebbles that could be collected by wading in a short distance when the tide went out. Canals didn't have tides.

Twit-whoo, twit-whoo!

Richard gave a shiver. "George," he whispered. "George, an owl just whooped."

"I know," replied George, who was busy examining his outfit in the mirror, a gift from Philip the Good.

"But it's only noon. Does that mean woe? Does it mean Marguerite has killed Edward?"

George arranged his green velvet hat on his golden curls at a jaunty angle, adjusted the black feather, and looked at him. "Dickon, you worry too much. Remember last night, when you saw a star fall from the sky? You thought it meant the death of one we loved, but you were wrong, weren't you?"

"Aye," Richard said with relief. "You said it means a *foe* falls, not a loved one."

"And this owl in daytime comes to bring us tidings of joy." He came to Richard's side, rested a gentle hand on his shoulder, and leaned close. "I daresay, Dickon, victory bells are about to peal for us."

"Victory?" Richard's heart almost leapt out of his breast. "That means we're going home, doesn't it, George?"

"Aye. How about a game of butts?" George said, picking up his archery set, a Yuletide gift from Caxton.

Richard regarded him uncertainly. How could George be so casual about such wonderful news? It didn't make sense, unless he had just made it up. George sometimes did that, thinking to cheer him. He felt suddenly wretched. He shook his head and watched George leave for the courtyard, his bow slung over his shoulder. A moment later, there was a shout of glee. An arrow must have hit its mark.

How he wished he had George's light heart. Nothing ever seemed to bother him, when all he himself could do was worry. How went the war for the Yorkists? Was his brother Edward safe or had he been killed like Edmund? Warwick—how did he fare? What would become of him and George if Edward and Warwick were dead? They'd be alone in the world then, without money or means. Would Caxton keep them, or would they be thrown into the streets to fend for themselves like the ragged orphans he saw begging their bread in the depth of winter? Worse, would he and George be handed over to Henry of Lancaster's savage queen?

His breath caught in his throat. Without Edward, they were lost. Edward was everything, all that stood between them and the horrors of Lancaster. Edward was their last hope. O, Edward…

Pray God his brother still lived!

With a trembling hand, he drew his Latin book close and bent his head to memorise the Latin verse his tutor had assigned for the afternoon.

~*~

Easter came and went. Richard found solace in his lute and the missives that came from England. His mother had written that Edward had won a battle at Mortimer's Cross early in February, but his sister Meg wrote days later that Warwick had lost one near St. Alban's. Warwick's own captain, Trollope, who had turned traitor at Ludlow, had led the Lancastrians against him and, in defiance of both honour and convention, had attacked at night, catching Warwick by surprise and routing his army. The Queen's seven-year-old son, Edouard, in a suit of golden armour covered with purple velvet, had judged the captives and watched their executions.

Thankfully, better news followed. Before the month of February was out, Edward had entered London to cheering crowds and was proclaimed King. The last Richard had heard, in early March, both York and Lancaster were recruiting large numbers of men. Edward himself had written this time. There would soon be another battle, he said, and Richard should pray for him. Edward had added a postscript. He'd put a high price on Trollope's head, and no doubt the ravens would be dining well shortly.

Richard laid aside his lute. That was Edward. Always trying to make him laugh, even when matters were at their worst. He hugged his knees and swallowed hard. There had been no word since. Nothing. The battle must have been fought by now. What if York had lost? He screwed his eyes tight and began a prayer.

"My lord..."

Richard jerked up his head. Edward Brampton, his brother's trusted man-at-arms, who had fled London with him that awful Yuletide months ago, stood at the door. Brampton's face was pale and very grave. Richard's heart began to pound.

"My lord, you are wanted in the Hall. A messenger has arrived. There is news from England."

CHAPTER THREE

"And Arthur yet had done no deeds of arms,
But heard the call and came."

In the tender spring of 1462, amid the dust of falling pebbles, as sheep bleated gently and church bells rang the hour of Sext, nine-year-old Richard ascended the steep slope to Middleham Castle's east gate. His cavalcade of knights followed, horse hoofs clattering and harness bells jingling. For three hundred years this northern castle, which the Earl of Warwick favoured above his many others, had dominated the rolling hills and meadows of Wensleydale. Richard had expected an imposing grey fortress, not the pearly jewel-box framed against the azure sky, and he stared, as wonderstruck as when he first crossed the River Trent.

His journey from London had unfolded a North that was like a song. There was music in the rustle of aspen leaves, the rushing of rivers, the thundering of waterfalls. Winds swept the endless moors and dales with a loud roaring in the ears, bending low wildflowers, heather and flowering may. Even birds sang a fiercer note in the North and wheeled with wilder freedom.

He drew a deep breath and inhaled the scented air of May. He had feared leaving London, for London was familiar and safe, but now he didn't care to see London ever again with its crowded streets and evil smells. As his brother Edward had said—King Edward the Fourth (he would never get used to thinking of him as *King*)—Middleham Castle lay in the loveliest part of England, Wensleydale: the heart of North Yorkshire near the Rivers Ure and Cover.

Richard squinted expectantly into the sun. Pennants fluttered from the turrets but Warwick's Bear and Ragged Staff was merely a splash of scarlet and gold in the distance. His herald galloped ahead to trumpet his approach. In spite of his excitement he was seized with fright. What if he disappointed his cousin? He held no hint of another Edward, and Warwick would be shocked at how little he'd grown since Burgundy. To worsen matters, a spring shower had soiled his grey velvet doublet and his boots were caked with mud from the journey. He looked like a stray cat.

Richard flushed with shame, remembering how disgusted Warwick had been with him on that night two years ago when they'd fled for Burgundy. *A snivelling coward,* he'd called him. Warwick was right. Only cowards were afraid, and since Ludlow and the storm at sea, his own shadow could send him trembling like custard pudding. He hated being afraid. It was as though he'd been born with a piece missing—a hole in his gut where his courage should be. If only he hadn't asked to come. If only Edward hadn't agreed to send him! But Edward *had* agreed, and heartily so. With a slap on the back that nearly felled him, Edward had declared it was time he left Nurse and his sister Meg to be with men, lest the constant companionship of women weaken his character.

Richard glanced up at the captain of his guard anxiously.

"Did you know," said Sir John Howard, his broad face creasing into one of his easy smiles, "that it was right here, in your royal cousin Warwick's household, that King Edward learned to be a great knight? And so shall you, m'lord." He was a powerful warrior and one of Edward's most favoured knights, a jolly man with a wavy mane that the years had darkened from yolk to amber and dusted with silver. Richard thought of him as Sir Friendly Lion.

But his words brought no comfort. Though Edward had knighted him on his return from Burgundy, Richard didn't feel like a knight. He couldn't wield a sword, and if he didn't grow, he might never manage it. Then he'd never sit at the Round Table that Edward had promised him he'd bring back. Tightening his hold on the reins of his palfrey, and chewing his lip as he did when he was nervous, he returned his gaze to the castle.

33

They were less than a bow shot away. *Kingmaker*, people called his cousin Warwick, for it was Warwick's support that had made Edward king. *Kingmaker*, too, because Warwick was richer and lived more like a king than Edward, who was always fretting about money, for Edward had many debts from the war he'd waged to win the throne from Henry of Lancaster.

The iron-barred portcullis rose with a loud grinding of chains that sent a flock of doves scattering from the ramparts. He bit his quivering lip and reminded himself that his cousin Warwick, though proud, stern, and courageous, was only an earl, while he was a duke, and Warwick was descended from only one of the five sons of Edward III, not three, as he was. But that scarcely helped.

The lowered drawbridge clanged into place. With a flourish of trumpets, he clattered through the arched stone gateway, followed by his knights. Crowds of people lined the inner court, the ladies in colourful silks, the knights in furs and velvet, the squires and servants in bright red jackets bearing the Warwick badge. He'd never seen such a retinue, even at the royal court.

Richard tightened his grip on his tasselled reins and strained his back trying to appear tall, for everyone was staring. But the eyes disappeared as he drew near, swept away into deep bows. Flooded with relief, he trotted past the chapel to his left and onward to the massive stone Keep. His gaze fell on a group at the foot of the sweeping outer staircase that led to the great hall. They held themselves as erect as he and their eyes never wavered. With a mixture of fascination and dread Richard realised that here, in their golds and scarlets, stood the awesome Nevilles. He recognised Warwick, and his youngest brother George who was Edward's chancellor and came often to court, but he wasn't sure about the tall, lean knight in silver with a hound at his feet. The knight stood straight as a lance, a hand to the dagger at his belt, his tawny hair blowing in the wind, reminding him of the rendering of Sir Lancelot in his illuminated manuscript.

Far too soon he closed the gap to find himself face to face with the Neville family. Fearing to speak in case his voice trembled, and not daring to look at Warwick, he focused on Lancelot. Close up, the silver knight was not young. He had the weathered face of a soldier and there were crinkly lines around his arresting blue eyes.

Lancelot grinned. "Welcome to Camelot, my fair cousin," he said with a twinkle. "I'm John Neville. And this…" He looked down at the bright-eyed wolf-hound who sat wagging his tail, "is Rufus." The hound barked in greeting.

So this is Warwick's brother, the famous Lord Montagu! thought Richard. He had a prince's bearing to go with his lion's heart, this military genius of courage and chivalry. Feeling his colour rise, Richard dropped his gaze to the chirping sparrows flitting about the stone steps. Lancelot could probably see straight through his stomach to his missing guts. Then, unable to hold back his curiosity, he braved a look up at John Neville's face and was surprised to find Lancelot surveying him, not with the contempt he expected, but with a kindly expression. "Is it true you cannot be bested in a feat of arms, like Sir Lancelot, my Lord of Montagu?" he blurted out, voicing the question always linked to his famed cousin.

John Neville laughed, a deep laugh that dimpled both sides of his generous mouth. Richard's heart warmed. His Cousin John's good looks reminded him of his mother Cecily, called "The Rose of Raby" for her beauty, though his mother's hair was gold, and John's the colour of sand, and her eyes were blue periwinkles, while his were a twilight sea. There the resemblance ended. John's brow was lofty, his jaw square. He was well-made and sun-bronzed, as someone would be who spent much time outdoors. For this reason, and in some other intangible way Richard couldn't explain, he reminded him of his dead father, the Duke of York. Richard sensed that here was someone worthy of trust. Someone who could be a friend.

"I may have shared Lancelot's good fortune on the field of battle," John Neville smiled, "but Lancelot never had the pleasure of being entertained in a dungeon."

His eyes looked sad to Richard beneath his merriment. Now Richard remembered that John had been taken prisoner when he chased a fleeing Lancastrian straight into enemy territory after a victorious battle. For his recklessness he spent time in a dungeon in the city of York and was freed only when King Edward won the city back from Henry of Lancaster and his vicious queen, Marguerite d'Anjou.

Rufus barked, and Lancelot's voice cut into Richard's thoughts. "My lord Duke, may I assist you to dismount?"

Shy as he was, smiles rarely came to Richard, but he gave one to John, and put out his arms.

"Benedicite," said George Neville, the youngest of the three Neville brothers and a bishop at twenty-three. "'Tis joy to see you again, fair cousin of Gloucester."

Richard thought the holy smile hovering on his lips strangely out of place on his rosy, youthful face, and he inclined his head in solemn greeting, unwilling to risk speech again.

With a flash of jewels, the majestic Warwick bowed. "Joy and good wishes, worthy cousin Gloucester." Like his brother Lancelot, Warwick was handsome, but the lines of the Kingmaker's face were sharply drawn, his demeanour stiff, and the nasal quality of his voice hinted of his famous arrogance.

"God's greetings to you, my lord," Richard said with a courtly bow, remembering his manners.

"May I present my Countess, Your Grace..."

Anne Beauchamp, Countess of Warwick, curtsied, rustling her high-waisted gown and fluttering the gauzy veils of her butterfly headdress.

Warwick continued. "My eldest daughter, Bella. And Anne."

Richard made a proper bow to Isabelle. She was skinny and,

though near his age, towered over him by almost a full head, making him feel uncomfortable. He didn't like her bright pink dress or her pasty complexion; and anyway, he didn't like girls. Girls were always preening like cats or jabbering like magpies—all except for his sister Meg. He turned to Anne.

He blinked as if he gazed into captured light, so bright a glow bathed seven-year-old Anne Neville. She wore a gown of shimmery golden gauze that floated in folds from the high waistline, and her hair, unbound beneath a flower circlet, flowed behind her bright as a field of buttercups. Her eyes were huge and reminded him of flowers. *Violets,* he thought, for their lavender was flecked with brilliant blues and ringed with deepest purple. She dropped her gaze and Richard had a moment to observe her unnoticed. She was about his height—not quite, though, he was pleased to realise—and she brought to mind not jabbering magpies, but an angel he'd once admired in the dazzling coloured glass of Canterbury Cathedral.

She curtsied with grace. He bowed, and caught the scent of lavender. Then the angel lifted her lids and gave him a shy look from beneath her lashes, as if she feared her full gaze would be too bold an intrusion, and what he saw there stunned him. The violet orbs shone with terror. Richard stared, speechless. Never had he expected a Neville to fear meeting him. He was seized with a fierce protectiveness towards the girl as he turned to climb the stairs of the Keep with his cousin Warwick.

CHAPTER FOUR

"But those first days had golden hours for me."

Anne followed her parents and Richard into the great hall, seized with excitement. She had dreaded the Duke of Gloucester's arrival but when she'd looked up into Richard's clear grey eyes, her anxiety had melted like icicles in the sun. The young duke was not what she had expected the King's brother to be—not big and blond, loud and bold like Edward, whom she had once met and found fearsome. On the contrary, he wasn't much bigger than she, and he seemed as shy as she was. She liked his thick dark hair and the funny little dimple in his chin, but there was a look about him that made her think he'd been hurt somewhere, though she didn't see a bandage.

She watched him enter the huge chamber beside her father and uncles. He stood awkwardly in their midst as if he'd lost his way. Suddenly, she wanted to make him feel better. Forgetting her manners for the first time in her seven years, she said, "I have a pet squirrel. He eats marchpane out of my hand. Would you care to see, my lord?"

Richard was startled by the breach of etiquette, but even more by the sound of her voice, which was as sweet as the song of the lark on the morning air.

The Earl of Warwick swung around at the interruption.

"Very much, my lady," Richard replied hastily, before Warwick could censure Anne. "If your gracious lord father permits?" He looked up innocently.

Warwick knitted his thick eyebrows together, obviously torn between his desire to be a gracious host and the need to reprimand his daughter. "Is the Duke not tired from his journey and in need of refreshment? We have a table prepared." He motioned to the dais, which was laden with silver trenchers, fruit and wine.

In as firm and grown-up a voice as he could manage, Richard replied, "My lord, I am not really hungry or tired, although I've been riding a long time. I'd enjoy meeting the squirrel."

Anne grabbed Richard's hand with excitement.

"Nay, lady," said the great Warwick sternly. "I believe your friend lives on the moors..."

Anne's smile faded. She looked up at her father with anxious violet eyes.

"Therefore," the Earl of Warwick continued, "it will be necessary to change your dress."

With a shriek of delight, Anne pulled Richard by the hand and out of the hall.

~*~

Later that afternoon, wearing the crimson and royal blue colours of the House of York, Richard was escorted to the tiltyard by the Master of Henchmen and introduced to Warwick's thirteen other apprentices in knighthood. They all came from noble families whose names Richard recognised, and they were all much taller. Richard's discomfort grew as he joined them around a table outfitted with a variety of vicious weapons, terrifying in spite of their blunted ends. Panic flooded him. He wanted to run back to London.

"Have you chosen your weapon yet?" inquired a rusty-haired boy, whom Richard knew to be Robert Percy. Richard shook his head. A Percy was a strange sight in a Neville household, since the Percys and the Nevilles were bitter enemies, but the fellow, whose load of freckles reminded Richard of himself when he'd caught the pox, no doubt came from a branch estranged from the main line. Such a thing was not uncommon. Warwick himself had an irreconcilable feud with his cousin, Sir Humphrey Neville, a staunch Lancastrian and even stauncher foe.

"I suggest the battleaxe," whispered another boy who bore the emblem of a hound on his breast. This was Francis Lovell, whom Richard knew to be fatherless, like him. He had a swath of wavy dark hair that fell over his forehead, and deep brown eyes that reminded Richard of a troubadour. The boy added, "Since it's your first time, 'tis a bit easier than the mace."

Richard nodded his thanks. The troubadour moved ahead in line with a jerky gait. Richard was stunned. He had a club foot! How could he even think of making knight? Admiration and a sense of kinship flooded him. They were both reaching for the same dream against great odds, and they were both outsiders. Except Francis wore his difference like a badge in plain sight, and his own lay hidden, a secret fear that stirred in the murky waters of his mind and which he suppressed by force of will. It was at night, when he lost control over his thoughts, that his demon emerged to haunt his dreams and accuse him of being a bastard.

As far back as Richard could remember, he'd suspected he was no Plantagenet. In a family of blonds, he was dark. His brothers were all young lions: large-boned and self-confident. He was short, puny, unsure of himself, and ill at ease in a world in which he found no true place. Yet his problems paled next to the troubadour's, for they were in his head and he didn't have to walk on his head. If the troubadour were willing to battle to be a knight, he *had* to overcome his fears and deficiencies!

The Master of Henchmen strode into the centre of the tiltyard, placed his muscular arms on his hips, eyed the boys, and roared, "Don your helmets and choose your sides!"

Someone called out, "What's the prize for winners, my lord?"

"An hour's hunt in the woods," came the reply. A cheer of approval rose from the boys.

"And for losers?" demanded someone else.

"An hour's ride in full armour." This was met by a chorus of groans.

The troubadour gave Richard a mischievous wink. "Our backsides will be raw for a week if we lose." Richard picked up his weapon and followed his new friend with a smile.

"My Lord of Gloucester!" the Master of Henchman roared.

Richard gave a start. What had he done wrong already? There had scarcely been time to do anything.

"Your axe must be held in the right hand, not the left!"

"But," Richard protested, "I'm left-handed, my lord; I can do nothing with my right."

"Then you must learn! *Learn!* 'Tis what you've been sent here for."

A nightmare followed. The weapon proved unwieldy in his right hand. His aim was poor, his reaction slow, his blows without force, and he found himself on his knees as soon as he engaged an adversary. To rub nettle into the wound, the Master of Henchmen called the apprentices' attention to each of his many mistakes.

At the end of the session, his face smeared with dirt, Richard lay down his weapon, unable to look his new friends in the eye. They'd lost because of him. *God's bones, lame would be better than left-handed! I'll never be a knight; never be able to serve my brother the King.*

When everyone left for refreshments in the great hall, Richard disappeared around a corner and sat down in a small recess of the wall, between two water barrels. Resting his cheek on his knees, he relived his dim performance. Eventually a distant door creaked open. Footsteps crunched on the hard ground, grew louder. He dug deeper into his recess, praying that whomever it was would pass him by. But the footsteps turned the corner and stopped. Then a hound barked.

"My lord, so there you are. I've spoken with the Master of the Henchmen. There's been a grievous error," said John Neville, the brilliant general and valiant soldier who, like Lancelot, had never lost a battle.

Richard held his breath. He knew what John Neville had come to say: *A grievous error, my lord. You were never meant to be a knight. We are sending you back to London at once, to spare you further humiliation.*

Richard shrank back. John crouched down beside him.

"My lord, we didn't know you were left-handed. That changes everything."

Startled at the kindness in his tone, Richard lifted his head and looked at him.

John Neville's heart twisted at the suffering in his little cousin's face. To his astonishment, faint lines ringed Richard's eyes and mouth. But why not? These wretched wars of succession between York and Lancaster had stripped the boy of childhood. He had been born in violence, had learned early that men died and that the world was a dangerous place, full of cruelty and wickedness. At six he'd been taken prisoner at Ludlow; at seven, he'd been left fatherless; at eight, he was an exile. Each blow had taken him a stride away from infancy until he'd sloughed off innocence like a mantle that no longer fit.

He tore his gaze from the heartbreaking dark eyes. "You're left-handed. That can't be changed. The question is, what's to be done? Most believe that such a person must learn to overcome his deficiency. That's the view of the Master of Henchmen."

Richard nodded. "He said that until I learn to use my right, I shall always be beaten. And if I do learn, I'll never be as good as those who are born right-handed."

"Because you'd be going against your inclination and would always be at a disadvantage. But I believe there's another way."

Richard held his breath.

"Your left-handedness, far from being a handicap, can serve you well. See, while an opponent has to reach across his body to get at you, you can use the hand nearest your foe and take him by surprise. 'Tis a natural advantage."

Richard's heart thumped wildly in his ears.

"The best soldier I knew was left-handed—it was camp fever that killed him, not the sword. I learned a thing or two from him myself. So it seems I'm the one to instruct you."

"You?" Richard exclaimed in delight. Then his heart sank. "But aren't there battles you must fight?"

"There are always battles I must fight, but only one Richard of Gloucester who needs to learn to wield his sword like a true knight. I shall tell my brother Warwick that the King's brother has urgent need of my services here at Middleham. He can't refuse the request."

"My gracious cousin," Richard said, scrambling to his feet, "I shall never forget this."

John grinned. "'Tis no more than I'd do for any great Duke."

CHAPTER FIVE

"In that fair order of my Table Round,
A glorious company, the flower of men,
To serve as model for the mighty world."

From a high window at Barnard's Castle, John Neville watched Richard as he sat on a ledge overlooking the forests and river. His lute was laid aside and his arms were clenched tightly around his knees. A humiliating defeat at the mock tournament the day before had devastated him and he had left the field to laughter and snickers. Worse, from the barricades crowded with common folk, someone had called out, "Hey, Gloucester—*duke* you may be, but *knight* you're not!" Then something had struck Richard's breastplate. A rotted apple. The small figure, so vulnerable and solitary, tugged at John's heart.

"Richard asked me again how his father died," he said, almost to himself.

Warwick looked up sharply from his ledger. "You didn't tell him, did you?"

"No."

"Good. He's not ready yet. Now, about this accursed war. It's making a pauper of me." Warwick scribbled into his ledger. "Aah, wait… perhaps we can cut expenses here. Aye, this way supplies will last the men much longer. Excellent." He looked up. "Well, John? Is it agreed?"

John shook himself free of Richard and gave a hasty nod. Since his brother always thought his own answers best, there was no need for him to have heard the question, only to agree. He inhaled a deep breath. The time had come to broach the subject he hated before he lost his nerve.

"Dick—I need a loan. Could I borrow fifty marks?—only until the harvest, you understand. What with the repairs to the roof at Seaton Delaval, and the sickness that killed the sheep… Well, it's been difficult for the family."

Warwick offered him a forgiving smile. "Seems to have become a regular problem, John."

"I regret that," John said in a small voice. "I'll repay as soon as I can, I assure you. It's just that the house is old and the girls are growing. If they didn't need new gowns…"

"As I said, this infernal war is draining my resources, but very well. I'll do what I can." Warwick slammed the ledger shut.

"My thanks, brother… By your leave, I'll take some air." Relieved to be done with the unpleasant matter, John made for the door, anxious to be off to Richard's side. Ever since the tournament on the previous day, his little cousin had avoided him, but there was no time for the child's wounded pride to heal. The Scots border beckoned and he had to do something for the boy before he left. As Rufus bounded to join him, he halted sharply. In his haste to leave, he'd almost forgotten the matter that had weighed on his mind of late.

"Dick—one more thing. Is all well between you and Edward?"

This time it was Warwick who hesitated. "That confounded wanton drunkard?" he muttered finally.

John glanced around, relieved to see no servants. He closed the distance between them and grabbed his brother's sleeve. "Dick, be careful, I pray you. Remember, Edward is king now."

Warwick snatched his arm away. "And I am *Kingmaker.*" He gave John his back and picked up a document from the desk.

John burned to swing him around and shake sense into him. *God's Blood*, he wanted to cry, *your damned rivalry with Edward to prove yourself the better man will be the ruin of us all! Edward's not just a lad with an eye for women, as you think he is. His victories in battle are not just due to luck, as you say they are. He's a man who's done the impossible, and he's not to be taken lightly—or provoked.*

But he said nothing. His brother hated to have his judgement questioned, and any effort to reason with him always ended in a shouting match. And why should Dick respect his opinion when he always came hat in hand, begging for loans he had trouble repaying? The truth was, he could ill afford a fight right now. He desperately needed the money.

Cursing his brother's pride and his own helplessness, John swung on his heel and crossed the hall, followed by his faithful wolf-hound. He took the privy stairs down to the courtyard and left by the postern gate. The cold wind blew in his face and the river thundered in his ears as he circled the castle walls to the ledge where Richard sat staring miserably at the River Tees rushing below.

"May I?" John inquired, feeling almost as despondent.

Richard shrugged without looking up.

John sat down and clasped his knees like Richard, while Rufus stretched out to watch them. "'Tis a fierce wind that blows, isn't it?" *A damn fierce wind,* he thought.

No response. The silence lengthened. "We younger sons have much in common," said John. "'Tis not easy being a younger son." Indeed, it wasn't.

Richard lifted his head.

John threw a pebble into the angry river below. "Younger sons have nothing given to them. They must earn by care and pains what comes to first-borns without effort." Richard's dark grey eyes were fixed on him. *Such intelligent eyes—so wise, so old*, John thought. The boy might be only nine, but he knew much of life, and he was gifted beyond his years. "Younger sons must be inured to self-denial and dependence, for they shall not inherit. They can't have their will in weighty matters…" John broke off. Damn Dick's pride! Why was he always so certain he was right?

"They can't have their will," prompted Richard.

"In matters such as marriage," John resumed, dragging his thoughts back to Richard. The boy's obvious affection for Anne had led Warwick to hope for a royal marriage alliance but Warwick had been unable to get Edward to discuss the matter. Poor child. Much heartache lay in store for him. How well he remembered his own misery! The girl who'd won his heart had been the orphaned daughter of a Lancastrian knight, a ward of the Bitch of Anjou, and the Bitch had demanded almost a queen's ransom to give her hand in marriage to the son of a Yorkist lord. Never had a year seemed so long, or life so pointless and irrelevant. Then his father met the Bitch's price, though he was a younger son and not entitled to the consideration. No such impediment faced Dickon, but his case did not look hopeful. It was becoming apparent that Edward might not care for his brother's happiness in the way John's own father had cared for his.

He realised the boy was staring at him, waiting for him to continue.

"Younger sons tread a harder path in life and so they become reflective. 'Tis the younger sons who dream of righting the world, of riding the path of great knights of yore, of making their mark by deeds of chivalry… The world denies us much, but not the chance to do good with our lives. To win honour."

"Like Sir Galahad, who went in search of the Holy Grail?" Richard offered.

In spite of his heaviness, John smiled. In some ways the little lord who thought himself a man still retained the innocence of childhood. "Aye, like Sir Galahad, and all King Arthur's men who burned to right the wrongs in their path." He picked up another pebble and threw it over the cliff, noting that Richard copied him. "Sometimes I think first-borns are like gaudy peacocks, and we younger sons like dowdy wrens. No matter what they do, the world will applaud and admire, and no matter what we do, the world will as likely forget us."

"So we're useless?" demanded Richard. In his royal blue tunic, with his sun-bronzed face and tawny-gold hair, John looked anything but a dowdy wren.

"Nay, fair cousin. No man is useless who betters the lot of others. We can never turn our feathers to flame and jewel colour like our older brothers. But if we're true knights, and let honour and conscience guide our lives, we'll face God without shame when the time comes, and that is the best any man can do."

Richard burst out passionately, "But what if you can't be a knight?"

"You're a knight already. A Knight of the Bath, knighted by the King himself on his coronation day."

Richard averted his face. Hungering for a win, he'd trained hard for his first mock tournament, rising long before the castle stirred and stealing away to the woods to practise his tiltyard routine in rain and cold. Winning would have helped him shoulder the memory that had haunted him since Ludlow: that, scared witless, he had wet himself like a babe. A year later, Edward had dubbed him knight and had handed him his golden spurs. The solemn pride of the ceremony had made him dream of redemption, of erasing his shame. The old archbishop's words still echoed in his heart: *A knight must throw down his gauntlet to the Devil and fight for right against the servants of sin. Whether*

47

you win or lose matters not, only whether you follow the quest.
Remember that virtue always prevails.

"I'm not a real knight," said Richard. "'Tis hopeless."

John rested a hand on Richard's shoulder. "Nothing is ever hopeless, Dickon. You fought well. An accident threw you— you tripped on a rock and fell, is all. 'Tis only your first year in training. Power comes from speed and leverage, and can be taught. It's *heart* that makes the difference. And that you have."

Richard knitted his brows together. "'Heart'?"

"Resolve, Dickon. Have you never seen a mother wren defend her nest against a cat? Or a wounded boar attack a man in armour? It's will that gives them strength to drive off the enemy." John gave him an irresistible smile. "You're as fierce and determined as a boar. Before you're through, you'll throw a man twice your size."

"Do you really think so, Cousin John?"

"I do. Never look back on your failures, Dickon. It matters little how we begin, provided we are resolved to go on well— and end well. 'Tis not what you were that matters. 'Tis what you will become."

Richard had a wonderful thought. Maybe courage was contagious and he would be like John one day! "You're as a brother to me," he blurted.

"Aye, we're much alike, we four Nevilles and you four Plantagenets," John laughed. "We've two Georges and two Richards among us, and all are fair except for you and Thomas…" It was the first time in a year that his dead brother Thomas had slipped into his speech as if he still lived, and suddenly all joy left him. "Much alike… We share the same blood and our lives seem to take the same turns. Four brothers are made three, and our fathers dead on the same day, struck down by the same accursed hand: the Frenchwoman who calls herself our queen."

Gone was John's smile. His eyes were dark with emotion

and a muscle quivered at his jaw. *Aye,* Richard thought, *blood and loss unites us.*

"Knights of yore exchanged rings and mingled blood to seal their bond," Richard said. "My fair cousin of Montagu, I should like to do the same with you."

John's mouth curved at the corners. Removing a heavy gold band shaped into his emblem of the golden griffin, he offered it to Richard. "My lady gave me this. Had our babe lived, it would have gone to him. You're not only as a brother to me, but also a son, Dickon."

Richard took the ring and gave him a sapphire from his own hand. With his dagger, he cut John's palm, then his own. They clasped hands, mingling their blood. "Brother to brother, yours in life and death," they intoned solemnly. John rose from the ledge, and said with a smile, "Now I have two brothers named Richard."

But Richard didn't hear. The talk of death and family had turned his thoughts to his father as he had looked the last time ever he saw his face; and to Edmund, tall, slender, and seventeen. He saw them in his mind's eye, mounting their horses in the courtyard of their London house. Pigeons were cooing, the sun was shining, the bells on their reins were jingling softly. They rode out through the gates with a smile and a wave, and never returned.

"Remember, Dickon," John said gently, "you can't go forward if you keep looking back. In last year's nest, there are no eggs."

Framed against the sky, John stood looking down at him with twilight-blue eyes, a hand extended in help. The sun had gone behind a bank of clouds and the wind had risen, whipping his hair and sweeping the trees with a fierce rustling. Richard knew that he'd never forget this moment, that in some strange way it marked his life forever. He accepted John's hand and pulled himself to his feet. There was truth in what John said. No use looking back. The future lay ahead, beckoning brightly, and could be whatever shape he willed. He eyed the birds shrieking across the hills. *In last year's nest, there are no eggs.*

CHAPTER SIX

"The teeth of Hell flay bare and gnash thee flat!"

Anne couldn't sleep. She shared a bed with Bella, who always caught cold at the change of seasons and was snoring heavily. Bells from nearby Jervaulx Abbey clanged periodically, owls hooted, and through the open window the October sky glittered with stars. Her thoughts turned to Richard.

Eighteen months had passed since he'd come to Middleham and so much had changed. Life was exciting now. Before Richard she had been so afraid. Messengers always brought bad news, villages pretty in the spring were charred ruins when she returned in the fall, and young men who left the castle to fight returned wounded and drenched in blood, if they returned at all.

Voices murmured and hushed footsteps fell in the stone passageway. She tensed. Bella stirred. For a moment, light fell through the crack under the door, then it was dark again. Anne exhaled with relief.

"What is it?" Bella demanded, still half asleep.

"Only Mother, going to the village to help a woman give birth."

Bella sat up on an elbow and rubbed her eyes. "Why are you still up?"

"Because you're snoring."

"I don't know what you see in Dickon," Bella replied, guessing the truth. She fluffed her pillow. "He's so glum."

"He's… different…" Anne replied dreamily. "Like the knights the troubadours sing about."

"Pooh. He doesn't laugh or like to dance." Bella pulled up her covers.

"He likes music and books."

"I hate books," Bella retorted. "They make me sneeze—except for the one with the pictures of the nude statues in Padua." She giggled. "I dusted that one carefully."

Anne's eyes flew open. "Where did you see such a thing?"

"In Father's chamber. Cousin Tiptoft brought it back for him. Father hasn't any idea he has it. He never reads, unless it's a treaty or something. Do you want to see it?"

Anne blushed a furious red. "No."

"You're well suited to Dickon, sister. You're no fun either. They say his brother George is handsome and witty and loves to dance. I think I shall like him much better than Dickon." She turned her back on Anne and soon began to snore again.

Church bells tolled for matins. Anne wiped her nose and closed her eyes. A cool breeze stirred in the room. She snuggled under the cozy feather comforter and heard Merlin, her pet raven, flutter on his perch. *I'm glad Richard was able to heal the injured baby owl I found in the woods,* she thought. Richard was clever, and kind. She supposed he took after his father, the Duke of York, who had been much loved and respected. The noble duke had died bravely, but cruelly, and his head had been nailed to the gates of York. That much was common knowledge, but the manner of his death remained a secret. Adults spoke of it in whispers and fell silent whenever she approached. She only knew that he died at Wakefield Castle, with her uncle Thomas, who had been so much fun, always making playful faces and twirling her around.

She shut her eyes tight to banish the image that suddenly came to her: Thomas's rotting head, caked with dried blood and buzzing with flies, nailed to the gates of York beside the good Duke of York's. She tossed in bed. Poor Richard. It must be horrid to lose a father. She would be so sad if she lost hers.

She was always so glad to see her father after he'd been away that she couldn't stop herself from shrieking with joy and running to him with open arms, though her nurse said it wasn't ladylike. But her father didn't mind. He always smiled and swept her up to him. Poor Richard had no father to run to.

Anne saw him again, wielding his sword and shield in the rain. In her mind, he turned and smiled at her. *Richard, Richard...*

She saw him dreamily as she floated through the woods like a leaf in the breeze under the branches of the chestnut in the woods she and Richard had made their own, past the gentle River Ure with its banks of lilies. The breeze lifted her over Yorkminster's ornamented towers and deposited her in the nave. She gazed up in wonder at the stained glass glittering around her like jewels. The jewels enlarged, fractured into pieces, and she laughed as they twirled around her. It was then she realised something was wrong.

She was no longer in the nave but in a dark space outside. Demonic gargoyles danced around her as her father struggled to balance on a steeple. He stretched out a hand for help but they reared up between them, snatched him away, and sent him hurtling to earth. She heard weeping and thought it was her father, but when she looked down, there were no tears, just blood. It was sticky and it smelled sour, and it rose like a river, tearing at her skirts. She opened her mouth and started screaming. The demons laughed. She covered her ears. They yanked up her head to cut it off. She saw their faces and let out one last, shattering scream. They were all Marguerite d'Anjou.

She opened her eyes to find Bella shaking her. Merlin was beating his wings and squawking noisily.

"Stop it, stop that shrieking!" Bella was yelling. "What's the matter with you?"

Anne swallowed dryly. "It's the dream again, Bella."

Bella froze. "Oh, God's mercy..."

Anne crossed herself and hastily pushed out of bed. The

dream was an omen that always preceded disaster. "We must pray," she said. "Hurry, Bella, hurry!" The two sisters rushed to their prie-dieu, knelt on the velvet cushion and, placing their trembling hands together, prayed to the Holy Virgin.

They continued their urgent prayers through Mass the next morning, and silently through breakfast. When the King's messenger arrived with a missive for their father, Anne reached out for Bella's hand.

He cut the white ribbon with his jewelled dagger, broke open the seal, and read. He seemed relieved, for his taut face relaxed when he looked up. "Good news, my lords and ladies. The King will visit us next week on his way north to deal with the Bitch of Anjou."

Bella almost laughed in relief. But Anne turned her eyes to the far hills from whence the King would come riding.

CHAPTER SEVEN

"Live pure, speak true, right wrong, follow the King—"

On the last day of October 1463, All Hallows Eve, King Edward IV arrived on a gleaming ebony stallion caparisoned with crimson velvet and embroidered with the golden suns-and-roses of York. He dismounted before the castle and stood with hands on his hips, grinning at his brother Richard. His startling blue eyes were brighter than the summer sky, his smile dazzling as sunlight, his golden hair more brilliant than the wheat fields of August. He stood six foot four in his stockinged feet and was so tall and broad-shouldered that he blotted out the sun behind him.

"Dickon—you've grown!" Edward laughed. "God's mercy, look at those muscles—I daresay you'd do me damage with those!" He gave Richard a playful punch on the arm.

Richard wanted to run to his great golden brother in his joy, but that would have been unseemly. He was eleven years old, almost a grown man. When Edward was twelve he'd successfully led an army and rescued his father, the Duke of York, from Queen Marguerite's clutches.

"Aye, my lord brother," Richard replied proudly. "I've been learning much of knighthood here at Middleham."

"I seem to be sinking ever deeper into your debt, cousin," smiled Edward as he embraced Warwick, but it seemed to Richard that his brother's tone had lost much of its warmth. Whether Warwick noticed he couldn't tell from his mumbled acknowledgement.

"My Lord of Gloucester is becoming a fine warrior," Warwick said after a pause. "My brother of Montagu is much impressed." He gave Richard a smile and, turning back to Edward, dropped the formality. "John hopes to be with us this night, Sire. He comes to brief you on matters in the North and to request permission to take Dickon back with him to observe the siege of Bamborough."

Startled, Richard glanced up at them joyfully, his heart stirring with gratitude to John.

Warwick said, "My lord King, you are journey-tired. Come, rest and take refreshment. We have a fine banquet prepared."

Followed by Richard, the Neville family and the glittering Knights of the King's Body, the King and the Kingmaker led the way into the castle, their heads together, talking in hushed tones of Marguerite's invasion. Richard overheard part of their conversation.

"There's a rumour the Scots have promised to send an army to Bamborough within the week," Warwick said.

To this Edward laughed. "Fear not; the Scots keep no promise."

Nothing daunts my brother, Richard thought with admiration.

~*~

Dark fell over Wensleydale. Villagers and townsfolk gathered outdoors to celebrate All Hallows Eve with bonfires and revelry, and in the snow-covered castle minstrels struck a lilting melody to commence the festivities. The Kingmaker's guests rose from their banquet tables with a rustle of silks and a flash of gems to greet the King entering the great hall. Crushing rushes and dried lavender underfoot, King Edward strode forward alone at the head of the procession, greeting his subjects with easy grace. The Nevilles followed. Richard escorted Anne, and a small retinue of trusted knights and councillors brought up the rear.

The massive chamber dazzled like a jewel for the royal visit. A fire roared welcome from the new-styled hearth on the dais and torches threw dancing lights over gilded pillars, tapestries, and coloured glass windows. All the tables were covered with white cloths, and where the nobles sat there were gold trenchers, small boxes of precious salt, and silver bowls piled high with apples and pears.

Richard's eyes followed his brother. Resplendent in his golden crown of points and a tunic quartered with the Lilies of France and Leopards of England, Edward, who had turned twenty-one in April, was every inch a king. A jewelled girdle with the white rose emblem of York worked in pearls glinted around his narrow hips, and the Yorkist collar of golden Suns and Roses flashed across his broad shoulders. The Sun in Splendour had become his emblem after his defeat of Queen Marguerite at the Battle of Mortimer's Cross, when three suns appeared in the sky. By God's grace he'd triumphed over insurmountable odds that day, and the five-pointed rose on a sunburst was a reminder to all that Fortune had chosen him her champion.

Edward eclipses everyone, Richard thought proudly, trying to imitate his swagger. *Even the stately Kingmaker in his opulent white damask attire, furred with sable and dusted with jewels.* He turned his glance on Anne.

In contrast to Bella, who looked an apparition in a pumpkin-coloured gown, Anne seemed clad in living flowers and was never more fair. Now he noticed the startling resemblance she bore to the image of their mutual ancestress, Joan Beaufort, that hung on the east wall. It was from Joan that the Nevilles inherited not only their royal blood, but their good looks.

Born out of wedlock to their common ancestor, John of Gaunt, Duke of Lancaster, and his mistress, Katherine Swynford, Joan was an unsuitable bride for a Neville. Before he died, John of Gaunt wed Katherine and legitimised their four children, giving them the name Beaufort. Never before had royalty married a commoner. The marriage scandalised Europe and outraged the nobility, but allowed Joan to wed her Neville.

Despite the stain of illegitimacy, the Beauforts gained such respectability and wealth over the next sixty years that they became the rivals of the Nevilles for power. Little did Joan and her brothers know when she married Ralph Neville what enemies their descendants would become as the thirst for power cut its way through blood ties. The Neville and Beaufort cousins feuded for decades before the rift broke open into civil war in 1453. But for the Lancastrian Beauforts, mad Henry would have been deposed years earlier. But for the Yorkist Nevilles, Edward wouldn't be King now.

They took their seats at the royal table. Drums rolled and servants carried in silver trays laden with food, followed by hounds begging for scraps. Within the first half hour Richard counted more than seven courses, including peacocks and swans decorated with their own bright feathers, roasted wild boar, finches, larks, and the more edible pheasants. Never at the royal court had he enjoyed such a selection. Only to impress merchants who might lend him money did Edward throw banquets, and none so lavish. Richard knew Edward was both impressed and irked by Warwick's wealth. To swell his own treasury, Edward had resorted to trading in wool, tin, and cloth like a common merchant, and his royal ships roamed as far afield as Italy and Greece, seeking high prices for his goods.

A troubadour came to sing of Arthur. Richard noted that Anne was absorbed in the tale, unlike Bella, who was busy making cow-eyes at a new apprentice-knight. But then, the sisters were different. Anne loved to learn, enjoyed reading, and could recite passages from Virgil and Ovid. There was only one blessing that Heaven had forgotten to bestow: If only she weren't so frail! To make matters worse, she picked at her food and never touched flesh. He'd tried to persuade her to eat meat, hoping it might help her grow strong, but she'd refused. "Would you eat your friends?" she'd demanded, shocked.

He almost smiled as he watched Anne choose fruit and decline flesh. He nodded to a server and the man heaped roasted boar on his gold trencher. A hound nosed under his elbow. Richard fed him a slice. Anne smiled in secret approval. He returned her smile as he devoured the boar and accepted a pheasant leg to share with the hound.

A sharp crack of thunder startled him. The night had turned stormy. The wind had begun whistling and part of a shutter banged against a window, raising an eerie chorus around the troubadour's song as he told of Arthur's love for Guinevere. Suppressing his unease, he sipped wine from a gilded wine cup and glanced down the table.

Next to the King sat Lord William Hastings, who had married one of Warwick's many sisters. Hastings was Edward's bosom companion and Richard thought they made an odd pair, since Hastings was eleven years older and his hair was already silvering at thirty-two. But, like Edward, he laughed easily and his blue eyes raked women boldly. Richard had heard the ladies talk and he knew they thought Hastings irresistible. Men found him genial, too, yet Richard had always felt uncomfortable around him. Maybe because Hastings was too rowdy for good company, or maybe because he reminded him of what he wished to forget...

Ludlow.

He'd met Hastings at Ludlow Castle on his sixth birthday. On that same October day he'd also met his two eldest brothers, Edward and Edmund, who had been sent away to learn knightly conduct in another noble household. Edward was then seventeen, Edmund barely sixteen. There had been much joy at Ludlow.

And fear.

Richard's goblet slackened in his grip. It was at Ludlow that he'd first met Queen Marguerite. He blinked to banish the image of the fiery queen astride her horse in the marketplace, looking down at him with loathing and contempt. God's curse on her, all England's woes flowed from her evil doings—hers, and her corrupt favourite, Henry Beaufort, Duke of Somerset. If Marguerite d'Anjou hadn't wed mad King Henry, or if King Henry had kept his wits, Richard's father would never have died. It was Marguerite's mortal hatred that forced his father to remember that he—by his descent from an older son of Edward III—held better title to the throne than King Henry himself. By the time Richard had turned six, there had been several bloody battles between the Yorkists and the Lancastrians. Fearing that Fotheringhay Castle was no longer safe, his father moved them to Ludlow, his stronghold on the Welsh Marches.

Ludlow. Absently, Richard picked up the candle before him, brought it close and stared into the flame. He could feel its heat in his face. *Danger,* it warned. *Danger...*

Aye, there had been danger at Ludlow. And treachery. And unspeakable horror. The world had changed after Ludlow. He stared into the flaring flame. The bright hall dimmed and receded, laughter faded; time hurtled backwards and Ludlow rose up before his eyes.

Standing high on a hill near the River Teme, Ludlow Castle had been cold and damp, the walls thick, the windows narrow. The castle had been crowded with his father's soldiers, friends and servants. Since there was little furniture besides some trestle tables and a few benches and stools, they sat on the stairs, slept on rushes and lounged on cushions. The air was pungent with the smell of horses, dogs, sweat. And the scent of fear. Death lurked in the shadows at Ludlow.

Besides his father and three brothers, Edward, Edmund, and George, there was Richard's uncle, the Earl of Salisbury, and his son Warwick, and many others whose scarred and pockmarked faces flitted in and out of the shadows in the castle. As the gloom deepened, torches and tapers were lit. Richard crouched in a corner, trying not to notice the grotesque shapes the candles threw on the walls, concentrating instead on his nine-year-old brother George, who sat at his mother's feet by the cupboard, bare because his father had pawned his plate to pay his soldiers. As she embroidered a war banner, George waved a plume, shook his golden curls, laughed his merry laugh, and regaled her with tales of how he would single-handedly vanquish their enemies. Richard remembered that she had smiled.

But there was no smile on his father's face. Tense and drawn, he carefully went over the battle plans with Salisbury, Warwick, and the fierce leader of the Calais regiment whom Warwick, the Captain of Calais, had brought over with him. Andrew Trollope reminded Richard of a pirate with his scarred cheek and blackened teeth. Hideous as he was, Richard knew his father felt lucky to have this fighter of known repute. Without Andrew Trollope and his seasoned fighting men, he had no chance against Marguerite's forces.

"We're outnumbered," said the Duke of York.

"Fear not," grinned Trollope. "We've something the Bitch's army 'as naught of. *Heart!* Bah, we'll chop 'm up like raw liver, for they're naught but gutless swine and know not what real fighting's about!"

The corners of the duke's handsome mouth lifted slightly. "Nevertheless, we'll accept their terms if they offer us any concession at all."

"Nay, Father!" Edward broke in. "You must fight and seize the throne! You knelt to them after our victory at St. Alban's, and here we are again. Nothing can be resolved as long as that she-wolf rules idiot Henry."

"Idiot he may be, but king he is," the Duke of York replied. "And if there's a way to preserve my oath and save my men, I shall do so, my son, and you'd be best advised to hold your tongue."

At nightfall the envoy returned for the last time. There were no concessions, only demands. The castle prepared for battle.

"See you at dawn, my lord," said Trollope with a confident bow as he left to guard the bridge.

At dawn, Trollope was gone. He and all his men. Crossed over to Marguerite's side.

"We can't flee," said the Duke of York. "'Tis dishonourable."

"We can't fight," said the Earl of Salisbury. "Trollope knows our plans."

"But the townspeople—if we abandon them..."

"They've had no part in this. Marguerite will let them alone."

"Marguerite spares no man. Hers is a blood lust I've seen in few."

"We've no choice," Salisbury said.

Everyone fled as best they could. The duke and the earls made it safely away but some of their men were slain and the prisoners were hung and quartered. Then came the punishment of the townspeople...

Richard's grip tightened on the candle. He closed his eyes. There was no refuge; no refuge anywhere. People were running, horsemen in pursuit. Swords and axes swung. Men, women, and children staggered, fell. Blood overflowed the gutters as it did on Butchers' Row before a feast day. The sky was on fire, houses ablaze, blackening the air. From the church came the squeals of animals and the cries of people trapped inside. Shouted orders rang out, mingled with the wails of the dying in a din torn from the bowels of Hell. He felt sick, his knees buckled, and hot urine trickled down his legs. He grabbed his mother's hand tightly and pushed up against her skirts to keep from falling off the steps of the high market Cross. The sickly sweet odour of burning human flesh stung his nostrils…

"Richard, you've burned yourself!" cried Anne. She dabbed at his hand with a wet cloth. "Richard, you look strange. What's wrong?"

Richard grabbed his wine cup unsteadily and downed a gulp. "Nothing," he lied.

Anne slipped her hand into his. "Don't look back, Richard. I get scared too when I look back."

He hated that she could see his fear, but she was right, of course. What was it John had said? *In last year's nest, there are no eggs.* Yet he couldn't help wondering whether he'd ever forget; ever feel safe again. Ever feel one of them. His gaze flicked the table. He didn't belong here. Everyone here had forgotten. They were all laughing. Not only could he not join in, but he caught menace in their laughter. What was wrong with him?

He turned his eyes on the arched entrance of the hall and fidgeted with his ring. He wished John would come. John understood. Not that they had ever spoken of fear. The closest they had come was a remark John once made, something about fears of the past breeding fear for the future. Aye, there was naught to be done about the past. One could only do one's duty and hope for God's blessing. He gave Anne a nod and fixed his gaze on the entrance.

"He might be detained at the front, Richard," said Anne softly, reading his thoughts.

At that instant, trumpets blared and a herald's voice announced, "John Neville, Lord Montagu!" All below the rank of lord stood, and though he was a duke, Richard half-rose from his chair with excitement, almost spilling his wine. Anne jumped up from the table with a squeal of delight and ran to her uncle. Richard watched with an ache as John scooped her up in his arms, laughing, and she gave him a kiss. It seemed to Richard that he'd been thought too old for that since the day he was born. Followed by his ever-present hound, John strode to the King and went to kneel, but Edward rose and embraced him warmly.

"What joy to behold you, fair cousin!" He turned to motion for a chair and caught Richard's expression. Under his breath, he muttered, "It seems you must sit with Dickon or break his heart, John."

A servant set a chair for him between Richard and Bishop Neville.

"How goes Bamborough, John?" demanded Edward from down the table.

"We've not made much progress, my King. The weather's been against us."

"We should learn from the Italians," Edward called out. "By gentleman's agreement they never fight in winter!"

John grinned. The table dissolved into laughter.

Richard's gaze fixed on his golden brother. How he envied Edward. Nothing troubled him. Already he'd put the unpleasant subject of Bamborough aside to engage in carefree conversation with Warwick on his right and Will Hastings on his left. Every so often there was a burst of laughter from the three at the centre of the table. Amid one of these, Will Hastings rose. He stood for a moment, a tall, glittering figure in purple satin slashed with black velvet. The minstrels hushed their instruments and all eyes turned to the royal table.

Waving his flagon unsteadily, swaying on his heels, Hastings performed a pantomime. Pointing in front of him and pretending to hide his eyes, he shrilled, "Fie, fie, for shame and forsooth, cover thy b-b-b-breasts, shameless maidens!"

The hall roared with laughter and Richard's mouth curved at Hasting's imitation of the monk-king Henry—whom some called Holy Harry—and his horror of nudity. Hastings tilted his dark brows at Edward. "Laugh not so hard, my lord, or your crown will fall off as mine does. And without my crown, who would guess I was king? 'Tis a good thing my servants catch it for me."

Playing along with his friend, Edward exclaimed, "Too bad Somerset couldn't catch you when you fell off your throne, Harry!"

The company in the hall hooted with approval. Richard grinned. Henry Beaufort, Duke of Somerset, was the leader of Queen Marguerite's forces. Some said he was also her lover and the father of her son, Prince Edouard.

A grizzly-bearded friend of Warwick's, Lord Wenlock, yelled, "But no doubt Somerset caught your queen when she fled from your bed—if ever she was in it." He gave a loud burp.

Beside Wenlock sat Sir Friendly Lion, John Howard, who had escorted Richard to Middleham nearly two years earlier, and next to him a former Lancastrian, who had avoided taking sides in the wars by leaving England to study in Italy. Richard knew Warwick distrusted the Earl of Worcester, John Tiptoft, even though Tiptoft was married to one of his fleet of sisters. Their end of the table lay far from Richard, yet a fragment of Tiptoft's comment reached him.

"I could make Somerset regret he was born," Tiptoft was boasting to Howard. "They have a cage in Padua, you know, that is used to…" His voice was drowned out by the noise in the hall, but its ominous quality and the strange flash of his protruding dark eyes fascinated Richard. He noticed that even the seasoned warrior John Howard had paled. He couldn't help wondering what happened to a man in a cage. Maybe vultures pecked out his eyes and flesh like they did to Prometheus. That had to hurt a great deal. Now that he thought about it, Tiptoft's bony face resembled a vulture's. He could see him pecking out someone's eyes with that curved beak he had for a nose.

With a glint of gold and gems, Warwick leaned back in his velvet chair. Directing himself to Hastings, he said dryly, "Aye, Harry, as you can't tell a hart from a hind, you've sent us much trouble by letting Somerset do your husbandly duty. Now there's a bastard prince claiming the throne."

Will Hastings looked down his nose at Warwick. "Prince Edouard is the child of the *Holy Spirit!*" he sniffed.

Howls and shrieks shook the hall. Anne, who understood little of this, peered at Richard.

"When mad Harry was shown the queen's new-born babe," he explained, "instead of claiming the child as his, as is the custom, he said it was the child of the Holy Spirit."

"Oh," Anne said, filled with admiration for Richard, who knew everything.

Edward dried tears of laughter from his eyes. "Indeed, Harry, the boy's not likely to be yours—unless you found a way to get into Marguerite without removing her clothes." Whistles and the loud stamping of approving feet met this remark.

As the company in the hall resumed their conversations, the minstrels took up a lively tune and servants returned to their duties, clearing tables, filling wine cups, and bringing sweet courses. There was pudding to choose from, and marchpane, stewed fruits, and almond cakes. Richard chose cheese and Anne selected cake. Smiling at one another, they ate in silence.

From his royal seat beneath the canopy, Edward observed Richard. His baby brother had changed much, he thought, watching him tear into the bread and cheese he loved. His dark hair, bobbed at the ears, shone with a healthy lustre; his grey eyes were clear; and his complexion no longer dead white but lightly bronzed by sun. Tonight he was attired in bright crimson and gold, a stunning change from his favourite dull greys and wines. He could scarcely substitute this new Dickon for the sickly child he remembered two years ago, after the battle of Towton, standing on the deck of the ship that had bought him home to England from his exile in Burgundy.

Dickon had been wearing a plain dark tunic that made him seem sadder than ever. In the dimness of dusk, with his dark hair and pallid face, he looked like a waif. "Are you going to bring back Camelot?" Dickon had asked, gazing up at him with his solemn eyes.

"I certainly hope so," Edward had replied.

"Then I wish to be one of your knights of the Table Round."

"Indeed?" Edward had smiled. "But such a knight must have training." He exchanged a look with Bishop Neville who had come along to greet the royal brothers, Dickon and George.

Barely suppressing a smile, Bishop Neville said, "Sire, may my brother Warwick have the honour of training a future knight of the Table Round?"

"I can think of no better household, fair cousin," Edward had replied. "Dickon, go to Middleham and there learn to be a knight so you may serve your King and seek the Holy Grail when you are grown."

Edward came back to the present slowly, looking down the dining table at his young brother. Dickon had grown into a broad-shouldered boy with muscular arms, and about him there was a quiet strength. Edward thought of frivolous George, three years older, who seemed such a child in comparison, and wondered again how his two brothers could be so different. He frowned, as thinking of George always made him frown.

Leaning past Warwick, he addressed himself to the Countess. "Middleham's been good for Dickon. He looks well and seems to be mastering the accomplishments of knighthood."

"He practices hard, my lord. I've never seen a boy his age

65

work so earnestly at his lessons."

"Does he relish the art of war so much then?"

"No, my lord. He relishes peace. He says he does it for you, for to keep peace in the kingdom you will have need of strong and loyal men. It seems the little duke has a wisdom far beyond his years."

"Indeed," replied Edward thoughtfully. "Indeed."

"Edward," said Warwick, his proud head held high, "Dickon and Anne are fond of one another, as you know. They desire to be wed. A marriage would..."

Edward's roar of laughter interrupted him. "You're the one who keeps reminding me that love has nothing to do with marriage—that it's solely a commercial transaction, a means of acquiring wealth or extending power. How many times have you said that, cousin?"

"But their union would benefit our two great families and show the realm we Yorkists stand firmly united," Warwick countered, his face flushed. "Let us be joined. Delay gains us nothing. 'Tis a good time to announce the betrothal, cousin." His eyes pierced the distance between them.

"My Lord of Warwick," Edward said coldly, using formal address to put distance between them, "marriage is a weighty matter. We shall consider it another time."

He turned away, irked by Warwick's manner and his nasal voice, which underscored his insufferable arrogance. Even his motto was arrogant: *Seulement un.* The only one to what? To have made a king? The only one who was always right? Fit to govern? England had anointed him her hero and sung his praises so loudly that he thought himself a deity. Since his cousin had helped him gain his throne, Warwick thought he owned him. In the past year the Kingmaker had decided that the King should marry, and had bandied the King's hand around Europe as if he were so much meat to be auctioned to the highest bidder. *Your people fear that their sovereign lord has been long without a wife and not chaste in his living,* he had scolded. *They do not approve, Edward.* The audacity! Louis of France had turned out to be the winner and Warwick fixed his mind on wedding him to Louis's sister-in-law, Bona of Savoy. Persistent and tireless, he urged the marriage alliance at every turn.

A pox on his marriages! Edward thought, throwing his knife across the table. Turning to his friends Hastings and Tiptoft, he engaged them in conversation.

At the end of the table, Anne said to Richard, "I fear my father is displeased."

Richard's eyes flew to the Kingmaker, who a moment before had been deep in conversation with the King. He now sat stiffly as his brother, Bishop Neville, talked with the Countess. Though Warwick pretended to be listening, his face was set in a hard line and his eyes smouldered. Richard's stomach clenched tight. The King and the Kingmaker had glanced at them several times as they spoke, and Edward's expression, normally so good-natured, had darkened. *They were discussing us,* Richard thought.

"And it bodes us no good," Anne said, finishing his thought, as she often did these days.

Richard had no heart to reply. He pushed his plate away and looked up to find Edward beckoning.

"I wish your company a while, Dickon," Edward said, patting the chair a servant placed beside him. "The entertainment is about to begin."

Drums rolled and a dwarf led a huge brown bear into the hall. The minstrels struck up a Saracen melody. The dwarf pulled on the bear's chain and the bear clapped her hands with a jangle of silver bracelets. He tugged again and she twirled and somersaulted around the floor, veils flying, coloured glass necklaces flashing. Edward threw his head back and roared with laughter. Richard loved the sound of Edward's laugh, so joyous, so exuberant. That was part of his charm—the ability to enjoy life, to revel in the moment and never to worry about the past or the future. He wished he could laugh like that and always be so *sure* about everything, instead of being shot through with doubts. He had so many doubts—about his future, about whether he'd marry Anne, about whether he'd measure up. He even had doubts about his paternity.

When he was small, he used to study his mother, hoping her guard would drop and he'd learn who his father really was. But after the death of the Duke of York, she withdrew from the world and spent most of her day in prayer, living almost a monastic life, and Richard resigned himself never to know the truth of his birth. Instead, he sought comfort in the tales of the Round Table, for the legendary Arthur had suffered the same doubts. It was another reason why he had taken King Arthur to heart.

"Why so sombre, little brother?" Edward demanded. "Is the wine not good? Is the bear not amusing?" He raised his ruby-studded cup to his lips.

"Tomorrow you leave," Richard said.

"But you're coming with me," Edward exclaimed with surprise.

"Not to fight Marguerite. To observe the siege. I'm not in danger. You are."

Edward regarded him a moment. "More reason to laugh today, Dickon." He drained his flagon and set it down with a resounding clang. In one agile leap, he was across the table, making a sweeping bow to the bear. Gasps of horror sounded around the room and mouths fell open. Women clutched their crucifixes; men unsheathed their daggers and leapt to their feet. The dwarf blanched, took a step forward. "But my Liege…"

Edward waved him away. The hall fell deadly silent. Her eye caught by a jewel twinkling in Edward's crown, the bear stared at him as if bewitched. Edward turned, picked up a bowl of custard from a table, and held it out to her. Sniffing the air, she ambled over, stuck her snout into the silver bowl and licked noisily. When she looked up, yellow custard covered her face. Slowly laughter erupted, softly at first, then rose in volume until it filled the hall. For a moment Richard forgot his worries and laughed as happily as any child.

"Dickon laughs," Edward announced. "My little brother laughs!" He leapt over the table and back into his seat. "Now, Dickon, 'tis your turn to perform. What shall it be? A dance? A song?" He looked around and a chorus of *Aye's* swept the room. "Sing for us, Dickon!" he demanded.

A minstrel hurried to the table with a lute. Richard's eyes met Anne's. Then he bent his ear to the instrument, strummed gently, and sang:

"Love, thou art bitter; sweet is death to me,
I fain would follow love, if that could be;
I needs must follow death, who calls for me.
Call and I follow, I follow...."

So pure and melodious was his young voice that the hall remained quiet for some moments after Richard set down his lute. Then loud applause shattered the silence. Edward said, "Dickon, that was splendid—but far too sad, little brother. Play a gay ditty."

"I don't know one, my lord."

Edward gripped his shoulder. "Then learn, Dickon. Life can't be all grief or we couldn't survive it." He tousled Richard's dark hair and rose to his feet. The hall hushed. "On the second of October, the feast of St. Thomas, His Grace the Duke of Gloucester celebrated the eleventh year of his birth, in honour of which we wish to make an announcement." He turned to Richard. "My gracious brother, we appoint you Admiral of England, Ireland, and Aquitaine."

Richard blushed. Edward lifted his gold and ruby cup. "To Lord Richard of Gloucester!"

"To Lord Richard of Gloucester!" echoed the hall.

When he sat down, Edward leaned close and said in a low voice, "I regret I had to take back the lands I gave you in August, Dickon, but George raised such a fuss, I felt compelled to transfer them to him. This is compensation."

Richard nodded. Lands, titles, money didn't mean as much to him as they meant to George, who never seemed to have enough to suit him.

Edward smiled and shifted his large frame in his chair. His bright blue eyes swept the room. Abruptly his expression changed. He moved forward in his chair with interest, and stared as if mesmerised. Richard followed the direction of his gaze. It had caught on a golden-haired beauty at a table below. He watched Edward give the blond a slow secret smile; watched her smile back; watched Edward's gaze return to his own table and encounter Warwick. A knowing, half-contemptuous smile fluttered on the Kingmaker's lips. Edward clenched his jaw and turned away.

Richard was seized with foreboding.

CHAPTER EIGHT

"Young as I am, yet would I do my best."

King Edward was in the antechamber of his private apartments at Windsor enjoying a cup of wine in amiable conversation with Hastings and some of his lords when Warwick burst in, unannounced.

"My lord king, how can you rest easy when there's such trouble in the realm?" Warwick growled, throwing his gauntlets on a nearby table. His obeisance was scanty, a bare acknowledgement of the royal presence. "1464 has been nothing but trouble since the clock heralded its first accursed hour!"

The lords stared in shock at the impropriety of Warwick's manner, but Edward grinned. "Ah, Warwick, a cold wind blows you in. Here, have some wine." He pushed his own cup into Warwick's hand. "To answer your question, let me see… Last I heard, there was trouble in Wales, unrest in the Midlands and Lancashire, and rioting in Gloucestershire… Then Somerset, whom we captured and pardoned—in January, I believe—went back on his oath last month—can't think why!—and fled to Scotland to rejoin Her Grace, the Bitch of Anjou. Ah, yes, and Bamborough, which we twice won back from gentle Marguerite, fell to her again a week ago… Has something happened that I should be concerned about, fair cousin?"

Warwick gave an uncertain smile. "I'm glad you can jest, cousin. The fact is, we'll have no peace in the kingdom until we rid the North permanently of Lancastrian troublemakers. I know you haven't much taste for the soldier's life, but there's no other way. And no time to lose."

Edward threw himself into a chair and propped his feet up on the table, displaying thigh-high boots of gleaming black Spanish leather. He indicated the silver flask and a server rushed to pour him a cup of wine. "Wars cost money, cousin. Since we have none, can you suggest what we can use to pay the troops?" He drank deep, and gave a smack of appreciation.

Warwick gripped the table, eyed him urgently. "We have no choice, Edward. We must raise the money by any means possible. Until we do, the crown's not truly ours."

Edward twisted in his chair and looked up at his cousin. *"Ours?"* he said with the lift of an eyebrow.

Warwick reddened, but offered no explanation or apology, and Edward didn't demand one. He turned his attention to the window, staring out silently. Snow was falling more heavily than before, blanketing the banks of the Thames with crystalline brilliance in the March dusk. Abruptly he slammed down a palm.

"Very well. I'll see how many pence I can scrape together.

71

Then I'll dispatch commissions of array to the south and order conscription. Will that content you, Warwick?"

Warwick set his wine cup down. "It's the only way, Edward." He bowed. "By your leave."

"Incidentally," Edward called out to his retreating back. "The crown is mine, and mine alone, cousin."

Warwick halted stiffly, then resumed his steps. Laughter followed him out the door.

~*~

On a sunny Sabbath afternoon, Warwick returned to Middleham with startling news.

"Dickon's been appointed sole commissioner of array for nine counties."

The Countess ran to keep pace with him as he dismounted and marched up the outer staircase into the Keep. "Sole? He's but a child. Raising an army is work for grown men."

"Evidently the King has supreme confidence in our Dickon."

"Why not George? He's three years older."

"You know as well as I that George interests himself only in clothes and enjoyment—and Bella. I never knew two brothers so unalike. Where's Dickon? We must get the word to him. He has much work ahead."

~*~

In the blossom-laden month of May, Richard led his troops north to meet the royal army, his head high. He wished Anne could see him now. His mind strayed to their last afternoon together, when they'd played Crusaders and Infidels in the melting snow with his friends, the two Toms, Francis, and Rob. "Make up your mind, Anne. Are you in?" he'd demanded. She'd pouted, looking at him shyly from beneath her lashes in her endearing way. "Only if I don't have to be a horse again." He'd shrugged. "There's but one other choice, then. Are you willing to be a damsel in distress?" With a sigh, Anne had gathered her cloak of violet wool around her and climbed into position on a low branch of a crab-apple. "You always rescue me," she'd complained, "but one day I'll rescue you. See if I don't!"

Richard smiled, remembering. It was only because she'd refused to be a damsel in distress that he'd come up with the idea of the horse so many times.

They were nearing Leicester, the point of muster with Edward's army. The air hung heavy with a coming storm and thunder rumbled distantly. They climbed through heavy yellow fog and all at once Richard caught a glimpse of a hillside village to his left. He felt as if he gazed through gauzy veils, for the picturesque cluster of church steeples and whitewashed cottages lay half-hidden by curls of faint, floating mist. Cows grazed among purple wildflowers, and orange clouds glowed with flashes of jagged lightning, illuminating the sleepy village in spasms of glittering, uncanny light.

Richard blinked. "What is that place?"

"Bosworth, my lord," the Friendly Lion replied.

"Bosworth," Richard echoed softly, unable to tear his gaze from the scene. "It doesn't look real, does it, Howard? Like a faerie place."

"Faerie? Frankly, my lord, I find it a strange sight... Makes me think of phantoms."

Richard considered the thought for a long moment before glancing away to find Edward waiting ahead at the bow bridge that led into Leicester. Edward was grinning, and it irked him that his brother should be so amused to see him leading an army. He might cut a small figure among all these men, but he had done man's work though he was not yet twelve years old.

"My Lord of Gloucester," Edward said, greeting him from the saddle in a formal, royal manner that helped to mollify Richard. "Your King thanks you for the army you have delivered. However, there's no longer urgency. We've received excellent tidings. Lord Montagu defeated the Lancastrians at Hedgely Moor."

Richard felt his disappointment as keenly as if he'd been struck a blow on the tiltyard. He had burned to see action, burned to distinguish himself as Edward had at his age, and now that chance had been snatched away. "Our noble cousin Lord Montagu is a valiant general," he said with dignity. Then, with a crack in his composure, he added, "But what now?"

Edward exchanged a look with Hastings. "Now we celebrate," he laughed. "And, at our leisure, we'll head north to help John finish off the Lancastrians."

~*~

Richard followed expectantly as Edward and Hastings led the way into a dimly lit townhouse in Leicester for the surprise they had planned for him. They were treating him differently now. Like an equal. A bosom companion. One of the men—no longer just Edward's baby brother. He took care to walk with a swagger.

A black-clad woman with hair on her chin met them in the hall. She led them up a staircase and along a passageway to a room decorated in red velvet and heavy with the odour of sweet spices. Candles flickered and maidens with unbound hair reclined on silk pallets, laughing and eating grapes, pouring wine and proffering goblets. Richard stared, his heart pumping erratically. The women were bare-breasted.

Edward grabbed a goblet from a fair-haired girl and up-ended the cup. He bent and kissed her full on the lips, fondling a breast in one hand. Then he released the girl and draped an arm around Richard's shoulder. "Do you know what this place is?"

Richard gulped. "A brothel?" He'd heard the palace whispers.

"Aye," laughed Edward. "The best in the county. Isn't it, Will?"

Will Hastings grinned.

Edward led Richard to a small raised platform that served as a dais, propped his long elegant bulk on a brocade pallet, and patted the space beside him. Richard sat down, and Hastings took a seat on Edward's other side. "We've prepared a show for you, Dickon. Never will you forget this night, little brother."

He clapped his hands. Half-nude girls brought in wine, fruits and sweet tarts, and minstrels struck up a tune from their dark corner. A red curtain parted and a group of dancing girls entered. Like the others, these were barefooted and bare-breasted. Bodies weaving, hips swaying to the beat of drums and tambourines, they danced to the high melodic notes of the haunting flute. A delightful shiver ran through Richard at their writhing motions and he felt that giddy pleasure which had lately come to him when his eyes met Anne's, but this time the blood was surging through his veins like a thundering river. He glanced at Edward and Will Hastings. Their faces were flushed as they stuffed their mouths with sweetmeats, and they were clapping loudly, their cries of approval growing lustier with drink. He settled back proudly.

Two men and another girl joined the group. The men were bare-chested and he noted with surprise that though they wore tights, an opening between the legs exposed their manhood. The girl set the silk cushion she carried down on the floor and stretched out gracefully. Moving to the rhythm of the music, they entwined limbs in a pantomime that left Richard breathless.

When the dance was over, the bearded woman made her way past the flickering candles to the dais. "My lords, all is prepared."

Laughing and drinking from a flagon, Edward and Hastings stumbled after her. Richard followed, swaggering. In a small chamber adorned in black and red, a woman sat on a bed playing a stringed instrument. Richard's jaw fell open and his knees went weak. She was completely nude.

"My lord King, I would rise but I know you prefer me in bed," she smiled.

Edward laughed. "You've wit to match your charm. 'Tis what

I love about my little Maud..." He broke off, interrupted by a moan from the curtained alcove in the corner of the room.

"She awaits, my lord Hastings," the bearded woman smiled. She turned to Richard. "My lord of Gloucester, this is Maggie." She led a naked maiden forward to Richard. The girl was young, pretty, with small pink nipples that kindled feelings of fire. Maggie smiled and the bearded woman withdrew with a bow.

"Go with Hastings, Dickon," Edward said. "I don't like to be watched, but he does."

Will Hastings pushed back the curtain and Richard moved to the alcove. He halted abruptly, scarcely aware of Maggie's hands stroking his thigh. A young girl lay naked on a table. She was not much older than Anne and he saw with shock that her wrists were chained to the wall. Desperate to free herself, she moaned as she thrashed, her eyes as terrified as a wounded deer's. Richard jerked around to look at Hastings.

"She's naught but a village girl," Hastings said thickly, pulling off his shirt and casting it aside. "They always fear it the first time, for they know not what pleasure awaits."

He looked strange, Richard thought, with his red face and glazed eyes, puffing like a winded stag. As though she sensed an ally, the girl twisted her head and fixed her eyes on Richard. They were beseeching, bewildered eyes that held a strange, unfocused expression. "M-My lord!" she whispered hoarsely, "S-s-save me—I b-beg you..."

She not only stuttered, but her words were unclear, half-formed, as though she had difficulty uttering them, and Richard didn't comprehend immediately. Then realisation came. The girl had been abducted and drugged, to be ravished by a lord! The warmth of desire vanished, drowned by the sudden lurch of his stomach and the bitter taste of bile that rose in his throat. He thrust Maggie from him and backed away.

The girl fought Hastings with her legs but he pinned her down, heaved his body into hers and began to grunt. Her back arched. She let out a shrill cry. The sound, blood-curdling and filled with terror, washed over Richard in chilling waves. Not since Ludlow had he heard such a scream, such a desperate, tormented scream. He closed his eyes, averted his face. With a sick relief, he realised that the cries had eased.

When he opened his eyes again, the bearded woman was clamping a damp cloth over the maiden's nose. Slowly the agonised movements stilled, the muffled cries hushed. The woman stole away. Hasting's body shook with spasms but the girl lay deadly still.

Richard's gaze fixed on the blood oozing down the girl's thighs. His stomach gave another lurch. Blindly he ran out of the alcove, past Edward, who never glanced up, through the empty red hall, down the narrow staircase. Unable to restrain himself any longer, he turned to the wall and retched. Leaning his head against the wood door, he gasped for breath and passed a hand over his face to banish the obscene image of Hastings thrusting with mounting pleasure.

Edward was right. Never would he forget this night.

CHAPTER NINE

"A storm was coming, but the winds were still."

Richard didn't return to the brothel again, though Edward and Hastings lingered there for the next several nights. Sullen and miserable, he pondered the fate of the maid who'd had no one to speak for her. She'd died that night, overdosed by opium administered by the bearded lady. To Hastings, who'd done the same before, it was a small matter, soon forgotten. Edward, too, regarded it lightly, but in Richard's heart, the girl's fate festered. *I should have done something,* he thought; *I should have helped her.*

So ran Richard's thoughts as they rode to Pontefract Castle.

It troubled him more than he cared to admit that Edward had taken the girl's death so lightly. He could have saved her; he could have stopped Will Hastings. *But Edward was in a different room*, Richard argued with himself. *He didn't know what was going on. By the time he found out, it was too late. What good would it do to chastise Hastings then? Even if it were not the first time a girl Hastings abducted had died this way, Edward wouldn't blame his friend. He was too loyal. He always believed the best of others, and he always gave them the benefit of the doubt. Especially those he loved.*

Still, nagged a small voice in his head, he wished Edward had helped her. As for Will Hastings, he'd never see him again with the same eyes. Merely to be near him caused discomfort. He longed to be with John Neville. John, who was as different from Hastings as the North was from London.

When they finally arrived at Pontefract, it was too late for Richard to see battle. While Edward and Hastings had been whoring at Leicester, John had vanquished the Lancastrians.

"We crushed Somerset's forces at Hexham, Sire!" John informed Edward on bended knee. "Two dozen leaders were captured and executed by sentence of the Constable, John Tiptoft, the Earl of Worcester."

"And Somerset?" Edward demanded.

"I personally had him executed on the spot, my Liege." John hesitated, debating whether to tell Edward of the heated argument he'd had with Tiptoft, who had wished to impale Somerset's men on stakes in the Byzantine manner. He decided on silence. Though cruelty warped Tiptoft's character with a viciousness he'd not thought possible in a sane man, Edward favoured him, and it was wise to tread warily where favourites were concerned. "Holy Harry fled so quickly, he left his crown behind." He held out Henry's golden circlet.

Roaring with laughter, Edward took it. "Poor Henry, always losing his crown." He raised John to his feet and held him by the shoulders. "Such a splendid service deserves a splendid reward... My fair cousin, John, Lord of Montagu, I grant you the earldom of Northumberland. We shall invest you at York in a proper ceremony on Trinity Sunday."

Joy exploded in John's breast. He dropped to his knees. *Earl of Northumberland,* he whispered silently in his heart, bowing his head to hide the happiness that choked him. *Earl of Northumberland!*

With the princely income of the earldom, he'd move his family from the draughty manor house that had been his father's wedding gift into a spacious castle. Isobel would have servants; she would embroider tapestries instead of darning robes. Their daughters would make good marriages. All was changed. All was now possible. He had not failed his family.

"Sire," he managed. "Thank you."

~*~

In June Richard returned to Middleham, anxious to see Anne. But only the Countess stood before the Keep, dressed in drab grey, looking older than he remembered.

"My lady, what has happened?"

"Anne has been sorely ill, Dickon. She caught the ague and her neck swelled so... I barely recognised my own child. But she is recovering, thanks to the Holy Virgin. 'Tis a miracle."

Richard heaved a sigh of relief. He had been struck with fear for a moment, but there was no cause for concern. As the youngest of twelve children, he himself had been so sickly at times that he hadn't been expected to survive, and whenever the steward of Fotheringhay Castle had written his parents, he'd always included a postscript: "Richard liveth yet." Now he was hardy as a young oak. In time, Anne would outgrow her weakness, as he had done. "May I see her?"

"Later, perhaps. She's resting."

Richard followed her upstairs into the hall. That Warwick, tough as he was, should beget two frail daughters was a source of constant amazement to all. "And my Lord of Warwick, how fares he?"

The Countess led him to a window seat. She clasped her hands together nervously. "Dickon... I must tell you, I fear all is not well between your gracious brother and my Lord of Warwick. My lord husband made a fine arrangement with the French for their Princess Bona of Savoy, and with Castile for the hand of Princess Isabella. The King has only to choose, and he will not."

"But there's much to be gained from an alliance with Louis XI," Richard exclaimed.

"I know, my lord... I know," said the Countess. "There is also another matter..." She bit her lip, then rushed on. "Thrice now my lord has asked for your hand in marriage to our Anne, and thrice the King has refused it, as he has refused George's request to marry Bella."

A suffocating sensation tightened Richard's throat. It had not occurred to him that Edward knew about his feelings for Anne. Why was he against the match? Age couldn't be a factor. The Earl of Warwick and his Countess were not much older when they'd wed. The blood of Edward III ran in Anne's veins as it did in his own, and she was heiress to the richest, most powerful magnate in England. Their marriage would only strengthen the Yorkist bond. So *why?*

Something was wrong. Terribly, terribly wrong.

CHAPTER TEN

"It is the little rift within the lute
That by and by will make the music mute."

Never will I forget this moment, thought Richard. *Never, so long as I live.* He stared at Edward, stunned, unable to comprehend what he had just heard. The moment was accompanied by a strange silence, a kind of thundering lull during which a shadow seemed to steal forward, casting an ominous darkness over all who sat around that council table in Reading Abbey. Sick with dread, he saw the fear he felt reflected on everyone's face. No one could believe it. They all sat still as alabaster. What did it mean for them, and for the realm, that Edward had chosen a wife for himself and married her in secret on May Day? John, in particular, had taken the announcement hard. *He looks,* thought Richard, *as if his heart is frozen in his chest.*

Horrified, stunned, and swept with fear, John himself felt as if a hand had closed around his throat, and for a moment he could not breathe. He knew his brother's fierce pride; he knew how hard Warwick had laboured to secure an alliance with the French, and how heavily his pride relied on that success. The depth of Edward's own pride was only just becoming apparent. The boy had grown into a man testing his power. And these two mighty forces had just collided.

A stony-faced Warwick broke the silence. "Who is she?"

"Elizabeth Woodville," replied Edward.

Shocked voices protested. Warwick drowned them out. "She's a married woman!"

"A widow," corrected Edward. "Her husband, Sir John Grey, was killed at the second battle of St. Albans."

"She's of low birth!" Warwick shouted.

Richard heard the uncomfortable rustle around the table.

Anger hardened his own jaw. No matter what he had done, Edward was king. Warwick had no right to take that tone. But Edward seemed strangely unruffled.

"You forget, my lord of Warwick, that they said the same about Katherine Swynford, from whom we are both descended. Besides, her mother is a Princess of Luxembourg."

"Our noble ancestor, John of Gaunt, was an honourable prince who did his duty to the realm! Twice he married for dynastic reasons. Only late in life, when it no longer mattered, did he marry the woman he loved."

"The woman I love refused to be my mistress," Edward replied.

"So you offered her the crown of England?" Warwick blustered. "You offered the crown of England to a woman whose family is despised throughout the realm?"

"I offered the crown of England to a woman of virtue whose father is a lord and whose mother is of royal blood," Edward said coldly, his patience clearly at an end. "May I remind you, my lord Warwick, that Elizabeth Woodville's mother, the Duchess of Bedford, was the first lady in the land before Marguerite d'Anjou married Henry?"

"And may I remind you, my lord King," Warwick retorted acidly, "that her father was nothing but a low-born knight before the Bitch of Anjou raised him to lord? As for Elizabeth Woodville's mother, the Duke of Bedford stooped to marry her—she brought him no dowry and her family is descended from the monstrous serpent, Melusine. 'Tis even said she's a witch, that she consorts with alchemists and occultists!"

"You don't believe that folly any more than I do, Warwick!" Edward hurled back. "The House of Luxembourg traces its lineage even further than we Plantagenets—all the way to Charlemagne, no less."

"Luxembourg means nothing to England! Charlemagne less!" Red-faced, Warwick slammed a hand on the table and pushed to his feet. Hunching over the table, he rested his weight on his fists and stared down at Edward. "An alliance with Burgundy would have cemented our ties of commerce. An alliance with France would have prevented the Bitch of Anjou from invading us with a French army at her back."

"We had a French queen once, and she brought us neither peace nor riches." Edward's tone had chilled and his narrowed eyes held warning. "Besides, too late now—'tis done. We shall have to find other means to pacify Louis and Marguerite."

"For God's sake, how could you? She has two sons."

Edward's sensuous mouth curled into a smile. "That means she can have many more."

"She's five years older than you."

"And the most beautiful woman in England."

"Her father and brothers fought for Lancaster—her husband died for them. My father and brother gave their lives to make you king!"

Edward scraped his chair back and rose. His brilliant blue eyes flashed dangerously. "And king I am. Best you remember that, Warwick."

The two glared at one another. Then Edward swung on his heel and strode from the room, leaving Warwick and his councillors staring at the open door. Warwick's friend Lord Wenlock heaved himself from his chair. "The King is right, my lord." His shrewd eyes looked up at the Kingmaker from beneath their craggy brows. "'Tis a *fait accompli*. We must accept it."

John knew he must add his warning to Wenlock's before more damage was done. After the initial shock, he had become more concerned by his brother's reaction than by Edward's marriage. So a treaty was lost. No real harm was done. But a feud with a king...

"My lord brother, 'tis well known that Elizabeth Woodville's mother is a sorceress. She must have cast a spell on the King..." A medley of voices cried, *"Aye, sorcery!"*

"The King is bewitched," John added. "He knows not what he's done."

"What he's done, brother, is to make a fool of me before all of England and Louis of France!" Warwick stormed, his bright blue eyes pained, his sharp-etched face taut. "He's treated me like a common varlet."

Aye, Edward had made it clear to the world that he ruled alone, that he deferred to no one, not even to the mighty Kingmaker. He had brought his proud cousin down in men's eyes knowing that, more than any man alive, Warwick measured himself by his reputation. He was richer than Edward, a famed soldier and a friend to foreign kings, but now Edward had tarnished the image. No longer would men bow as low to the great Earl of Warwick, or kings embrace him as an equal.

"You're no varlet," said John. "You're the most powerful baron in the land. It's not a mortal blow, brother. Men will forget this insult. And I pray you to forgive… For England's sake."

Warwick turned his proud head and stared at the open doorway through which Edward had left. Slowly, he sank back into his seat. John rested a hand on his shoulder. His brother had suffered a sore wound. A worthier ruler he might make— more dedicated, capable, and wiser than Edward—but he was not born to the throne. By birth God had appointed Edward king and Warwick his servant. Edward answered to no one. Warwick answered to the King—like a common varlet, aye; in that his brother was right. Even a baron, mighty though he be, was not master of his own destiny. And that knowledge, striking its mark with this day's work, had to taste as bitter to Warwick as a cup of hemlock.

John felt compelled to add, softly, "There is no way to go over the wall without bringing it down, brother."

Warwick twisted in his chair and gazed up at him with unseeing eyes. He had heard, but whether he had understood, John could not be sure.

CHAPTER ELEVEN

"...she hung her head...
the braid slipped and uncoiled itself
and the dark world grew darker towards the storm."

*J*ohn's wise counsel prevailed. Warwick decided to accept
with as much grace as possible what he couldn't change.
On Michaelmas Day, ten days after the council meeting,
Elizabeth Woodville was escorted into the chapel of Reading
Abbey by the Earl of Warwick and the King's brother, George,
Duke of Clarence, and honoured as queen. Though of common
stock, she looked very royal in her gold and blue brocade robes
with an ermine cloak over her shoulders and her abundant
white-gold hair loose in shimmering ringlets down to her knees.
Warwick himself knelt before the lovely bride and kissed her
hand. He even paid assiduous attention to her throughout the
event. Edward, in gratitude, raised Warwick's brother, George,
to the Archbishopric of York.

Everyone rejoiced at the amity between the King and
Kingmaker, but John was unable to shake his unease. In the
recesses of his mind, a small voice warned that all was not well.
Still troubled, he left for Carlisle after the ceremony to meet
with the Scottish embassy, who wished to sue for peace.

At the same time, Warwick left for York to inform the
members of parliament gathering there that Parliament was
adjourned. Explanations were unnecessary. Everyone knew the
King was frantically making love to the bride who had withheld
her virtue for a crown. "My Liege," Bess Woodville was reported
to have told Edward, "full well I know I am not good enough to
be your queen. But ah, my Liege, I am far too good to be
your mistress."

They had met after the battle of Towton in 1461, when
Edward paused at Stony Stratford, a few miles from Grafton,

where Bess Woodville's father, Lord Rivers, lived with his wife, the former Duchess of Bedford.

John, Duke of Bedford, the most able and trusted brother of Henry V, had been a mature widower when he met Jacquetta of Luxembourg, daughter of the Count St. Pol. He'd never expected to marry again, being quite comfortable and set in his ways, but he fell hopelessly in love with the lively, beautiful, fifteen-year-old French princess and married her in France while presiding over the trial of Joan of Arc. When he died soon afterwards, the lovely Jacquetta was escorted to England by a guard of English knights under the command of Sir Richard Woodville, the handsomest man in England.

Without the royal permission necessary for a royal to marry a commoner, Jacquetta married Richard Woodville. Parliament was furious and confiscated the duchess's lands. Later it was restored by a sympathetic young Frenchwoman who'd just become Queen of England—Marguerite d'Anjou.

Jacquetta and her handsome knight took up residence in Grafton Manor. Elizabeth was the first of twelve children born to them and a dazzlingly lovely child. When she was old enough, she was appointed lady-in-waiting to Marguerite d'Anjou and at twenty-one married a Lancastrian knight, Sir John Grey. Grey was commander of Queen Marguerite's cavalry and died in battle, leaving his widow with two sons. As soon as Edward became king, he confiscated Bradgate, seat of the Grey family, and Bess Woodville and her sons found themselves in poverty.

It was Bess's mother, Jacquetta, who devised a way to get back her lands.

"They say the new King is more ardent in the pursuit of ladies than of the deer in the royal forest," she told her daughter in her sweetly accented English. "*Alors*, don your prettiest mourning dress and go to him and plead our case, Bess."

"God's mercy, *Maman*, they'd never let me see him."

"Ah, that is why you must go to him when he is hunting in

Whittlebury forest."

"But…"

"Listen to me, *ma fille*. I am always right, no?" she demanded, bustling about the chamber, checking coffers and wardrobes. "I have found out he is hunting there today. Take the boys and wait for him under the oak tree—you know the one. For certain, he will come. Then he will see you, eh?"

Bess nodded. Her mother was French and used to intrigue, and so far most of her schemes had worked. She'd had no relatives to protect her, she'd fought her own battles, yet she'd married the man she loved against the will of powerful men and had him made lord. It was why they called her a witch. Her success defied all other explanation.

"Fortune favours us, *m'enfant*. The midnight blue of mourning is your best colour," Jacquetta said, removing a gown from one of the coffers and helping her daughter into it.

Bess regarded herself in the mirror and eyed the glittering ruby at her mother's throat with longing. "A pity I can't wear jewels. I suppose it wouldn't be seemly, would it?"

Her mother fingered the necklace that had been a gift from a queen. "*Ma fille*, your violet hood is more flattering than any gem. Only be certain to let the King see your so lovely hair." Jacquetta combed the abundant masses of silver-gold locks that rippled down to her daughter's waist. "Angel hair, soft as petals of the lily." She met Bess's eyes in the mirror. "They say the King, he is most handsome."

"They also say he's debauched and sports with wanton women," Bess said, lifting her chin with disgust. "I am no harlot."

Jacquetta watched her daughter slyly. "*Non*, you are certainly not. Your head is always clear to reason."

"He favours merchants' wives." Bess lifted her chin higher. "I'm no lowly merchant's wife."

"*Non*, indeed. He has never met anyone like you. You can manage him."

Bess smiled coldly. "The King is a man, and men are fools. They think with what hangs between their legs. If I play the part with timid glances and soft words, I shall get back my lands without compromise."

"And he can go back to his merchants' wives," said Jacquetta, suppressing a smile. She threw her daughter a glance that was part admiration, part pity. Admiration for the cool remoteness that protected her from the pain of emotion. Pity that she'd never know the ecstasy of passion. She tied her daughter's hair loosely with blue ribbons to match her dress and carefully arranged Bess's violet satin cloak over her graceful shoulders. "*Alors*, go now and save our fortune!"

With a child in either hand, Bess walked the short distance to the stately oak tree, a landmark of Whittlebury forest. Massive and splendid, it stretched out its branches as if to bless the woods it dominated. Her two sons, six-year-old Thomas and four-year-old Richard, could scarcely contain their excitement at the prospect of seeing the King. Taking up her stance beneath the oak, she waited.

The morning wore on. The children grew impatient. Bess had almost despaired when barking dogs and galloping horses emerged from the trees and headed towards her, the King alone in front, leading the hunting party. Her heart racing, she stepped out from the shade into the sun.

Edward saw her standing there with the sun streaming through her pale gold hair and shimmering over her violet cloak, reflecting a rose aura around her so that she appeared almost an illusion. He blinked, focusing his gaze. He pulled up sharply.

"Good God, lady! What do you here?"

She knelt with her sons. In the sudden motion of bending her head, her cloak loosened and her glorious gilt hair tumbled out and swept the ground. She raised her head slowly and her emerald eyes met those of the King. Edward saw that her face was pure oval with a milk-and-roses complexion, the line of forehead and nose carved with perfect symmetry, her lips full as rosebuds. But it was the eyes that held him, those cool green eyes that looked at him lazily through half-closed lids and exuded an erotic magnetism. He stared, unable to drag his gaze away. Beneath his red velvet riding jacket, his heart pounded wildly.

"Lady, I bid you rise," he said.

The hunting party arrived and waited nearby, exchanging covert grins. They knew how Edward felt about beautiful women. And this one was a beauty, indeed.

Bess rose and Edward's eyes clung to her. She looked a goddess in her simple gown with her cape flowing from her statuesque shoulders.

"What is your name, fair creature?"

"Lady Elizabeth Grey, my lord."

"Grey," he said, noting the sweep of golden lashes against smooth skin, the lift of the red lips, the short, perfect white teeth and pointed chin. Nor did his practised gaze miss the fullness of the breasts that hugged her closely fitted gown. "And what would you have of me, my lady?"

"Your Grace, my husband was killed at the battle of St. Alban's and I come to beg you to restore my husband's estates to me, and to grant my father an audience."

"Your father?"

"Lord Rivers, Sire."

"Ah, Richard Woodville," said Edward, who never forgot a name. He glanced around at Hastings, sitting comfortably in his saddle, leaning on an elbow, watching them. Hastings quirked an eyebrow and they exchanged an amused glance. Richard Woodville was the lowborn knave who'd managed to marry royal blood and get himself made lord. While outfitting Holy Harry's ships in Sandwich, he and his son Anthony had been surprised in their beds and taken prisoners to Calais, where Warwick and his father, Salisbury, had given them a tongue lashing and called Anthony "a knave's son." All England had laughed at their shame.

Edward turned his attention back to the widow. "Your husband and father fought against me, Lady Grey. Why should I help you?"

"Because my father sees the error of his ways and wishes to serve you loyally, my lord, and because my children and I are innocent of any crime against you and in dire poverty."

Edward smiled. "Well spoken, my lady. I shall think on it." He turned his horse. Over his shoulder he called out, "Come tonight for my decision."

Snickering followed this invitation and Bess blushed furiously as she watched him ride away.

~*~

"You should have heard him, *Maman!*" Bess raged, pacing back and forth. "As if I were some merchant's wife! And they were all laughing…"

"We will both go," Jacquetta said. "With me there, he would not do something rash. We royals respect one another."

"I don't wish to go at all!"

"But you will. There is money at stake." She arranged an emerald cape about her daughter's shoulders and, putting on her own black cloak, she tied it firmly around her chin. "*Alors,* let us go!"

Escorted by a male servant, the two women rode into Stony Stratford and made for the King's halting place on Watling Street.

"We seek an audience with the King," said Jacquetta.

"Indeed?" Lord Hastings smiled derisively at Jacquetta's accent. He glanced at the tall slender woman beside her, trying to see her face, but her head was bowed and he could make out nothing beneath the riding hood. "And what name shall I give him?"

"The Duchess of Bedford."

Ah, River's wife—the witch, Hastings thought. *And this is her daughter from the forest.*

"Wait here," he said with a smirk.

~*~

Hastings entered without knocking. Clad in a loose shirt, Edward rolled on a pallet with a buxom lass. Hastings cleared his throat. Edward looked up

"The damsel from the forest is here to see you, my lord," Hastings leered.

Dismissing the girl, Edward tucked his shirt back into his hose, downed a draught of wine and smacked his lips. "By God, bring her in. I am good and ready," he laughed.

Surprised when two women entered, he ignored the one who bent to kiss his hand, his eyes following Bess's every move as she dipped in and out of her obeisance. A heavy scent of lilies assailed him.

"My lord, we are here for your decision," Jacquetta said, rising.

"Do I know you?" he asked, finally registering her. The woman seemed an oddity beside the girl, like a crow guarding a rose tree.

Jacquetta smiled. "I don't think so, my lord, but I remember you very clearly. I was attending on your mother when you were born in Rouen."

His face split into a wide grin. "I knew you looked familiar!" She laughed at his jest.

He regarded her warmly. Her sweet French accent evoked happy memories of his childhood in France, and her grey hair and slender frame reminded him of his nurse, Anne of Caux, whom he'd loved, and who'd been French. "My first language was French," he said. "My ladies—would you care for refreshment?"

"My lord King," replied Jacquetta when Bess made no answer,

"we shall be delighted."

As Jacquetta and Edward laughed and exchanged stories about France, Bess and Edward exchanged glances. He was clearly reluctant to let them leave, yet by the end of the night they still didn't know his decision.

"My lord, the hour is late and we must return to Grafton," Jacquetta said at length. She waited expectantly.

"I've never seen Grafton Manor," the King replied, avoiding the hidden question.

Jacquetta realised there was nothing to be done about it. They'd have to endure another evening with him. "Perhaps you will sup with us tomorrow night?" she said with her best smile. Surely that would be the end of it. He couldn't stay forever. He had to get himself to London to be crowned one day.

Edward glanced at Hastings, who stood with arms folded, leaning against the doorframe. "Will, do we have a battle engagement tomorrow?"

"Not that I'm aware, my lord," he grinned.

"In that case, my ladies, we shall be honoured to accept," Edward said.

~*~

Before Edward started on his way back to London, he sent word to his Chancellor, Bishop Neville, that Bess's father, Lord Rivers, and her brother, Anthony Woodville, were pardoned all offences and that the Duchess of Bedford was to be paid the annual stipend of the dower she held of the Crown—in advance.

He returned to Grafton often during the next three years, at first with Hastings and a party of friends, later alone and in secret, but his visits continued to be unfruitful to him. He wished he were more like Hastings, who thought nothing of abducting unwilling women, but he could never resort to force. His honour forbade it, and until now—with one terrible and deeply regrettable exception—women had flocked to him willingly. At last, in desperation, he pulled Bess down on the bed in her chamber and held a dagger to her throat.

"You may kill me if you wish," she said, "I'm willing to die for my virtue."

"What do you want?" he demanded hoarsely. "You know I'm deep in love with you, Bess!"

"'Tis best if you leave and never come back, my lord. I was a virtuous wife to my husband and I won't be any man's mistress. Not even yours."

Edward froze. He'd heard those words before. For an instant, with striking clarity, he saw *her* face, the face he wished only to forget. He put the dagger away with an unsteady hand. "What do you want, Bess?"

"Nothing you can give me," she said. "Farewell, my lord."

He watched her leave and he felt as though the sun had left with her, turning a bright world of blues skies and flowering fields into a grey, barren stillness. He rose from the bed and went to the open window. Linnets twilled and a soft breeze fluttered through the room. It was spring, the season of love, and the scent of flowers hung heavy on the air. He sank down on the window seat.

Jacquetta appeared. She heaved an audible sigh and stood before him.

"'Tis the curse of royalty to have everything but love," she said. "Only your noble ancestor John of Gaunt was able to marry his Katrine... and Kate of Valois, she had her Owen Tudor for a time, poor soul." She stole a sly glance at him from the corner of her eye, and sighed again. "Thanks be to the merciful God I married my knight in secret and nothing was to be done about it. But then, I was only a princess. You are King..." She turned her eyes on Edward, who was gazing at her silently. "'Tis the curse of royalty to have everything but love," she repeated, pleased at how sad she sounded.

CHAPTER TWELVE

"Thro' the peaceful court she crept
And whisper'd."

*E*dward had expected to tire of Bess Woodville once he'd bedded her. He'd expected to leave her as he'd left the others, without a backward glance. If she had tried to expose the marriage, he would have laughed her out of the hall. As far as the world was concerned, only a mad woman would dare to claim that a King stooped so low to wed her.

To his surprise he found himself more desperate for her than ever before. She was a perfume and he was intoxicated. The more he made love to Bess Woodville, the more he had to have her. Against this frenzied, tormenting passion, he struggled in vain. Eventually he knew he had to proclaim the marriage, though it meant scandal, and worse—opposing Warwick and drawing his ire. Fortune, crown, future and soul were as nothing before the mysterious force that possessed him.

Despite his perennial money woes, he spared no expense on his queen's coronation, making it the most lavish in living memory in the hope that people might forget her low birth. The streets of London were hung with bright banners, rotting traitors' heads were removed from their poles above New Stone Gate, and London Bridge was spread with sand to cover filth and feces. Tall-masted ships, carrying the Duchess of Bedford's royal relatives from Burgundy, including the Count de St. Pol and a hundred of his knights, rocked at anchor in the sparkling Thames. Edward had stressed to Bess Woodville's royal kin the necessity of making an extravagant display.

After eight months of planning, two days before Whit Sunday in the year of 1465, all was ready. Bess Woodville came to London from her palace at Sheen, one of many Edward had given her. Through the gaily decorated streets she progressed to the Tower of London, past the mummers and colourful pageants, past the singing minstrels and the two angels with wings assembled from a thousand peacock feathers. On the next day, seated in a velvet litter drawn by white horses, she was led to Westminster Palace by fifty newly created Knights of the Bath dressed in blue robes with white silk hoods.

There, on the eve of her coronation, she rewarded Edward with a night of lovemaking more violent and passionate than any he had ever known.

~*~

Jacquetta watched her daughter's graceful figure enter Westminster Abbey under a canopy of gold cloth borne on silver spears. Bess carried a sceptre in each hand and her gilt hair flowed over her ermine cloak and scarlet robe. Beaming, she followed Bess's train, borne by the King's sister Meg. Wariness crept into her pride when they entered Westminster Abbey and her gaze fell on the King's brother, George, Duke of Clarence. In crimson and cloth of gold, and mounted on a stallion caparisoned with gold spangles and embroidered velvet, he rode through Westminster Hall, making way for the queen to be led before the Archbishop of Canterbury. Of the King's two brothers, Richard of Gloucester had stayed away on some pretext or other, and though George had come, he'd been vociferous in his condemnation of the marriage. Edward's tongue-lashing had cowed him into submission for the time being, but she feared George's good behaviour wouldn't last.

Jacquetta stiffened at the moment of crowning and held her breath until she thought her lungs would burst. When the blue-veined old hands of the Archbishop of Canterbury set the crown on her daughter's head, she exhaled with such violence that she thought all Westminster had heard. Her head swam, the light falling through the brilliant coloured windows blinded her sight, and her face felt as if it would split with the breadth of her smile. *Her daughter was Queen of England!*

When she finally recovered her composure, she became aware of the dark looks around her. She glanced uneasily from the old craggy face of Archbishop Bourchier to the young Neville next to him. The new Archbishop of York was the only Neville present. Warwick was conveniently away on a trade mission to Burgundy and his brother John was chasing down Holy Harry somewhere in the North. She pressed her lips together. The Nevilles were trouble. Bess must watch them.

In response to a gesture from her daughter, Jacquetta stepped forward and lifted the heavy crown from Bess's brow. During the long ceremony she performed the service several times. Though Bess exchanged the crown for a coronet at the banquet, even that proved such a crushing weight that she removed it while she dined. As Jacquetta listened to the music from a hundred minstrels and tasted one of the sixty dishes served at the feast, she heard the tittering and the snickers. "The crown would not sit on her low-born head!" they whispered. *Pardieu,* people were always whispering. Not until the next day when she attended the tournament did the whispers concern her. There had been a prophecy, the whispers said, made by a ragged old woman outside the jousting ground. She gave a shudder as she took her seat in the crimson-striped royal loge with her husband. The wise woman had crossed herself when Bess had passed and said, "Where she treads, evil follows, and as the Crown tottered on her head so will England totter beneath her weight."

Jacquetta was superstitious, and for good reason. On several occasions she found herself foretelling events that later came true. She hugged her fur-lined mantle closer, only dimly aware of the braying of trumpets and the marshals shouting the rules for the melee. *The wise woman has to be wrong,* she told herself. As mistaken as those who'd foretold disaster for Edward because he'd chosen to be crowned on Childermas, the ill-omened anniversary of the massacre of the innocent babes by Herod. So unlucky was it considered that the King of France refused even to discuss business on Holy Innocents Day.

Yet Edward was secure on the throne. All was well.

She rested her eyes on him. He was in high spirits, laughing, making jests, and drinking frequently from a gem-studded golden cup presented by one of his Knights of the Body. Edward cared as little for unlucky days as he did for holy days, and he had insisted on being crowned on that Sabbath because it suited him.

We worry too much, mon Dieu, she thought. *'Tis the times, they are so uncertain.* She adjusted her veil to shield her from the bright sun. The heralds yelled *"Laissez allez!"* and scampered from the field. Trumpets brayed again and two knights rode in, one in shining black armour, the other a gigantic figure in silver. They took up their stance at opposing ends of the field, lances in hand. Hoofs thundered and dust rose as they ran the course, then came the shock of steel and groans of disappointment from the crowd, for neither knight was unhorsed. Furnished with fresh lances by darting squires, they cantered into position once more.

As she turned to watch the second course, she noticed the dagger glances slyly cast at her and the snickers quickly checked from the adjoining loges. Many among the crowd of old nobility resented them, but today she was determined to enjoy her happiness and dwell only on the positive. Had untold honours not been heaped on her family these past eight months?

A loud chorus interrupted her reverie. The black knight had been unhorsed and the silver pronounced the winner. Hoisted to his feet by his squires, the black knight strutted angrily off the field as the silver knight advanced to the royal box for his prize. "Well done, Cheyney!" cried the King, tossing him a jewelled medal of St. George. "A fair course!" Twenty more knights entered the field on foot for the general melee and hand-to-hand combat. The prize was a ruby to the winner.

Amid the cheers of the crowd and periodic blare of the heralds' trumpets, Jacquetta's glance swept the boxes and rested proudly on her brood of thirteen children. Thanks to Bess, they had all made splendid marriages. *Pardieu,* but no one could fault her for not looking out for her family! One daughter had married a duke, one an earl, and four had married earl's sons. Her eldest boy, Anthony, was now a baron, having wed the heiress of Lord Scales. Another had married the richest duchess in the kingdom; yet another was betrothed to the King's niece, who had earlier been promised to John Neville's new-born son.

Jacquetta smiled inwardly. Warwick's humiliation of her husband still rankled her after all these years and it gave her pleasure to see the Nevilles brought low. She patted her husband's hand. He cast her a smile and her harsh thoughts fled. After all, they'd had the last laugh. Lord Rivers was now Earl Rivers and riches had gushed into their hands. She turned her eyes to the centrepiece of the lavish ceremony: cool, remote, beautiful Bess, seated on her velvet chair in the centre of their row. Once she had been lady-in-waiting to a queen; now she herself was queen. Her daughter was not only the fairest in the land, but very clever, she thought, reflecting on their conversation earlier that day...

"To think, *ma fille,* of all that is now yours," Jacquetta mused as she clasped a necklace of flashing gems around Bess's smooth white throat. "The crown imperial of gold and pearls to which my husband, the Duke of Bedford, was heir would have made me queen. Now you are the queen in my place. When I fell from grace, I had no relatives to protect me. Now our relatives are everywhere and the land complains of it! How strange is life—as if it turns in circles as it moves along. 'Tis like a dream."

"Nay, 'tis the Wheel of Fortune, and the Wheel can bring us down again as quickly as it took us up," Bess replied. "What you lost and I won back has come to us at a cost—everyone is against us. They say I'm lowborn. That I'm not good enough to be queen."

"That will change now we are linked in marriage to the most powerful of the noble families."

"That will never change, *Maman,* until people learn they cannot laugh at us."

"*M'enfant,* what does it matter? They laugh because they can do nothing else. The important thing is we are safe. You are crowned now, and blessed by God Himself." Jacquetta fastened the last ruby button of her daughter's gown. "No one dares harm us."

Bess turned her cool green eyes on her mother. "No, *Maman.* Not until Edward is mine—*all mine*—will we be safe. When he turns away from his friends—from the Nevilles, from his brothers—then are we safe."

"And when is that, Bess?" Jacquetta demanded, surprised again at her unpredictable daughter.

"When I have a child, *Maman.* If anything happens to Edward before I have a child, George will destroy us—but when I have a child, then are we safe. Then shall we settle old scores with our foes. Then shall Warwick rue the day he called my father a knave! A child will make Edward a puppet in my hands. A child— a *son*—'tis what we need, but why does one not come? I've been trying, *Maman.* Oh, how I've tried!"

"I have no doubt you will get your child soon, Bess. None of us is plagued with the barren condition, but for sure we can use the help of God. First, we will buy more prayers to win His favour. Then I shall consult Friar Bungey. His spells are said to be the most powerful. Meanwhile, *m'enfant,* you must endow a college. That is what queens do, and since it takes much money, God will look with favour on the sacrifice."

She placed a hand on Bess's arm. "But most important, Bess, remember: Use only soft words and sweet ways with the King. 'Tis unwise to demand from him. He is stubborn, that one. If you try to push him in one way, he will go in the other, like a mule. But if you accept everything, he will deny you nothing, *ma fille.*"

Bess peered at herself in the looking glass Jacquetta held. Carefully she rubbed cochineal paste into her high cheekbones. She lifted her chin.

"You need have no fear, *Maman.* I know how to manage Edward. I'm prepared to wait for my revenge, but I shall have what's mine, though I walk through Hell to get it."

A roaring cheer brought Jacquetta back to the present. She lifted her hands and clapped for the champion of the tournament, Lord Thomas Stanley. The stout bejewelled baron stepped up to claim his prize. Bess rose to award him the ruby. Jacquetta watched with approval as the powerful lord bowed most humbly to her daughter. The King watched, too, but he was gazing only at Bess, an adoring look in his brilliant blue eyes. Having fulfilled her duty, Bess sat back down in her velvet chair. Turning to her husband, she smiled shyly at him with lowered lashes.

Ah, indeed, we need have no fear, Jacquetta thought. Her daughter was very clever.

CHAPTER THIRTEEN

"I found Him in the shining of the stars
I marked him in the flowering of His fields
But in His ways with men I find Him not."

In the Painted Chamber of Westminster Palace, Richard waited by the gilded entrance, listening to the minstrels and watching guests assemble for the banquet. Plump bishops, their robes sewn with jewels and gold, conversed with lords richly arrayed in satins and fancy shoes, some with points so long they were caught up at the knee with golden chains. Ladies swept past, holding their fur-trimmed trains and nodding their headdresses in greeting. Their perfume assaulted his nostrils. He sneezed.

"Ah, Dickon," said a gentle voice, "you've caught another cold and you've no handkerchief again."

His sister Meg proceeded to wipe his nose. He pushed her away. "It's not a cold, Meg, and I'm not a babe anymore."

She drew her hand back awkwardly. "Pray forgive me, Dickon. Old habits die hard."

"Well, indeed, they may," said a high bright voice behind her with a trace of laughter. "But are you too grown now to give your long-lost sisters a kiss, Dickon?" It was his second-oldest sister, Liza, bouncing a toddler in her arms. "And your new nephew, Johnnie?"

Regretting his rudeness, Richard embraced Meg warmly, gave Liza a hug, and admired her first-born.

"Have you seen Nan?" inquired Liza, referring to their oldest sister. "I've been looking for her all evening. She hasn't met my Johnnie yet either."

"She's over there, talking to St. Leger," replied Meg.

Through an opening in the crowd, Richard saw his eldest sister standing by one of the many windows, deep in conversation with a knight. Richard had seen Nan but three times in all his life, which suited him well enough. He didn't think his haughty sister liked him much, and he always found himself ill at ease and tongue-tied in her presence. Meg claimed Nan's coldness was not personal, she was just bitter at having been abandoned by her husband, the Lancastrian Duke of Exeter, who'd fled to France with Marguerite d'Anjou. Richard wasn't so sure. Guests milled between them and the opening closed like a folded spyglass.

"Time you met your oldest aunt, isn't it, sweet babe?" Liza

cooed. "Come with me, Meg, tell me your news. I'm dying to know; is there a handsome prince hovering on your horizon?"

Richard bowed as Liza led a blushing Meg away. When he lifted his head, his sisters were gone but he heard an echo of Liza's merry laughter. Aye, laughter was everywhere tonight, for there was cause to celebrate. Much good news had arrived on the heels of the queen's coronation. On St. Swithin's Day, in the warm month of July, Henry of Lancaster was captured in the North, where he had hidden for a year disguised as a monk. Warwick had tied Henry's heels beneath the stirrups of his horse and paraded him around London for the people to mock him. Then Edward had locked him up in the Tower to pray to his heart's content. That same month, the deputy lieutenant of Ireland, the Earl of Desmond, came to make his report to Edward.

Richard had heard a great deal about the Earl of Desmond, Thomas Fitzgerald. So close a friend had he been to his father that even Richard's mother, who rarely attended court functions anymore, had come to pay her respects. Warwick, of whom little had been seen at court since Edward's marriage, had also made the journey. Only John was absent, though he'd sent word that he'd attend if the border remained quiet. The festivities in Desmond's honour were to be spread over several days, with hunting, feasting, and much music making and reading of poetry, for the Earl loved music and was a patron of the arts in Ireland.

George appeared out of the throng and closed the distance between them. Richard smiled happily. "Edward has made everything very fine tonight, hasn't he, George?"

George cast a bored look around. "He's spent a few groats, but even with that, he can't match Warwick's splendour."

Richard threw him a sharp glance. Besides the hall's magnificent painted walls, tracery windows and gilded angels, cartloads of flowers perfumed the air and candles flickered over the gleaming marble pillars and tapestries by the hundreds, while the colourful murals around the room that set out scenes from the Old Testament and Edward the Confessor's coronation sparkled from the scrubbing they had received. Richard decided to ignore George, who was obviously in bad humour for whatever reason, and turned his attention to the paintings.

As he looked, the smile that had begun to curve his lips faded. A grave series darkened the wall with bloody battles and beheadings that depicted the Vices in harrowing detail, and every glint of gilt and jewelled colour seemed to tell a tale of violence and suffering. All at once he wished he was back in the North. He had never cared much for court. Court was like a beautiful song—full of trills, rippling and gay, but beneath the lilting melody rumbled distant chords, warning of danger to the straining ear.

Trumpets sounded. Amid a swish of silks, lords and ladies bowed as the glittering King and Queen entered the hall. As always, Edward looked as handsome as a god. He wore a tunic of yellow shot silk beneath a tabard of heavy brown velvet edged with sable. The puffed sleeves and open sides suited his broad-shouldered frame, but it was not a style for the short of stature, like Richard. He favoured the simple doublet, such as the dove grey he had chosen for the evening, embroidered with motifs of black and gold.

His mother, Duchess Cecily, followed Edward and Bess on the arm of the guest of honour, the darkly handsome Irish earl, who was attired in white velvet tissue of gold, and they distributed themselves on the steps around the canopied throne.

A movement caught Richard's attention. Ten-year-old Thomas Grey, the queen's older son by her first marriage, was snickering with his younger brother. Richard thought Thomas looked like a gillyflower in his short doublet of orange and lime with alternating green and orange stockings. The fashion was the rage at Edward's court but Richard found it lewd, for it was cut above the buttocks and manly organs, leaving little to the imagination. Hastings, standing nearby, was another who chose to sport the disgusting new fashion.

Around the queen's two sons clustered more Woodvilles: the Duchess Jacquetta and her husband, Earl Rivers, with their brood of seven daughters, five sons, and newly acquired noble spouses. Among these the queen's oldest brother, Anthony Woodville, stood out like a peacock in a field of pansies as he conversed with his youngest brother, John.

John Woodville and his new wife made a ridiculous looking couple, Richard thought. The marriage between the sixty-year-old Dowager Duchess of Norfolk—who could barely stand even with the aid of a silver cane—and the queen's eighteen-year-old brother had scandalised the world, and infuriated Warwick. The duchess, his aunt, had fallen prey to the Woodvilles because she was the richest widow in the land. Richard recalled Warwick's rage. "A diabolical marriage!" he'd roared, stomping back and forth across the great hall in Middleham like an enraged bull.

Warwick was right. The Woodvilles were looting the land like locusts, and their greed was all the more revolting because they made no effort to hide it. His glance moved to the queen. She had grown even more haughty in these months and sat with her back rigid, gripping the gilded armrests of her throne, her chin held so high she seemed to be looking down her nose through closed lids. He knew she was displeased. There were many here tonight whom she disliked, including him.

Trumpets blared again. "George, Duke of Clarence!" the herald announced.

Richard watched his brother saunter up to the throne in his pointed plum-coloured shoes. George cut an elegant figure in his ducal coronet, his cloth of gold surcoat blazing with the royal arms, but his manner bordered on insolent. A hush fell over the crowd and there was an uneasy rustle. George threw Edward and his queen a perfunctory bow, made no move to kiss their hands, then greeted Desmond with marked warmth. Unlike Warwick, George didn't cloak his feelings, and everyone knew that he despised his brother's lowborn wife. Richard thought his show of hostility unwise and had said as much. But George had laughed. He was heir to the throne, he said, and could do as he pleased.

Heir to the throne, aye, Richard thought, *but heir only until the queen has a child—doesn't George think that far ahead?* Yet, in spite of himself, he admired his brother's courage. George wasn't afraid of anyone. Richard wished he had his guts. His glance moved to the queen's mother, Jacquetta, near the dais, and he felt a stab of unease. He didn't like the way she looked at George.

"Richard, Duke of Gloucester!" cried the herald.

Richard marched up to the King's chair. He knelt before Edward and the queen and kissed Bess's icy hand. Edward leapt from his throne and embraced him. "Dear Dickon, how joyous we are to behold your face! You've been gone too long from my sight, fair brother."

Richard beamed at Edward as he took his place a step below George, but his glance, moving back over the dais, touched, and held, on the queen. Her hooded green eyes regarded him coldly, and for a fraction of a second—so quickly that he might have imagined it—a thin smile twisted her mouth into an ugly line. He thought of Melusine, the serpent from whom she claimed descent.

One after another gorgeously dressed nobles and their ladies came up to the dais, gems glittering, silks shimmering, gauzy veils flowing, but the queen's malicious look had spoiled his pleasure in the evening. He chewed his lip as he always did when he was nervous, and forced his attention back to Edward, who rose to give a speech of welcome. When he was finished, the minstrels and jugglers began their performances. Without warning the music ceased and a shocked murmur ran through the crowd. Heads turned towards the entrance. A man with a long white beard and leather pants cut high above knobbly knees thumped his way through the room with the aid of a staff.

Edward's hand froze with his wine cup halfway to his lips. "Whoa!" he called, the smile vanishing from his lips. "What's this?"

The man ambled up to the King.

"Why, 'tis George's Fool!" muttered Edward.

"Fool I may be," replied the Fool, "but tonight, Sire, I am the King of Fools!"

"A dubious honour, I assure you," said Edward with narrowed eyes. "Tell me, Your Foolish Grace, why are you dressed in this bizarre fashion?"

"Sire, my journey here was full perilous as any knight's. Many times I came near death."

"How so?" demanded Edward, warily.

"I was near swept away by the currents, so high were *the Rivers!*"

A deadly silence fell over the room. Everyone stared at the rigid Queen. Then Edward let out a roar of laughter. The silence shattered, and everyone laughed. Music sounded in the minstrels' gallery. With relief, Richard fled the dais. *Jesu,* but George had made his Fool take a dangerous chance!

Richard danced a pavane with the Countess of Desmond, his mind returning to the queen. She was smiling now and seemed to have forgotten her displeasure at the jest, but Richard suspected she rarely forgot or forgave anything. When the dance ended, he retired to a corner beneath the minstrel's gallery to observe the revelries. He wished he knew where Anne had gone. He hadn't seen her all evening.

A feather tickled his ear. "Can you never be still?" laughed a voice behind him.

"Anne!" he exclaimed. Then, lowering his voice to a whisper, he added, "Let's leave." He seized her hand, but as he dragged her to the door they bumped into the Earl of Desmond. Behind him came Bella, and, spotting Anne, spirited her off to see a newborn hound, leaving Richard alone with Desmond.

"You've made quite an impression on my Countess, my lord of Gloucester," the Earl said, a twinkle in his brown eyes. "She seems unable to talk of anything but you. No doubt all Ireland will soon know the King's brother is near as handsome as he is."

Desmond was a fine-looking man, Richard thought, with his generous mouth, aquiline nose, and touches of humour around his eyes and mouth. "My lord," Richard replied, "the Countess is kind."

"Nay, Lord Richard, not so. You resemble your dear father whom we all loved, God absolve his soul."

Richard knew the rush of gratitude he felt showed on his face. "You knew my father well, my lord. Could you—would you..." Richard braced himself. "Tell me how he died?"

Desmond gave him a long, appraising look. "Aah... you don't know? A bitter tale. No wonder they have kept it from you. But perhaps it is time..." He rested a hand on Richard's shoulder and drew him aside from the circulating crowd.

Richard listened in rapt attention. It had happened during a Christmas truce at Wakefield Castle. Snow had been falling lightly as a small number of the Duke's men left the safety of the castle to forage in the nearby woods. Suddenly there were shouts and calls for help. A party of Lancastrians had fallen on the Yorkists and were cutting them down mercilessly. The Duke of York never hesitated. Grabbing his armour, he rushed to save his hapless men. Along with him had ridden his son Edmund, Warwick's father, Salisbury, and Warwick's brother, Thomas. They were winning the foray when out of nowhere appeared a thousand-strong Lancastrian force, led by the iron-faced Lord Clifford. Heavily outnumbered, the Duke of York and his men had no chance. The Duke and Warwick's brother fell, fighting bravely, but the Duke's son, Edmund, seventeen, disarmed and unhorsed, was brutally cut down by Clifford as he fled across the bridge to Sanctuary. Warwick's father, the Earl of Salisbury, was taken alive and beheaded the next day. Further atrocities followed. The bodies of the Yorkist leaders were mutilated and their heads cut off and borne to York, to be nailed to the gates. Amid derisive laughter, Marguerite had placed a paper crown on the Duke's head, since he had wished to be king.

"It was despicable... breaking the truce, the double ambush, murdering an unarmed man—a youth, no less—and defiling the bodies of those who had fallen honourably in battle... The world changed after that."

Silence.

"England lost a good man that day, Lord Richard. A fair-minded man, free from the greed and ambition that plagues others. Ireland only had your father a year, but he governed us with justice, something we had not known before... We will never forget him."

"There you are, my Lord of Desmond!" came George's voice. "I've been searching for you."

Desmond's smile widened. A special tie bound the two since George was born in Ireland and Desmond was his godfather. George was also Lord Lieutenant of Ireland while Desmond was his deputy. The arrangement worked well, since Ireland was governed by an Irish lord for a change, and George, who had neither the interest nor the ability to govern, enjoyed his title.

"My dear George, how well you look," Desmond said.

"'Tis no doubt due to my dress," said George, with a futile effort at humility. "Gold flatters me. I have fourteen gowns of tissue of gold alone."

After exchanging information about the health of absent friends and relatives, George spotted a familiar face. "Sir Thomas! Pray, join us."

The portly old gentleman hitched up his silver girdle around his ample belly and, excusing himself from his company of ladies, came stoutly to their side. Richard had met him before. Sir Thomas Cook was a former mayor of London. With a sweeping bow, the old man introduced himself.

"I hear you've sold a fine tapestry to the Queen, Sir Thomas," said George. He took a pasty from a page with a silver tray and popped it into his mouth.

The old knight coloured. "Nay, my lord, it was the Queen's mother who asked to buy my arras. But I didn't wish to sell, though she offered me eight hundred marks for it."

"Aha," Desmond said, sipping his wine. "Then it's a fine arras, Sir Thomas."

"I can vouch there's none finer in England," George interjected before Cook could respond. "A scene of the Siege of Jerusalem, exceptionally well wrought in gold and worth far more than what the thrifty Duchess is willing to pay."

"Money's not the question, in truth," Cook said quickly. "It reminds me of my youthful fighting days in France. Sentimental of me, I daresay, but I can't bring myself to part with it."

"No reason why you should," George replied, draining his wine cup. He held it out to a page for a refill. "The Duchess has no need of your arras. She has others."

Richard looked in Jacquetta's direction. She stood on the dais with her daughter and Tiptoft, the Earl of Worcester. Tiptoft, whose sharp movements were tinged with controlled violence, was deep in conversation, and making a curious gesture. Hammering his fist into the palm of his hand, he twisted it around as if to crush something, while the queen and her mother nodded. Richard felt uneasy. What could they be discussing?

"I meant no offence to the Duchess of Bedford when I refused her offer, my lords—indeed no offence was meant," Sir Thomas insisted, clearly uncomfortable.

"Indeed not," Desmond said, and changed the subject. "The King has planned much entertainment for the morrow, then I depart. Urgent tidings summon me back to Ireland sooner than anticipated."

"I hear you have a particularly fine manuscript of Tristan and Iseult, my lord," Richard said quickly. "If you should return again, would you bring it with you? The tale of Tristan is one of my favourites."

"Then you are fortunate," announced a voice in his ear. "For I have it on the best authority that tonight the tale shall be told by the finest raconteur in France, fair cousin!"

Richard swung around. "John! I thought you'd not come! I feared the Scots might keep you."

"They tried. But since the King was so good as to include me in the Earl's festivities, I got away from them. I grow dull alone in my tent with only my maps for company. Besides, I wish to finally meet the Earl of Desmond, who has long been a loyal friend to the House of York."

John's deep blue eyes twinkled as they always did, but he looked different. Richard had never seen him so splendidly attired. The fabric of his azure velvet coat was thick and rich, his furs magnificent, and around his neck hung the golden collar of York sunbursts and roses that Edward had given him.

There was another change that was not as flattering. In the months since Richard had last seen John, he'd grown leaner and the lines about his mouth were more deeply etched. Too much campaigning in bad weather, Richard supposed. He remembered the bone-chilling cold of Northumberland, the soaking rains, the sleet and icy snows that made the mud-mired paths they traversed so laborious during the siege of Alnwick and Bamborough. A soldier's life was not an easy one. Not even when the soldier was an earl.

"My lord of Northumberland, I regret we didn't meet earlier. I believe you were otherwise engaged when the Duke of York came to Ireland?" Desmond said with a hint of amusement.

John laughed. "Aye, fair Marguerite insisted on entertaining me in the York dungeons at the time."

Richard looked at him with renewed admiration. He had not known until Desmond told him how John had saved the city of York. But for John, York would have been razed to the ground like Ludlow, its women raped and its men put to the sword. No one had dared beg mercy for the citizens in the face of Edward's rage after he had seen his father's and brother's rotted heads—no one except John. Yet John's own father and brother had been beheaded and their heads nailed to those same gates.

A voice added, "Count yourself fortunate. You might not have lived to enjoy her hospitality if I hadn't been holding Somerset's brother prisoner in Calais myself." It was Warwick. He was with his brother, George Neville, the newly created Archbishop of York, and his majestic presence commanded a rustle of attention, not only from the nobles nearby, but from the queen and Tiptoft across the room. "That stroke of good fortune was all that kept your head attached to your shoulders, John." Warwick's thin smile was forced and it was clear that other matters weighed on his mind.

After a short silence the conversation turned for a while on the neutral topic of manuscripts. Richard, who delighted in books, listened with rapt interest, but George had heard enough.

"Tell me, my lord Desmond," he said, choosing a sweetmeat from a tray presented by a page. "How do you find our new Queen?"

"Very beautiful," Desmond replied, startled at the abrupt interruption.

"Edward would agree with you, of course, but to me she looks like a rat with that pointed chin."

The Earl of Desmond, in the motion of taking a sip of his hippocras, froze with his cup at his lips. Silence fell. Heads turned. A woman's laugh floated across the room. It was Bess Woodville. At that precise moment, she turned and stared directly at them. On her face was a look so malevolent that

Richard understood why she was called a sorceress. Beside her, Tiptoft also met their gaze, his stony black eyes protruding over his hawk nose, giving him the appearance of a vulture that had just sighted its prey.

Sir Thomas Cook immediately excused himself on a pretext and slipped away. Richard noticed that the Earl of Desmond and the Nevilles had turned a sickly grey colour, but George held his head high, staring at the queen as if issuing a challenge. Richard hoped she hadn't overheard his words, impossible as it seemed from across the room. Yet some instinct told him that despite the distance and the crowds that separated them, despite the music of the minstrels and hubbub of conversations, somehow she had.

Desmond broke the silence that held them in thrall. "There is danger in words, my lord," he said to George in a voice so low that Richard had to strain to hear. "At court even murals have ears."

"She can't touch me," George replied, making no effort to lower his voice. "I am heir to the throne!"

Richard realised that George, who was overly fond of sweet wine, was half-drunk on his favourite malmsey. He knew he should leave, but he couldn't just abandon his brother.

The Earl of Desmond had no such hesitation. "My lords, pray excuse me. I find the room exceedingly warm. I shall seek air in the garden." He bowed deeply.

Hastily, Warwick said, "The blooms are profuse this time of year. Allow me to give you a tour, my lord of Desmond."

Richard watched the two earls leave. So did the queen, he noted. A sick feeling churned his stomach. John, still pale, left in search of his wife with whom he said he wished a dance, and George Neville, the Archbishop of York, suddenly decided to consult the Archbishop of Canterbury on some point of clerical law.

"Come, George," said Richard gently, taking his elbow. "I'll take you to your chamber."

George shook off his arm. "The night's young, brother!" Richard realised it was useless. He couldn't save George from himself. He excused himself without preamble and left the room.

~*~

Outside it was refreshingly cool. A brisk wind blew from the river, rustling the trees. Except for a small group of maidens sitting around a young man playing a lute on the stone steps, the garden was empty. Richard headed past the clipped yew hedges to the river's edge and sat down by a clump of lilies. The Thames was inky black and deadly still. He preferred to look up at the stars. God was up there somewhere. Maybe his father, too. Maybe even looking down at him.

In the distance, a barge passed, torches flaring. Men's voices came to him, distant and muffled, then grew more distinct. At first he thought they came from the barge, then he knew that he was mistaken. They came from somewhere behind him, from one of the walks behind the hedges of yews.

"Edward asked me what I thought of her when we were hawking today."

"I hope you didn't give him the same answer you just gave me?" There was humour in the tone. The voice seemed familiar to Richard but was still too faint to place.

"If I had, I wouldn't be here talking to you now, would I, Richard?"

Richard jumped at the mention of his name, then realised that it was the Earl of Desmond, Thomas Fitzgerald, addressing the Earl of Warwick, Richard Neville. They had drawn close now and their voices came to him clearly on the night air.

"No, you'd be in the Tower, Tom," Warwick replied.

"Minus a head." A chuckle.

"So how did you respond?" Warwick asked.

"What I told George. That she is very beautiful."

"Was he satisfied with that?"

"No. He pressed for my true opinion."

"And?"

"I told him nothing he doesn't know himself," Desmond said. "That a royal French bride would have brought the country peace and an alliance of trade."

There was a long pause. Richard's unease grew and his heart began to pound. When Warwick spoke again, his voice was low, anxious. "What did he say?"

"That the last queen was French and brought the land no peace and no trade."

"Aah… He told me the same." Warwick's tone evidenced relief. *And I'm still alive,* it suggested. "How did you respond?"

"I told him that a marriage negotiated by the Earl of Warwick was not the same as one negotiated by that traitorous fool Suffolk, who sold out England by marrying Henry of Lancaster to a penniless princess for his own ends," Desmond said.

"True," replied Warwick. "Marguerite had only a single soiled dress when she arrived in London. Henry had to supply her wardrobe before he could receive her. It was a disgrace." He paused. "So how did Edward react?"

"He took it well enough. He laughed. You know Edward."

"I thought I did, once. Now I'm not so sure."

"He's a good man, Richard. All will be well, I've no doubt," Desmond said.

Here they began to move away, for their voices became muffled, grew faint, and faded into the night, leaving only the gentle lapping of the waves to break the silence. Richard looked up at the sky, crowded with stars. He wished Desmond had not trusted so much in the truth. It was not safe to speak freely about the queen. *At court even the murals have ears,* Desmond had warned George. Why hadn't his father's loyal friend taken his own advice?

Because he trusted Edward, came the answer unbidden

to his mind.

He turned his gaze back on the river and frowned. Strange, but in that deep black water, he could not see the reflection of the stars.

~*~

Bess stood naked beneath her shift while a lady-in-waiting brushed the hair that fell to her waist. In the mirror she watched Edward as he entered the bedchamber, came to her side and, with a wave of his hand, dismissed her lady-in-waiting. The door clanged shut.

Edward wrapped an arm around her midriff, and met her eyes in the mirror. She could feel his uneven breathing on her cheek. Winding a fistful of her hair around his hand, he lifted it to his lips. "I can't decide whether it's silver or gold. 'Gilt' they call it, did you know?"

She smiled at him in the glass. He kissed her neck.

"How do you like Desmond, my love?" he murmured, his breath hot against her ear.

"Did Warwick appoint him, my dear lord?" she asked.

Edward jerked his head up. "I appointed him. On Warwick's recommendation."

"Oh."

"It was one of Warwick's better pieces of advice," Edward said, relaxing. His hand slid under her shift to skim her hips and thigh. "Desmond's done well in Ireland. There's peace there, for a change. But let's not talk about Desmond." He bent his golden head and kissed her shoulder.

Bess reached behind her and explored his thigh. He gave a gasp, sought the ribbon of her shift and untied it. The gown fell to the floor in a silken heap, exposing her naked body.

"Bess, oh, Bess," he murmured, brushing her cheek, her neck, her arms with hungry kisses. "I don't understand your power over me, but if it's witchcraft as they say, never let it end..." He gazed at her in the mirror, face flushed, eyes glazed with passion. "There's no one else in the world like you. I love you, Bess." Suddenly, he looked up and laughed.

"What amuses you so, my dearest lord? Not my body, I hope?"

"Never your body, which grows sweeter like ripening fruit," He cradled a smooth, plump breast in one hand.

"What then?"

"Desmond said I shouldn't have married you," he laughed. "That a royal princess would have brought me a trade alliance. 'Tis funny, eh, Bess?"

She lowered her eyelids so he wouldn't see the expression in them. "Very funny."

He swung her around and crushed her to him. "No trade alliance this side of Christendom can compete with your charms, Bess. Marrying you was the best thing I ever did."

Bess pulled away and looked up at him, a smile on her lovely lips. "My dearest lord, I've been waiting to tell you. We're going to have a child."

CHAPTER FOURTEEN

"they… that most impute a crime
Are pronest to it."

On a chilly March afternoon, the day after he had returned from attending a council meeting in York with Warwick, Richard stole away with Anne to the stately chestnut they had made their own. Pine needles swished under their feet and the din of the castle receded into a gentle quiet, broken only by birdsong and the sweep of the wind through the woods. A running brook gurgled nearby with water so clear the speckled gravel at its bottom glistened like shiny gems. The brook marked the boundary of their stronghold, their secret place, their own mythical kingdom of Avalon where as children, they had ruled supreme as king and queen, with no grown-ups to tell them what to do.

But they were children no longer. It was 1466 and the cares of the real world could not be banished so easily. On this day a sense of dread enveloped Richard like a pall.

"All will be well," Anne said, watching him. "The King has asked my lord father to be godfather to the newborn princess, and my gracious uncle to baptise her. Surely that's a good sign?"

Toying with the ruby ring his father had given him, Richard made no answer. Aye, to all outward appearances all seemed well enough. Edward made gestures and Warwick accepted them. In February, three days before the feast of St. Valentine, the queen had given birth to a girl she named Elizabeth, in her own honour, and Edward had made Warwick godfather. He sent the three Neville brothers to negotiate a truce with the Scots and let Warwick head embassies to Burgundy and France. But Richard had spent time in both camps and knew the truth. He'd been with Warwick and Edward as they passed through London and the villages. He had heard the crowds cry, "Warwick! Warwick!" as though the Kingmaker were a god dropped from the skies. And he'd been with Edward in his private chamber and seen him pace back and forth, angrily shouting that the people loved Warwick more than they loved him, their King.

Then there was the queen. She lost no opportunity to fan Edward's jealousy. In his presence she'd questioned Richard about Archbishop Neville's feast in the North, which Edward had been unable to attend. It had been held at Cawood Castle on Michaelmas Day, a celebration of George Neville's promotion to the Archbishopric of York.

"They say it was the largest feast ever," Bess said, playing a game of ninepins with her son Thomas Grey in the garden at Windsor. "More splendid than any royal feast in living memory, correct, Dickon?"

Thomas Grey looked at Richard sideways and a corner of his mouth twisted upwards. With his insolent eyes and permanently mocking grin, Bess Woodville's elder son was nearly as unpleasant as his mother, Richard thought. And he hated that the queen used the familiar with him. She had a way of making it sound demeaning. Richard knew she regarded him as her rival for Edward's favours, and though she pretended affection in front of Edward, she made her disdain evident when he wasn't present.

"I don't know what they say, my lady," Richard replied courteously. "I don't listen to gossip." He watched Edward step up to take his turn at the pins.

The Queen smiled sweetly. "You sat at the head table in a chief chamber of estate—with Lady Anne. A high honour, wasn't it, Dickon?"

Richard hesitated, an eye on Edward, who was readying his club. "Aye, my lady," he replied. Edward missed.

"Good that you are better on the battlefield, my lord," the Queen remarked to Edward, then turned back to Richard. "How many guests were there, Dickon?"

There was no relief for him, he thought. "Many, my lady." He watched Edward ready his club for another throw.

"Was the great hall full?"

"Quite full, my lady."

"The great hall at Cawood is known to hold seven thousand. So six thousand—which is the figure most mentioned—would be no exaggeration?" Edward threw and missed again, his wooden club landing with a great thud against the stone base of a fountain. A servant ran to retrieve it.

"I suppose not, my lady," Richard said as Thomas Grey stepped into position.

"And what did these six thousand guests eat?" she asked.

"Bulls and boar mostly, my lady, and some swans and

peacocks," Richard replied. Thomas Grey knocked down an ivory pin.

"Well done, Thomas!" the Queen exclaimed. She turned narrowed eyes on Richard. "There were four thousand sheep, and hundreds of bulls and oxen. Even porpoises and seals, were there not?"

"Aye, my lady."

The Queen stole a glance at Edward, who was examining a platter of refreshments offered by a servant. Porpoises and seals were a delicacy, expensive and difficult to come by.

"A dozen porpoises and seals, in fact," she continued relentlessly. "Four hundred swans, and over a hundred peacocks. For dessert there were thirteen thousand sweet dishes and a magnificent marchpane subtlety depicting St. George slaying the dragon. Life-size, so I hear." Bess Woodville took a step forward and readied her club. She addressed herself to Edward with a sigh. "It must be wonderful to be as rich as Warwick and never have to worry about money, as we must do, my lord."

Richard could have strangled her. Edward's eyes were blazing. She threw her wooden club, knocked down five of the nine ivory pins, gave a gleeful cry, and clapped.

And so it continued the entire time he was at Windsor. Bess told Edward about a rumour on the Continent that Warwick had become his enemy, and Edward kicked a dog. When Bess informed him that King Louis of France sent Warwick copies of all his official correspondence with Edward and that on one of the embassies Louis had received Warwick as if he were King himself, not an emissary, Edward yelled at Richard and found fault with his soup, his squires, his scribes, and his tailor. "He even sent Warwick a hound, my lord, and asked Warwick to do him the honour of sending him a fine English hunting hound," Bess persisted as she worked on her embroidery. "Why did he not ask you, my lord? You are King Louis's equal. Not Warwick."

Edward had thrown his goblet against the fireplace.

Then there had been that scene between Edward and Bess when Richard sat unnoticed, reading a book in a corner alcove of the royal apartments at the Tower.

"I've had a belly-full of your spies and their reports about Warwick!" Edward had stormed. "Lady, I order you to stop meddling in my affairs!" She had thrown herself at his feet. "My dearest lord, pray forgive me," she'd wept. "I shall never speak of such matters again. The reports come not from spies—for I employ none—but from my royal uncle, the Count St. Pol, who was at the French court and learned of these matters. He bade me tell you for your own good. But never shall I mention them again, for never would I distress you."

Seeing tears sparkling on Bess's lovely face, Edward had taken her into his arms and begged forgiveness.

Richard knew that Bess lied. She employed an army of spies. He'd overheard her give them instructions on several occasions, and how else could she have known about his conversation with Desmond? She had asked Richard whether the Earl of Desmond had ever sent the tale of Tristan and Iseult he'd promised. A seemingly innocent question, but in that same conversation George had likened Bess to a rat. It was the Woodville's way of telling Richard she knew. The Earl of Desmond had been right. There were no secrets in a castle—except from Edward. He was blind when it came to his queen.

Richard bit his lip. Whatever his misgivings about Warwick and Edward, he had to allay Anne's fears.

"No doubt it's a good sign that your gracious father will be godfather to my niece." He looked up at her standing before him. She was twelve now, looked more a maiden than a child in her fitted russet gown and flowing blue mantle. Her fair hair was tied back at the nape of the neck with pearls and a gauzy veil, and the summer sun glinting through the leaves of the huge chestnut threw darts of gold through her silken tresses. Behind her the little brook babbled gently. Unable to restrain himself, he added with a rush of emotion, "I wish I could stay here at Middleham forever, Anne!"

Anne sat down and rested her cheek against his hand, suffused by joy, then quickly by guilt. At least Richard came often to Middleham, even if his stays grew shorter in duration as strained relations between their families made the King claim his presence elsewhere, but poor Bella lay pining for George, whom she hadn't seen in months. "Has the King changed his mind about George and Bella?" she ventured. "Is there hope they might marry?"

Richard hesitated. Implicit in her question was the thought, ever at the back of their minds: *Is there hope we might marry?* He didn't want to tell her the truth. She'd find out soon enough that Edward had tried to marry George to the daughter of Charles of Burgundy. The negotiations had failed. Warwick had headed the embassy to Burgundy and everyone knew he was against the marriage. He wanted George to marry Bella, not nine-year-old Mary of Burgundy, and he wanted Richard's sister Meg to marry a French royal, not the recently widowed Charles of Burgundy, whom he despised. But while Warwick favoured France, the queen favoured Burgundy, the ally of her mother's family, the St. Pols of Luxembourg. The question was, Who would win? France or Burgundy?

Warwick or the Queen?

And if it were the queen, would Warwick the Kingmaker accept a second humiliation at Edward's hands?

Richard decided to tell Anne part of the truth. "Edward won't hear of a match between George and Bella. He fears a union with your mighty father will make George more powerful and fill his head with even more dangerous notions. I think Edward would like to see George abroad. He'd be less trouble there." He fidgeted with his ring. "Anne... I leave for London tomorrow."

"So soon?"

"I must attend the queen's churching with your lord father.

It is politic, Anne."

"Will you be back?" she asked in a choked voice.

A silence.

"Whatever happens between our families, Anne," he replied at last, "know that I will raise Heaven and Earth to see you again." A sickening sensation knotted his stomach. Nowadays each time they parted, he feared he might never see her again, and without Anne, the world was such an empty place. He looked up through the leaves at the shining sun. A bird stirred in the branches and a gust of wind rustled the leaves.

"Remember the afternoon we picnicked in the heather by the windmill?" he said, reaching into the past for comfort.

Anne smiled down at him.

There are moments you never forget, he thought. *Images that are forever.* Part of the music of the North that would always be with him, like the roaring of the winds through the trees, the rushing of the rivers, the pine-scented freshness of the air, the cries of birds over the moors. And Anne, smiling at him with her flower-eyes.

He stood up, and took her hand into his own. "London is a foul place. Filthy. Malodorous. The court swarms with greedy, grasping, scheming Woodvilles. There's whispering everywhere, deceit everywhere. I loathe London. If I had my way, I'd never leave you… never leave Middleham, or the North." Under his breath, he added, "I fear trouble, my lady. If you go away, leave me a message here, on our tree. I shall do the same." He fumbled in his doublet, and drew out a ring. "Wear this for me, Anne. As a remembrance."

Anne gazed at the delicate ring worked in a motif of silver leaves. The gift meant one thing: trouble lay ahead. Tears welled. She averted her face blindly.

Richard put his hand under her chin and turned her head to the old tree that had been struck by lightning in its youth. The deep gash had never healed, and there, in its hollow heart, they had sheltered in many a rainstorm. "Look, Anne… it's survived all kinds of storms, and so will we." He slipped the ring on her finger. "Someday we'll be together and never have to part. We must believe that."

He couldn't deny he had his own doubts sometimes, but like a beacon that guides a sailor safely back to shore at night, there was a certainty at his core that saw him through the blackness of his fears. Somehow, like their tree of Avalon, they would survive. Someday, somehow, they would be together.

CHAPTER FIFTEEN

"The meanest having power upon the highest,
And the high purpose broken by the worm."

The frantic blare of trumpets, the galloping hoofs through the gatehouse, and the shouts of men in the courtyard drowned out the mellow chanting of monks in the chapel. Archbishop Neville, in Middleham for the weekend, interrupted the Mass he was conducting to hurry to the courtyard with Warwick. The Countess followed with Richard and Anne. They reached the west door in time to hear Warwick groan. Beside him the Archbishop stood as if turned to stone, ashen as a ghost. Two messengers were kneeling, heads bowed, sobbing. A crowd had gathered around them, faces wet with tears.

"What is it, my lord?" the Countess cried, running to her husband's side.

"Evil, evil tidings, my lady…" Warwick took an unsteady step towards her. She seized his hands and looked up into his stricken eyes.

"The Earl of Desmond is dead. Executed by Tiptoft. His two small sons with him."

The Countess blanched. "How could such a thing happen?" Silence.

Richard's stunned gaze flew from the Countess, to George Neville, to Warwick. Events had moved swiftly after the birth of the little Princess Elizabeth and messengers had streamed to Middleham for weeks. The most disturbing report was that Edward had relieved the Earl of Desmond as Deputy Lieutenant of Ireland and appointed in his stead the Earl of Worcester, the harsh Tiptoft, to the post. The move bore the mark of the queen's hand, for Tiptoft had carved himself a fearsome reputation for cruelty since his return from Padua and was a man distrusted by everyone —except the Woodvilles.

The Countess turned on one of the messengers. "Tell me this is not so!"

"I fear it is too true, my lady. The Earl of Worcester accused the Earl of Desmond of treason and Desmond came in bravely to answer the false charge. He was immediately cast into prison and condemned to death. His two sons, mere schoolboys, eight and ten years old, were sent to the block with him." The messenger paused. "One of the boys had a boil on his neck. He asked the executioner to pray be careful, for it hurt." His voice cracked; he dropped his head.

The second messenger spoke. "'Tis said that the Queen stole the King's signet ring to seal the Earl's death warrant, my lady. The King was not pleased."

"But why should the Queen wish such a thing? It makes no sense..." The Countess searched their faces: all were blank, except her husband's. He said nothing, but fury now mingled with the grief in his eyes.

Silently, wretchedly, Richard made his way into the chapel to pray for the dead Irish earl, his father's beloved friend. Anne followed him, tears rolling down her cheek.

~*~

"So what that Edward was angry with her? He forgave her soon enough, didn't he?" George fumed to Richard on a visit to Middleham. "She's a witch from the bowels of Hell, she and Jacquetta both! 'Tis said they practise the Black Arts with the help of a certain Friar Bungey, who is in truth a Warlock."

I wouldn't doubt it, thought Richard. Aloud, he said, "Don't believe that foolery, George."

"It's true! She's a sorceress. If I were king, I'd burn her at the stake." His blue eyes blazing, he added, "And I *should* be king! Edward has no right to the throne. He's not our father's son."

"You're mad, George. Why do you say such things?" Richard rushed to the open window and looked down at the foot of the tower, where a gathering of nobles stood talking in the garden. He slammed the window shut, his heart racing with guilt. It was not Edward who was the bastard.

"Because it's true! Our mother was with child when our father married her. Why do you think Edward's so tall—so much taller than our father? So much taller than the rest of us? Because he's no Plantagenet!"

"Edward takes after Mother's grandfather, Lionel, who was a giant. You're losing your mind, George. For the Blessed Virgin's sake, you must stop this. 'Tis treason what you speak! If Edward knew…"

"Edward does know. I've made no secret of it." He plopped down on a bench.

"More fool you, George. If he hasn't clapped you into prison, then he's a better man than you."

"Why do you always defend him, Dickon? Are you so blind to what he is?"

"He's our brother—and King. You're wicked to slander him with lies. Have you no gratitude? Have you forgotten that he came to our lodgings every day to visit us when we were alone in London? He was fighting Marguerite, yet he came every day— because he knew we were frightened. When Father died, he was our lifeline—all that stood between us and the revenge of Lancaster. Does that mean nothing to you, George?"

"Edward was different then. Before that Sorceress sank her fangs into him."

"He's still our brother. Don't shame him. Aside from ingratitude, it's dangerous."

"He shames Warwick who made him king! He shames me by denying Bella and I the right to marry! *He* married for love but he won't abide anyone else doing so. Not even you, Dickon. I've seen the way you look at Anne—you love her, yet you'd give her up if he asked you to. You're naught but a milksop. A milksop, Dickon!"

"Edward is king. We took an oath. The king's word is God's law. To go back on an oath is to put your soul at risk."

"Then Edward broke his own oath and God's law by deposing Holy Harry."

Their eyes locked. Richard was the first to look away. He moved to the hearth and picked up a cherrywood branch. He stoked the fire. He had yet to win a battle of words with George. George was too clever.

The House of York had indeed unseated an anointed king, but Richard knew what that decision had cost his father. He'd been at Fotheringhay Castle, unnoticed, oiling his lute when the matter had been decided. His mother, Cicely, had sat in his father's bedchamber, at the foot of his trestle-bed, one thick golden braid falling over her shoulder, her posture as rigid as if she sat on a throne. The Duke of York had stood before her, his face anxious, his back to the fire that raged in the hearth, throwing light and shadow into the room.

"We must be patient, my lady," he'd said. "Sooner or later Marguerite's rash conduct will lead the people to call me to the throne and save me the hateful necessity of unsheathing my sword against Henry."

"My lord, there must be an end to patience, for where has it led you? As soon as you disbanded your army after the Battle of St. Albans, Somerset was reinstated in all his authority."

"Nevertheless, we can't act rashly. Too much is at stake. We must explore every venue to end this peaceably."

"Too much patience is as foolish as rashness. Your claim is stronger than the King's, and your army larger. Seize the throne that's rightfully yours, my lord. Another chance may not come again."

"If I do, my lady, I'll plunge England into civil war. Bloodshed must be avoided at all costs. It always leads to anarchy."

She leapt to her feet. "Look around you, my lord. There is already anarchy. County fights county, bishops are murdered, men are executed without trial."

"True. But I am Henry's heir. All will be righted in the end."

"Somerset was found in the Queen's apartments," she said quietly. "Soon there may be a bastard prince. Will you remain Henry's heir then?"

"By God, lady, if that should happen, I'll not stand by and do nothing!"

Richard dropped the cherry branch, turned away from the fire. "Father's mistake was waiting too long, not acting too soon," he said. "Holy Harry wasn't fit to be king."

"Neither is Edward."

"Your word that he's not our father's son doesn't make him unworthy of the crown."

"And Bess—is she worthy of the crown?"

No, Richard wanted to cry out. *No!* Aloud, he said, "I will not go against Edward."

He picked up his book, *Tristan and Iseult*, a tale of the conflict between loyalty and love. Good Desmond had sent his own treasured volume immediately upon his return to Ireland— Desmond, his father's faithful friend, murdered for the truth he spoke. He winced. George's epithets followed him to the door.

"Lily-livered coward! Faint-hearted milksop! Little rabbit—

we don't need you. Woodville-lover, damn you to Hell!

~*~

"Did you see her at her churching?" Warwick raged as he paced the gleaming tiled floor of the Chapter House at Yorkminster.

Richard sat on a marble seat carved into the wall, across the empty octagonal chamber from Archbishop Neville. Everyone was fuming about the Woodvilles. There was no escaping the subject.

"She lounged in a golden chair and ate alone, not deigning to say a word to anyone. She kept your royal sisters and her own mother kneeling for three hours. Power has driven the woman mad, by God! Now she's pushing for an alliance with Burgundy—'tis folly." He halted, looked at them, blue eyes flashing. "Philip the Good of Burgundy grows old. His son Charles is an idiot. Has the King met him? God's blood, I have—the man's almost as crazy as Holy Harry. If Louis wants Burgundy, I predict he'll have it one day. That fool Charles will deliver it to him on a gilded platter!"

He resumed pacing. "An alliance with Burgundy means we are against France, and France is a mighty enemy. They don't call King Louis the 'Spider King' for nothing. He'll spin his web and devour everyone against him, including Edward. What can Burgundy offer us? Trade, Edward says. But we can have that, and more, with France…" He halted, waved a hand broadly. "I've tried to make Edward understand that he can't turn his back on King Louis of France, not while the Bitch of Anjou and her confounded son dally there, waiting for Louis to nod support to a Lancastrian invasion. I tell you England must make a treaty of peace that will dash Marguerite's hopes, or England will pay!"

Richard had no wish to believe the dire prophecy, but he knew that Warwick believed it, and that it was tangled in Warwick's mind with his famous pride. An alliance with Burgundy would show the world—and Louis of France in particular—that Warwick was no longer *le conduiseuer du royaulme,* Master of the realm. Richard knew that if matters between the King and Kingmaker didn't go well, he might find himself forced into choosing sides. Warwick or Edward? *Anne or Edward?* His breath caught in his throat.

He lifted his eyes to Warwick. "Make my brother see the wisdom of sending you to France. Negotiate an agreement so favourable to England that he'll have no choice but to accept it, my lord."

An expression of surprise fixed on Warwick's sharp features. He stared at Richard as though seeing him for the first time. "You speak truth, Dickon. Will you come with me to London and support my cause?"

"Aye, my lord," Richard said quietly. "For much depends on it."

CHAPTER SIXTEEN

"The dirty nurse, Experience,
Hath foul'd me."

*E*dward was hunting when Richard and Warwick arrived at Westminster in the full sunlight of a late April afternoon. They awaited him in the White Chamber, crowded with glittering Woodvilles. As they stood stiffly at an oriel window, looking out at the river, the Woodvilles laughed and whispered together across the room and sent them barbed glances. Richard turned his back and tried to focus on the tall-masted ships that filled the harbour, some bearing English wool for sale to Burgundy, others returning with gold. Trade had flourished in these last two years of relative peace and the people seemed content.

Followed by his attendants, Edward strode in at last, magnificent in a topaz velvet riding jacket and high brown boots of Italian leather. He clasped Richard to him heartily and did the same with Warwick, as if they had never quarrelled. He removed his jewelled gauntlets and smiled at a group of damsels giggling nearby.

"Charming, aren't they?" he said, tearing his gaze away with marked effort. "So what brings you to London, my lords, pleasure or business? If it's business, I fear it shall have to keep till the morrow. The day's too fine." He turned and grinned at the damsels.

Richard averted his eyes. He had heard, and apparently it was true, that Edward was unfaithful to Bess, though it didn't seem to affect her power over him or lessen her charms. She was with child again.

"May we talk privately, Sire?" Warwick inquired.

Edward laughed. "I should have guessed it was business, Warwick. You and my solemn little brother are not made for pleasure, it seems. Very well, follow me."

The anteroom of Edward's royal chamber was scented with lavender and hung with lavish tapestries. A chess set of intricate coloured glass stood on a table between the hearth and a lancet window, the game unfinished. Edward leaned against the window seat, arms crossed. His gaze strayed as Warwick made his case, but the Kingmaker failed to notice. To Richard's surprise, Warwick quickly won his agreement to a diplomatic mission to France. Edward had given in too easily, Richard thought. There had been no argument, no counter-proposal, no need for compromise, yet Warwick suspected nothing. "That's the spirit, Edward!" Warwick boomed. "I knew you'd see that I am right." Flush with his effortless victory, he smiled broadly as he left.

As soon as the door had shut, Edward laughed. "Let him go to Louis with his magnificent retinue. No doubt the Spider's eager to spin his web of flattery around this splendid fly!"

"But you must give him a fair chance, Edward," Richard exclaimed.

Edward's eyebrows lifted a fraction. "So it's true, Dickon. You love his daughter."

"That has nothing to do with it," Richard said hotly. "There's much to recommend France over Burgundy—particularly in securing the crown you wear. Yet you choose to ignore the issues at stake here—only because the advice comes from a Neville, not a Woodville."

Edward's blue eyes darkened ominously. "When I was in exile in Calais the year before Father died, I ate with Nevilles, drank with Nevilles, and slept with Nevilles—I could never get away from Nevilles. They think they bought me the crown and that I owe them for the rest of my life. But I'm their king, not their puppet, and they'll damned well do as I say or I'll wipe those Nevilles off the face of the earth!" He swept an arm across the chess board. The delicate figurines smashed to the floor and shattered. One landed at Richard's feet.

He picked it up. It was a white knight. At first he thought it had survived intact but when he turned it over in his hand, he saw that the face had been obliterated. He stabbed his finger on a jagged edge, surprised at the quantity of blood that oozed. He wound a kerchief around the cut and looked at Edward. His brother stood staring out the window. Richard laid the broken knight gently on the board. "You've forgotten, Edward. You're a Neville, too."

Edward turned, his anger spent. "Warwick assumes that because I don't pick a fight, I'm easily managed. I am not."

"Then why Burgundy, if France has more to recommend it?"

"What matters is trade, Dickon. Look there… See those ships bearing gold? Trade generates gold—gold to be spent on enjoyment, comfort, security. Merchants live well because they have gold. Our father had land aplenty and no gold to pay his troops. For that he had to pawn his plate to merchants." He fell silent, a faraway look in his eyes. "I've decided on Burgundy," he resumed, "not because my queen favours it, brother, but because trade with Burgundy will make England rich. However much my subjects grumble against Burgundy's embargo on English cloth, the fact is, they hate France. We fought a hundred year war and she gave us the Bitch of Anjou. Not since Boudiccea, Scourge of the Romans, has England known such a queen... Besides, the English still expect their king to make good Henry V's claim to the French throne." He went to a wine flagon on a sideboard and poured two goblets. He held one out.

"Too early in the day for me," Richard said sullenly.

Edward returned with his cup and dangled an arm around Richard's shoulders. "Little brother, let me give you some advice. Drink with a man and you make him your friend. We of royal blood can't have too many friends!" He gave a laugh, winked and downed his wine. He returned to the sideboard for another long swallow. "You do love his daughter, don't you? Answer me; 'tis a royal command."

"Aye," Richard admitted miserably.

Edward threw his head back and roared. "And George loves Bella! Isn't that funny?"

Richard stared at him. Could it be his brother was drunk so early in the day?

"No," Edward grinned, waving his goblet. "I see you don't think so. But it does complicate matters, doesn't it? Warwick may be my enemy. Yet my brothers love his daughters. Divided loyalties are always complicated, aren't they, Dickon?"

Edward seemed suddenly very sober as he stared at Richard, his blue eyes piercing the silence.

"You know me better than that," said Richard.

Edward gulped a swallow of wine and wiped his mouth with the back of his hand. "Do I?" He swayed a little on his heels.

"I took an oath to you."

"Oaths are broken daily."

"Not by honourable men," said Richard, averting his eyes and suppressing the sudden discomfort that had come to him.

He had no real doubt what he would do, if it came to that, did he?

He stole a look at Edward. Edward was staring at the broken chessboard and its shattered knights. "We shall see," he murmured, sipping his wine. "We shall see."

CHAPTER SEVENTEEN

"...And rolling far along the gloomy shores
The voice of days of old and days to be."

How much humiliation could a proud man take? That was the question. Stroking a young black wolfhound, Richard watched the colourful fleet that had arrived from Burgundy as soon as Warwick left for France. The ships had sailed into the Thames, banners aflutter, bearing the Duke of Burgundy's illegitimate son, the Bastard of Burgundy, who had accepted a challenge to joust with Bess's brother, Anthony Woodville.

He picked up the wooden board he'd laid aside. The carving had claimed his attention over the past few anxious weeks, yet it remained unfinished. He shifted in his window seat in the White Tower and removed the dagger at his waist. The hound pawed for attention. When Richard ignored him, he lay down with his nose poking mournfully over the crimson cushion and watched Richard chisel.

Why hadn't Anne written? Her last letter had arrived over a week ago and there'd been no word since. Absently Richard refined the tusk of the boar he had chosen as his emblem. How did matters go with Warwick in France? He wished Archbishop Neville would visit, but he'd remained closeted at his palace in Charing Cross, preparing his speech for the opening of Parliament in June. Edward was expected in a few days, along with Anthony Woodville, officially, for the opening of Parliament and the tournament; unofficially, to seal their sister Meg's marriage to Charles of Burgundy. Did Archbishop Neville suspect Edward's duplicity? How about John?

The familiar sick feeling washed over him. He stabbed his dagger into the wood, pulled it out and stabbed again. He threw the carving aside. He didn't belong in London. He belonged in the North with Anne and his friends, Francis and Rob and the two Toms; with people who meant what they said and didn't conceal lies beneath their smiles. He'd never been able to feign what he didn't feel, yet that was what people did at court; how they got ahead—how they survived.

"My lord, here you are, I've been searching for you," a voice said from behind, rolling its r's in the way Richard remembered from his days of exile in Burgundy. Edward Brampton spoke haltingly, for he was of Portuguese origins and not at home in the common English. A swashbuckling naval hero who had captained Richard's return voyage to England from Bruges, he was a Jew, god-fathered at his baptism by Edward himself, and so he'd assumed the royal name.

The hound sat up expectantly. Richard took a moment to compose himself before turning around. Brampton was as cheerful as always and gave Richard a broad smile, white teeth sparkling in his tanned face. "Everything is prepared, m'lord. We can leave for Windsor as soon as you wish it."

~*~

At the head of his retinue, Richard clattered through the crowded streets, the dog that refused to leave trotting alongside. All London throbbed with excitement. It was at its most festive this May, with thousands of banners and tapestries decorating the bridges and streets. People thronged everywhere: lords, to Parliament; commoners, to the joust. As they passed Charing Cross towards King's Street and the Strand, Richard cast a glance at Archbishop Neville's palace on the River Thames. He wished he could halt his journey here, instead of going on to the tournament. Windsor would be crawling with Woodvilles.

He wondered what the Archbishop was doing this morning.

~*~

After a brief absence, Archbishop Neville had returned to London early that day from his Manor of the Moor in Hertfordshire. Still in his riding outfit, he stood with feet apart, hands behind his back, a sombre expression on his face as he listened to his messengers' reports. His sermon for the opening of Parliament lay half-completed on a brocade-covered desk.

"Antoine, Bastard of Burgundy, was accompanied up-river by many knights and ladies in barges decorated with arras," a messenger was saying on bended knee. "At Billingsgate he took horse and rode in a splendid procession past St. Paul's to his lodgings in the Bishop of Salisbury's palace. The Bastard's chambers have been hung with cloth of gold, Your Grace."

The second messenger continued. "King Edward plans to greet him with great ceremony. The sheriffs at Smithfield are rushing to complete the construction of the lists for the tournament, which are larger than any ever built—ninety yards long by eighty wide..."

"Enough!" Archbishop Neville barked. "I've heard enough." He dismissed them and waited for the heavy oak door to shut before turning to his companion. "What do you make of it, Will?"

Sir William Conyers, one of Archbishop Neville's many cousins, was from the wealthiest of all non-baronial families in the North. Gravely, he said, "You're right, my lord. Such a warm welcome is a guise for something more significant than a mere tournament. I fear the King has sent your brother Warwick to France only to get him out of the way while he connives with the Burgundians."

The Archbishop slammed a fist on the table, rattling the Great Seal. "We'll not stand for another humiliation!"

135

"The old nobles of the land are brought low, the commons oppressed, the people discontented, while the Woodvilles plunder and the King wastes our substance on concubines… These are ill times indeed." After a pause, Sir William Conyers added, "How go the negotiations in Rome?"

The Archbishop's tight expression relaxed. "Well. The King has written the Pope to request he deny the dispensation, but his brother George has outbid him. It shall be granted soon."

"Good. Once Bella is married to the King's brother, Edward will come to his senses."

"Let's hope so, cousin. For if Edward continues down this road, I fear the consequences…"

"Aye, civil war is too terrible to contemplate."

Archbishop Neville's glance fell on the Great Seal. "Pray Edward is as aware of that spectre as we are. Meanwhile, I'll show our displeasure by not addressing Parliament next week. I'll plead ill-health."

"Indeed," agreed Conyers. "'Tis time to let Edward know we'll not stand for more."

~*~

Edward was furious.

"Ill-health! Nevilles are never ill!" he roared. "George Neville is chancellor by my grace and he shall know it, by God! Come, Dickon. I want you at my side when I take back the Great Seal."

Richard put down his dog miserably. They rode to Charing Cross and waited in the cold, stinging rain for the Archbishop to come to Edward at the palace gate. In a tone of ice, Edward demanded the Great Seal from the Archbishop; with a face of stone, Archbishop Neville placed it into his hands.

Swinging his magnificent destrier around, Edward rode back to Westminster with his entourage and immediately conferred the chancellorship on Robert Stillington, Bishop of Bath and Wells.

"At least you're not a Neville!" Edward informed the stunned Stillington.

~*~

In the bright afternoon of St. George's Day, the day of the tournament at Windsor, Richard sat in the solar stroking the black wolfhound, his Book of Hours open on his lap, the prayers unread. Except for a few varlets, everyone from the castle had gone down to the lists. Though he'd promised Edward to attend, he was unable to stir himself from the apathy that gripped him.

The periodic blare of distant trumpets floated up from the lists followed by roars of excitement. He moved to the tall lancet window and gazed past the steep stone walls of the castle down to the dusty plain by the river. The forked pennants of the contending knights fluttered from their pavilions and the bright sun flashed off their armour. A knock came at the door, open behind him. The hound sat up, barked once. Sir Friendly Lion stood at the threshold, his silvering head gleaming in the dimness of the room. John Howard was in full armour and wore the ceremonial white silk jupon embroidered with his coat of arms, the Silver Lion, since he was an afternoon contender in the lists.

"You don't go to the jousting, my lord?" Howard's tone evinced surprise.

Richard shook his head.

"It would banish your cares," he said kindly. "If only for a while."

"Nay, my lord. For me, the management of weapons is not a sport, but a duty."

"In all my years, I've heard that only once before."

Richard looked at him uncertainly. He believed himself an anomaly, yet somewhere there was one other who felt the same. "May I ask who it was?"

"The last person I'd expect," replied Howard. "The Earl of Northumberland, John Neville."

Richard winced. Dimly he heard Howard excuse himself. The clink of armour faded down the hall. Clouds of dust kicked up by the horses obscured the field now but the roar of excitement from the crowds was louder than ever. Richard wished he could enjoy the things that brought others so much joy. He only knew that for him there was no such ease; for him the world resolved itself into a tangled mass of fears against which he struggled helplessly and for which he found no weapon except prayer. A deep yearning for John and Anne and Yorkshire swept him, leaving a trail of desolation in its wake. He picked up his Book of Hours.

~*~

In the late June dusk, a week after the Bastard's departure on St. Swithin's day, Warwick, flush with the triumph of his successful visit to Louis, stood at the bow of his ship as the *Grace a Dieu* sailed into London harbour. Not only had the King of France received him in a stately procession and showered him with gifts, but, wishing to prevent a Burgundian alliance at all costs, he had offered exceedingly generous terms to secure England's alliance with France.

Warwick's glance moved across the imposing array of French ambassadors crowding the ship's deck. "The King will be amazed when he hears what Louis is willing to offer, is that not so, Wenlock?"

Lord Wenlock rested his hands on his silver girdle and arched his grizzled eyebrows. "Indeed he will, my lord!"

"There's only one thing puzzling me, Wenlock—something Louis said; something strange which makes no sense."

"My lord?"

Warwick knew that most men in his own position would guard their tongue on such a delicate matter as the confidence of a king, but he had no doubts about Wenlock's loyalty. Wenlock was utterly his man. It was he, Warwick, who had raised him up to lord from his low origins, and because of those origins, Wenlock had no friends at court. They held his low birth against him.

Birth, Warwick scoffed inwardly. Birth had made a king of a madman and a lecherous youth. So much for birth! It was merit that mattered. He turned his back on the Frenchmen gathered across the deck, leaned close, lowered his voice to a whisper. "Louis said that if perchance I ever decided to restore Henry of Lancaster to the throne, he, Louis, my most devoted friend and admirer, would do all in his power to help. Strange, isn't it?"

"Indeed, my lord, 'tis the most curious thing I ever heard. To restore Henry is to restore Marguerite, the murderess of your most noble father and brother, God assoil their souls. Besides, you've been staunchly Yorkist from the first. Not like the others— bah!" He turned, spat. "How could King Louis entertain such a notion?"

"I know not, Wenlock. I mention it only because it has puzzled me throughout the voyage, for it makes no sense, and I know him to be a very clever man."

"That he is, my lord. Very clever."

The two stared out to sea thoughtfully. Moments later, as they drew near the wharf at Billingsgate, Warwick spied a familiar figure.

"Look, Wenlock, the Archbishop has come to greet us..." He broke off, frowned. "'Tis unusual that he should come himself. I wonder what news he bears."

CHAPTER EIGHTEEN

"Speak, Lancelot, thou art silent; is it well?"

At Middleham, in the month of July of 1467, the mood was tense and a strange silence pervaded the castle. In the kitchens and cellars the servants went about their tasks wordlessly while the chapel priests murmured their prayers and the chancery clerks buried their heads in their paper. The knights, squires, and men-at-arms of the great Earl of Warwick's retinue sat around the halls and on the staircases, polishing their armour and sharpening their weapons. Soon they might need them. The Kingmaker had summoned his brothers to a meeting.

"As you may have heard, John," Warwick said, "when I reached London from my triumphant embassy to France, my first discovery was that our brother had been deprived of the chancellorship, and the next, that Edward had concluded an alliance with Castile against France!"

Warwick stood with his back to a window in the antechamber of his high-vaulted private suite and John, across from him, by a table where a jug of blood-red roses had been placed.

"Though the French ambassadors stayed six weeks, all they took back with them were empty promises, a few hunting horns, and some leather bottles…"

As his brother spoke, John's glance kept stealing to the jug of red roses, an unnatural sight in a Yorkist household.

"The Burgundian envoys, meanwhile, were drawing up the marriage treaty as I arrived. They left loaded like mules with gold and precious gifts. Such is Edward's answer to us." Warwick's voice trembled. He fell silent, clenched and unclenched a fist. "For that we can blame the Woodville witch he married. Therefore, John, I plan to fight Edward and purge the realm of Woodvilles."

John's breath froze in his lungs. The sky darkened and across the court the stone tower grew irregular and wavered like a reflection in water.

"John! Did you hear me? John..."

His brother's voice came to John like an echo across a far distance. He felt Warwick's touch on his sleeve. He turned his head, looked at his face. It was strangely blurred. He swallowed painfully. "You've gone mad!" He heard his own voice, stifled, hoarse.

Warwick crashed a fist on the table. "'Tis Edward who's gone mad, brother! Mad with lust for the greedy witch he married. He pays with lands and earldoms each time he impales her. I didn't put him on the throne for this."

John leaned both hands on the table in an effort to steady himself but the roses gave off a sickly sweet smell that quickened the churning of his stomach. He drew himself up. With stiff lips, he said, "You put him on the throne, and he is *king.*"

"I put him up, and I can bring him down!"

"What then?" John demanded, loudly, over the roaring in his head. "Who would you raise in his place? Yourself? Surely you can't believe the people would accept you?"

"Not me. One other. Edward's own brother, George, who has cast his lot with us."

"George is a fool!"

"Fools are easy to control."

"So you think now. What if George turns against you as Edward has?"

"He won't. He's agreed to marry Bella."

"How? They're cousins and there's no dispensation—Edward has expressly forbidden it."

Warwick exchanged a glance with the Archbishop. "George has bribed his brother's own papal representative. The dispensation is being readied."

"What you speak is treason!" John breathed.

"Only if Edward remains king," Warwick said roughly. "And

if he remains king, we Nevilles are done for in any case."

"Aye," agreed the Archbishop. "Dick is right. The Woodvilles are like rats gnawing on the ship of state. They'll sink us unless we destroy them first. We Nevilles must stand firmly united—we rise or fall together."

John swung on his younger brother. "Easy for you to say! You've always backed Dick blindly in everything. You've no convictions of your own, George, only ambition!" He fought for composure. The roaring in his head was ferocious now, like a clashing of cymbals mingled with shouts. "But I'll have none of it."

Stunned, Warwick stared at him. "You're a Neville!"

"And have always done what you wished, Dick..." John managed. "Except in this. I cannot—I will not. My duty is to the King."

"What about your duty to your kin?" Warwick stormed.

"Tear down Edward and you tear down order with him, return us to anarchy—to the days when anyone with a sword and a few men at his back thought himself fit to be king. What will become of England then?" He felt drained, depleted. A vast weariness engulfed him, as if he'd been on the march for days.

The Archbishop scraped his chair back and rose. "You can't go against us, John. You'd be fighting your own flesh and blood."

"Like our cousin George?" demanded John. A silence fell. "I beg you to reconsider, my brothers! Don't plunge the realm into civil war. Think of the good men who'll die. Think of the suffering of widows and children dispossessed. Surely the cost can't be worth the gains, a few more lands here or there..."

"Cost? I know all about cost!" Warwick roared. "It was I who fought at Towton to put Edward on the throne, not you. I fought in that howling snowstorm, that hellish fourteen-hour battle! It was my men whose blood froze in the snow and melted with the spring to dye the rivers red while you were safe in your dungeon!"

John tilted his brows, looked at him uncertainly. He had the feeling they were all fools playing in some absurd, cruel farce. He wanted to laugh aloud but his insides hurt as if he'd been gutted by hot coals. "Then why... when you know the cost?"

"Because we can't live in peace with Woodvilles devouring the realm!" Warwick shouted. "Are you so blinded by your damned loyalty you can't see that?"

"All I've ever wanted is to serve. All you've wanted is to rule."

"I must be rid of this curse of service to Edward! 'Tis a question of being master or varlet."

"Have you ever given a thought to anyone else? Your ambition will destroy us all!" John shouted.

The brothers fell suddenly silent, glaring at each other. Then Warwick's shoulders slumped. "It must be done," he said wearily. "For the Neville honour."

"By Christ's sweet blood," John said in a strangled voice, "I beg of you, Dick..."

"We've gone too far to turn back now," replied Warwick.

John could no longer see his brother's face. Warwick was just a black shadow against the bright window and the light hurt his eyes. He looked down at the table and his own reflection stared back at him, ghost-like, blurred, distanced. *We're naught but shadows and phantoms in a world gone mad,* he thought, knowing he made no sense. He dragged his eyes back to his brother's face. "Then it must be done without me." He picked up his gauntlets, made for the door. He felt as if he walked in water, so strangely slow did his movements seem.

The Archbishop pursued him. "John—John—you will regret this!"

John hesitated, his hand on the door latch. Doves flitted at the windowsill and cooed from the velvet turf. Through the open windows, the warm summer wind wafted through the room, bearing the scent of flowers. From other regions of the castle came the tinkling of bells and the sound of children laughing. In a dark world, the sun still shone.

John gave a choked, desperate laugh. "I daresay, my good brothers, we all will." He thrust the door open and strode from the room.

CHAPTER NINETEEN

"And each foresaw the dolorous day to be;
And all talk died, as in a grove all song
Beneath the shadow of some bird of prey."

The August sun beat down. Richard loosened his collar and mopped his face, his eyes on his sister Meg. To keep up appearances, Edward had offered—and Warwick had accepted—the honour of escorting Meg on the first stage of her wedding journey to Burgundy. She rode pillion behind Warwick through the streets of London. Richard took in the faces of the people waving banners and throwing flowers. They had feared the Kingmaker's reaction to the King's duplicity, but to everyone's surprise, Warwick had accepted Meg's betrothal to Charles of Burgundy without animosity. Or so it seemed. Richard was deeply troubled by the graciousness the Kingmaker had shown. It was unlike him, and as unsettling as rain from a summer sky. But there had been little time to dwell on the matter, for yet another crisis created by the queen swept their way soon after Warwick's return from France. This scandal had pitted Warwick against the queen's blood and given the land fresh cause for concern.

Sir Thomas Cook, the rich merchant who had refused to sell his tapestry to the queen's mother, was implicated in a treasonous plot against Edward, along with Warwick's loyal retainer, Lord Wenlock. Meg had interceded for Cook, who was her friend, and Edward, suspecting Bess had something to do with the convenient charge of treason, and anxious to appease Warwick, took no action against Wenlock. He even appointed the queen's enemies, George and Warwick, to the commission investigating the case. The charges were dismissed. The realm breathed a deep sigh of relief.

A faint smile touched Richard's mouth as he remembered the light moment when the lumpish Mayor of London's snoring had disturbed the proceedings. "Speak softly, sirs, for the Mayor is asleep," George had warned a witness, grinning amiably. George could be endearing when he wished. Richard's smile faded. The crisis had passed and no doubt another would come along soon enough, but Meg, the sister he had loved like a mother, was departing his life. And there was no comfort, for this marriage promised little happiness. Her future husband, Charles of Burgundy, a long-nosed, wild-eyed man, was by all accounts so rash and unpredictable that—as Warwick had claimed—he could rightly be hailed as half-mad.

But Meg would do her duty, no matter what the personal cost. If that duty became too onerous a burden, for Meg, as for him, there was always prayer.

~*~

At the monastery of Stratford Langthorne in Essex, Richard shifted miserably in his chair at the banquet table. The three-day marriage celebration had been a nightmare. He looked to one side of the hall. There sat George and Warwick, whom he loved, but who would not speak to him because he couldn't turn against Edward. He looked to the other side. There sat the queen and the Woodvilles, whispering and throwing him burning, hateful glances. He looked to the middle. There sat his beloved Meg. When he'd see her again, only God knew.

At last the final banquet was over. With relief Richard retired to his cloistered room off the quiet courtyard, hoping for sleep, but the old dragon of his childhood nightmares kept him tossing fitfully. In the morning, as orange dawn streaked the sky, he embraced his sister on the wharf at Margate. "May God in His Heaven watch over you always, dear Dickon," Meg whispered, tears sparkling in her eyes as she gently smoothed his hair.

He watched her board the ship that would carry her from England forever. She cast back one last, lingering look. Then she was gone. Horses whinnied as the royal retinue and the knights departed for the castle, laughing. The wharf grew quiet. He stood alone, watching her ship until it was a speck of black against the dawn. It took all his will to crush the sob in his throat. Around him the cry of the gulls rose to an unbearable crescendo in his ears and the salt smell of the sea assailed his nostrils, threatening to choke off his breath.

As soon as he returned to Westminster, he begged Edward's permission to accompany Warwick to Middleham. He desperately needed to see Anne and to breathe the fresh air of Yorkshire.

~*~

Autumn came early, drenching the North in reds and golds, and the sun shone in Middleham more brightly than ever before in Richard's memory. But on this first October morning, Richard thought its peculiar brilliance foreboded rain, noting that a cloud had appeared in the far distance, marring the perfect blueness of the skies. The larks didn't seem to care, however, and sang with exceptional sweetness. The squirrels, too, were in a playful mood as they chased one another through meadows covered with purple heather. So were the hounds that bounded up the slope behind the castle, yapping as they followed. He hung his head, unsure if he were angry with himself, or with the Woodvilles—or with life. He was surrounded by beauty. He was with Anne. And he wasn't happy.

"The realm is uneasy, Anne," he said, picking up a stick and throwing it for the dogs to retrieve. "Holy Harry's Welsh half-brother, Jasper Tudor, landed in Wales and burned Denbigh. He's been driven out, but I fear it's just the beginning. Now that Louis of France has been spurned, there's nothing to stop him from aiding the Lancastrian cause and fomenting trouble in England."

"And Marguerite d'Anjou?" Anne queried with a tremor. "Do you think she'll return?" She smoothed her skirts and sat down in the heather. Richard joined her.

"There's always the chance. Her son, Edouard, is only a year younger than I. Soon he'll be of an age to rule. I fear he won't sit quietly in France. They say he's a beastly boy who thinks only of chopping off heads. I suppose it's because his mother had him watch executions since he was a babe."

Anne felt suddenly hot. Her stomach churned and the bitter taste of bile flooded her mouth. She leaned forward and retched.

"Anne, are you all right! Shall I send for wine...?"

Anne shook her head and swallowed back the nausea that had come so suddenly. To allay his fears, she said, "I'm fine, Richard—it was nothing. I was sick while you were gone, is all." Her stomach was still clenched tight and her head pounded, but she forced a smile as she looked at him. And for the first time in her young life she noticed the finely etched lines, lines that had no place in a face so young. His eyes, too, were different: darker grey, and sadder than she remembered.

"There's something else you must tell me, isn't there, Richard? You're going away again, aren't you?"

He nodded dully. He'd been at Middleham only three weeks before the queen managed to stir up more trouble. Edward had summoned him back to London. Even if he hadn't, Richard knew he had to leave. Warwick had made it clear that he was no longer welcome.

"Sir Thomas Cook has been charged with treason again and thrown back into prison. The queen's father, Earl Rivers, ransacked his house, and the tapestry has disappeared. There's to be a second trial for poor Cook. Edward wants me at his side."

Anne didn't know what to say. She only knew there was evil lurking in the world. Lurking, and reaching out for them. Richard's expression was one of mute wretchedness, and there was no comfort to offer, nothing she could do at all.

~*~

From the window in the Keep, the Countess of Warwick watched Richard and Anne as they sat among the purple heather. She turned back to her visitor.

"My heart twists so when I look at him. He seems so wounded."

While old Rufus kept careful watch, John Neville moved over to the window in time to see Richard gently place his arms around Anne's shoulders. He reflected a moment before he spoke. "They are both wounded, my lady, but they have youth on their side and, pray God, time to heal each other."

The Countess's eyes fixed on him in surprise. "Why, my fair brother of Northumberland, I didn't know you were a scholar of men."

"Nay, lady, merely a simple soldier. I only know the battlefields of life." Softly he added, "Sometimes 'tis on the ground we fight, and sometimes in the heart."

The Countess looked sharply at his face. Misery and despair lay naked in his dark blue eyes. Her heart squeezed in anguish and she reached out and touched his hand. "Aye, John," she said on a breath.

Together they turned their gaze from the young ones sitting among the heather, to the sky beyond where thunderous dark clouds hung on the horizon, immobile, waiting.

CHAPTER TWENTY

"...My knights are sworn to vows
Of utter faithfulness in love,
And utter obedience to the King."

The year of 1469 began with sinister portents of disaster. A shower of blood stained grass in Bedfordshire, and elsewhere a horseman and men in arms were seen rushing through the air. In the county of Huntingdon, a certain woman who was with child and near the time of her delivery, to her horror felt the unborn in her womb weep and utter a sobbing noise. And in the early spring, England heard about the first trouble, a rising in Yorkshire led by someone calling himself Robin of Redesdale, citing as grievances heavy taxes, injustice in the courts and the rapacious Woodvilles whose greed and impudence, they said, outraged honest men. No sooner did John put this down than a second arose in East Riding, led by a Robin of Holderness who called for the restoration of Henry Percy as Earl of Northumberland. John crushed it promptly and executed its leaders.

"I've earned my earldom, Isobel, and been a good lord to them," he told his countess. "Why should they call for Percy—what have the Percys ever done for them?"

From her window seat in her private solar at Alnwick, where she sat embroidering a green square of silk with John's emblem of the gold griffin, Isobel regarded her husband. In a fur-edged velvet tunic of her favourite emerald, his faithful hound curled up at his feet, John sat at an oak-carved table, writing a private missive to the King, which he didn't wish to dictate to a clerk. Her heart ached for him. She knew that the executions troubled him, that what he was really asking was whether he'd been justified.

Aye, he didn't deserve such ingratitude. Though he hadn't

149

the means of his brother Warwick, his kitchens never turned away a hungry mouth and his door was never closed to those in need of his help. He had in truth done many a noble deed. What Percy had ever sent firewood to the prisons or wine to the prisoners? What lord thought to do it in summer so men wouldn't have to cart the heavy loads through the bitter chill of winter? Such kindness was a rare thing, but John cared so for everyone: his soldiers, his servants, his family. His King.

She stretched out her hand and he came to her. She lifted her eyes to his handsome face. *Dear God, so much change.* His decision to support the King against his brothers came to him at fearsome cost. No longer did he sleep at night, or have heart for amusement. How different was this careworn face from the glorious countenance she had first fallen in love with! Grey dusted the tawny hair at the temples and deep furrows marred the once-smooth brow. From the nostrils of the fine straight nose, two lines ran down to the generous mouth, now grim-set and drooping at the corners, and a fresh scar cut through the left eyebrow over the deep blue eyes which had lost their twinkling light. She thought of the happy, dauntless youth he had been when she'd first met him, and her heart squeezed with anguish.

"Do not fault yourself, my dear lord. Robin of Holderness had no right to call for Percy's reinstatement… And Robin of Redesdale? Is he also against you?"

John turned. With a gesture of the hand he dismissed the servants. The minstrel hushed his harp in the corner of the room and rose from his stool. Isobel's tiring-woman, who had been moving quietly about her duties emptying chests and hanging clothes in the garderobe, set a hand basin of perfumed water down on a bedside table and withdrew.

John's eyes took on a pained expression as he met Isobel's questioning gaze. "I fear Robin of Redesdale is none other than our cousin, William Conyers."

Isobel gave a sharp gasp. With a rustle of silk, she rose from her place at the window. "Oh, my dear lord..." So the nightmare had already begun. So soon! She took his sun-bronzed hand into her own. Such a strong, fine hand. She pressed kisses to the long fingers.

John wrapped his arms around her and looked down at the full red mouth, straight little nose and honey-coloured eyes, luminous below their thick black lashes. In spite of his troubles, warmth flooded him. Thirteen years they'd been married and time had only ripened her beauty. She moved a little in his arms and he caught the flowery scent of her body. He pulled her tightly to him, marvelling that his passion for her was still unspent. Resting his cheek against her fragrant chestnut hair, he watched swans glide on the River Aln and sheep graze on the placid hills.

"Sunshine is always brighter when I'm with you, and birdsong sweeter, Isobel. You make me forget what the world is really like." It was the truth. At this moment, the stench of bloody battlefields and rotting human flesh, the shrieks of the wounded and the cawing of vultures, had surrendered their reality, along with the gales and the fogs, and the sighs of cold, weary men trudging over frozen earth.

Isobel snuggled closer in the warmth of his embrace. "And I, my beloved lord, feel the same now as when I first fell in love with you... I still remember the frightful days when you were taken prisoner by the Percys at Blore Heath and I thought I might lose you... Never would I relive them for all the earldoms in England." She pulled away and looked up at his face. "To think it was all so needless! You were taken prisoner after a battle you'd won only because you recklessly pursued the Cheshiremen into their own territory." She smiled at the image of John that came into her mind: a dashing Neville chasing a hated Percy with all the wild abandon of youth. "What were you thinking, my love?"

151

John grinned suddenly. "I wasn't thinking. That was the problem."

How good it felt to see him smile again; how long it had been since she'd seen those dimples she so loved! Isobel watched John's eyes go back to the window, the smile fixed on his lips. She turned in the circle of his arms and followed his gaze to the walled garden below, where their three-year-old son had suddenly appeared, romping and screeching with delight as his sisters made a game of chasing him around the hedges. After five daughters, God had granted them a son; George had been born on the feast of St. Peter's, the twenty-second of February, nine months to the day after John had won his earldom. She blushed, remembering that night in York. John had galloped back to their Abbey lodgings after the ceremony and, wild with happiness, they'd made love in the fierce heat of passion, known an ecstasy that can come but once.

"You've given me everything that's beautiful," Isobel whispered, her eyes returning to the children in the garden below. "Everything I cherish on this earth."

John tightened his hold around her waist. "One day our son will inherit my earldom. I'm thankful I have that to leave him."

Aye, Isobel thought, *the earldom with its annual income of a thousand pounds would greatly ease George's path.* Had his proposed marriage to the daughter of the Duchess of Exeter not been snatched away by the Woodville queen for her son, little George would one day have been one of the richest magnates in the land. She banished the thought. They still had many blessings. At least George would not have to take out debts in order to last the year, as they'd been obliged to do. And worse—far worse—carve his livelihood through bloody battlefields, like his father. John had sacrificed much for the earldom. He'd devoted his life to the King's business. Whether it was fighting battles or negotiating truces, the earldom of Northumberland had been hard earned. No one had a right to take it away.

"You are a good lord and the King's truest subject. Edward knows that, John, how can he not? As for me, I am the most fortunate of women to call you husband."

"And I, my lady, am the most fortunate of men to have an angel as my lady wife." A beautiful smile played on her lips, the same smile she'd worn the first time he'd seen her. How strange that he should remember it so vividly after all these years. He could still smell the air, feel the breeze on his cheek, see the Lincolnshire hills and sharp outlines of Lord Cromwell's castle...

The glow of sunset reflected off the western battlements as he clattered over the drawbridge into the inner court with his small party. Weary from the long, dusty journey from Raby, he'd dismounted and thrown the reins of his horse to one of the groomsmen, wondering as he did so why his brother Thomas hadn't come out to greet him. Surely they'd made enough noise? At that instant he'd heard a laugh light as silvery bells, a sound that seemed to fall from the heavens, like the beating of angel wings. He glanced up.

Framed by the violet sky, a face gazed down at him from a high window, the face of an angel, serene, beautiful, with a complexion white as lilies and hair dark as chestnuts. It was an oval face with a pointed chin, luminous smile, and extraordinary eyes. He stared, rooted to where he stood, unable to tear his gaze away from those two brilliant topaz orbs. He didn't hear the jangle of steel, the shouts of men or the neighing of horses as Thomas rode into the castle with Lord Cromwell and a troop of men-at-arms. He heard only the lyre and the angel's sudden laugh, sweet as chapel bells over the dales at morning time.

"John!" Thomas cried cheerily, leaping off his horse and running to him. His thick crop of dark hair was dishevelled and there were two streaks of dirt on his cheeks, but his brilliant blue eyes were alight with joy to see him. "My fair brother!" He clasped John to his breast and held him out at arm's length. "What a relief you're safe! You were so late, we rode out to search for you. One never knows with those damned Percys."

"Aye," Lord Cromwell boomed, "'tis good you're safe! Worried, we did. Damned Percys out there, you know…"

Isobel's laugh interrupted his reverie.

"All these years you've called me your angel," she said, "and all these years I've been telling you angels don't have chestnut hair. They have golden hair, as any painter or coloured-glass maker will tell you."

He grinned. "My angels have chestnut hair."

Isobel put her hands over his. "I love you, and have loved you from the first moment that I saw you."

John smiled into her hair. "That blessed twilight eve at Lord Cromwell's castle."

She threw him a startled glance. "Nay, 'twas not at Lord Cromwell's castle where I first saw you. I was twelve and riding past the River Ure with my cousins. We surprised you as you came out of the water after a swim."

John flushed, remembering the party of giggling young maidens that day long ago. "You mean you saw me…'"

She laughed. "Aye, naked as Adam, standing on the river bank! Thomas had the sense to cover himself, but you blushed as red as a beet and covered the wrong part."

"My face."

"That was why we were all laughing, my sweet lord."

John grinned. He clasped her tightly around her waist and bent his head tenderly to hers. "My love," he whispered softly, "you never told me."

CHAPTER TWENTY-ONE

"And in Arthur's heart pain was lord."

Richard watched Edward standing at the window with the queen's father, Earl Rivers. He was breaking the seal on a missive while Hastings, the Woodvilles, and their friend, a lord from Wales named Herbert, looked on from the council table. Richard hoped for good news. The past three months had been weighted down with troubles. The Thomas Cook affair kept recurring like a bad toothache, stirring fears throughout the land. Though the kindly merchant had been acquitted in his second trial, the furious queen had prevailed on Edward to dismiss the judge and retry him, after which poor Cook was assessed a ruinous fine. And Bess Woodville, by resurrecting the obsolete custom of "Queen's Gold," levied another.

His gaze went to Hastings seated beside the queen's son, Thomas Grey. *These two,* thought Richard, *had turned Edward from Camelot and led him into Sodom and Gomorrah.* At only fifteen, Thomas had already carved himself a reputation for wantonness and cowardice in arms, emerging to join Hastings as Edward's boon companion. The three spent their nights revelling with drink and bawdy women. Newly elevated to Marquess of Dorset, and flushed with his own self-importance, Thomas had demanded Richard address him by his title, and Richard obliged happily. The formality put distance between them.

Edward passed the letter to his father-in-law and took his seat at the head of the table. "From John Neville, my cousin of Northumberland. He's put down the rebellions and executed Robin of Holderness."

"But he fails to mention Robin of Redesdale, whose uprising seems to be of a more serious nature," said Earl Rivers. His rich gown of crimson velvet lined with green silk, loaded from shoulder to hem with jewels, flashed as he crossed the room to pass the missive to his friend.

"If John says it's under control, then it is, Sire," said Will Hastings. "John's a man of his word." Hastings's rivalry with Dorset sometimes ran bitter, and his wife, Katherine Neville, was John's sister. But always the consummate statesman, Hastings betrayed none of his dislike for Woodvilles on his broad-carved face.

Edward lounged in his chair, toying with his near-empty wine cup, which a wine-bearer quickly refilled. He fastened his gaze on Richard. "What say you, brother?"

"I agree with Will. Our Cousin John is a man of his word and loyal unto death."

"He's a Neville," spat the queen's father. "There's talk his brother Warwick may be behind this trouble in the North, even that Robin of Redesdale is his kin."

Edward tapped John's letter, which had been passed back. "He has assured me of his loyalty, in his own writing, no less. 'Tis sacred as an oath."

"Then, Sire, why did he not pursue the leaders of the Redesdale rebellion with the same zeal he showed Robin of Holderness?" demanded the Woodville's friend, Lord Herbert.

The queen's father guffawed. "Because Redesdale didn't call for the earldom of Northumberland to be given back to Percy!"

Dorset gave a snicker. "Nine years in the Tower has chastened Percy, Sire. Restore the earldom of Northumberland to him. Better a Percy than a Neville."

Trembling with rage, Richard leapt to his feet. "Better a Lancastrian turncoat than a man loyal unto death, eh, Dorset? Why does it come as no surprise you'd favour a turncoat?"

There was an uproar from the Woodvilles. Richard swung on them with murderous eyes. They recoiled and sputtered into silence at his expression. Without Bess they were not only out-ranked, but helpless against the King's favourite brother, and they knew it. They also knew their time would come when Bess, alone with the King, presented their case. So did Richard.

"Sire," Richard pressed, "our gracious cousin is your truest subject. He's a Yorkist, and of noble birth and noble intentions, unlike some others here in this room!"

Dorset gave a cry and lunged at Richard, a hand on his heavily jewelled dagger-hilt. In a lightning stroke, Richard had his own blade pointed at Dorset's throat. Edward came to his stepson's rescue, his long arms spreading between them like eagle wings. "Let it lie, both of you."

Reluctantly, Richard returned his dagger to its sheath.

"May I offer a suggestion?" said a voice silent until now. "These are troubled times and it would avail us much to make a pilgrimage and pray for God's help in our travail."

A hush descended over the group. Richard turned his eyes on the queen's oldest brother. He didn't know what to make of Anthony Woodville. The man was both like, and unlike, his kin. While sly of expression, as all Woodvilles were, he was dark, not fair, and his scholarly pursuits had won him notice and set him apart from his brothers, whose sole accomplishments were to marry well. He was also a chivalrous jouster, not chicken-livered like Dorset. On this day, in contrast to his gaudy nephew, he was sedately attired in a doublet of dark velvet edged with sable. Richard had heard that he had grown so pious that sometimes he wore a hair shirt beneath his silks and velvets. He wondered idly what had prompted such a change from his former flamboyant style. His manner, too, was sober, though he used to be as brash and boastful as his brothers. Indeed, he'd changed much since the Smithfield tournament two years earlier, and Richard almost liked the man. But it was impossible to forget he was a Woodville, and Woodvilles were not to be trusted.

Richard returned his attention to Edward, who now stood at the window draining his wine. "'Tis a good time for prayer, I doubt not," said Edward. "Therefore we shall make a pilgrimage to Walsingham, on our way north, to determine matters there." With a wave of the hand he dismissed his council. The chamber emptied.

Richard waited. "Do you really believe Warwick is behind the troubles in the North?"

"If he is, there'll be war before long. That's why I must leave as soon as possible and see for myself."

Richard swept up his gauntlets. "I'll go to him at once. He's at Warwick Castle…"

"No!"

Stunned, Richard froze in his steps. "You doubt me?"

"Experience is a hard teacher. I've already lost one brother to Warwick."

"I'm not George!"

"How can I be sure?"

Much as Richard hated to admit it, even to himself, the question was a valid one. Loyalty and honour were ideals. Men had died for them willingly from the time of Scripture. But Anne was real. Could he give her up? He'd never thought to be tested, had always believed it impossible for matters to reach this point. Safe in the cocoon of certainty he had spun for himself, he had felt confident of the choice he might be called upon to make. But in the end a man didn't truly know himself until he confronted the point of the sword.

"Do I have your permission to see Warwick, or not—*Sire?*" he demanded coldly so Edward would not guess how close to the mark he'd struck. He held his breath until his chest felt it would burst.

At last, Edward inclined his head.

With relief, Richard fled the room.

~*~

Warwick Castle, where Anne was born, Richard thought, anguish flooding him like a mighty river about to charge its banks. A suffocating silence filled the stone-vaulted chamber where he stood alone with the Kingmaker. Nothing he had said had moved this will of granite: this man who'd been a father to him, who'd been his guide and his family, whose daughter he loved, in whose household he'd spent the happiest years of his life. Warwick had remained resolute against Edward.

Splintered by the coloured glass border, the sun's rays poured through the tall lancet window like a funnel from heaven, brightening Warwick's hair and bathing his tall, crimson-brocaded figure in a strange play of light so that he appeared unreal, ghost-like. Richard could even see the tiny motes of dust that danced in the air he breathed. Behind him the River Avon wound placidly through the quiet countryside.

"Edward has taken a serpent to his breast that will destroy us all unless we strike first," declared Warwick in a tone ringing with finality. He moved out of the light.

Richard blinked to focus his vision. Now he saw that Warwick's face had an odd pallor, his skin was drawn tight across his cheekbones, and his mouth was set in a long tense line. In his vivid blue eyes an anxious question awaited Richard's reply.

Richard's head pounded. The hourglass had emptied. The moment he had dreaded, had hoped would never come, hung expectant for his answer. *Edward or Anne? Oh, God, Almighty Father in Heaven, no!*

Loyalty or love?

His mind, his heart, his soul, shouted for love. *For Anne.* Without Anne, there was no song, no joy. Only darkness, a vast emptiness.

Anne, Anne, Anne...

But had he not chosen as his motto, *Loyalty Binds Me*? Loyalty, the foundation of honour, and law, and justice; the principle of his life. If that were a lie, then all was a lie, and he was no better than Trollope, who had betrayed his father at Ludlow and unleashed a nightmare of death, destruction and misery.

Anne...

Was there no one to guide him? No one to take the decision from his hands?

No one. He alone held the answer. Could he truly turn against Warwick? His cousin was arrogant, aye, self-righteous and ambitious, aye. But he was Anne's father. He was generous and courageous beyond all limits. He had once risked his own life to save his. He owed Warwick, maybe as much as he owed Edward.

He stood in silence, the silence tearing at him, buffeting him in a desolate darkness, and gradually, out of the murk, formed an image from the misty past. It took shape dimly at first, then with increasing clarity, until he stood face to face with the truth; a truth he'd always known in some secret core of his being and had not wished to embrace. *Lancelot had broken his oath to his king and chosen love over loyalty, and with that broken oath he'd shattered Camelot and destroyed all whom he'd cherished.*

There had never really been a choice. *Oh, Anne, forgive me, Anne...*

"Edward is my brother," Richard said.

"So is George," replied Warwick.

"Edward is my King," Richard said.

"A king unworthy of such loyalty."

"A king unworthy of such disloyalty." Richard felt as if a hand had closed around his throat.

During the silence that ensued, the distant hammering and clanging of the blacksmiths and armourers in the smithy rose to a din in the room, and the rowdy, drunken laughter of soldiers on the ramparts blended with the murmurings of the knights in the courtyard until they rang in Richard's ears with all the shrillness of a war cry. He dug his nails into his palms against the panic that assailed him.

Warwick smiled, a hard, tight-lipped smile. "We're at an impasse then."

In a hoarse, cracked voice, Richard cried, "I'd do anything for you except betray my brother!" He closed his eyes, and again it was night and he was dangling from a rope over a raging sea with nothing around but lightning and thunder, the grip of Warwick's hand on his own all that kept him back from the depths of oblivion churning below.

Silence was Warwick's answer.

Richard put a hand to his dizzy head. There was nothing more to be said, nothing to be done. He willed one leaden foot before the other and felt his way to the door like an old man. He clenched his jaw to stifle the sob in his throat and laid his hand on the cold iron latch.

Warwick called out, "Dickon..."

Hope flared in Richard's breast.

"She means to destroy us all. I fear she will succeed." Warwick flung the words out bitterly, with all the anguish of his soul. "You're either for me or against me."

Richard swallowed, summoned all his will. "Then I'm against you." He felt as if he had plunged a sword into his own breast.

Warwick's broad shoulders slumped and he looked suddenly tired, and very old.

"What man ever trusted Edward and was not deceived?" he said, almost to himself. "Take care they don't destroy you, too, Dickon. Farewell... son."

Richard felt as though the thread of his life had broken. He bit down hard against the crushing sense of loss that engulfed him. Not trusting himself to speak, he thrust the door open and left the great Earl of Warwick standing there, staring out the window, alone in the empty room.

CHAPTER TWENTY-TWO

"...I care not to be wife,
But to be with you still, to see your face,
To serve you and to follow you thro' the world."

Through the sleepless nights of the year of 1469, Richard lived on hope, prayers, and dreams. Edward and Warwick had to reconcile. War was impossible. Somehow they would put aside their differences.

Three days before Midsummer Eve, in Norwich, where they had stopped on the way to Walsingham, Richard sat in a window seat in a secluded corner of a hall that teemed with courtiers and men-at-arms. He didn't feel well; he was nursing a bad chill and his physicians wanted to confine him to bed, but he'd refused. He hated admitting he was sick. He'd been sick too much as a child. Picking up his lute, he strummed an old melody. Music offered solace and softened the gloomy mutter of conversation in the hall and the dismal patter of rain against the windows.

Sweet is true love, though given in vain, in vain, he sang softly in his deep voice. *And sweet is death who puts an end to pain...*

A girl stood before him.

"'Tis beautiful," she said. "But sad. Do you know a gay ditty?"

Richard stared at her. "Someone else once asked me that same question."

"Well, 'tis indeed sad," she said, taking a seat beside him, uninvited. "Too much is sad these days."

Richard suddenly realised she didn't know who he was. He laid his lute aside. "Are you new to court?"

She nodded her auburn curls. "I arrived yesterday. You're a stranger here, too, aren't you?"

"In a way. How did you guess?"

"You look as lost as I feel."

Richard's drooping mouth curved up at the corners. "May I inquire your name, my lady?"

"Katherine," she replied. "Katherine Haute. You can call me Kate."

"What brings you to court, Kate?" inquired Richard, intrigued by her innocence and enjoying his newly found anonymity. It was refreshing to be able to talk to someone as an equal, without ceremony. As he used to do with Anne.

"I'm to be trained as lady-in-waiting to the Queen."

Richard stiffened. "Are you related then?"

"Very distantly. A cousin of a cousin of a cousin, by marriage. You know, that sort of thing. I imagine everyone at court is related in some way. If you dig deeply enough, I'll wager you'd find you were related to the Queen yourself."

Richard suppressed a smile. "Would that be good or bad?"

She cast a quick glance around and leaned close. "Don't you know you mustn't talk like that?" she demanded in a low, horrified whisper. "You'll end up in a dungeon."

"So it's good?" persisted Richard.

She straightened primly. "Unless you enjoy dungeons."

Richard found himself smiling. He studied her profile. He judged her age at fifteen, like Anne, and though she was nothing like Anne with her red hair and green eyes, there was a sweetness about Kate that brought Anne to mind.

"You've not told me your name," she said, blushing beneath his steady gaze.

"Richard."

"Are you training to be a knight, Richard?" she asked, lowering her lashes shyly.

"Aye," sighed Richard. "I'm training…"

~*~

From Norwich they went to Newark, arriving a week before St. Swithin's Day. Five weeks had passed since Richard had seen

Warwick, almost a year since he'd last seen Anne. Only letters connected them now. He knew that Merlin, her pet raven, had caught a fever and died suddenly one night; that she'd found a stray kitten and named her Elaine. He knew that Anne longed for him, as he longed for her. But letters didn't fill the emptiness of his life. They were no substitute for the sound of her voice, the warmth of her company. The months pressed down on him like lead. He was seventeen, as lonely as he'd been at seven when he'd lost his father and brother and fled into exile in Bruges. He'd spent those months with George, not knowing whether Edward lived or died, whether or not he'd ever see England again. But George had comforted him and made him laugh. Only now, George was lost to him, too.

Maybe due to loneliness, he had become prone to bouts of panic that sucked the air from his lungs and sent his stomach churning, drenching him in sweat and leaving him at once burning hot and shivering with cold. When herbal cures failed to help, and the oppression that accompanied these fits became more than he could bear, he took his horse and galloped from the safety of the castle into the surrounding countryside, his hound from Westminster at his heels. He'd named the dog Percival, and many a lonely hour had been made bearable by his company. At other times he drowned himself in music, even allowed himself a smile when Percival howled in accompaniment. But more often, he distracted himself with Kate's company. The fits eased when he was with her, and he had found that if he closed his eyes, he could pretend he was with Anne.

With Anne. Even when they made love.

He'd come a long way from that first night of initiation with Edward and Hastings, though he would always bear its mark. Except for Anne and Kate, he was still ill at ease with women. But when despair swept him, need overwhelmed him; and he had learned that women could make him forget. If Kate's arms failed to give him respite from the pain, he sought out the painted whores of the taverns. They, with their artful ways, drove the memories away—for a time. He'd become a good lover, so they told him, able to give pleasure as well as to receive. Though he no longer kept his lips closed, or pushed his teeth against their mouths when they kissed, he suspected their flattery flowed not from his expertise, but his generosity. A generosity that owed as much to guilt as to gratitude.

Poor Kate. He called her friend, listened for her coming, regretted her leaving. He held her tenderly, but he couldn't love her. Dear Kate. No matter how hard he tried, the shackles of the old love would not be broken. And Kate, Richard knew, loved him as he loved Anne.

The world was a harsh place, he thought. No pity in it.

~*~

It was while they were in Newark that the stunning news came. In Calais, two days before the feast of St. Swithin in July, George had been married to Bella by Archbishop Neville, in the presence of Edward's sworn enemy, the Earl of Oxford, and five other Knights of the Garter.

Edward was astounded. "'Tis impossible that Warwick—that George—that they openly defied me! For all our differences, Warwick's my friend, George, my brother—surely, 'tis all some mistake?" He turned bewildered eyes on Bess, who lowered her lids, a barely perceptible smile on her lips. Anthony Woodville averted his gaze. Edward turned to Richard, and Richard gave him a bleak look.

"And the Earl of Oxford," Edward muttered under his breath. "I returned his title and estates after his father's treason— intervened when Tiptoft would have cut off his hand. Only last year I pardoned him a second time! Is there no gratitude in men's hearts? No loyalty left?"

Silence. He picked up a silver wine flagon and flung it across

165

the room. It landed with a shrill crash, drenching the rushes with red wine. "Warwick is indeed behind the troubles in the North! We must round up more men—Dickon, Anthony, get to work. No, wait—first, a drink! Wine…"

Servants scurried in with flagons, hurriedly poured the cups and passed them around. Edward lifted his in a salute. "Drink, my friends! Drink till we roll on the floor and vomit."

~*~

In later years, whenever Richard looked back on this period of his life, he saw it as a blur, a tangled maze of events whose timing and sequence appeared confused, muddy. What news there was came in the form of rumours brought by peddlers, wandering minstrels, and itinerant friars; one rumour contradicting another. Even official messengers bore reports that were scarcely more reliable. To Croyland they came as the king's small army of two hundred horsemen pushed through the watery fen country; to Fotheringhay, the place of Richard's birth and his father's burial; through Stamford, and Grantham, where Edward attempted to raise troops: Warwick had landed in London, the messengers said; nay, Kent. He is the King's enemy, sworn to rid the land of Woodvilles, they declared; nay, he is the King's friend and will aid him in crushing the rebellion in the North. Warwick's reception in London was warm and the people cheered his cause, they said. Nay, it was warm in Kent, and London is for the King.

Through the blur, only one memory endured: his wrenching misery at the decision he'd been forced to make, and his loneliness without Anne.

On a bright July morning, a week after St. Swithin's Day, while the court still reeled from the news of George's marriage, the queen's young brother, Sir John Woodville, burst into the King's solar at Newark, a messenger at his side. "My Liege…" he panted. "There's shocking news!"

The messenger swept off his cap, sank to his knees. "The Earl of Warwick entered London yesterday and Robin of Redesdale is rapidly marching south to meet him with an army twice the size of yours, Sire. The Earl has issued a proclamation damning the Woodvilles and their friends Lord Herbert and Lord Stafford as avaricious favourites. One of his proclamations fell into our hands." He presented a rolled parchment.

Edward snatched it from him in an angry motion. He glanced down briefly and looked up, his face dark as thunder. "Warwick and George have likened me to the deposed monarchs Edward II, Richard II, and Henry VI—and we all know the fate that awaits deposed kings!" He crumpled the proclamation in his hands, hurled it across the room. "Traitors!" He turned to the Woodvilles. "Anthony, John, Rivers—seek your own safety; I can assure you none with so few men." He swung on Hastings. "Send missives to Herbert and Stafford, tell them to hurry to our aid with what forces they can muster. We'll meet them in Nottingham." He gripped Bess by the shoulders. "My love, get back to London at once—this is no place for you. Dorset, go with your mother." He strode to the door. "Come, Dickon. We're off to Nottingham."

~*~

Through the month of July, Edward waited in vain at Nottingham Castle for reinforcements. On the day after Lammas in August, he left for the south himself. Instead of aid, he encountered fugitives fleeing for their lives who panted devastating news: Robin of Redesdale had defeated Herbert of Wales and Stafford on their way North. On George and Warwick's orders, the two lords had been beheaded at Northampton. Edward turned in his saddle and looked at his men. Of the two hundred who'd set out with them in the morning, fewer than thirty remained. It was hopeless. "We're outmanoeuvred but undaunted," he said. "This is not the end. Seek safety and live to fight another day!"

They galloped away in a cloud of dust.

Hastings leaned on his pommel. "What now, Edward?"

"We go to Olney and wait," replied Edward. "They'll soon find us, I doubt not."

"And then?"

"Then, as I can no longer play the lion, I shall play the fox," laughed Edward.

Richard sat on his saddle rigidly as they trotted their horses to Olney, fighting his inner turmoil, still disbelieving that it had come this far. He'd hoped for reconciliation between those he loved—and prayed, begged, bartered, and promised God to endow innumerable chantries, to perform innumerable good deeds. To wear a hair shirt and make a dozen pilgrimages. When it became clear that he wouldn't be spared the ordeal and that Anne might be lost to him forever, he'd prayed for strength to bear his cross. But the burden was proving a crushing weight. The fits of panic came more frequently now and were harder to vanquish. The expenditure of energy left him drained, but he fought on, though inside it was as if he were scraped hollow.

They neared Olney. He scanned the horizon. There was no movement on the hill, only the stir of poplars in the wind. Hastings and Edward had fallen silent and their expressions were guarded. What would happen in Olney? Regicide was a mortal sin. But, then, what would Warwick do with the captive king? He tried to focus his mind on the glorious scenery around him. Rolling hills of hedgerows and wild poppies bordered wheat fields beginning to golden for harvest. Birds soared across the azure sky and sang in the trees that dotted the meadows. Aye, life went on. The world was beautiful. But the wind was bitter cold, though it was August.

CHAPTER TWENTY-THREE

"...now I see the true old times are dead."

In the solar at Warwick Castle, Edward removed his jewelled gauntlets and casually peered out the window at the formidable castle. "So, here we are, cousin. Captor and captive."

Red-faced, glowering, Warwick snapped, "You've only yourself to thank for that—and your love of the accursed Woodvilles."

Archbishop Neville wrung his hands. "Brother... cousin, I pray you..."

Edward plucked a grape from a silver bowl and munched. "I suppose I should love Nevilles better?" he grinned, addressing Warwick.

Warwick's colour deepened. "You're half Neville yourself. We're of the same blood—kinsmen, no less! For your cause, my father was executed, my lands seized, my wealth spent, all to place you on the throne. I risked everything and remained true to York in adversity. I gave you the Crown, and you gave me shame. For all your qualities, you're nothing but a lewd lad with an eye for women!"

Edward's turquoise eyes glinted. "Lewd I may be, but I'm no Holy Harry. No puppet king to be worn as your crown. No crowned calf or stuffed wool sack to be pushed around by you. I, too, risked all for the throne and lost a father—but I never lost a battle." He paused long enough for the insult to sink in. "At Mortimer's Cross my men would have fled, but I rallied them. I told them the three suns they saw in the sky were not a sign of God's wrath for turning against Henry, but a sign of the Trinity, and His blessing.

"You, on the other hand, made an arse of yourself at St. Alban's, cousin. All your fancy new guns, the stakes you drove into the ground, the traps you set expecting the enemy to charge straight into them, came to nothing by oversight—your flank lay open and the enemy took you by surprise at night! You failed to expect the unexpected, didn't you, cousin? Yet you always attribute my victories to luck. Lucky for me the wind-driven snows of Towton blew my arrows straight into the face of my enemy; but I, not you, placed those archers there. It was my cool head and leadership that won the Crown, not yours. And I, only I, am king!"

"You're king now, but will you keep your throne?" The veins in Warwick's forehead bulged with fury and beads of moisture shone on his lip. "The Woodvilles have infested you like a disease. You're rotting, my prince. Heed my words—sooner or later they'll bring you down and destroy you. Your queen is a woman reviled throughout the land. No son of her blood will ever be permitted to mount the throne of England!"

"By Christ's holy wounds, do you think they'll accept George? He's more despised than Holy Harry."

Silence. Then Warwick gave a burst of laughter. Edward and the Archbishop looked at him.

"I've just come to realise," Warwick said with a smirk, "that England has two kings, Lancaster and York, and both are my captives."

As the King and Kingmaker glared at each other, Archbishop Neville advanced uncertainly. "But we are kin. Our father—your mother, Edward—were brother and sister. Surely, surely..." He looked at them helplessly.

"George is right, Dick," Edward relented, dropping the titles, calling on remembered friendship and reverting to names he'd used in their youth when they'd laughed and cavorted together. "Blood binds us, and I can't forget you were my father's friend. But I am king. You owe me obedience, Dick, as God has willed. I'm prepared to forget many things, but not that I am king."

Warwick stood rigid, his shoulders squared, his hands clasped behind his back. He didn't respond for a time, though his expression softened.

"Indeed, we are of the same blood, and you are my best friend's son. I gave your father my solemn vow I'd look out for you, and I shall, Edward. You've made a mess of things, but I'll set them right. In the meantime, you are indeed king, but a king who is my captive and will do as I say."

For a long moment Edward appraised Warwick. Then he flashed a grin and draped himself comfortably in a chair. "You're a strange man, cousin. It's not my crown you crave, it's my power... Very well, each to his own potion. What would you have me sign?"

"You can start with this right here." Warwick nodded to a scrivener who brought him a document.

Edward glanced down. "Aah... so you wish to be made Chief Justice of Wales? I had no idea, cousin," he said amiably, bending his head to sign.

~*~

The news that Edward was a prisoner ran like wildfire through the land and shocked the people. They loved Warwick, but Edward was their king. London teetered on the verge of mob violence and Meg's husband, Charles of Burgundy, threatened the city with dire consequences if it deserted his brother-in-law.

Warwick and George captured Bess's father and brother, Earl Rivers and John Woodville, and beheaded them outside the walls of Coventry. Almost in unison people all over England took advantage of the breakdown of order to settle old scores, and a renegade branch of the Neville family stirred up a Lancastrian uprising along the Scots border. John in Northumberland refused to lift a finger to help his brothers, and Warwick could raise no troops. The men of England would not answer his call while their king was captive. The Kingmaker had no choice. He released Edward. Only then was the rebellion on the border crushed.

While Edward returned to London in a splendid royal procession, Warwick and George retired to Middleham, and Archbishop Neville sped to his manor of the Moor in Hertfordshire, so named for the exotic influences it reflected, built as it was in Saracen fashion with slender pointed arches, filigreed stonework, and elaborate fountains and gardens. There he was met by his sister's husband, John de Vere, Earl of Oxford.

"What now?" demanded Oxford, his back to the roaring fire. The misty September day held a chill and he was still cold from his rough sea voyage back from Calais. He poured a cup of hot spiced wine from a flagon on the table and downed a gulp.

The Archbishop regarded his Lancastrian ally. His brother by marriage was fit, dark-haired, rugged and likeable, but a bit too stubborn for his own good, and though he was family, he'd been an enemy for most of his life. Oxford's father had fought for Lancaster at Towton, accepted Edward on his accession, but remained Lancastrian at heart. Eventually he was executed for treason, along with his eldest son. Many disbelieved the charge of treason, however, for the son was tortured until he implicated his father, and their judge was the brutal Tiptoft who denied them a public trial. There was no appeal from Tiptoft's court, and father and son were executed on the same day; the father on the block wet with his son's blood. The Earl's wife was thrown into prison for three months, but his nineteen-year-old heir, John de Vere, was allowed to inherit his title and estates. Soon afterwards, young John, the new Earl of Oxford, got into a fight with another lord and he himself was brought before Tiptoft, who condemned him to have his right arm severed at the elbow. Fortunately for young Oxford, Edward commuted the sentence. Oxford had turned against York only recently, when he himself was arrested and thrust into the Tower.

Aye, Oxford had cause to hate Edward, and his imprisonment had further embittered him. After his release from the Tower, he'd come to Warwick to express his undying enmity for Edward and to declare that he would never again submit to the House of York. But the penalty for treason was death—a sobering consideration for any man. Taken to the gallows, a traitor was hanged, cut down while alive, then castrated and disembowelled while he still breathed.

Imprisonment was a lesser punishment, but many a prisoner had reason enough to wish he were dead. If a man were lucky enough to escape England, to be in exile was to be a pauper, and life was harsh, uncertain, dependent on the charity of strangers. It was said that the king's Lancastrian brother-in-law, the Duke of Exeter, had been found barefoot and in rags, forced to beg his bread until he was recognised and taken to Louis of France. And Louis was not known for generosity. Those who had seen Exeter said his clothes were near threadbare and his room in Louis's palace was a miserable, cramped, windowless chamber.

For the first time in his life, Archbishop Neville was glad to be a cleric. Clerics were not treated as harshly as the lay, and rarely was the death penalty invoked, even for treason. If he'd had his wish, he'd have been a scholar, married, had a family. But he was a younger son with no inheritance of his own, and scholars earned no bread. He'd have had to become a knight, like John, and seek glory in blood. That was hard enough for John. Sickened by the slaughter, John vomited after battle. It was why he always directed the fighting from a mounted position at the rear of his army, though he claimed he could better observe the battle this way. No one but John's squire and he himself, John's confessor, knew his shameful secret.

Aye, better to find glory in the church, where beds were warm, food was hot, and women were plentiful. He'd be glad enough for reconciliation when it came, as it was sure to do. Beneath the King and Kingmaker's enmity ran bonds of affection, and shared memories, too deep to be severed. The prospect of death and exile seemed to hold little fear for Oxford, but no cause was worth such sacrifice, and no sensible man would willingly embrace such a fate. Rash as Oxford sometimes was, he was no fool.

Archbishop Neville tore his gaze from the beauty of the autumn day and looked back at Oxford. *What now?* he'd asked.

"We've lost this round," the Archbishop replied, "but we've accomplished much. Two Woodvilles are dead, and Bella's married George. We've taught Edward a lesson he'll not soon forget…" he made the sign of the Cross, "and he'll come to terms with us to avert the calamity of civil war."

Oxford stared at him thunder-struck. *"This round?"* His rosy cheeks turned a shade of beet. He slammed down his goblet, splashing ruby wine over the table. "By Christ's holy wounds, this is no game! In case you missed it, George, Towton was the calamity: forty thousand dead, the bloodiest battle on English soil—the result of York reaching for a throne that had belonged to Lancaster for fifty years! We came to terms with the Yorkists and it cost my father and brother their lives! I came to terms with Edward, and what did it avail me? I was arrested, taken to the Tower, put in irons…"

His knuckles whitened around the back of his chair. "I gained my freedom at the expense of a friend's life. His only crime was to be heir to the earldom of Devon and to hate the queen and Tiptoft as much as the rest of us. He died because the man who judged him was Edward's friend and wanted his earldom…" In a hoarse whisper, he added, "And there was no mercy. He died a traitor's death."

He took a moment to compose himself. Then he closed the space between them and snatched his gauntlets from the sideboard. "Edward owes me a blood debt for murdering my family. I'll go to France now, but when I return it'll be with an army at my back. I don't play games like you Nevilles. Not until the House of York is ground to dust beneath the heel of my boot will I rest. And that, George, is a vow—something I hope even you understand."

He was gone.

A gust of wind bore a drift of dead leaves past the window with a rustling cadence. For some inexplicable reason George Neville thought of the sighing of lost souls swept by the Fates to their doom. He gave a shudder. Clutching his golden crucifix, he went into his private chapel to pray.

~*~

Despite the queen's vengeful urgings, Edward made an accommodation with George and Warwick for the peace of the realm. On Christmas Day, as a soft snow fell, they attended a feast of forgiveness at Westminster and agreed to forget their past differences. Edward ushered in the new year of 1470 with a general pardon for all those guilty of taking arms against him.

Though God had finally sent Richard the reconciliation for which he'd prayed, nothing changed. He had been unable to see either Anne or John. The usual border troubles kept John busy in the North, and Warwick kept Anne in Middleham, far from court, and far from him. Even her letters had stopped. Richard had written her almost daily for weeks, and she hadn't answered. Either her father intercepted their mail or he'd commanded her to stop writing, and she had complied, as she must. Richard knew Warwick was punishing him. *You're either for me or against me,* he had said. Richard feared he'd never be forgiven for choosing Edward, yet whenever he thought back to their confrontation, he remembered that Warwick's sharp, accusing eyes had softened at the end, and that he had called him "son." Hope would sweep his breast. Then, as crocuses broke through the March snows, everything changed.

In Wales, Richard read a letter from Edward. "Sweet Christ!" he exclaimed. Percival bolted upright and Rob Percy nearly dropped the hand of cards he was dealing to his friends, Tom Parr, Tom Harrington, and Richard's squire, John Milewater.

Richard waved the letter. "Warwick's mounted another rebellion!"

The shock brought Rob and the others to their feet.

"There's more… As Constable of England, Tiptoft has the power to try cases without a jury." He hesitated, forced himself to go on. "Tiptoft once spoke of a custom he had observed in Rhodes where Turkish prisoners were impaled alive— He caught twenty-three of Warwick's men in a sea battle and drove stakes through their buttocks and out their mouths. They're calling him the Butcher of England."

The two Toms blanched; Milewater's mouth dropped open. Rob moved to the table, splashed himself a drink, and downed it with a trembling hand.

"What of George and Warwick?" Rob asked, his goblet shaking visibly.

"They fled to Calais. Edward has proclaimed them traitors." Richard took a moment to compose himself. "Edward is marching north in pursuit of Redesdale. We are to join him."

A tense silence enveloped the room. Six months had passed since Warwick's rebellion and much had been accomplished to settle the land—now this! Richard hurled his goblet against the wall, startling Rob and the servants. Percival leapt to his feet with a low growl. Richard turned his back, clutched the cold stone mantle of the empty fireplace, and dropped his head.

CHAPTER TWENTY-FOUR

"When now we rode upon this fatal quest
Of honour, where no honour can be gain'd."

In his tent high on the Cleveland Hills of north Yorkshire, wrapped in a fur-lined mantle, John sat on a campstool and poured himself a tankard of hot ale. Around him were gathered Lord Cromwell and two trusted knights, Sir Marmaduke Constable and Sir Thomas Harrington. His faithful squire George Gower hovered nearby, while old Rufus watched him from a corner. Two days earlier, on Ash Wednesday, John had successfully persuaded Robin of Redesdale—his cousin Sir William Conyers, as it had indeed turned out to be—to put down his arms and seek the king's pardon.

We should be celebrating, John thought, *so why aren't we?* A strange dull ache lodged in his stomach and around his heart, and try as he might, he couldn't rid himself of it. He knew the others felt the same; no one had made an effort at conversation. Nor did it help their mood that the March night was bitter cold and foggy. The fog seeped in, misting hands and feet, dimming the light from the lantern, and throwing an eeriness over the dark that, like a sorcerer's spell, cast gloom and conjured foreboding.

How he hated fog!

Hated it, aye—and feared it, too, if the truth be known. Spawned by dread of dying in battle, his dreams took on all the appalling terrors his unconscious mind could devise and cloaked them in fog. Always he was alone in the fog; so terribly alone. The fog would swirl and thicken around his feet and rise to engulf him till he could no longer see or move. Cold and damp, it clung to him until it froze his heart and became a shroud that stopped his breath and stifled his screams. Out of the mist a shadow would appear and dissolve into the hilt of a sword, and then—

He always awakened in a panicky sweat.

He heaved a sigh. He longed for spring when frost gave way to dew. Winter had lingered long enough this year. It was already the twenty-fourth day of March, with no sign of spring anywhere. No sign of peace…

He picked up his tankard.

John's friends watched as he touched the tankard to his lips and set it back down on the rough plank table without drinking. They knew he was thinking of Lord Latimer's young son, Henry Neville, and Sir John Conyer's son, and Greystoke's son, and many other sons of kinsmen and friends who had died fighting against him, and for whose deaths he held himself responsible.

Marmaduke Constable said gently, "Remember, John, it was their decision to go against the King."

"Aye," John replied, staring at the tankard in his hand. After a moment, he raised it in a toast. "To the memory of the brave we loved."

A chorus of murmurs echoed his words.

He drank thoughtfully and rested his tankard on the table. "I fear I'm getting old. Lately every battle feels like a loss, though it be a victory." Indeed, it seemed he could no longer distinguish between triumph and disaster, between friend and foe. He looked up with tired eyes and his glance fell on his sword, lying on his pallet. He reached over, picked it up, held it to the lantern. He turned it this way and that, watched its shadow shrink, enlarge, and move across the canvas of the tent.

"Strange, isn't it, how the hilt of a sword resembles a crucifix?" John marvelled.

The men exchanged glances. Thomas Harrington said, "My lord, you've seen far too many battlefields of late. Go to Alnwick. Your lady-wife would be happy for a visit and will dispel your gloomy thoughts."

John laid down his sword with a heavy sigh. "You speak

truth, Tom. I haven't seen Isobel, my sweet daughters, or little George for months now, so busy I've been quelling risings for the King."

Lord Cromwell nodded his white-bearded countenance, eyes bright in his rosy face. "But remember, John, while the cost of victory's been high, there's comfort knowing the King will be well-pleased with you."

Shouts, galloping hoofs, and the whinny of horses interrupted their conversation. Rufus struggled to his feet. John's squire thrust back the flap.

"A messenger from the King, my lord!" George Gower cried, spying the Sun-and-Roses insignia on the crimson tunic.

The tight expressions in the tent relaxed into smiles of anticipation. The messenger entered, went to John and knelt. Opening his pouch, the man extracted a folded parchment tied with a white ribbon and impressed with the bright red royal seal. "My lord, for you, from the King."

John took the letter, glancing uneasily at the messenger. The man had avoided his eyes, strange for a bearer of good news. Had not the King received his tidings of victory? He had sent it with his most trustworthy servant, a canny lad who could worm his way through the thick of a rebel uprising. Cutting the ribbon with the tip of his dagger, he broke open the seal and began to read.

He looked at his friends in puzzlement. "The King is in York and summons me there on a matter of great urgency—nay, not the Conyers pardon. Another matter, unrelated. I'm to make haste to go to him." John spoke the words absently. He was lost in thought, for at the back of his mind old fears and terrible uncertainties had begun to stir.

It was the fog, he told himself. The fog, with its secret terrors; the fog, creeping in under the tent. He gave a shudder. How he hated fog!

CHAPTER TWENTY-FIVE

"But help me, Heaven…
I have sworn never to see him more,
To see him more."

On the eleventh day of April in the year 1470, the Earl of Warwick's vessel, the *Mary Grace*, hit rough seas while fleeing England for Calais. Drenched to the skin, Warwick stood at the helm of his tossing ship as one steep wave after another washed over the deck. Even his expertise could not stop the ship from listing so far to its side that it almost failed to make it back up.

"God's curse, we've no choice but to ride out the storm!" he shouted to the captain against the wind. "Put out the anchor!"

Below the poop at the stern of the vessel, in a small wainscoted cabin, Bella lay on her bunk, clutching her mother's hand and groaning in misery. Occasionally she lifted her yellow face to vomit into a basin that Anne held. The stench mingled with the dank smell of saltwater and fumes from a bucket of waste in the corner of the cabin. Anne's frightened eyes moved from her sixteen-year-old sister to the Countess mopping Bella's brow. She had always been able to find comfort in her mother's quiet strength, but now those gentle eyes were filled with tears and her mouth quivered as she gazed at her suffering child. Bella lifted herself on an elbow, retched again, and dropped back, exhausted. Anne passed the basin to the midwife who staggered to the corner and emptied it into a bucket secured to the wall by a chain. Like everyone else, Bella had ridden like the wind from Warwick Castle to the ship at Exeter. Bella, who was seven months with child.

Blessed Virgin, Anne cried inwardly, *help Bella, I beg you!* Aloud she said, "There, dear Bella, it will be better soon, we shall be in Calais soon, and then you shall have every comfort, my dear sister…"

A wave hit the ship. With a hideous creak, it lurched, then plunged downward so fiercely that Anne was thrown across the cabin floor and thrust against the hull. The horn lanterns suspended from a beam in the ceiling swung wildly, flickered, and went out, and the small wooden coffer carrying their belongings slammed into walls as it skidded along the floor. In the corner, the bucket of waste rattled against its hook. Bella screamed and the midwife cried to Holy Martyred St. Peter and St. Christopher to save them.

Anne dragged her aching body across the plank floor back to Bella, catching a splinter of wood in her finger and touching something slimy and malodorous with her outstretched hand. She realised with horror that waste had leaked from the bucket despite its tight lid. She bit down against the revulsion that heaved her stomach and wiped her palm frantically against her skirt.

Bella moaned in a frenzy of pain. Anne reached her sister, took her hand, and didn't cry out when Bella squeezed her sore finger. The ship heaved again with the shock of the great sea that broke over her. There followed another angry roar of water and a faint shouting for all hands on deck. Anne screwed her eyes shut and tried to stem her growing panic with prayer. All was hauntingly familiar. Long ago, when she was a child, she'd fled from Marguerite d'Anjou on a cold stormy night. The seas had been violent then, and she had experienced the same terror, but the years between had added a cruel dimension. A pregnancy for Bella. A broken heart for her.

A stream of Aves and Paternosters streamed from her lips while her thoughts ran on in confused images of home and the day in March when a kinsman had galloped to Middleham with the evil tidings that Edward had proclaimed her father and George traitors. There was no time to lose. They had to flee to Calais with all speed. Her anguish had been shattering as she hastily wrote Richard a last letter and ran to the chestnut in the woods.

"Blessed holy Virgin, Mother of God, grant us your abiding mercy," Anne prayed, raising her voice to drown out the image of Richard as she had last seen him, riding away from Middleham. "Have pity on us sinners, unworthy as we are…" In her mind's eye, she saw Richard turn, raise his gauntleted hand in farewell. Her voice faltered.

Her mother picked up the prayer. "And deliver us from peril, Holy Blessed Mother of Christ, who is our God and Lord, our redeemer and our reward, the promiser and the prize…"

Even Bella joined in now, though all she could manage were halting whispers. Anne forced Richard from her thoughts, found her voice again, and let the words tumble from her lips. All at once there was a shattering clang. The cabin door burst open and cold salt spray blasted the room. Her father stood at the threshold, wind and rain howling about him. She shrank back. At this moment, in his soaking robes, with his eyes dark and sparkling and his hair matted to his head, he looked not like the father she knew, but an apparition. Struggling against the wind, he forced the door shut. Her mother rose.

"See to what pass you've brought your daughter! See…" the Countess cried, her voice trembling. In the throes of labour, Bella writhed on the bed while the midwife hastily adjusted the soiled bed sheets. "I never let the meanest village women go without clean linens and warm water! At night, I tended to them myself, to lessen their pain, to ensure they had every comfort! Now my own daughter—my own daughter…" Her face crumpled.

Warwick turned his stricken eyes from his daughter back to his wife. He tried to speak but no words came. He opened his arms wide, a pathetic gesture begging forgiveness. His Countess went into them. Cradling one another, they stood sobbing softly. Anne averted her face. She had never seen her father weep before.

After a time, Warwick held his wife out at arm's length. "The storm is easing," he said. "The wind should shift easterly soon. We'll be in Calais by dawn, God willing."

"Calais," her mother whispered reverently, dabbing a handkerchief to her eyes. "Thanks be to Him and to the Blessed Virgin both."

Aye, Anne thought, *Calais was salvation.* Calais was refuge, comfort, safety, and blankets, warm water, and potions for Bella. Calais was sleep. Oh, to sleep, to lie still, and close one's eyes, and drift away into blessed, blessed sleep! Her father had been Captain of Calais since before she was born. They loved him there. His friend, Lord Wenlock, whom he had left in charge of Calais, would give them joyous welcome.

Her father turned to leave. His eye fell on the bucket of slop in the corner. "I'll send someone for that."

Anne closed her weary lids. Oh, to sleep, to sleep... A loud knock jolted her out of the languor into which she was sinking. She extracted her hand from Bella, and went to the door. A yellow-toothed, long-haired, half-naked sailor grinned at her. "Coom for the pail, lady," he said, lisping through gaped teeth. She held her breath, thinking he smelled worse than the waste he'd come to remove. He limped over to the pail, loosened it from its chain, and hoisted it up. He was staggering back to the door when his legs buckled and he dropped his load, seized by a violent spasm. Coughing and heaving for air, he fell against Anne, enfolding her in a stench so vile it knocked the breath from her body. She shrieked, flung him from her, and fled to a corner of the cabin. Her hand shaking, she tore a strip from the cambric shift beneath her gown and wildly, desperately, wiped at her face. She didn't need a physician to tell her infections and deadly sicknesses lived in bloody phlegm and offal.

The sailor collapsed against Bella's bunk, clinging to the wooden post like a drowning man and coughing as though his chest would split, while the midwife cowered against the wall and the Countess shielded Bella with her body. The spell subsided at last. The sailor cleared his throat with a rough gurgling sound, forced open the lid on the bucket, and spat out a wad of bloody slime. "Forgive me, m'ladies," he said, shamefaced. "I did'na mean no harm. A fit it is that comes on me chest at times. Nothing ta concern ye about." He secured the lid back on. "Aye—I'll be off, thank 'e, ladies.'"

Anne ran to the door, barred it behind him and leaned against it, trembling. No matter what he said, the man was dying. She prayed she hadn't caught his fearful condition, whatever it was.

~*~

Throughout the night Anne and her mother kept vigil at Bella's side. She quieted somewhat and managed to fall into an exhausted sleep, but as the grey light of dawn filtered into the cabin, her pains began anew, with violence. Anne's heart nearly burst with joy at the welcome cry, *"Land Ahoy!"*

"Bella!" Anne cried. "We're safe! We've reached Calais! All will be well, dear Bella!"

The Countess sank to her knees in prayer to the Blessed Queen of the Sea, the words spilling from her grateful heart.

All at once a thunderous, earth-shattering explosion shattered the tranquillity of the April morning. The vessel shivered. Shouts and clamouring broke out above deck and there was much running to and fro. Someone beat on the door. Bella groaned.

"'Tis nothing, don't fret child, all's well. We're in Calais," the Countess murmured.

Anne rushed to unbar the door. It was flung back with a resounding bang. George stood at the threshold, his blond curls dishevelled, his rich brocaded azure cote ripped. But it was his expression that made her recoil. His nostrils flared like a lathered stallion's and his brilliant blue eyes burned with a hatred that twisted his fine features into a demonic mask. He looked like

184

a madman.

"He'll pay for this!" he roared. "He'll pay, I swear it!"

The Countess rushed to grab George's elbow. "Hush, my lord, I pray you—think of Bella!"

Bella tried to rise. "George!" she panted. "Oh, George…"

George's expression changed to horror at the mass of tangled hair and the two wild eyes glistening in Bella's yellow face. The eyes were encircled in purple, the lips cracked, and the frail white body with the huge swollen belly was covered with bloody sheets. "Bella," he murmured. "Oh, my poor Bella…"

Warwick appeared at the door, a dazed expression on his face. The Countess's hand went to her breast. "My lord, what has happened?"

He stumbled into the room, collapsed on a stool. He looked up at his Countess with blank eyes. "We cannot land. They are shooting at us."

She shrank back with a cry and reached out for support to the wall. "But Lord Wenlock…" she managed.

"The garrison's orders are to turn us away. The Merchants of the Staple pay the troops' wages, and they favour Burgundy. Wenlock has sent us a secret message. Calais is a trap. If we enter, Charles of Burgundy will attack by land, and Edward by sea. We've no choice. We must go to France."

"Bella," she cried. "Do they know…?"

"They know. Lord Wenlock is sending wine."

She looked at him dumbfounded.

"'Tis all he can do, lady," Warwick said. He dropped his head into his hands.

~*~

The baby was a boy, and he was born dead. They wrapped his little body in a shroud and buried him in the sea. It was a beautiful spring day; a soft wind blew and the sky was as clear as if angels had washed it that morning. In the distance stretched

Calais with white sandy beaches and a long line of defensive wall studded with gun-holes. The red tiled roofs of merchants' houses glittered in the sun, reflecting purple shadows onto the Beauchamp Tower and the massive Woolstaplers' Hall. Across the water, the bells of two church towers tinkled sweetly.

Anne lifted her eyes to her father's face, bleak with sorrow, and to her mother, standing silent and immobile as a waxen image. She turned away, overwhelmed by a raw, primitive grief. She didn't look at George, who stood beside her, but she heard his words.

"Edward," he hissed between his teeth, "you'll pay. I vow it on our father's soul."

He reeked of wine.

~*~

All was quiet in the little cabin as they sailed to France. Even the seas, Anne thought, staring out the window whose wooden shutters stood open to the warm breeze. She let her gaze rest on Bella. Her sister lay on her bunk, eyes open, staring at the ceiling, as she had during the past four days since the babe's death. Beside her knelt the Countess, a drab figure in darkest grey, lips moving in silent prayer, fingers busily working her rosary beads.

Anne looked at the shining blue sea. She had no interest in France, which was the future, and she didn't allow herself to think of England, which was the past.

The waves are so gentle, she thought. *Like a blue silk banner blowing in the breeze.* She felt strangely calm. Maybe one day she'd be able to sleep.

CHAPTER TWENTY-SIX

"'Yea, lord' she said, 'Thy hopes are mine,'
and saying that, she choked,
And sharply turned about to hide her face."

On May Day the passengers aboard the *Mary Grace* awakened to glorious sunshine and cries of *Land Ahoy!* The Countess looked up from her rosary, and Bella turned her head, but the sound came to Anne only dimly, as though it travelled across a vast distance. She rose to prepare for landing, barely conscious that she moved at all and oblivious to the church bells along the river banks clanging the commencement of the festival of love.

Louis of France had arranged a warm reception in Honfleur, a sunny town with half-timbered houses and cobbled streets where the scent of lime blossoms perfumed the air. The streets were filled with people celebrating the spring. Minstrels played merry tunes and pretty girls danced around the gilded Maypole. Wine flowed, and mummers and men on stilts tried to make them laugh. But the wine made Anne's head ache, the glaring sunlight hurt her eyes, and the song and laughter that echoed long into the night kept her awake.

From Honfleur they were conducted through Bayeux to an abbey in Caen. Set in flowery meadows that sloped to the River Orne, and surrounded by blossoming apple trees, the limestone abbey was serene, the cloistered gardens fragrant with violets and roses. At night the nightingale's song mingled with the tinkling of the fountain, and in the early morning the cooing of turtledoves filled the dewy air. Punctually at Prime, Laud, Vespers, and Matins, church bells tolled and voices sang praises to Heaven. The soothing chants spread balm over Anne's dark, sleepless nights. For the first time since leaving home, she found a measure of peace.

Soon after their arrival, they were joined by Warwick's cousin, the daring Bastard of Fauconberg, bastard son of the Kingmaker's uncle, the Earl of Kent. There was much jubilation since Fauconberg, an admiral of Edward's fleet, had brought many of Edward's ships, and also several Burgundian vessels he'd seized on the high seas. Sorely in need of money, Warwick accepted the plunder gratefully.

Many conferences followed behind closed doors.

In June, Warwick and George journeyed to Amboise expressly to meet the King of France. In their absence, the Countess spent much of the day in the chapel, and Bella remained secluded in her room. Anne strolled the gardens, perused books in the vaulted library, and helped the nuns make an apple drink they called "cider." Often she assisted with their charitable deeds—feeding the hungry, caring for the sick, sewing for the poor. The nuns were kind and called her *"petite angel."* She welcomed their friendship, which helped allay her loneliness, and she was reluctant to leave them, even at Compline, when they prayed in the gloomy pillared crypt of the abbey church of La Trinite.

Nearly five hundred years had passed since William the Conqueror's wife Mathilde built the abbey in hope of saving her soul after committing the godless sin of marrying her cousin without a dispensation. Anne found herself drawn to Mathilde's stark black marble slab tomb in the chancel. Wondering what had driven the queen to take such a risk, she would murmur prayers for her soul.

On June 11, her fifteenth birthday, Anne sat quietly by the window in the empty warming room, watching the nuns pass below in the open arcaded court. The foliage glittered in the afternoon sunlight; squirrels chased one another across the emerald grass; and birds bathed in the fountains and twittered in the trees. Almost from the day she was born the world had proved a dread place, but in this house of God, she'd found refuge. When her father returned from Amboise, she would request permission to take her vows. If she couldn't have Richard, then she would have God.

Gratitude warmed her heart at the thought of her father. Marrying her to Richard had been his dream, too. Memories flooded her. She saw herself as a child, running to him in joyous welcome, and she saw him bending down, opening his arms wide to receive her, his face lighting with pleasure. He'd always had a smile for her softer than for anyone else. If there were one surety in this world, it was her father's love. He understood. He had always understood.

She gazed at the River Orne, where a cluster of colourful sails dipped gently beneath an azure sky. A life of meditation might bring her contentment once she learned to forget Richard. These weeks of prayer had served to heighten the healing detachment that had first come to her aboard the *Mary Grace,* a detachment that shielded her from the arrows of Fortune as effectively as fine Milan armour shielded a knight from the arrows of war. No longer did a melancholy melody rip her heart with the sharpness of a knife's blade. No longer did gargoyles terrorise her dreams. Now all she remembered when she awoke was blessed blackness.

Nothing will touch me ever again, she thought, absently twisting Richard's ring around her finger. The knowledge comforted her.

~*~

On Midsummer Eve, near the end of June, Warwick and George returned from Amboise. With them came Fauconberg, and Anne's uncle by marriage, the Earl of Oxford. In the solar at Caen Castle, where they had gathered for the reunion, Anne stood by her mother's chair on a Saracen carpet in the middle of the room. Her father had a smile on his lips; Oxford and Fauconberg seemed pleased, but George was in a foul mood.

"We have reached an agreement, King Louis and I," announced her father. "Louis will reconcile Marguerite to me, and I will restore Henry of Lancaster to the throne."

Anne heard Bella gasp. She looked behind to where her sister sat. George stood beside Bella, already half-drunk. He gave Anne a brutal stare, a look that would have struck fear into her once.

The Countess rose from her velvet chair in stunned surprise. "But Marguerite hates us. You brought Henry down."

"It appears that her thirst for revenge on the House of York is greater than her loathing for us," Warwick said dryly.

"Why would Louis…" her mother broke off in bafflement.

"Louis's reward is an alliance of England and France against Burgundy," said Warwick.

A silence fell. Finally the Countess spoke again. "And your reward, my lord?"

Warwick smiled, reached out his hand to Anne. "Mine, my dear Countess, is the marriage of our daughter, Anne, to Marguerite's son, Prince Edouard. One day, my Anne, you shall be Queen of England. Think of it; *Queen of England!*"

Anne felt a terrible weakness in her body. The faces around her blurred and dimmed; the room tilted and began to spin. Everything went black and she sank to the floor in a heap.

~*~

Anne pleaded with her mother and fought with her father, but nothing moved them. Her father threatened to throw her out into the streets if she refused to comply, but she came to realise his bluster and fury hid a terrible truth: He himself had no choice, so he could offer her none.

In the days following her father's announcement, Anne learned that he had lost faith in George, as it became clear to him that the people of England would rather keep Edward their king than accept his vain, foolish brother. Since her father found his position under Edward untenable, and he couldn't place George on the throne, there was only one alternative left to him: Restore Henry of Lancaster. By this marriage, the Kingmaker would achieve his heart's desire. His daughter would be queen. Only it would not be Bella. That was why George followed her around with jealous, hate-filled eyes.

At Angers, in the solar, the Countess added another instruction to the many she had already given Anne. "The King of France is not like Edward, dear child," she whispered. "Take care not to show your feelings. Do you understand?"

Anne stared at her blankly.

Wringing her hands, the Countess turned to a lady-in-waiting. "She is so thin, so pale—she has been ailing. God's mercy, can nothing be done for her? Prince Edouard…" She broke off helplessly. So much depended on this meeting. She pinched Anne's cheeks to force colour into them. The child was as white as a phantom.

The lady-in-waiting rummaged through her ointments and pulled out a vial. "Juice of the pomegranate fruit," she said, rubbing a few drops into Anne's cheekbones and lips. She adjusted the pearl coil holding Anne's hair and stood back to regard her handiwork.

"Better," the Countess agreed. "Now, child, let us go to the King… and remember my warning."

Anne heard her mother as through a mist. When she'd recovered from that day in Caen Castle, she found that life came to her in broken pieces, hushed and distant, as though a thing apart, evolving around her but not through her. It was like the early days at the abbey, except without the pleasure or the hope. She sat listlessly in the abbey gardens where she once used to stroll. She no longer took down the books from the shelves, or looked in the mirror, or cared what she wore. Her gauzy veils and the sea-green satin dress sprinkled with silver stars that her mother had laboured on for this special occasion meant nothing to her; the jewels loaned her by the Queen of France, nothing. Even her prayers brought her no comfort and seemed to come from lips not her own. Only one aspect of life seemed real and would not be silenced no matter how many prayers she uttered, how many candles she lit.

Her fear of Marguerite d'Anjou. The dreams had returned.

Dutifully Anne fell into step behind her mother as she led her out of the solar and along the gallery to meet the King.

~*~

Two men-at-arms thrust open the doors to the King's bedchamber. Now Anne understood her mother's warning.

In stark contrast to the opulence of their own quarters, the royal bedchamber was bare of furniture and gloomy, lit by only one candle on a mantle over a high fireplace. A foul stench struck her as she stood blinking in the darkness and she nearly coughed. Slowly, her eyes adjusted. She saw that the King of France lounged on a pallet on the floor instead of a throne, and in lieu of a golden crown he wore a filthy, odd-shaped dark hat. His black hair was matted to his brow with sweat and his shrewd dark eyes were hooded and bulged like those of a toad. His features were coarse, his face made ominous by an enormous crooked nose. Instead of splendid robes, he wore a cheap grey coat, and instead of courtiers, he was surrounded by dogs.

Louis of France, Anne thought, was the most hideous creature she had ever seen.

She approached, moving carefully along the rush-strewn floor to avoid stepping in excrement. She sank into a low curtsy before the King and held her breath as she kissed the hairy hand he offered.

Louis XI examined her while he stroked a narrow-faced grey dog. He smiled, showing a mouthful of gaps and blackened teeth. "My gracious cousin, the Setter-up and Plucker-down of Kings, did not tell me his daughter is beautiful like a rose. That makes our task more simple, *n'est-ce pas?* You are fifteen, *m'enfant?*"

Anne replied with downcast eyes, "Aye, Your Grace."

"Good, very good. You may 'ave children right away."

Anne blushed.

"Do you like my dogs?" he demanded suddenly.

Startled, Anne didn't respond for a moment. The dogs were a motley group who stared at her haughtily, unwilling to accept her right to be there. "Aye, my lord," she finally said.

"I prefer them to people. They are—'ow you say it? Predictable." He rose. He was a tall man with a slight stoop. "*Alors*, let us go now and meet the Queen Marguerite."

Anne followed the strange figure down the gallery, feeling as though she were following a glistening spider into his dark and terrible lair.

~*~

The doors to the great hall were drawn open to receive the King. Anne saw a huge chamber bright with tapestries, vibrant paintings and beautiful sculptures, the walls lined by Lancastrian exiles, their shabby dress a stark contrast to the surroundings. Their faces were turned to Anne as she waited in the entrance, and in their fierce looks she read their memories of blood and wrong. Most were unfamiliar, but below the dais stood certain faces she recognised.

There was her uncle, the Earl of Oxford, black curls falling over his pale brow, his emblem of the Star and Streams blazing on his jacket. There was King Henry's Welsh half-brother, Jasper Tudor, tall, austere, greying, a frown on his craggy face. And King Edward's brother-in-law, the Duke of Exeter, a long angry scar slashing his cheeks, his garments nearly threadbare. Nearest the queen stood the Duke of Somerset, scowling across the hall at Anne, his hand on his sword hilt, as though he would slay her if she dared step forward.

Sunlight poured through the windows; candles and flaming torches lit the hall. Yet it seemed to Anne the place was dark and cold, and she shivered. Her glance fell on Richard's little

193

ring of silver leaves quivering on her finger and she averted her gaze. Bugles blared. The King's herald announced him. Louis strode up to the dais, nodding to his courtiers as he went. Anne heaved a breath, murmured a hasty prayer, and stuck out her chin. She was next.

The herald shrilled his bugle.

"Lady Anne Neville, daughter of the mighty Earl of Warwick, Maker of Kings!"

Anne made her way up the long hall to the throne with stiff dignity, dragging her legs towards the woman in black velvet who sat beneath the royal canopy and the youth in red and purple who stood beside her. On the far side of the dais, Louis lounged casually against the window, arms crossed. He reminded Anne of a spider watching flies struggle in his web: a gigantic, ugly spider.

A gargoyle.

She felt dizzy and the figures began to blur. *No!* She must not faint. To faint now would be to dishonour the House of Neville! She had to keep going—for her father's sake. She was his only hope of salvation, the only way out of his anguished predicament. To such desperate lengths had he been driven that he had paid Marguerite's brutal price for this marriage. He had knelt at her feet, begging her forgiveness and singing her praises. And Marguerite had savoured his humiliation by keeping him prostrate a full quarter-hour before granting him permission to rise. He had grovelled and abased himself at the feet of his father's murderess, knowing full well how all the world would laugh at the once-proud, once-mighty Kingmaker. He had done that, and she must do this. She could not fail him in his hour of greatest need. She fixed her eyes on him, to draw strength from his strength.

He stood below the dais, to Marguerite's left, a majestic figure in blue and gold, his shoulders stiffly erect, a frozen smile on his taut face. His blue eyes were riveted on her, but it was not strength she found there. It was fear.

Dear Mary Mother, help me...

She turned her eyes on the Queen. Like an eagle circling prey, there was a wild and dangerous beauty to Marguerite d'Anjou. Her netted brown braids were twisted like wings beneath a circlet of gold, and from a wide angular face glittering dark eyes stared out with scowling intensity. As Anne approached, she saw that the Queen sat so rigidly, gripped the carved side arms of her chair with such force, that her knuckles were bloodless white. For an instant Anne expected hatred to rip the Queen from her seat and send her flying at her with the scaly wings, hissing breath, and venom of the gargoyles in her dreams.

Blessed Mary, she thought, averting her gaze from the Queen. She turned to the Prince with a measure of hope, for nothing could be as terrible as the monster on the chair. He was seventeen, almost Richard's age, she thought. A year younger. *Think not of Richard now; he is gone, gone, gone...* She staggered, caught herself, and continued forward. She saw that Prince Edouard was tall, handsome, muscular, with wavy brown hair, fine bone structure, and green eyes that glared at her from a face contorted with loathing.

She shuddered. Her legs shook, collapsed beneath her, and she dropped to the floor, her face in her skirts. The action might well have cast disgrace on the Nevilles but for the fact that she had reached the dais. Thankfully, the Queen kept her on her knees a long moment before granting her permission to rise.

Anne raised her eyes shyly, hesitantly, and looked up at the royals through half-lowered lashes. She was surprised to see the contemptuous smile on the young prince's lips falter, but the face of the woman her father had once called the Bitch of Anjou did not soften. Marguerite examined her with the coldness of a surgeon about to disembowel the condemned. Then she whispered something to her son, who recovered himself enough to smile at her with contempt.

"So you wish to be queen one day," Marguerite announced in a husky voice thick with the accent of her native Anjou.

Anne braced herself before she spoke. "'Tis not what I wish that matters, but what God wishes for me, Your Grace."

Marguerite d'Anjou gave a dry chuckle. "Ah, the little mouse can speak," she said to her son over her shoulder, loud enough for the hall to hear. "Well, there is hope, I dare say."

Derisive laughter swept the room. Anne blushed a vivid scarlet. She had survived what had promised to be the hardest part. Now she knew the worst lay ahead.

CHAPTER TWENTY-SEVEN

"From my own earldom foully ousted me."

The June sky was a flawless turquoise; birds chirped and squirrels chased one another around the trees. Near a circle of green in the Archbishop's palace, the once Lancastrian Henry Percy, clad in flaming reds and golds and surrounded by an elegant retinue, came up to John as he gave his squire instructions. John's new wolf-hound pup, Roland, that he'd adopted after Rufus's death, rose to his feet with a low growl.

"So, *Marquess of Montagu*, I see you can still afford a horse and a squire," Percy said with a glance at George Gower saddling John's horse. "But your man is gaunt, your horse mangy. It must be difficult to feed both on forty pounds a year. Evidently the King places a high value on your services." Percy grinned at his retinue. His men snorted.

John winced. Laughter and snide remarks had followed him from that ill-starred day in March when the King had stripped him of his earldom of Northumberland. He clenched his fist, dug his nails into his palm until he drew blood. He'd trusted Edward, set him above his own brothers, and Edward had betrayed him by taking away the earldom for which he'd bled. That was the urgent matter on which his royal cousin had summoned him to York after he'd crushed the Redesdale rebellion. To inform him that the earldom was restored to Percy, who'd been released from the Tower and had sworn an oath of fealty to Edward.

John remembered little after the King's announcement. He'd stood rooted to the floor, stunned, reeling from shock while the room darkened and the stone pillars around him wavered like reeds in a river. He barely heard Edward's explanation, that his object was to bring peace to the unruly North, which was Lancastrian in sympathy and clamoured for Percy's return. In exchange for the earldom, Edward promised John's son George the hand of his eldest daughter, Elizabeth, and conferred on the little boy the title of Duke of Bedford. John was elevated to the marquisat of Montagu.

But no lands were bestowed. No means with which to support the marquisate were provided. Nothing but forty pounds a year from the county of Southampton. Edward claimed he was short of money and promised to take care of the matter one day. But Edward was always short of money and months had passed since John had lost his earldom. He couldn't live on hollow titles and empty promises. With his coffers drained, he'd borrowed to survive. If it weren't for the generosity of his friend and kinsman Lord Scrope of Bolton he'd have been reduced to beggary.

John swallowed the bitter gall that flooded his mouth. Lord Scrope had sided with Warwick and led the Redesdale rebellion with Conyers. From a foe, he'd received succour; from a friend, a foul blow.

He looked at Percy, remembering the tearful day when his family had quitted Alnwick and moved back into the leaky manor house his father had given him. As they could no longer afford many servants, Isobel and his daughters helped with the chores. Now Percy lived in Alnwick. Such was Edward's thanks to him for going against his brothers, for fighting his kinsmen, for labouring day and night to crush rebellions in the North and keeping the border safe so Edward could take his ease.

Such was his thanks.

John didn't respond to Percy's taunt lest the pain and rage in his heart sound like fear, but his eyes blazed over the hostile crowd as he took the reins of his horse.

"Your clothes have seen some wear since we last met," sneered Dorset over Percy's shoulder. His ice-blue eyes glinted with amusement as they raked John's chaperon and cote. John's hat was devoid of gems, for he had long since pawned them, and though his cote was of finest blue velvet, there was a stain on the shoulder, the silver embroidery was frayed, and the fur was matted by weather. Hatred and humiliation coursed through John's veins and the muscles of his forearm hardened beneath his sleeve. He turned his back and mounted his horse.

But Percy was relentless. "How fares your brother, Montagu? I hear the Bitch of Anjou kept him on his knees a full hour while he whined his pardons and begged her forgiveness." Raucous laughter met the report sweeping England.

John trotted his horse closer and looked down on Percy's sallow, pockmarked face. "The only whining I hear, Percy, is your womanly voice," he said, breaking his silence at last.

Percy's group jeered, but from the corner of his eye, John saw his squire smile.

"Your niece…" Percy shot back with a sneer. "I hear it took all Louis's arts to persuade Marguerite to agree to the marriage! Called her a little mouse and wanted nothing to do with her—said the match was not to her profit and even less to her honour."

John stared at Percy, but it was Anne he saw: tiny, fragile Anne, hiding her tearful face. "Why so sad, my little lady?" he'd asked as he'd scooped her up in his arms. "I'm nearly four," she'd wept, "and I still can't touch the moon." He clenched his fist around his bridle, his breath burning his throat. How dared that lily-livered turncoat insult Anne! He met Percy's rat-like eyes. Slowly, meaningfully, finger-by-finger, he drew the gauntlet from his hand. For fear of thinning the ranks of his supporters, Edward had forbidden the issue of challenges, but once offered, a challenge could not be rejected without dishonour.

John leaned on his pommel and curled his lips. "Any time you wish, Percy, we can settle this man to man." He threw his gauntlet at Percy's feet.

Percy's mouth twitched. He gave no reply. Like everyone else, he knew John had yet to lose a fight, be it a battle, or man-to-man. John's gauntlet was a death warrant.

"As you're so reluctant, Percy," said John, "perhaps Dorset here—renowned through the land for his valour—is willing to take your place?" He turned hard blue eyes on Dorset, who blanched and backed away. John smiled coldly. "I'll take both of you snivelling cowards at the same time. What say you?"

At that moment a window was flung open on the second floor of the palace and someone yelled, "Northumberland!" The window slammed shut again.

Percy recovered, leered at John. "I must go, Montagu. The King needs me."

John watched him swagger across the courtyard with his retinue. Revulsion tightened his stomach into a painful knot. He swung his stallion towards the gate. His squire handed him his dusty gauntlet and mounted his horse to follow him. John raised a hand. "I go alone."

"'Tis not safe, my lord! You are a…" George Gower broke off.

John knew what his squire was about to say. *You are a Neville!* He spurred his horse and galloped blindly out of the palace gates, Roland following at his heels. Men ran, chickens clucked out of his path, a cart nearly overturned, dogs barked, children fell. John heard nothing, saw nothing. He had only one desperate wish.

To leave behind the painful world of men.

CHAPTER TWENTY-EIGHT

"He walked with dreams and darkness."

At Westminster Richard took the narrow stone steps up to the private chapel of the royal apartments. The beautiful room had octagonal walls, many windows, and a reed mat on the tiled floor. A wooden cross stood on one windowsill between an icon and an urn of blue periwinkles, and a Bible lay open on a stand before the small altar. Richard shut the door and drew the crimson velvet curtain for privacy. He knelt and said a prayer of thanks for the safe delivery of his newborn daughter Katherine.

The child had been born during the spring revels in May, in the small house he had bought for Kate on Beech Hill near Pontefract Castle. He was proud of the sweet babe with the rosebud mouth, yet his joy in fatherhood was tainted by an inexplicable guilt. Somehow, he felt unfaithful to Anne.

That was ridiculous, of course. Nobles begot bastards. It was the way things were and there was nothing shameful in that. If Anne had not been lost to him, he would never have known the need that drove him to other women. And that need existed. He was no anchorite. He was made of flesh and blood. While he didn't revel in orgies as Edward did, he didn't spurn the women of the taverns. But Kate was no bawdy wench to be paid and dismissed. He cared about her, knew she hoped for more than he could give her. Had not Edward made Bess his queen? Had not his own great-grandfather, the Duke of

Lancaster, married Katherine Swynford, a herald's daughter?

With hope in her heart, Kate had named the babe Katherine—but not in her own honour, as haughty Bess had done with her first child. Kate's thought had been for the lowborn girl who'd wed a duke. But there had been love between Katherine and her duke. He loved only Anne. He would go to his death loving only her. He made the sign of the Cross and rose from the altar. Taking a seat on the velvet-cushioned window seat, he slipped his hand deep into the bosom of his doublet and withdrew Anne's letter from a pleat pocket in his shirt.

After Wales he'd gone north to aid Edward against Robin of Redesdale, but once again their cousin John, that valiant soldier, had quelled the rebellion without help. Returning to London, he went by way of Middleham. He'd received no word from Anne in months and he needed to know if she had left him a letter.

Gulping deep breaths of cold fir-scented air, he'd panted into the woods and made for their tree. Leaping over the gorse, stumbling over rocks, he'd run past the grove of poplars, across the gushing brook. Twice he fell in his haste. The chestnut finally loomed into view. He stumbled to a halt. It hadn't changed. Split down the middle and hollow at its heart, the old tree still stood tall, wounded but healed, stretching out its limbs with the proud dignity he remembered. His eye fixed on the carving he'd cut into the gnarled old bark as a ten-year-old boy: *Richard and Anne, King and Queen of Avalon, where all is Justice and Joy.* Here had stood their mythical kingdom where, in their childhood innocence, they had ruled supreme. His heart began to race. Inside the hollow a white ribbon fluttered down from the little shelf he'd nailed there so many years ago, in that other lifetime. Trampling the stinging nettles he didn't feel, the brambles that ripped his hose and pierced his flesh, he made his way to the tree and reached up into the hollow. He flung the stone aside and seized the letter. He slashed the ribbon and bent his head to read.

201

Beloved,

My heart is heavy and the world filled with darkness since I learned the news. Father says we must flee for our lives, that there is no other way. God has chosen to part us, but you will be with me always for I will carry you in my heart until we meet again. If that day comes not on this earth, I shall wait for you in Heaven, for you are my love, my only joy, all that I treasure in this world and the next.

Anne

He slid to the hard ground, clutching the letter. In a bramble bush, an animal squealed and darted away. Deer approached and fled, cracking dry twigs underfoot. The woods fell silent again except for the cawing of ravens. The light grew cold; the sky lit with purple and darkened. He got up stiffly. Folding the letter with cold, clumsy fingers, he slipped it into a breast pocket deep inside his velvet doublet.

He had carried it with him ever since.

He looked down now at the delicate, evenly-formed black script and traced the small flowing letters gently with a fingertip. Resting his head against the window, he shut his eyes, his mind flooded with Anne. Her warmth came to him, and he could hear her voice, feel her touch. He was closer to her than at any time since their parting, closer even than when he'd found her letter by their tree. The love and the longing he felt overwhelmed him, and for a moment he forgot where he was.

He tucked the letter safely back into his doublet. Despite everything that had happened, despite all the doubts that at times drowned his hope, he continued to believe they'd be together some day. How or when he would win Anne, he couldn't fathom, but the old conviction was still there at his core, radiating hope amidst the darkness, giving him will to go on.

~*~

"Sire! An emissary from the Duke of Burgundy with urgent tidings!" cried a herald.

"Send him in," commanded Edward, seating himself on his throne in the Marculf chamber at Westminster.

Richard hurried to his stance beside Edward while his old friend Howard, the Friendly Lion, and other knights gathered at the foot of the dais. It was the morning after the Feast of St. Swithin, three months after Northumberland had been restored to Percy. They had been conferring with Edward on the situation in the North, which was as unsettled as ever, but news about Warwick took precedence over all other troubles.

The messenger strode in, knelt before Edward, and confirmed that a pact had been made in Angers and that the proud Warwick had indeed prostrated himself before Marguerite d'Anjou for a full half-hour.

Edward laughed. "Warwick will be as true to Marguerite as he has been to me."

"Sire," the messenger said gravely. "The Earl of Warwick swore on a splinter of the True Cross to be Queen Marguerite's faithful subject."

A choked gasp escaped Richard's lips. Gone was hope of reconciliation; gone, all hope of winning Anne! Warwick had chosen his side and now his choice bound him unto death. Before he could stop himself, he exclaimed, "The Cross of St. Laud has the power to strike him dead within a year if he breaks his oath."

Edward slammed a fist on the armrest of his chair. "I'll strike him dead myself if I get the chance!" He signalled the messenger to continue.

"The Earl of Warwick agreed to place Henry of Lancaster back on the throne. In return, on July 25th at the Cathedral of Angers the Lady Anne Neville was betrothed to Prince Edouard of Lancaster."

Richard's pulse pounded in his ears and his legs buckled beneath him. He clutched hold of the throne. Edward's words came to him dimly. "Marguerite agreed to that?"

"She would not hear of the marriage at first, Your Grace. King Louis is a persuasive man but it took all his powers to get her to accept the offer. In the end, the King prevailed, though two conditions were placed by Queen Marguerite. First, as Prince Edouard and Lady Anne are cousins, that a papal dispensation be obtained before the marriage is consummated. Second, that—that…"

"Proceed, good man. However ill the tidings you carry, you are pardoned," Edward said.

The messenger swallowed. "Second, that the marriage not be consummated until the Earl of Warwick has won England for Lancaster."

"I see," said Edward, a hard edge to his voice. "I don't envy Warwick. Marguerite neither forgives nor forgets. If he succeeds in getting Henry back on the throne, I wouldn't wish to be in his shoes… What of my royal brother, Clarence?"

"He and his Duchess were at the betrothal, Sire. The agreement declares him heir to the throne if the Lady Anne and Prince Edouard have no issue. 'Tis said he is not happy with the arrangement."

Edward's mouth twisted. "Nothing short of the crown will content George, but clearly he's gained naught by this that he didn't already have. Is that not so, Dickon? Dickon, are you all right?"

Richard looked up, tried to reply, but no words came. He was in the thick of one of his fits, drenched in sweat, gasping for air. He tugged at his collar.

"Wine!" Edward roared. He pushed Richard into his throne, loosened his doublet, and made him drink.

Slowly the shivering ceased and warmth stole back into Richard's frozen body. Edward dismissed the emissary and waved the others away. "Dickon, you know that if I could, I would change all this."

"'Tis God's will," Richard managed hoarsely. "But to fight George…"

"I know. But George has turned his coat twice, Dickon. He can be made to turn it again." He paced.

Richard's head began to clear. Ill at ease on the throne, he made an effort to rise, but his dizzy head forced him down. Edward whirled around. "I have it…" He pounced on Richard like a lion and gripped his shoulders. "It's a good plan, Dickon. It'll work, I know it. But first things first." He lowered his voice. "There's unrest in Yorkshire and I've had no word from John or Percy. We must secure the North before Warwick returns." He hesitated. "Can I count on you, Dickon?"

Richard lifted his head, met his eyes. Never in his darkest moments had he truly believed he would lose Anne. He had always believed things would come out all right in the end; that in the end, he and Anne would wed. He had been so certain.

He had been so wrong. *You're either for me or against me,* Warwick had said. And he had meant it. Aye, Richard thought; he had regrets, but had he ever had a choice?

"Loyaulte me lie," he whispered. Loyalty Binds Me. His decision, made long ago.

Edward squeezed his shoulder in a gesture that spoke more than words. Then, in an abrupt change of mood, he said, "Now, Dickon, it's time to vacate my throne. I trust you didn't enjoy it too much?" His blue eyes, though smiling, held a wary look that reminded Richard of the tiger at the Tower zoo.

"As a matter of fact, brother, I found it distinctly uncomfortable," Richard replied.

Edward threw his head back and let out a great peal of laughter. With a slap that nearly felled him, Edward declared, "I knew I could trust you, Dickon!"

~*~

"Sire, sire, wake up! Your enemies are coming for you!" cried a voice in the night.

Edward stirred, rubbed his eyes. Torchlight smoked in his face. He couldn't make out who was shaking him. "Go... away..." he mumbled, turning on his side. "Go... away..."

More hands grabbed him, shook him, shouted at him. He rolled back. Richard was leaning over him, a desperate look in his eyes. "What are you doing, brother?" Edward yawned. "I was dreaming... a nice dream... nipples, red as berries..."

"Wake up, Edward!" Richard demanded. "There's no time to lose!"

Edward forced himself up on an elbow. "What are you talking about, Dickon? Why do you worry so much? Can't you see I'm drunk?" He fell back, closed his eyes again.

A bucket of cold water splashed over him. He sat up, spluttering. "I'll have your head for that, whoever it is!" Someone threw a towel at him. He dried his face.

"We've got to go, Edward," said a familiar voice. "Your enemies are indeed on the march."

Edward grinned playfully. "What enemies, Hastings? I have no enemies, have I?"

"Tell him, Carlisle!"

Now Edward recognised the man with the torch. The sergeant of his minstrels. "What are you doing here, Carlisle?" He yawned. "You're... supposed to be... up north with Montagu..."

"The Marquess of Montagu, Sire—he's espoused his brothers' cause! Warwick has landed at Plymouth and the Marquess is marching to join forces with him. He's coming here, to Doncaster, with his army of six thousand men at his back. There's no time to be lost."

"Now I know you're mad! Be gone, let me sleep."

"My lord, 'tis true! He said you sacrificed him. That you took

206

away his earldom and gave him a magpie's nest to live on. You must flee—he's coming south, he and all his army, for they're loyal to him."

"You have it all wrong, Carlisle. *We're* the ones going *north* to join forces with *him*. Montagu's my friend, and truer than a brother..." he broke off at the irony, gave a chuckle. "Yet your sorry tale has a touch of truth. He's much loved by his men, and if ever he turned his coat they'd stand with him to a man... Now leave me. We've a hard day's ride tomorrow." Edward collapsed on the bed, drew his blanket up to his chin.

"By God, 'tis the truth! Fugitives are pouring into the camp, and all tell the same story," Hastings bellowed.

Startled by Hastings's harsh, uncustomary tone, Edward's eyes flew open.

Richard pushed Hastings out of the way. "Edward, it's true... John's turned traitor."

Edward reached up, grabbed his brother's neck, and stared into his eyes for a long moment. He flung him back. He'd seen what he needed to see. He seized the cote Anthony Woodville held out to him, threw on his boots and strapped his sword to his side. Without a word he thrust open the shutters and leapt out the window of the farmhouse where they had halted for rest. The others followed. Vaulting on their horses, they fled east through the night.

~*~

"Holland!" the captain announced.

"'Tis a relief, Sir Captain. For a while, I almost doubted we'd make it," grinned Edward.

Richard's gaze swept the dirty, hungry, downcast faces of the men who huddled in the cold, driving rain, before fixing on his brother. Edward was at his best when things were at their worst. He had fled his land and left his pregnant wife in Sanctuary. He had been pursued by enemy vessels of the

Hanseatic League and had almost drowned in a gale off the shores of Norfolk. Were it not for Edward's friend, the Governor of Holland, who'd appeared by the mercy of God to ward off the Easterlings, he and Edward and their seven hundred men would now be dead or captive. Yet Edward could still jest, while beneath his wet cloak he, Richard, trembled with dread to taste the bitter cup of foreign exile for a second time. He didn't know how Edward could take so little in life seriously, when he himself could take nothing lightly. The world thought them brothers. The world was wrong. Edward was fearless. A true Plantagenet.

"We're a sorry lot, are we not?" Edward laughed, giving Richard a hearty slap on the back. "A throne's been lost and between us we've not enough coins to fill a wine cup!"

Aye, Richard thought. That was yet another problem: how to pay the ship's master for the trip. Even as the thought occurred to him, Edward removed his fur-lined cloak and offered it to the captain. "Sir Captain, will you accept this as payment?"

"Sire, I've no use for such a fine cape but I'll take it, for I know 'tis all you have. Mayhap I can find a king with a throne and sell it to him!"

Edward threw back his head and roared with laughter. He hung an arm around the man's shoulder. "Sir Captain, I tell you what—when I get back my crown, I'll buy it from you myself! And at a pretty price—how's that?"

"May God make it soon, Sire, for as the Blessed Virgin knows, I've sore need of the money."

Edward roared again. Still laughing, he sauntered down the gangplank. On the wharf, he turned. "See you in London before the year is out, good Captain!"

"Aye, Sire!" the man called from the deck. "You surely have my prayers on that."

CHAPTER TWENTY-NINE

"A doubtful throne is ice on summer seas."

Richard felt as if time had rolled back, so little had changed in Bruges in the ten years since he'd walked its cobbled streets. It was still as cold as he remembered, and the canals looping through the walled city were still crowded with swans and boats as before. The only difference was that more arched stone bridges and windmills had been built in the meanwhile.

In the tavern of The Blind Donkey, near the Eglise Notre Dame where he had gone to meet his old friend William Caxton two days before All Hallow's Eve, Richard slipped Anne's letter back into his doublet. Until that moment at Westminster when he'd first learned of Anne's betrothal, he'd believed with utter certainty that they would wed some day. Even now he dared to hope, and he wondered at the incredible foolishness of the human heart, and the stubbornness and tenacity of hope.

He drew his worn cloak close and looked around him. The inn was boisterous with laughter and the din of clanging dishes, the air thick with the odour of sweat and the aroma of freshly baked bread. His stomach growled again and he was reminded that he was hungry. For a moment he thought about ordering a portion of mutton leg, but the few coins he carried jangled thinly in his purse, and he quickly decided against it. At this point in his life, meat was a luxury he could ill afford. He swivelled on his bench seat and warmed his hands on the fire behind him. He was not only hungry, but thoroughly chilled from the short walk from the Governor's Palace where he and Edward lodged at the governor's invitation. Bruges was no colder in winter than Yorkshire had been, but in Yorkshire he'd had fine furs and heavy mantels. Here he had only debts and favours he might never be able to repay.

He lifted his eyes to the window. Snow flurries were falling and people hurried past, bent against the wind. On such a day in 1460 he'd arrived in Bruges, mourning the death of his father and brother, leaving another brother behind to fight for his life. He raised his cup and downed a gulp of wine. He hated Bruges and the memories it brought back. The city erased the years between his two exiles, made him feel as confused and helpless as he'd been at seven, and flooded him with a blind, painful anger. Even now, the great cry of his childhood was welling up again: *It isn't fair!*

Absorbed in his thoughts, he didn't hear the whinny of horses, feel the blast of cold air that admitted his friend, or see the old burgher thread his way to the far corner table where he sat. He looked up with a start at Caxton, who had given him refuge when he'd fled Lancastrian vengeance as a boy. Time hurtled backwards and he forgot where he was, forgot that a decade had passed between. Unable to move or speak, he stared at the blue eyes twinkling in the red-cheeked, white-bearded face. Recovering his composure, he bid Caxton welcome and gratefully accepted the secret letter from Meg that the rich English merchant delivered.

They bantered. Richard drained his cup and tried to drown his thoughts and noisy stomach, while Caxton sipped hippocras and spoke of a printing press he'd seen in Germany and his hopes of owning such a machine one day. "Then I would print books by the hundreds," the old merchant said. "And if I live long enough, everyone will own a Bible…" He broke off, grinned sheepishly. "A dream, I know. Merely a dream."

"We must all have our dreams," Richard said. "We could not go on without them." He poured more wine.

"I know of your predicament," the old burgher said in a different tone, "and can offer you money, my lord, but alas, not enough to launch a navy against Lancaster. For that you need the support of the Duke of Burgundy and the rest of the English merchants of Bruges. All else I have is yours."

"I thank you, my friend Caxton, but for now all is provided us most generously by the Governor of Holland, who has given us warm welcome in his home. Seigneur de Gruthuyse rescued us from the Easterlings, you know. He's a true friend—as you are—and will be richly rewarded when Edward regains his throne."

Richard spoke with a confidence that belied his fears. They had been in Bruges two months and the truth was their debts were mounting, their future never so uncertain as now. To their stunned surprise, Meg's unpredictable husband, Charles of Burgundy, had entertained the Lancastrian dukes of Somerset and Exeter at his court, but had refused to see them.

Like Henry of Lancaster, Charles was a descendant of Edward III through John of Gaunt and, despite his marriage to Meg, his heart remained Lancastrian. He had supported Edward against Warwick in the summer, but Warwick's espousal of the Lancastrian cause had won his sympathy. When Gruthuyse had informed Charles that he'd saved Edward from the Easterlings, Charles had cursed, not thanked, his Governor. What would happen if Charles ordered Gruthuyse to throw them out? Where would they go? Who would help them then? Meg sent them money and letters by the hand of their mutual friend Caxton, but even Meg couldn't go against Charles if he demanded they leave Burgundy. The old burgher's voice cut into Richard's thoughts.

"'Tis hard times we live in… Is it true the Kingmaker executed Tiptoft?"

"Warwick appointed Oxford Constable of England, and Oxford condemned Tiptoft to death, just as Tiptoft had condemned Oxford's father and brother. His execution pleased the commons. They hated Tiptoft for his brutality, said he could weep at a manuscript, but not at the suffering of men."

"Yet I regret his passing… He was a fine scholar." Caxton shifted his girth on the bench and brightened. "God be thanked, the Earl of Warwick has shown moderation. Tiptoft's is the only execution. Other Yorkists have not been harmed and he's honoured the queen's Sanctuary at Westminster."

Richard mulled his wine. Warwick hadn't attainted a single Yorkist. Not even Richard or Edward. His vengeance was limited to Woodvilles, and even then he exempted women.

"And the poor queen, delivered of a son in Sanctuary… How fares she? Have you had reports?"

Richard said dryly, "The child is a healthy boy, and the Queen does as well as can be expected. Warwick sent Lady Scrope to aid in the birth."

They fell silent, ruminating on their thoughts. At length Caxton gave a soft sigh. "So many changes, the Wheel of Fortune ever turns… My lord, may I take the liberty of inquiring after the Duke of Clarence—he was dear to my heart. Such a golden, laughing boy, so full of life; I loved him well."

Aye, George had been a merry child. Richard remembered how he had always looked on the bright side of things. In Bruges he'd brought him comfort and soothed away his fears with his optimism. *A star shot.* "That's a foe falling, Dickon!" *An owl whooped.* "Victory bells are going to peal for us, Dickon!"

No, he couldn't have made it through those dark days without George.

He came out of his thoughts abruptly and realised he hadn't given his old friend a reply. Here in Bruges he was as cursed by memories of George as he'd been that other winter by memories of Edward and Edmund. He downed the last of his wine and rose. "Clarence is well, as far as I know. We pray for him."

The old merchant heaved himself up. "'Tis right queasy the times we live in," he sighed.

~*~

Letters came from England. Francis had written. Since he was a minor at fifteen, he was still Warwick's ward, still at Middleham learning the art of war, but too young to participate in any real killing. And Percival was with him. A fond smile softened Richard's taut features. That was good. Percival liked Middleham. He'd be safe there. Kate had written, too. She was with child again. The babe would be born in April. A wise woman had said it would be a boy and she wanted to know what name he wished. The news had brought a smile to Richard's lips that lasted for days and prompted much teasing from Edward. "Must be a woman," he laughed. "Only a woman can make a man smile in a storm."

And the storm was showing no signs of abating. More letters followed from their sister Meg over the next months, but nothing from Charles except excuses. Finally Meg admitted the truth. Charles did not wish war with England and hoped to reach a settlement with the House of Lancaster.

Only after Christmas, when Warwick foolishly joined Louis in declaring war on Burgundy, did Charles throw his support to Edward. Richard could not understand what had prompted Warwick into such a rash blunder. He was too wise a statesman to commit political suicide, yet he had irrationally, inexplicably, turned the tide against himself by throwing support to his ally's enemy. Charles immediately gave Edward the audience he had refused for months and a fleet was outfitted in the port of Flushing. Richard and Hastings went to work victualling the ships. They were ready to leave on the second of March, but weather detained them. "Marguerite can't join Warwick for lack of a fair wind," Edward had laughed. "May it blow for us before it blows for her!" And it did. There were those who said that Edward always had unholy luck, and some who never failed to add that the Devil tends to its own. Richard had no doubts: God was with Edward.

On the eleventh day of March, aboard the *Anthony*, while Marguerite waited in Honfleur, Richard watched their little flotilla of Burgundian and Hanse ships with fifteen hundred men aboard hoist their painted sails. The coastline of Holland faded away into blueness. Edward lounged against the wooden rail and set his face west, to the sunset bleeding into the sky. "Now for the enterprise of England and another turn at the Wheel of Fortune!" he grinned.

Richard stared at the fiery horizon, unable to return his smile. The Grand Vicar of Bayeux had granted the dispensation Warwick had sought. Anne had married Edouard of Lancaster on December 13th.

CHAPTER THIRTY

"Farewell; think gently of me."

On the fifteenth day of March, 1471, in the fortress of Pontefract, before the hour of Vespers, a sergeant-at-arms burst into John's chamber in the Constable's Tower.

"My Lord, good news!" he cried.

John looked up from the map he had been studying with his captains, and in the corner of the chamber, Roland pricked up his ears.

"Edward of York and Gloucester have landed at Ravenspur with two thousand men. They plan to slip around our army under cover of darkness to reach Sandal Castle where a group of retainers await them."

"Sandal Castle," remarked the Lancastrian knight Sir John Langstrother with a cold smile. "Their father and brother were killed at Sandal. 'Tis fitting that the sons should also die there."

"You forget," said John quietly, "my father and brother also died there, fighting for York."

A silence fell. John moved to the window. He refrained from adding that what was not fitting was that he and Warwick should now be aligned with the same savage queen who had ambushed the Yorkist leaders ten years ago. From these very walls of Pontefract the Lancastrians had set out for Wakefield to fall on his father's tiny party as they foraged during the Christmas truce. Laughing as their heads were nailed to Micklegate Bar, the queen had called out, "Leave room for Edward of York, for he shall be next!" John winced. He could deliver her wish.

Grey twilight was settling over the quiet countryside, fading the land into a dreamy unreality. From somewhere in the distance came the faint, plaintive bleating of sheep. So Edward had landed at Ravenspur. Strange... Ravenspur was where the Lancastrian usurper Henry of Bolingbroke had landed seventy years earlier to press his rights against Richard II. From there he'd set in motion the train of events that had led to the Wars of the Roses. John sighed heavily, rubbed his eyes. Now his gallant cousins were within his grasp—to crush them, to silence them forever, all he had to do was reach out his fist. Then amiable Edward of March, his golden Sun-King, and Dickon, his brother-in-blood, would be no more.

He looked down at the ring Dickon had given him that long-ago day at Barnard's Castle. An image of the frail, determined boy flashed into his mind, and he saw himself in the castle tiltyard at Middleham, aiding Dickon with the battleaxe. The child whom he had loved as a son had grown into a man he cherished as a brother.

Without turning, John said, "We shall follow them tomorrow."

"But..." the sergeant sputtered, taken aback, "My lord—they are marching south with all speed! Tomorrow will be too late. We must go after them now."

John was not listening. He was thinking of all the battles he had fought, so many never-ending battles. Always he had hoped for peace, and always there was only war. And always he had to choose between those he loved. The old wound in his right leg, which had never truly healed, began to ache again. Absently, he rubbed his thigh.

He placed his hands on the stone embrasure of the open window, and rested his full weight on his arms. A cool wind caressed his cheek and stirred the branches of a beech below. A hint of spring was in the air; it smelled fresh and clean. No blood tonight. High above, two birds soared across the dusky sky in perfect harmony. A terrible yearning for Isobel seized him. He remembered that sunny day at Alnwick when they had stood together watching little George play on the turf and swans glide past on the River Aln. There had been too few such days in his soldier's life. He shut his eyes, swept with sudden desolation. Oh, how he needed the comfort of her arms at this moment!

He looked back at the birds, remembering the raven that had alighted on his shoulder that very morning. A dire omen, some said. He knew that it was. He would never see Isobel again. He tightened his grip on the ledge. It felt cold and damp to his touch. He heaved a deep breath and bowed his head. He felt old and weary, and his thirty-nine years weighed like stones on his heavy heart.

The sergeant looked helplessly at Langstrother. The knight took a step forward, his hand clenched on the hilt of his sword. "My lord, 'tis madness to let them get away! We outnumber them three to one…" He spoke loudly, to shake John out of his listlessness. "We'll make short work of them if we take them now, before they rally troops. Who knows if the chance comes again?"

John made no response. *Three to one.* His father and brother had been outnumbered three to one. He stared at the darkening fields, seeing the faces of dear friends long dead in old battles.

Langstrother strode up to him, sword clanging. "If we don't get them, they'll get us!"

Silence.

"My lord of Montagu, *they* are the enemy."

John turned his head and Langstrother was startled at the suffering look in his eyes.

"Tomorrow," John repeated thickly, his handsome face pale and pinched in the gathering darkness. "We follow them tomorrow."

Langstrother stiffened. "My lord, I must say it. Some would call this treason."

John hesitated. Aye, he thought, he had a choice. To be a traitor, or an executioner. His lids came down heavily over his eyes. He nodded that he understood. He turned back to the window and beneath his faded tunic his shoulders sagged. Outside all was dimness and gloom; no stars lit the sky and the moon was obscured by clouds. He fixed his eye on a point beyond the northern battlements.

Fare thee well, cousins, he whispered in his heart. *May God be with you and keep you.*

CHAPTER THIRTY-ONE

"The cup was gold, the draught was mud."

Ravenspur was not where Richard and Edward intended to land. The ill winds of Fortune had blown them off course, far too north and close to Lancastrian lines positioned around the fortress of Pontefract, a stone's throw to the west. They had spent an anxious night awaiting capture or death.

The attack never came. Morning dawned cold but bright with birdsong. Edward threw up his arms gleefully, as if to embrace the sky and the angels who resided there. Turning to his men, he laughed, 'John's scouts must have been snoring like pigs!"

Richard averted his face. He knew the truth, sensed it with

every fibre of his being. John had let them go. He hadn't the heart to fight them. Nay, it would have been no fight. It would have been a massacre.

"Where to now?" Hastings's voice.

"York," said Edward. "We need cash, and the duchy of York owes me, as their liege lord."

York refused Edward admittance.

"Never mind," said Edward to his men, attaching a feather to his cap at a jaunty angle. "There's more than one way to skin a rabbit."

"But—Sire!" exclaimed Edward Brampton, the Portuguese Jew and swashbuckling sailor whose steady hand at the ship's helm had guided them through the storm that had swept them to Ravenspur. "The white ostrich feather is Prince Edouard's insignia!"

"And that, good Brampton, shall get us into York," grinned Edward. He looked around at his men. "You scoff, but seventy years ago the ruse worked for Henry of Bolingbroke. And from York he went on to win the throne for Lancaster!"

His men mounted their horses and followed him to the city walls. Their mouths twitching with the need to laugh, they watched as Edward, lustily cheering for King Henry, swore he came only to claim his rightful inheritance, the duchy of York. And with their hearts bursting with gladness and relief, they watched as the gates were thrown wide to receive them. The angels had to be guarding Edward, thought Richard. How else to explain this second miracle in as many days?

From York they marched south, saddlebags bulging with gold, and on their way they stopped in Nottingham for the night. They had just finished dinner at the inn when a missive came. Edward read carefully. He leaned forward on the greasy table. His men huddled close. "Marguerite's due to arrive at any moment," he whispered. "The foul weather that kept her stranded in Honfleur has lifted and she's set sail for England at last. We must draw Warwick into battle before she arrives."

"Aye, aye," a chorus replied. Someone said, "For once they unite their armies…"

Edward finished the thought. "For once they unite, we're dead men, slaughtered like fish in a barrel by their superior numbers… So why in Heaven's name Marguerite delayed leaving Honfleur before the winds turned foul, I'll never fathom."

"What does it matter?" said Richard. "We're still only two thousand strong against Warwick's twelve. How can we fight him, even without Marguerite's reinforcements?"

Edward met his grey eyes with his own periwinkle blue. "This missive I received—it's from George, Dickon. My plan has worked, brother. Our intermediary, a lady who shall remain nameless, has persuaded him to desert Warwick. He, and his five thousand men!" A broad grin split his face.

"That only gives us seven thousand. Scarcely even odds."

"Aah… the voice of reason. Or doom," laughed Edward. "Well, you can cease your worries for once, little brother. Remember Bolingbroke? Men fell behind him by the thousands as he marched against Richard II. And they didn't even know Bolingbroke. I'm their king. The people love me."

But Richard found Edward sadly mistaken. While men had flocked to Bolingbroke's banner seventy years earlier, few joined Edward's against Warwick. Edward was in turns astonished, wounded, and angry.

"It's not that they don't love you, my lord," said the Friendly Lion, Sir John Howard, as they rode along. "But the realm, it's weary o' war. Weary o' choosing between York and Lancaster."

Richard was puzzled by the tremulous quality of the Friendly Lion's tone. Surely this seasoned warrior had no qualms about fighting? There was glory in war. But soon Richard realised with relief that not everyone felt as John Howard did, for Edward found better fortune as they hurried south. In Leicester twenty-five hundred men came to his side, and in Coventry George and his men pinned the White Rose to their lances and swept to Edward's side with a thunderous roar, swelling Edward's band of followers into an army of nine thousand men. Wasting no time, Edward boldly marched to the gates of Coventry.

"Warwick!" he called. "I'm here to settle our little argument! Come out and do battle!"

"I'll do battle when I'm good and ready, Edward! Not a moment sooner!" shouted Warwick from the snow-dusted ramparts.

"What are you waiting for?" called Edward. "The butterflies to hatch?"

No answer.

"Very well, Warwick!" Edward called out. "Let's talk terms. I'm prepared to offer you pardon of life only—you and all your men. If you surrender now!"

"You'll have my answer by Tierce!"

~*~

"Edward sends fair terms. End this feud, brother, this damned unholy alliance," pleaded John.

The Earl of Oxford turned glittering eyes on Warwick. "Surrender, and Louis will curse your name, Warwick. Next time Edward turns on Nevilles, there'll be nowhere to flee. Accept Edward's terms and—heed my words, fair brother-in-law—you'll pay for your double treason, and pay dearly."

Warwick led John aside to a window. A colourful sea of banners bobbed gaily through the falling snow. Above the clamour of voices and whinny of horses, men drank wine and ate heartily, laughed and made jest, as if it were a feast day. Some paused every so often to greet a long-lost Yorkist friend, now a Lancastrian enemy, and others to shout an insult, as if to incite battle. Warwick's eyes rested on the Yorkists almost gently.

"Oxford's right, John. We'd have nowhere to turn. Otherwise, I might be of a mind to accept Edward's offer." A pause.

"Desmond's crime was a slight of words. I beheaded Bess's father and brother. We could never rest easy with that vengeful Woodville witch panting for our blood, fair brother."

"And Marguerite," John said quietly, "is she famed for compassion?"

"There's something I can tell you now, John. Louis and I have a secret pact. In return for my support against Burgundy, Louis will carve out a realm for me from Burgundian lands. Once he's crushed Charles, I shall be Prince of Holland and Zeeland, brother. So we need only survive Marguerite for a short space."

"I don't like it, Dick," John said uneasily. "I don't like what we've done, and I don't like Louis. From all reports, he's not to be trusted. Take Edward's offer, my brother..."

"You worry too much, John. Louis is my friend. All will be well. Trust me."

He sent back a refusal.

Edward could not linger for a siege. He turned his troops south to London. By a stroke of incredible good fortune, there was no resistance. The Duke of Somerset, hearing of Queen Marguerite's imminent arrival on the south coast, had left London to greet her. And London, the city of merchants, gave their merchant-King a roaring welcome. Joyously Edward released Bess from Sanctuary, where she'd given birth to their fourth child. "Behold your son," she cried. "I have named him Edward!"

After recapturing Holy Harry, whom Edward found muttering to himself in a chamber at the Bishop's Palace, he imprisoned him in the Tower.

~*~

As soon as Edward abandoned Coventry, Warwick set out to join Marguerite. On the way he was deluged with bad news. While he had been disheartened at George's desertion, the blow had not been unexpected. But he didn't expect his brother George to seek Edward's pardon with such speed, or his Lancastrian ally, Somerset, to leave London open to the Yorkists or his other Lancastrian ally, Jasper Tudor, to land in Wales and not seek to join forces with him—both so distrustful of him that they'd rather see Edward march through the heart of England to the gates of London, unopposed. Nor did he expect his brother by marriage, Lord Stanley—who rode into London at his side on his triumphant invasion of the kingdom the previous year—to hide out now, at the moment of his greatest need. And he didn't expect the last shattering blow. The devastating, ultimate betrayal from the man he considered his dearest friend in the world.

He didn't expect King Louis, who had sworn friendship to him forever, and to whom he had remained steadfastly loyal these many years, to make peace with Burgundy behind his back. In one blow Louis had destroyed his fragile base of power and everything he had trusted in. Gone was his dream to be Lord of Holland and Zeeland. Gone, the dream that had prompted his struggles and sustained him through the darkest hours of his tossing, plunging fortunes: To be rid of the yoke of service to Edward. To be master of his destiny.

"Leave me!" he barked to his men.

"But, my lord—your decision?"

"Later!"

A clink of spurs, the thud of boots, then silence.

In his tent at St. Albans, Warwick sank down on a campstool and dropped his head into his hands. Was it wrong to want to control one's own life? So great was his desire that he'd failed to see past its glitter to the fatal truth: *That there are only kings and fools, and he, who had thought himself the friend of kings, had been their pawn. The maker of kings had been undone by kings. His life had been a walk down a hall of masks and mirrors where nothing had been what it seemed—he'd seen only what he'd wanted to see, and never heard the mocking laughter.*

Anguished and alone, with only a flagon of wine for company, he pondered his dilemma: *Marguerite or Edward?* There was a sea of blood between him and Marguerite—St. Albans, Northampton, Towton. He had called her "Bitch of Anjou," impugned her honour and cast doubts on the paternity of her son. They had set aside their hatred to achieve a common goal, but the hatred between them ran too deep to be suppressed. If Marguerite trusted him, or forgave him as she'd sworn to do, she would have departed France long before foul weather stranded her. United, they would have been invincible... But she had delayed. Now it was too late.

He poured wine from the flagon and emptied the cup. He poured another, and emptied that. Wine made everything clear, he thought. He understood now with a lucidity that had eluded his other, sober self, all these years. Marguerite had never meant to keep her vow. She had merely used him. As Edward had used him. As Louis had used him. Once back on her throne, she would exact her vengeance.

As for Edward...

Warwick stared into his empty golden cup. He had come to the end of the long twisting road that began when Edward married Bess Woodville. There was only one decision left. Would it be Marguerite's revenge, or Edward's sword?

He poured more wine. Marguerite's arrival was imminent. The Duke of Somerset and Jasper Tudor would join her with their forces. If he delayed battle even a matter of hours, they would combine. Three Lancastrian armies would converge on London. Edward would be caught in the visor grip of his enemies; crushed like an ant beneath the heel of a boot.

And he, himself?

He drained his flagon and rose. He thrust back the flap of his tent. The Lords Wenlock, Scrope of Bolton, Fitzhugh, and faithful Conyers swung around to face him.

"We go south," he said. "To Edward."

~*~

In his tent near the village of Barnet, where Warwick had decided to await Edward, John sat at his makeshift desk, his pup Roland asleep at his feet. He arranged the candle and spread out a piece of paper before him, rubbed his weary eyes and picked up his pen. He dipped it carefully into the ink. In his thoughtful, even script, markedly devoid of flourish, he wrote to Isobel.

My Beloved Lady,

Tomorrow we give battle. Lest I be unable to write you again, I send you this missive so you may know my thoughts when I am no more.

Isobel, you have been the deepest love of my heart. Memories of the joys I have known with you crowd me tonight, and I feel so grateful to you, and to God, that I have been allowed such happiness. But how fleeting, and how few, those precious times now seem—like a handful of gold dust scattered into the darkness, visible one moment, gone the next. If only our hourglass had not emptied so soon, and we could live on together to see our George grown to honourable knighthood!

Alas, Isobel, I have the sense that the last night's candle has been lit. If tomorrow should prove me right, tell the girls how much I loved them. And never forget how much I have loved you, and know that when my last breath escapes me on the battlefields, it will whisper your name.

Forgive my many faults and the many pains I have caused you. How thoughtless and how foolish I have sometimes been! But, O Isobel, if the dead can return and visit those they love, I shall always be with you, on the brightest day and the darkest night; always, always! And when the soft breeze caresses your cheek, it shall be my breath, or the cool air your throbbing temple, it shall be my spirit passing by.

Isobel, my angel, do not mourn my death. Think I am gone and wait for me. For we shall meet again.

John stared straight ahead, seeing a vision of Isobel as she read his missive. He shook himself, drew his attention back to the letter and carefully affixed his signature. He added *Barnet, Easter Saturday, 1471,* and put down the pen. Wearily he reached for the sand cup and scattered a few grains across the paper. He rubbed his eyes, pushed away from the desk and went to the entry of his tent. He lifted the flap.

The day was almost ended, and fog was rolling in.

CHAPTER THIRTY-TWO

"Now must I hence.
Thro' the thick night I hear the trumpet blow."

On Easter Eve, as dusk fell on the little village of Barnet ten miles north of London, Richard sat with Hastings and George in the tavern that Edward had appropriated as his headquarters.

"'Tis a foolish thing that Warwick has done, to come to me, when all he had to do was wait," Edward reflected in a distant voice, toying with his wine cup. Abruptly, he shed his dismal spirits and smiled. "Well, he's played into my hand." He glanced out a window, to the north.

Richard followed his gaze. Through the dim blossoms of a pear tree, a small church was visible on the crest of a distant hill. Somewhere near that church, a mile north of the village on a high plateau, Warwick had encamped his forces across the main road to London.

Edward drew an imaginary horizontal line across the greasy table. "We must place our three battalions opposite his, east-west across St. Alban's road. Will, you'll command my left wing. Dickon, you'll command my right."

Richard cast a shocked, uncomfortable glance at Will Hastings. The veteran soldier had to be offended by Edward's decision to give command of his vanguard to a novice. "I—Edward—I have no experience…"

"You have courage. It'll be enough, Dickon."

"What about me?" demanded George, his face flushed, his eyes glinting. "What do I command?"

Edward gave him a smile that never reached his eyes. "You, George, shall be at my side." It was obvious what he meant. He didn't trust him. Under his watchful eye, there would be no opportunity for George to defect to Warwick in mid-battle if things went badly for York.

George's colour deepened at the implied insult. "I brought you four thousand troops. I should command the vanguard, not Dickon."

"Then you might be killed, George."

George opened his mouth to object, changed his mind and shut it again, rendered mute by what he saw in his brother's eyes.

"We'll wait till dark," Edward resumed, "and crawl into position so close to Warwick that he can't escape battle on the morrow."

"How close?" demanded Hastings.

"Five hundred feet."

"But—isn't that dangerous?" demanded Richard. Such proximity was a daring, unorthodox move and went against everything he'd been taught. If they were discovered, they'd be butchered by Warwick's superior numbers.

"A gamble, admittedly, but take heart, Dickon," replied Edward, reaching for his gauntlets. "For all his talents, Warwick never expects the unexpected... Besides, we have no choice. In surprise lies our only chance of victory."

The bells of the little church on the hill chimed for Vespers.

~*~

Under cover of darkness, following Edward's urgent instructions to avoid making noise or showing light, the royal army climbed up the St. Alban's Road. At the top of the hill, they crept silently into position on the treeless, heathery plateau of Gladmore Heath. Not until they were close enough to hear the voices of Warwick's men did they halt. No campfires were lit. The night was cold, the moon shrouded by dense clouds. The sudden boom of cannons shattered the darkness.

"Should we respond, Edward?" demanded Hastings.

Edward stared in the direction of Warwick's troops and his eyes blazed open with joy. "My plan worked. Warwick thinks we're further back than we are—his cannons are going over our heads! Hold your fire! Christ, what a surprise he'll have in the morning!" He gave Richard a hearty slap on the back. "Now get some sleep, little brother." He turned to Hastings. "Fog rolling in, Will, and it's cold." He rubbed his hands. "But we've fought in worse and won, haven't we?"

Hastings drew an audible breath. "We have indeed."

Richard had heard the stories. Howling ice-winds; driving, blinding snow; dead men so frozen to their horses they had to be buried on them; blood that had melted with the ice. Towton had been fought on Palm Sunday in '61, in a fierce snowstorm. Ten years later, almost exactly to the day, this battle at Barnet would be fought in fog. He could hope it was an omen. Edward had always been lucky in battle—at Towton he'd been outnumbered, all odds against him, yet he'd won the day.

Not only did they face a superior force this time, but Edward had entrusted the command of the precious right wing of his army to Richard. He was only eighteen years old, without experience of warfare, not even powerfully built. He had little to offer his brother besides his life, and his will to succeed or to die in the attempt. That, and what he had forged at Middleham under the loving guidance of the two brothers he must fight come dawn. His misery closed in on him like a steel weight. He crunched his way across the hard earth to the right wing under his command.

~*~

Richard stretched out on his pallet in the mist. They were so close to the enemy he could hear all the sounds of their camp: the neighing of their horses, the tramping of their feet, the banging of their pewter mugs, even their oaths. As Edward had said, in this proximity lay safety and their only hope of victory. Warwick's cannon fire was passing over their heads because he thought them further back than they were, and by attacking before first light, they would catch him unprepared.

But victory and safety came at the cost of comfort and warmth. As they were so close, they couldn't pitch tent. There would be no time to dress in the morning, so they had to sleep in their battle gear. Richard's suit of white armour, a gift from Edward in happier days, was wrought in Milan and represented the finest that could be bought. But steel was steel, and nothing could make it less than cold and clammy. He lay awake all night, listening to the booming cannons, thinking of those on the other side who had once shared his dreams. He wondered what John's thoughts were, whether he slept or wept. He wondered whether they would meet in battle, and prayed they would not.

He thought of Warwick, who had been a father to him, whom he had hoped to have as a father-in-law. He thought of Anne, and drove her away by force of will, for she brought more pain than he could bear. Instead, he conjured up an image of Edouard of Lancaster and clenched his hand around his sword. If only Edouard were here and he could engage him in battle! But Edouard was safe at sea with his mother.

At four o'clock in the morning the camp stirred. It was April 14th, 1471. Easter Sunday.

Richard sat up with stiff joints and looked around him. An eerie fog blanketed the night. He peered into the floating whiteness. Men were rubbing their bleary eyes, or taking out from their bags the dried meat they had brought with them and munching grimly.

Richard prayed for strength and lined up his men for battle. He took a westerly position on Edward's right wing. Edward's order came through the mist: *No quarter for the commons!* Richard was stunned; he hadn't realised the depth of Edward's bitterness. The cry before had always been to slay the lords and spare the commons. But then, the common man had always loved Warwick.

The King's trumpets sounded the battle cry. Richard advanced his banner.

CHAPTER THIRTY-THREE

"Confusion, since he saw not whom he fought,
For friend and foe were shadows in the mist,
And friend slew friend not knowing whom he slew."

John and Warwick stood together in thick fog. Behind them ranks of fighting men stretched away into the mist, their plumes limp, their banners sodden in the heavy dampness. Warwick's Dun Cow of the Nevilles was barely visible, the normally bright tones of his scarlet and silver Bear and Ragged Staff drained of colour. An unnatural stillness hung over the field. Cannons boomed, horses neighed, and there was the clink of metal, but no murmur of voices. No human sounds.

Warwick looked steadily into his brother's face. Beneath his raised visor, John's face was set and haggard, and his dark blue eyes held a curious expression, almost as though John didn't see him. The unease that had kept him company all night mounted into a stark cold fear unlike anything he'd ever experienced. He forced a long steady breath. "Are you all right, John?"

"Never better," said John in an odd tone.

"I don't understand," said Warwick anxiously. "You wish to lead your men on foot when normally you direct the battle mounted, from the rear."

"Normally there is no fog."

Warwick gave a terse nod. "Of course."

"Men's minds are uneasy, they fear treason," John said in a voice that seemed to come from a long way off. "I recommend you follow my example and tether your horses at the rear."

Warwick hesitated. A man in armour had little likelihood of escaping alive without a horse. Fighting on foot would put the lie to rumours of treason, show the Lancastrians the Neville commitment to their cause, and give their own men heart. They had little love for the cause for which they were risking their lives, and the Lancastrians returned their hatred. But the truth was, he didn't want to die. What if traitors had sold him out? How would he flee without a horse? There had always been bad blood between the Beauforts and the Nevilles, yet here they were, aligned with one another. Even Exeter, who commanded the left wing of their army, had feuded with them for years, and Oxford, who commanded the right, distrusted them though he was married to their sister. Both had fought against them in earlier battles.

Aye, a twisting road had brought them to Barnet. Treason was what they all feared, what they whispered about John, his conduct at Pontefract, letting Edward slip past unmolested like that. John had always been a bit too fond of Dickon, a bit too loyal to Edward. Yet John had chosen to fight on foot, condemning himself to death if victory were not his.

Could he follow his brother's example?

His own chances of survival were better. He'd be behind his brother's line, in charge of the reserves, close to the trees in Wrotham Wood where the horses were tethered. Despite George's desertion, he still outnumbered Edward by a generous margin: twelve thousand to nine. And he had artillery, while Edward had few guns. Comforting odds. So why was he not comforted? Maybe because Edward had something better. Unholy luck.

Already luck had played in Edward's favour. Fog had helped the Yorkists. He couldn't even be sure that the cannons, which had fired blindly through the night, had done their work and inflicted damage before they closed in for hand-to-hand combat. Moreover, he hadn't been able to discover Edward's battle position. That alone was cause for unease.

I recommend you follow my example and tether your horses at the rear, John had said. He glanced uncertainly at the powerful bay destrier that his squire held for him. *Fortune.* He hadn't realised until this moment how aptly he had named him. He searched John's face but it was as though his brother were carved of stone. He seemed to have lost awareness of him, of all around him. He had been acting strangely all month, ever since Pontefract, Warwick thought, noting the pallor of his skin. John had the look of a man who stood beneath the shadow of the great black wings that open above the dying.

And that was the question, wasn't it? Could he commit himself to fighting on foot if it meant he was signing his own death warrant? Warwick swallowed, found his voice. "I'll tether Fortune in Wrotham Wood."

He gazed at John, mindful of the others who had failed him:

231

his son-in-law George, who had deserted at the first opportunity; his brother George, who had wasted no time grovelling before Edward to save his own skin. Only John was at his side now— John, who had opposed him... Only he had answered the call of kinship, would fight for him, though his heart lay in the enemy camp. Without warning he was stricken to the core, swept with a curious mingling of gratitude, brotherly love, regret, despair, fear, and a strange longing for he knew not what.

"Maybe I should have accepted Edward's terms..." he said, breaking the silence he had never broken before; admitting to doubts his pride would have crushed before. His brother made no acknowledgement, and for a moment he thought John hadn't heard.

Then John said, "In battle there are easy answers to everything."

Warwick knew there was no more to be said, that he should bid his brother farewell, but he found himself unable to leave. He stood motionless in the milky grey dawn, thinking how strange it was that this battle should fall on Easter Sunday, the day his great treaty with King Louis creating him Prince of Holland and Zeeland was to have been ratified. King Louis, who had professed admiration and affection, called him "cousin" and "brother," then mocked him by making peace with Burgundy.

Strange, too, that even now, even after all the disappointments of his life, the disillusionments, the perfidy of kings and betrayal of kin, hope still stirred in his heart. Hope of survival; hope that somehow all would be well in the end, would be put back as before. In a dry, cracked voice, he said, "Then this day will decide all." It was a question.

John made no reply.

A wild panic seized him. He heard his brother's voice like an echo from an empty tomb, "God be with thee, and keep thee," and watched his tall, shining figure move ghostlike into the murky gloom. "And God keep thee, my fair brother of Montagu!"

cried Warwick suddenly after him.

But his brother was already gone, swallowed up by the swirling fog.

~*~

From his command position in the centre, John stared into the fog ahead, unable to see anything through his narrow visor slit but solid white mist. How he hated fog! The small noises of the Yorkist army came to him vaguely, muffled by his armour, nearly drowned by the sound of his own laboured breathing in his ears. He was hot, his face flushed, already covered with tiny beads of perspiration, yet he was so cold he shivered inside his clammy armour.

Warwick's trumpets blared. Gunfire crackled. A hail of arrows whistled overhead and quickly vanished. From beyond the wall of mist, Edward's trumpets responded. John gave a start. They sounded surprisingly close. Out of the blankness, a great shout went up. The Yorkists were coming on the run.

They were indeed close! Less than five hundred feet away instead of the customary five hundred yards. He wondered dimly what other surprises the battle held. He made the sign of the Cross, and plunged forward at the head of his troops.

The two armies collided with a mighty crash of steel.

~*~

Richard heard the sounds of combat to his left, on John's line, and knew that something was wrong. Why hadn't he closed with the enemy? Why hadn't his arrows been answered?

The ground had grown wet and muddy and was sloping steeply down beneath his feet. Realisation dawned. He froze. This was not the plateau. This was the marsh! In the dark, Edward had misjudged their position. The three Yorkist battalions were not directly opposite the three Lancastrian battalions, but misaligned—much too far to the right—and he was descending down into the marshy ravine that protected Exeter's flank. If they were discovered, they'd be trapped, slaughtered like pigs in a pen.

His men had fallen silent, were looking at him. He saw that they understood all too well. He pointed left, to the west, towards the woods. Grimly they turned, groped their way up blindly, silently, into the fog. If they could make it up the slope without being discovered, they'd surprise Exeter on his rear.

~*~

As Richard was making his discomfiting discovery, the Earl of Oxford, who commanded the right wing of Warwick's army, was learning the same and revelling in the knowledge. His right wing far outflanked Hastings, and he had no harsh terrain to contend with. He immediately swung eastward, behind Hastings, and smashed into his flank.

Men were taken by surprise. They cried out in horror, dropped their weapons, and ran. Hastings's left wing collapsed. With Oxford himself in hot pursuit, the Lancastrians chased the fleeing Yorkists ten miles to Barnet, where the Lancastrians stopped to pillage and celebrate their victory with drink. Some of the fleeing Yorkists managed to reach London and awaken the citizens with shouts of a Yorkist defeat.

~*~

Surrounded by his squires and household knights, Richard emerged from the ravine. He'd taken Exeter by surprise, won a brief advantage, but now he and his men were fighting desperately to keep from being forced back into the marshy hollow below. Reinforcements from Warwick's reserves had poured into Exeter's wing, swelling his ranks. Richard's men, outnumbered, were pressed up against a thicket of steel. His squire, John Milewater, was dead at his feet, struck down by an arrow. Beside him one of the two Toms—Tom Parr, whom he had made his new squire—was battling three yeomen at once and losing. Richard wanted to go to his aid but he himself was fighting two steel-capped yeomen. Tom fell to his knees. Richard heard his plea for quarter. He tried to cut his way to him but the yeomen were putting up too fierce a fight. He saw the poleaxe plunge downward, saw Tom's body twitch convulsively. With a howl, Richard bitterly drove his battleaxe into the nearest stomach. One of the yeomen staggered, clutching his belly. There was a look of surprise in the man's eyes as he crumpled, spurting blood over Richard's armour.

Richard froze for an instant, watching in horror, then the second yeoman charged him like a madman with his spear. Richard recovered, quickly sidestepped the blow by putting out a foot to trip him, a manoeuvre he'd learned years ago under John's tutelage. He cleaved his battleaxe into his back. Killing a man in battle was not what he had expected, not glorious and heady. He swallowed the bile that rose to his mouth and turned to engage the next adversary who was already upon him. They fought hard. The knight went down, but Richard was wounded. The knight's broadsword had pierced his pauldron, slashing his right shoulder. Thankfully, it was not his good arm. Thomas Howard, the Friendly Lion's son, appeared at his side to ward off other challengers, and his household knights closed around him in a wall of steel so he could consult with his battle captains.

"We're hopelessly outnumbered! We must have reinforcements!" they gasped.

"No!" shouted Richard over the crash of steel, the screams of terrified horses, the cries of dying men. He couldn't move his right arm; his shoulder had begun to throb and his gauntlet was filling with blood. For a moment his head swam. He shook himself to clear it. "Hastings's wing has collapsed! My brother needs his reserves! Send word to the King not to commit his reserves, that we will hold!"

"We cannot hold! 'Tis folly! We're fighting both Exeter and

235

Warwick! We cannot hold!" they shouted back.

"We'll not deplete the King's reserves!" he roared. "'Tis an order!"

~*~

In the centre, the fighting was savage. John's green and gold Crowned Griffin, emblem of the ancient Montagues, bobbed in the fog amid a sea of spears, swords, battleaxes, and struggling men who now writhed forward, now fell back like a gargantuan tide. They were holding, but no more than that. Each time he tried to break through the Yorkist centre, Edward would appear leading reserves, an awesome mighty figure on his black warhorse, hewing a path before him with his strokes of death.

Panting for breath, John stepped back after a kill and called for a messenger. At the signal, his knights closed around him like a steel hedge.

"I need more men!" John shouted above the din of clashing metal, thundering hoofs, and cries of battle. "Send to my brother Warwick! I need more men from his reserves!"

The messenger, scarcely more than a boy, dug in his spurs and galloped off into the fog. John went back into the fray, engaged the next adversary. While he was still locked in combat, Warwick materialised out of the fog, fighting his way forward, leading men to the front. John retreated, let his knights converge around them so they could confer.

"Edward's left wing under Hastings is destroyed!" cried Warwick. "But fighting is fierce on Exeter's wing—Dickon continues to inch forward, though he's heavily outnumbered!"

Beneath his visor, John couldn't suppress a smile.

"Oxford's sent word! When he rallies his men in Barnet, he'll return to the fray and strike at the rear of Edward's centre!" Warwick's voice held a rasp of excitement. "Victory's in sight, brother!"

John nodded his plumed helmet. Warwick withdrew to bring

up more men and John went forward to exchange blows with a Yorkist knight. The knight gave ground, stumbled backwards, fell. John raised his sword. The man died. John pushed ahead, stepping on bloody dead men, severed limbs, and a sprawling body in a padded leather jerkin, ripped hideously open from throat to stomach, exposing violently red gutted entrails.

John caught his breath, momentarily unable to move. His stomach was heaving in the old familiar way and the sour taste of bile, bitter as gall, stung his throat. This was his nightmare. This was the world gone mad. This was Hell. This screaming of dying men, suffering horses; this stench of blood and gutted entrails. This vile fog that stank of offal and hid unspeakable horrors. Once he hadn't minded killing—once, when he was young, fearless, and had fair cause. A friend's death at the battle of St. Albans, on this very road, had changed that. Seventeen years old, sliced through the belly, disembowelled like that man, his friend had died cruelly in his arms. Since then, he'd been unable to abide the stench of blood. Just so, they told him, had his brother Thomas died at Wakefield. Sliced open. His head cut off.

Sweat was blinding him. He could taste its pungent salt on his lips. In his gauntlets, his hands were sticky, his fingers stiff and cramped from wielding his sword. The fog swirled around him. Swords flashed; men fell. Cries of York and Neville mingled in the murk. He stumbled forward, nearly tripped over the body of a man without arms. The man moaned.

O God, my Creator, how much longer? cried John silently.

~*~

Richard's throat was raw from shouting commands, his ears deaf from the din of clashing metal and the shrieks of men and animals. His right arm hung limp, useless at his side, the pain was shattering now. Cannon shot and arrows rained down through the dense clouds that shrouded the field. Many of his household men were dead. Thomas Howard had taken an arrow in his gut, had fallen at his feet, and strangely, he'd had time to think of the Friendly Lion, that Thomas was his only son.

He didn't know how much longer they could hold. With the help of Warwick's reserves, Exeter was pressing them back, foot-by-foot back down the steep hill that they had climbed. But he had to hold! Edward needed his own reserves. By sheer force of will he gathered his failing strength and directed it into each blow of his battleaxe.

Then he heard it, the roar that came from somewhere far away in the mists, somewhere along John's line. A thunder that first started as a growl and built into a fury that shook the earth. Richard and his adversary both lowered their weapons, turned towards the sound.

~*~

John halted when he heard it, swung around, stared into the misty reaches to the right of his line. He could see nothing of what was happening on his wing. The ground shook beneath his feet, the roar grew into a ferocious clamour. Men were cursing, shouting angrily. "Treason!" they cried. His flank guard sent a flock of arrows suddenly hissing into the milky greyness. "Treason!" came the shouts, louder now. Out of the mist rode a cavalry force bearing the Yorkist emblem of the blazing sun, cutting down his men. John pushed up his visor, turned back. Something was wrong! Terribly wrong! The Yorkist emblem loomed ahead of him. There could not be two!

In a flash, he realised the appalling, tragic error.

This was not Edward's crimson and gold banner of the Sun in Splendour! This was Oxford's crimson and silver banner of the Star and Streams! The two emblems were much alike. These were Oxford's men returning from the pursuit to what they thought was the rear of the Yorkist flank! In the fog, they couldn't see—didn't know—that the collapse of Hastings's wing on the

238

east and Dickon's flank attack on Exeter in the west, had wrenched the battle lines from east-west to north-south.

They were killing their own side!

Even as Oxford discovered his error and reared up his horse with an oath, John's archers sent another volley of arrows into his midst. Curses and shouts of betrayal shrilled in the air. Oxford and his men recoiled, turned their horses, galloped off into the fog. John's men picked up the cries of *"Treason!"* and ran after them.

Confusion broke the Lancastrian ranks. Throwing down their weapons, men turned and fled. Voices yelled in triumph as the Sun banner erupted from the fog and smashed through John's centre. Weapons beat down his pennon; beat down his men. All about him they were falling. He parried the blows as best he could, but they were raining down with stunning force. Through his visor slit, he could see his enemies' murderous eyes, hear his own panting breath. Blood was bursting in his ears and nose. The blows smashed through his armour. He slumped to his knees.

The fog thickened around him like a shroud; he couldn't see, couldn't breathe. A fierce pain exploded in his head. His mind filled with broken images of his life: his father leading Isobel to him, eyes alight with pride; Thomas, grinning; Dickon at Barnard's Castle, handing him the ring. Edward jesting that Italians had the right idea of war, they never fought in winter. He saw Warwick frown; heard Percy laugh. Alnwick Castle rose above the River Aln, and he had a vision of swans and Isobel's smile.

For one soft moment he felt her arms around him.

Suddenly it was very quiet. There was blood in his eyes and he thought he'd lost his sight. Then he realised he wasn't blind. He could make out the shadow of a crucifix in the fog. The crucifix grew, loomed large, blotted out the fog behind it and ushered in a shining bright place. He had a faint sense of surprise that he could have been so wrong, that he had so misunderstood. He had dreamed it many times, had feared it always. But there was nothing fearful in that shining place. He turned his head and smiled.

The Yorkist who stood astride John's body plunged his sword down into John's heart.

CHAPTER THIRTY-FOUR

"Such a sleep they sleep—the men I loved."

It was sunrise; it was over.

The battle had lasted three hours and three thousand men were dead. Most of the slain came from the rank and file on Warwick's side. In their padded tunics, sometimes without even a steel cap to protect their heads, they were easily killed by a sword thrust and, in sharp contrast to other battles, Edward did not spare them but cut them down as they fled. The common people had loved Warwick too dearly.

Edward stood amid the carnage and pushed up his visor. "Where's John?" he yelled. "Where's Warwick?" He looked around, shouted to a yeoman of his household, "Save Montagu and Warwick—find them and save them!" The man galloped off into the floating whiteness. Richard stumbled up to Edward's side, panting, depleted.

Edward said, "I came face to face with John. He turned away. He wouldn't fight me, wouldn't fight his King."

"Does he live?" cried Richard.

"I don't know, but I saw his pennon go down myself..."

Richard shut his eyes.

"Sire!" a horseman cried, galloping towards Edward. He flung himself from the saddle, knelt at Edward's feet. "John Neville, the Marquess of Montagu, is slain! He was separated from his men and fell fighting bravely in the thickest press of his enemies."

Richard felt as if a hand closed around his throat.

A second horseman appeared, leapt from his horse, ran to the King. "Sire! The Marquess is slain! The Lancastrians struck him down, calling him a traitor."

"First reports are always wrong. We'll probably not know the truth for days, until we talk to survivors," said Edward, meeting Richard's eyes.

The King's yeoman returned. "Your Grace, the Earl of Warwick is dead," he panted. "I was too late. They caught him trying to reach his horse in Wrotham Wood and killed him on the spot."

"Blessed Heaven," Edward murmured. After a moment, he said quietly, "I want the body of the Earl of Warwick treated with respect."

"Your Grace, we have found the body of the Marquess," the yeoman said. "You should know…" He hesitated.

"Aye?" Edward prompted.

"The Marquess, Sire. He wore your colours beneath his armour."

"*Jesu…*" whispered Richard, reeling

Fighting bravely beneath his brother's banner, John had died in the colours of his King. Torn by conflicting loyalties, he'd not wanted to live. Instead, he had chosen a death that bespoke his love for both his brother and his King. To some, John would always be a traitor; but they didn't understand as he did. In doing their duty, in fighting for their blood kin, they'd each betrayed their own hearts. John had tried to remain true to both, to the end, as best he could.

He swung on Edward. John had ever been a Yorkist—would never have turned from York had Edward not sacrificed him for Percy! And where was Percy now? Safe in some castle somewhere! Percy had sent word that the best he could do for Edward was to keep his men from siding with the Lancastrians.

Edward's face was hidden. Before Richard could accuse him, his brother turned. What he saw drained his anger. The sun was breaking through the fog and soft morning light fell on Edward's fair hair, illuminating his towering figure, glittering on the blood-drenched sword lowered in his hand. He looked like a god of war, but his grief-stricken face and bowed head spoke only of hatred of war. *It wasn't Edward's fault!* he thought. A miscalculation, aye, but not malice. Edward had not wanted John or Warwick to die. He'd tried to save them both.

Others were riding up. Hastings and John Howard dismounted. Howard came to stand by Richard. He was grim-faced, his horse and armour red with blood. Richard wondered miserably if he knew about his son. He didn't have the heart to tell him.

Hastings said, "A great victory, Edward." He sounded tired. To Richard, he added, "Well done, Richard. Had it not been for you, we'd have lost the day, I've no doubt."

Richard nodded his thanks. The compliment was generously given since Hastings should have been the one to command Edward's vanguard. But then, Hastings was a generous man, well liked by all except the Woodvilles, and for good reason. He was not given to pettiness, grudges, and rancour, was admirable in all aspects of his character except one, and that had coloured Richard's view of him to the exclusion of all else. Hastings's uncurbed lust for women was an evil that had encouraged Edward's wanton ways and led to the death of the innocent maid in Leicester. Richard could neither forget, nor forgive.

"You did well, no question, little brother," Edward smiled gently. "But you should have sent for my reserves. Courage is one thing, recklessness another, Dickon."

Richard couldn't return his smile. Grief pressed too heavily on his heart. Hastings spoke again. "You know about Warwick?"

Edward nodded.

A knot rose in Richard's throat. Feeling Howard's scrutiny,

he lowered his head and bit his quivering lip. Then the gruff, old soldier laid a gentle hand on Richard's shoulder. Richard raised his head and their eyes met in quiet understanding.

Howard's sudden kindness, conveying the kind of fatherly concern of which Richard's life had been so bereft, had an unexpected effect. Richard's iron resolve, which was all that had kept him upright and composed, crumbled. All at once he was acutely aware of the burning, throbbing pain in his right shoulder, the whining of flies and the stench of blood, the moans of the dying and the frenzied cries of vultures. His stomach churned. Blood rushed to his feet.

Howard said quickly, "May I escort you to the surgeon's tent, my lord?"

Richard shook his head. "My squires..." Then he remembered that the two Toms and John Milewater were dead. The sudden wrenching pain in his arm knocked the breath from his body and sent a sickening wave of nausea to his throat. He swallowed hard, nodded his head, and leaned on Howard's arm.

Behind them the silvery bells of the little church on the hill tolled for Lauds and Edward's voice rose above the chimes. "Fortune is fickle... No man can escape his fate. May God have mercy upon their souls."

In the distance, a dog howled plaintively.

~*~

After a brief visit to the surgeon's tent, where he had his arm cleansed with wine and treated with a salve of centaury and the wild yellow nettle, Richard took to horse. Despite the surgeon's entreaties, he refused all other treatments, and though still weak from loss of blood, refused even rest. While Hastings and Howard accounted for the dead and organised the army's return to London, Richard rode to Hadley Church. There he dismounted, looped the reins of his warhorse around a tree at the edge of the graveyard, and followed its curving path to the entry. With great effort, he pulled open the iron-hinged parish door. The church was empty. A fitful grey light came through the coarse glass windows, and the dank, musty air stank of burning mutton fat from the votive candles at the altar. He took a step down into the nave and felt suddenly faint. He put out an arm and leaned heavily against a pillar. Drawn by the clanging of the door, a pimply acolyte came out from the vestry. He gave a start at the sight of Richard.

Richard suddenly realised how frightening he must appear with his bloodied hair and clothes, his bloodstained, bandaged arm, and his face that had to be as pale as a phantom. His taut mouth softened. The boy recovered, came towards him. "Do you seek Sanctuary, my lord?" he asked, recognising Richard's high estate despite the condition of his clothes. Richard was unable to respond. He was fighting a terrible fatigue, a pounding head and blurred vision, and stood erect only with great effort. He rubbed his eyes in a desperate attempt to clear his mind. One day, he thought with a stab of fear, the moment would come when he would no longer be able to exert will over body and he would break. He shook his head with determined effort. "Priest!" he demanded more harshly than he intended. The flustered boy ran off into the nave and out the west door into the churchyard. A moment later an older man lumbered in the same entrance. He was gaunt, his grey hair thinning around his tonsure.

"My lord, you asked for me?" he inquired anxiously, his face flushed.

With a slow, clumsy motion, Richard withdrew a small bag of coins from within his doublet. The movement sent pain shooting along his right side. He grimaced.

"Pray, sit down, my lord!" the priest said. With concern for his benefactor, he dusted the steps with a corner of his gown.

Richard shook his head. "I wish... prayers... Masses... for one dead in battle." There were many dead in battle whom he would remember: his boyhood friends, the two Toms; his squire, John Milewater. And Warwick. Later, he would buy Masses for them, too, but this—this could not wait.

The priest took the purse, made the sign of the Cross. "It shall be done, my lord," he said. "And the name of the deceased, God assoil his soul?"

"John Neville, Marquess of Montagu," Richard replied in a choked voice. "He died honourably." Somehow, he felt it necessary the priest know that. Heaving himself around, he dragged himself from the little church.

~*~

Around the hour of Nones, Edward led his army slowly back to London. Insisting he was not badly injured, Richard spurned a cart and rode at Edward's side.

At St. Paul's Cathedral the next morning, Edward laid the torn and muddy banners of Warwick's Ragged Staff and John's Golden Griffin on the high altar and gave thanks to God for his victory. Later that day a humble cart rumbled to St. Paul's bearing the bodies of the brothers. For three days they lay on the pavement, naked except for a loincloth, so all would know the fall of the House of Neville.

CHAPTER THIRTY-FIVE

"Shall I kill myself? What help in that?
—What else? What hope?"

On Easter Sunday, within hours of the Earl of Warwick's death, his Countess sailed into Portsmouth and received the tidings. Shattered by grief, she sagged against the rail and stuffed a fist into her mouth to stifle her cry. At forty-four, she was suddenly aged, a broken woman. Dragging herself into Beaulieu Abbey, she begged for Sanctuary. She had loved her husband, admired him as one admires the North Star that glitters in the night firmament and guides the weary traveller safely home with its light. Now there was only darkness.

At almost the same moment, the news reached Prince Edouard and Queen Marguerite as they were about to disembark at Weymouth. The queen, badly shaken and fearing for her son, would have turned the ship around, but the Duke of Somerset insisted that victory was hers for the taking. As they argued, Anne mounted the steps from the cabin below and reached the opening to the deck at the stern of the vessel. Aware that the others hadn't seen her, knowing how they despised her, and dreading to offend with her presence, she stood humbly in the doorway, listening. At first she didn't comprehend. Then the appalling truth exploded in her heart with the thunderous violence of a cannon shot.

Dead, dead, all dead...

She swooned, sank to the plank floor in a heap. As her frail body was carried below deck, the queen, restored to her composure, exclaimed, "Would that she had died with Warwick!" Prince Edouard, who was staring after Anne, made no response at first. Then he recovered, twisted his mouth scornfully, and forced a laugh. "They say she loves Richard of Gloucester. I shall enjoy having her watch as I cut off his head."

~*~

Stricken with grief, alone in the midst of the Lancastrians she had been taught to hate, Anne had never despaired as she did during the two weeks Marguerite d'Anjou grimly raced westward towards Wales to join forces with Jasper Tudor. Even at night the queen did not halt, for Edward was clattering at her heels. Too ill to ride a horse, bewildered, shorn of hope, Anne rattled along in her wooden cart, barely noticing the harsh journey.

In thirty-six hours, Marguerite travelled thirty miles, but her desperate effort to unite with Jasper Tudor failed because Edward covered the same ground in less than twenty-four. In the process, however, Marguerite showed Edward that the bitch could be a fox as she led him first in one direction, then another, always turning the opposite way before he realised he'd been tricked. But the forced march in unusual heat exhausted her men. Hungry and thirsty, when neither they nor their beasts could take another step, they collapsed before they could cross the Severn. Cut off from escape, Marguerite swung around to confront the Yorkists, a cornered animal at bay, in an agony of fear for her son. "Come with me to Cerne Abbey, Edouard!" she commanded.

"No, my mother. My place is here with my men," he replied.

"But you—you are only seventeen, Edouard…"

"I am a man," he snapped, his pride bruised. "Now you must go, Mother."

She seemed to wilt, and stood silently, clearly unwilling to leave. Yet she made no further plea, as if she hadn't truly expected to prevail. Edouard relented, took her hands into his, bent and kissed her lightly on the cheek. "Farewell, Mother."

She nodded mutely and stepped into the small wooden boat. Lifting and dipping their oars, the boatmen splashed quietly away into the summer twilight.

The two armies collided near the Welsh border, at Tewkesbury.

It was at Cerne Abbey three days later that she was found by the Yorkists and given the news by a smirking Sir William Stanley. The Lancastrians had been routed. The Duke of Somerset, in a rage over some suspected treason, had galloped up to Lord Wenlock and struck him dead through the helmet with a battleaxe. The men, seeing their leaders butchering each other, had flung their weapons aside and run for their lives across the battlefield to the River Avon. There was a pursuit. Such carnage followed that the meadow turned red with blood. Her son Edouard, fleeing the field of battle, had called out for succour to his brother-by-marriage George of Clarence, and George had struck him dead. Somerset had escaped and found refuge in Tewkesbury abbey. From there he was taken, tried before Richard of Gloucester, and executed the next day.

All Lancastrian claimants to the throne, with the exception of her husband, Henry, lay dead.

~*~

Edward was elated when the news was brought to him that Marguerite had been found.

"What did the Iron Queen say when you told her that Prince Edouard was dead?" he demanded.

Sir William Stanley's thin lips, bracketed by a thin ginger moustache and closely clipped beard, curled into a crooked smile. "The iron seeped out of her, my lord. She sat drooping in her chair for a good space, silent as a sepulchre. Then she said to tell you that she is at your command."

Edward gripped Richard's shoulder. "Finally we have chastened the Bitch of Anjou... Finally we have avenged our father and Edmund, Dickon."

Richard tried not to grimace. The shoulder, which had been healing before Tewkesbury, had been made raw by the exertion of fighting too soon in another battle. "Not soon enough," he managed, pulling away. "Not before she made battalions of widows and left them to mourn their dead." Tewkesbury field, where so many of John and Warwick's men died, had run so red with blood that men had renamed it Bloody Meadow.

Edward leaned close. "There's one more widow waiting to be made, brother—or else more widows may yet be made."

Richard understood too clearly what Edward meant. Marguerite's husband must die, for there could be no true peace in the realm as long as Holy Harry lived. He had deep misgivings

248

about such a step and hoped to dissuade Edward, but there was another matter of greater urgency to be dealt with first. Another widow who mattered more to him than a string of Marguerites or Henrys.

"Stanley," Richard demanded. "What about the Lady Anne? What did she say when she was given the news of her husband's death?"

"She said nothing, my lord. She stood quite still, with downcast eyes, as if she had not heard a word of it. Until…" a small smile came to his lips, "your name was mentioned."

Richard turned to the King. "Edward?"

Edward looked softly into Richard's eyes, his own eyes moist. "Ask anything, Dickon. It is granted."

Richard broke into a broad, open smile.

~*~

Anne did not ride at the back of the triumphant royal army in the open cart with Marguerite d'Anjou to be pelted with dung and rotted fruit. She was sent a bolt of gleaming violet satin, a fine grey palfrey, and a flask of Damask rosewater for her toiletries, which Richard had great difficulty obtaining. He also sent a letter.

Richard had debated with himself whether or not to go to Anne directly, and unable to decide, had consulted Edward. He worried that Anne did not wish to see him. He was now her conqueror, and the mightiest man in the kingdom next to the King. She was the daughter of a traitor. In agreement, Edward had pointed out how her apparel, torn and filthy from the march, might add to her humiliation by serving in her eyes as a reminder of the gulf that had opened between them.

At his suggestion Richard sent the fabric and rosewater. What really held Richard back, however, was Edward's warning that Anne, no doubt still in shock, might hold Richard responsible for the fate of her father and uncle. If she blamed him for their deaths, if love had turned to hate, he could not bear it. To see that in her eyes would be worse than any death. And so, while they paused at Coventry, he picked up his pen and scratched out a letter.

My Dear Heart,

I regret all that has happened in these two years since we have been apart, and I would undo all, if I could. You once loved me, but I fear that, too, has changed. My feelings for you are as they ever were. Middleham was always my greatest joy. In memory, and in my dreams, I have returned there often during these bitter years and I am aggrieved with sorrow for the loss of those we loved, may God assoil their noble souls.

The King has made me Constable and Admiral of England, and Great Chamberlain. I go to London with him for one night, then north against the Scots. As soon as I return, I shall seek you out in London. You shall reside there with your sister Bella, and there I shall come and beg your forgiveness, and receive your comfort, I pray God.

Know that I love thee, and will always love thee. If you can no longer care for me, you still have a champion who will give his life for your happiness.

God and His Blessed Mother have you in their keeping.

Richard of Gloucester
Coventry, 19 May, 1471

Then, with an anxious heart, he awaited Anne's reply.

CHAPTER THIRTY-SIX

"These be no rubies, this is frozen blood."

Leading the King's army, clarions blowing, battle flags streaming, Richard entered London on the twenty-first day of May. His heart was swept with gladness, for he had received Anne's reply. There had been no greeting, only a single line, but it had been enough. His hand strayed to the letter inside his doublet. *If it takes forever*, she had written, *I will wait for thee*. A smile lifted his lips. He wished he could go to her tonight...

Not tonight. In an attempt to restore Henry of Lancaster to the throne, the Bastard of Fauconberg had attacked London from the river, firing his guns at the Tower, which sheltered Bess Woodville and her children, and burning London Bridge and the city walls at Bishopsgate and Aldgate. He had been driven off by Anthony Woodville but remained at large off the coast. Edward wanted Richard to deal with him as soon as he disposed of one other matter.

Richard winced.

All along the way to London, as Edward rode through towns and villages, smiling and nodding to the cheering crowds who waved kerchiefs and threw flowers, Richard had argued with him over Henry's fate.

"Edward, he is a holy man—almost a saint!"

"There's no choice. You know what's at stake."

"Aye. Your immortal soul."

"A king can't always be merciful and do the noble thing, Dickon. Sometimes he must simply do what needs to be done to secure a good end."

"What about principles, conscience... mercy?" Richard ground the words out between his teeth.

"Easy for you to judge me! Do you really think I want to kill the doddery old fool? I don't relish it, but it must be done. A land with two kings is a land with naught but strife. If Henry were dead, would the Bastard of Fauconberg have attacked London? While his son lived, nothing was to be gained by his death. Now…" He looked at Richard. "I've learned something being king, Dickon. Conscience is a disability, so are principles… and mercy. I was always ready to forgive, to trust. It almost destroyed me. A ruler must be ruthless. Otherwise he can't survive." Under his breath, he added, "To be a king, you have to kill a king. 'Tis the way it has always been."

Richard averted his face. Aye, the deposed kings Edward II and Richard II had been put to death to make room for Edward III and Henry of Bolingbroke. Henry of Lancaster had been allowed to live years longer than either of them. Maybe he was foolish, but he hadn't truly expected Holy Harry to share their fate. Never in history had there been two anointed kings in one realm. Since the old rules no longer applied, he had been lulled into believing Henry could continue to live in captivity.

They rode along in silence. "What will you tell the people?" he demanded at length.

"I'll tell them he died of grief," Edward replied. "As he damned well should have, for all the grief he's caused."

Richard's ruby ring caught the sun's rays and glinted on his little finger. He thought of blood. Blood kept seeping around them; Barnet and Tewkesbury had not yet staunched the flow. When would it end? What was enough? Edward would do what had to be done, but he himself could never accept the deed, though he understood the necessity for Henry's murder, and understood that Edward liked it no better than he did. Regicide was a mortal sin in God's eyes and repugnant to a man of honour. He tightened his fists around his reins and clenched his jaw until his muscles quivered.

Edward said quietly, "Very well, Dickon. I'll hold a meeting to determine my councillors' feelings on the matter."

"Your councillors will agree with you, naturally." Richard

met his eyes without flinching.

Edward drew a long, weary sigh. "If they do, you shall come with me to Henry tonight to see for yourself that there's no way around it… Lucky for you you're not king, Dickon. You wouldn't last the turn of an hourglass."

~*~

As Richard expected, the verdict of the council was unanimous. Henry must die.

Richard looked around the table, at Hastings, Howard, Anthony Woodville. At Edward's Chancellor, Robert Stillington, Bishop of Bath and Wells, to whom Edward had given the Seal he took back from Archbishop Neville. He looked at his brother George, and his brother by marriage, the Duke of Suffolk, John de la Pole, married to their sister Liza. Of all the men gathered in the council chamber at the White Tower, only Howard had voiced an objection, one quickly withdrawn when Edward turned on him angrily. No one but George drank his wine; no one but George moved. No one spoke—George from obvious indifference, though the others looked uneasy. Anthony Woodville and Suffolk had once been Lancastrian and had sworn an oath of fealty to Henry. At one point Anthony Woodville did open his mouth as if to protest, then shut it without uttering a word. Stillington, the cleric who should have pointed out the appalling enormity of the sin they were about to commit, made no effort to dissuade Edward, though he trembled visibly.

It was dark when the meeting ended. With grim faces, the men descended the steps of the Keep in silence and disappeared into the soft night. Guided by a torchbearer, Richard strode shoulder to shoulder with Edward across the inner ward, then up to Henry's apartment in the Wakefield Tower. A guard unlocked the heavy door with a jangle of keys and swung it open.

The vaulted stone chamber was dark, pervaded by a stale smell. Candles burned in the oratory opening on the east side and Richard could make out a dark figure kneeling at his devotionals. A green linnet fluttered on a wooden perch by a bed beneath a great stained glass window, watching as they crossed the room. Their boots clicked against the tile but the monk-King didn't turn. The bird squawked once, then fell silent.

"Forgive the intrusion, Henry, but I fear we do not have all night," Edward announced.

Bringing his prayers to a close, Henry of Lancaster made the sign of the Cross, shut his Bible, and heaved himself up from the tiled floor. He was dressed like a cleric in a long dark robe, and beneath his cap his hair was spare and grey, but he looked younger than his fifty years. He came to them, a smile on his mild face. He was of a good height, but stooped. Richard, who had no memory of the king he had met in his infancy, thought Henry's head too small for his body, and that it was strange he should resemble Edward.

"Ah, my dear Cousin Edward, you are welcome," said Henry. "'Tis a while since we last saw one another, is it not?"

"Aye, and much has happened between," said Edward dryly. "This is my royal brother, Richard, Duke of Gloucester, whom you met when he was a babe." Edward laid his gauntlets down on a table.

Henry of Lancaster turned his dim eyes and kindly smile on Richard. "Fair cousin, we greet thee well."

Richard inclined his head in acknowledgement.

"Do you like my bird? His name is Becket. He is good company."

"He's a fine bird," Richard replied, feeling oddly embarrassed.

"Our gracious cousin of Warwick gave him to me. How fares our Cousin Warwick?" Henry said, addressing Edward.

Edward exchanged a glance with Richard. The poor idiot no longer remembered '64 when Warwick humiliated him after his capture by tying his feet to his stirrups and parading him around the city like a common felon. He remembered only

Warwick's recent kindnesses. "Warwick is dead, Henry."

"Oh, dear, dear, a shame," Henry clucked sadly. "Poor Cousin Warwick, I shall pray for him. He was a good man."

"Good?" demanded Edward sharply. "Too ambitious for his own good would better describe Warwick!"

The comment failed to register on Henry. "How did he die?" Henry inquired on a note of surprise, as if the thought that had just occurred to him was of sudden great importance.

"In war, fighting for you."

Henry tilted his brow, looked at him uncertainly. "But war displeases me. I am a man of peace."

"For a man of peace, you've been the cause of a remarkable number of battles, Henry."

"'Tis God's will then," murmured Henry.

"'Tis not God's will, Henry. 'Tis yours!"

Henry smiled blankly. "I'm not wise or strong, but God tells me what to do."

"Not God, Henry!" raged Edward. "Marguerite—Marguerite and Somerset! Do you know how many died at Towton because of you? Forty thousand!" He slammed his fist on the table. The bird shrieked, flew from its perch in a panic. "Do you care how many died for you at Barnet, or Tewkesbury? At St. Albans, Hexham, Edgecote, Blore Heath, Wakefield?" Edward's bright blue eyes blazed. "Why didn't you renounce your throne for an abbey, Henry? Then you could have prayed to your heart's content and all would have been well with the world!"

"Fair cousin, you know a king is God's anointed until the day he dies. God put me here to rule, therefore everything that happens is His will."

"You half-wit, God also gave you a brain to reason with, therefore all evil that has been done is your fault!" Edward stormed. Then he fell silent, realising the folly of his remark. When he spoke again, there was resignation in his tone. "Henry, all would have been different had you renounced the throne to my father years ago. As you did not, I regret that Fate has forced us here, to this point."

He hesitated.

"Farewell, cousin."

Henry tilted his head again and gazed at him quizzically. The silver crucifix hanging from his belt glinted in the candlelight. "Farewell, Cousin Edward. Peace be with you." He moved back to his altar. Opening his Bible, he knelt again at his devotionals.

Edward swept his gauntlets from the table and strode out the door.

Richard stared at Henry's crouching back, seeing there merely a harmless old man mumbling his prayers. When Richard was newly born, Henry had made a visit to Fotheringhay, had cradled him in his arms, and blessed him. Pity twisted his heart. Poor, gentle Henry must die; he who had only wanted to feed the sparrows at his windowsill and pray to his God, who had never wilfully harmed a living soul, who'd been so generous a king that he'd bankrupted his treasury and once given away the only robe he owned. Henry, who had been so distraught at the sight of a traitor's torso rotting on a pole, he'd demanded that the body part be taken down, given decent burial, and the practice be stopped. Poor, innocent, saintly Henry whose only crime was to be wedded to Marguerite d'Anjou. Even that was not of his own choosing.

It wasn't fair.

Richard followed Edward out the door.

That night, Henry VI died in the Tower. The next morning, Anthony Woodville requested permission to go on pilgrimage to Portugal. After angrily denouncing him as a coward for wishing to leave while the Bastard of Fauconberg was attacking Kent and so much remained to be done, Edward granted his request. Throwing an arm around Richard's shoulder, he said, "Dickon, what would I do without you? Who would I send to deal with Fauconberg? With the Scots? Now that John's gone, there's no one to guard the border. God knows, Percy's too damned fond of his own skin to be a soldier. You're my best general, my most trusted advisor. The only one I can count on, brother!"

~*~

Richard had no need of his armour in Sandwich. When the Bastard of Fauconberg learned of Henry's death, he sought and was granted Edward's pardon. Richard received him warmly, called him friend, and took him into his service. After all, he was a Neville, and Nevilles would always claim his heart.

There was yet one more Neville who needed his help. On his return to Westminster in early June, he immediately secured Archbishop George Neville's release from the Tower. Of the other rebels, his sister's husband, the Duke of Exeter, while badly wounded, had survived Barnet and was imprisoned in the Tower; Oxford had managed to reach France; and Jasper Tudor was still in Wales, fomenting trouble with his fourteen-year-old nephew, Henry Tudor, at his side. But the Lancastrian threat was dead for the present. Only the Scottish threat remained.

Matters on the Scots border were so urgent Richard couldn't stay in London past the day, not even for a special ceremony dear to Edward's heart. Richard's little nephew, seven-month-old Prince Edward, born to Bess in Sanctuary at Westminster during the troubles with Warwick, was to be created Prince of Wales. Edward was sorely disappointed that Richard would be absent for the ceremony. Richard didn't share his regret. The child might be his brother's son, but Bess would see to it he grew up a Woodville, infected with her own destructive avarice.

Urgent as Scotland was, however, Richard had decided not to wait to see Anne, but to delay his departure and go to her after he spoke with Edward. He found Edward in a corner of the Painted Chamber, laughing with his courtiers and a blubbery cleric. Edward caught sight of Richard, disengaged himself from the group, and with an arm around Richard's shoulder, drew him to a far window where they could converse privately. He arranged his magnificent form comfortably in a tapestried chair, and Richard took up a position in front of him. Servants bore them wine, which Edward accepted and Richard declined.

"Who's the cleric?" Richard inquired.

"Bishop Morton," replied Edward, sipping his wine. "You've heard of him. He was one of Marguerite's advisors. Now he's seen the true way and wishes to serve me as diligently as he served her."

Something about the man bothered Richard. His face was hard as an iron pot and his protruding dark eyes watched them carefully across the distance in a way that made Richard uncomfortable. "I don't like the look of him," he said.

Edward laughed. "Neither do I, but what difference does that make, little brother? If I depended only on those I liked, there would be precious few to help me govern." He held out his wine cup and a servant hurried to refill it.

"I wouldn't trust him," Richard persisted. "There's something unsavoury about him."

Edward followed the direction of Richard's gaze. "Now that you mention it, he does resemble a toad somewhat. Nevertheless, there's a good brain behind that ugly face that I can use quite well. Now, tell me about Kent."

Richard made his report on Fauconberg and received his instructions regarding Scotland. Their talk concluded, Edward gave him a grateful smile. Then the smile faded from his face and his expression grew serious. "I suppose you're going to see Anne now, Dickon?"

Richard was caught off guard by the anxiety in Edward's tone. "Aye, briefly. I could make it to George's house and back by noon if I hurry."

Clearly uncomfortable, Edward rose, went to the window.

Richard followed. ""Dickon..." Edward said. "Dickon, I must ask you to wait."

"Wait?" Richard demanded, a trifle loudly. From the corner of his eye, he saw heads turn across the hall, but he didn't care. "Wait for what? God's curse, I've been waiting all my life! I'll not wait any longer. You said..."

"I know what I said, the Devil be damned!" Edward snapped. Aware of the sudden silence in the room, he lowered his voice. "Dickon, we have a problem. Can you not guess what it is?"

Richard frowned, his tension mounting.

Edward drew an audible sigh. "Then you're even more blind than I knew."

"What are you talking about?"

"George."

"What about George? He's been sulking more than usual lately, but that's just George. He's always been moody."

"He demands that you not see Anne."

Richard stared, dumbfounded. He found his voice at last. "*Demands?*" he echoed with disbelief.

"He fancies himself her guardian, and as her guardian he can deny her company to whom he chooses."

"You never appointed him her guardian."

"No. But 'tis how he sees himself..." Edward held up a weary hand to forestall Richard's heated protest and continued in the same tired voice, "because as her guardian, he is master of her wealth."

"She has no wealth. She's a traitor's daughter, for God's sake."

"I know that, and you know that, but George lives in his own mad world. Since I haven't attainted Warwick—and have no plans to do so—he thinks of Anne as her father's heiress, which I suppose she is, in a way." He passed a hand over his eyes. "Frankly, Dickon, I can't deal with him right now—his lunatic ravings, his insults, his tempers, his foul accusations..." He dropped his hand, met Richard's angry gaze. "I can't manage

him alone. I need you here beside me. I need respite, Dickon…
Grant me respite and I swear that nothing will keep you from
marrying the girl once you are back."

Richard opened his mouth to protest, but changed his mind.
In the morning light, Edward's mouth was deeply grooved, the
lines around his eyes merciless. He looked haggard and far older
than his thirty years.

"But once Scotland's behind me, I marry Anne."

"You marry Anne," Edward replied.

~*~

Richard stood amidst his packed coffers, rolled carpets, and
dismantled trestle bed being readied by the servants for his
journey north. Half-dazed by fatigue, weighed down with his
disappointment over Anne, he found himself unable to keep his
thoughts from returning to Henry. As Constable of England,
he'd had no choice but to carry the King's order to the Constable
of the Tower and arrange the matter with him. How he had
made his stiff lips utter the dreadful command, he could no
longer recall. He held himself accountable for Henry's death,
but now some in London were saying that he had murdered
him with his own bare hands.

He had always known that, for most people, rumours were
the spice of life, to be devoured with relish, but until now he
had not felt their sting himself. He found that it bothered him
more than he cared to admit. He lifted a hand to his brow, and
his glance caught and held again, as it often had in recent weeks,
on his father's ruby ring. The bright crimson stone glinted
wickedly. He rubbed his eyes. Had he Henry's blood on
his hands?

No more than Edward.

Poor Henry. *Peace be with you,* were his last words. Peace,
which had been bought with his blood. An uncanny choice of
words. A thought flashed through Richard's mind: Without

benefit of pilgrimage, would God forgive him his part in Henry's death, or would he send fitting retribution? He tore the ring from his finger and strode to his writing table. A servant hurried over with a key and unlocked the silver casket that held his jewels. He flung the ring inside. The servant locked the casket and withdrew a respectful distance. Richard clutched the edge of the table, and bowed his head. He was not some dread monster without conscience! Damn the malice inherent in men's nature that made them believe the worst of others. Damn his own helplessness to defend himself against their preposterous allegations.

It wasn't fair.

He slammed a fist on the desk. He was no longer a child to cry that life wasn't fair! He was a man who had seen battle. A man who had carried out his King's orders. He should have outgrown his childish terrors by now. God's blood, but Edward had reason, years ago, to fear that the company of women had softened his character! If Edward didn't fear God's wrath, why should he? He was no less a man.

He looked up. Everyone in the room was staring at him.

"Make haste!" he roared, taking his anger out on his servants for the first time in his life, as he'd seen Edward do. "The Scots will be rattling the gates of York if you make no more haste than this!"

Strange, but it helped. He felt calm, and in control again.

CHAPTER THIRTY-SEVEN

"O ye stars that shudder over me..."

At the end of September, as leaves turned red and gold beneath a cornflower blue sky, Richard rode home from Scotland with his army, his work on the border done. Much had happened in the three months he'd been gone. At the end of April, Kate had given birth to his second child, a son, conceived the September before he'd fled to Bruges. He had named him John. On the way south, he journeyed to Pontefract to see his babe and eighteen-month-old Katherine.

Green silk flashed at the window of the house on Pontefract's high hill as he dismounted in the walled close and gave his reins over to a servant. Laughing, Kate flew out the door and ran to him, arms wide, long coppery curls flaming in the fiery sunset and tumbling loose beneath a hair band of seed pearls he'd given her.

"Richard, Richard..." she cried joyfully throwing her arms around his neck. "Why didn't you send word? Oh, love, how long I've waited, and hoped, and now, at last, and now..."

Richard was unprepared for the surge of desire that charged through him at the contact with her. A year had passed since they'd last seen one another and he'd thought his feelings for her dead. He was mistaken. There was something between them that would never die, but he could never hold her again, not now that Anne would be his. He tensed, stood perfectly still, not trusting himself to move or speak. The joy drained out of her. She went limp, drew back, and searched his face. Her green eyes held a stunned, wounded expression. He swallowed, looked away. For a long moment, she said nothing.

"I see," she whispered at length. Her lip quivered, but she lifted her chin in resolve. She turned, led the way up the steps into the hall. He followed awkwardly, acutely aware of her perfume. The rose scent was familiar, one she'd worn ever since he'd first admired it.

The room was pleasant, even cozy, with chairs, a footrest, a table set with fruit, an urn of white roses, and two silver candlesticks that had been his gift to her. He recognised all the others—a book on Sir Lancelot bound in green leather, a chess set of agate and ivory, and two finger-high figurines of coloured glass, one a red image of his beloved St. Ninian, the other a blue of his favourite saint of the North, St. Cuthbert. On the wall over the fireplace hung a small tapestry Kate had worked of Lancelot and Elaine, the fair maid of Astolat who'd died for love of Lancelot. A white wool blanket, yet another gift, had been carefully folded and lay draped over the side of a chair by the empty grate.

His eye went to Kate and the gold locket around her neck that held a snippet of his dark hair. Guilt washed over him in a muddy flood. He felt wretched, utterly miserable. "Kate, I'm sorry... Maybe I shouldn't have come... Maybe I should have written... I didn't know what to do."

"I heard the rumours. I didn't want to believe them." There was a quaver in her voice, but she held her head high with dignity. "I knew you loved her before me, but I thought... I thought... I hoped you were over her—that I'd made you forget..."

"I never meant to hurt you, Kate."

"For the love of God, Richard!" she cried. Then she composed herself, said in a calmer tone, "Why have you come?"

"The children... And to see you, to explain—to make sure you're well and have everything you need..."

"I have everything I need. You've been very generous. You're a generous man."

"Kate—don't make this harder than it already is, I pray you. You know that I care—I'll always care."

"Not enough, apparently." A sob strangled in her throat. She clutched the chair fiercely. "You're right. We must think of the children. They're good children. So much like you, both of them…" She dropped her lashes, turned quickly, and rang the bell that stood on the mantle, rang a little too long, a little too harshly. A servant woman came to the door. "Bring the children," Kate said.

They waited in silence. Moments later a wail sounded in the passageway along with giggles and the hurried patter of little feet. Then the footsteps were halted, the giggles and wailing suddenly checked. The nurse appeared in the doorway, cradling an infant in one arm and holding a little girl by the hand with the other. The child was sucking her thumb and hid behind her nurse's skirts as soon as she saw Richard, though auburn curls and huge solemn grey eyes peered out intently from the folds of the woman's coarse brown kirtle.

Kate knelt. "Come here, sweet one…" She smoothed the child's unruly locks. "What have I told you about your father, Katherine?" She waited. "That he's a prince," Kate prompted, "and good and…"

"I lub…" the child managed, trying to remember.

"Love… aye… you love him…This is your father, Katherine."

Katherine stared at Richard a moment. Then, with a shriek of glee, she toddled to him, arms outstretched, smiling broadly. Richard swung her up in the air. Her little arms went around his neck in a strangling hold, and she smothered him with kisses wet as Percival's. Then Kate brought Richard his four-month-old son and tenderly gave the tiny infant over into his care. "And this," she said, "is John."

John. Born a week after Barnet. Richard swallowed. The babe gurgled and the memories fled. He was suffused with a sudden, almost intolerable joy, a wild, sweet happiness so unbearable that it threatened his composure. He buried his face in the babe's soft neck. "Thank you, Kate," he said in a choked voice.

A sob escaped Kate's lips. With a hand twisted to her mouth, she fled the room.

~*~

Riding in the autumn sunshine the next morning, Richard relived the scene, every vivid detail. He felt such guilt for what he'd done to Kate and wondered miserably if he'd ever forgive himself for the hurt he'd caused. Partly because of his heavy heart, he found himself reluctant to linger at Pontefract for the children, and instead, departed at first light after spending the night at the castle. They would never meet again. From now on, whenever he visited the house high on Beech Street, Kate would not be there. It was what she wished, and best for both of them. Poor Kate. Poor, beloved, dear Kate, who deserved so much better than he had given her.

He closed his eyes and swallowed on the knot in his throat. So many memories. So much pain he could not undo. All at once the children's smiling faces intruded, blotting at the sadness, chasing away the regrets. They were God's own miracles, these two little innocents, and he would never let them suffer. They would always have the best. They might be bastards, but they would never feel the sting of their bastardry. And, pray God, little John would never know the anguish of losing a father in battle as he himself had, or the horrors of war, as his namesake had. For peace had come at last to England.

The lesson he had taught James III was a harsh one, and there would be no more infractions of the truce for a long while. He was relieved. He had no wish to repeat the measures he'd been forced to take.

There had been scant fighting as James retreated before him, leaving him no alternative but to scorch the earth on the way to Edinburgh. Though he forbade his men to ravage and pillage, many Scots lost what little they owned. They blamed England, but in truth they should blame France, for Louis's hand was behind the troubles. Since Louis had supported Marguerite's invasion of England, he feared Edward's retaliation. To keep

265

Edward from invading France, the Spider King had stirred up the Scots and helped Jasper Tudor foment rebellion in Wales. But news of the truce had sent old Jasper fleeing, taking his confounded nephew Henry Tudor with him. God be praised, they never reached France. A storm blew them astray to Brittany where Francis, Duke of Brittany, granted the Tudors refuge. Now there was hope that Francis would ransom those two sorry Lancastrian remnants in order to spite Louis, whom he hated.

If Brittany did indeed hand over Jasper and his nephew, Edward could at long last bury the Lancastrian threat forever. That was something to look forward to. He wished he could look forward to returning to London. The image of Anne beckoned him back, but court was another matter, more like sticking one's nose up the chute of a privy. One could be sure to find trouble there, and trouble had two names: Bess and George.

While Anthony Woodville was away in Portugal, Hastings had been granted Warwick's old title of Captain of Calais, angering the queen, who had wanted the honour for her brother. For sure, Hastings would have to watch his back now. As for George, he was upset that Edward's seven-month old son had been made Prince of Wales, since that was the hereditary title of the heir to the realm and he considered it his. Had not the act of the Lancastrian parliament declared him heir to Edouard of Lancaster, if Edouard died without issue? Good old, mad old George—who could understand George?

There was one note of humour, though. The tiny Prince of Wales had been provided with a chancellor—no doubt on the insistence of Edward's pretentious queen, since a babe couldn't dictate letters and scarcely had need of a secretary. Unfortunately, George had ridiculed Bess and her affectations when he knew she was within earshot, and though it served her right, Richard feared George's tongue would surely be the death of him one day.

Ah, court, what joys have you in store for me? he wondered.

~*~

London's city walls came into view, dark against the glow of the setting sun. Richard shifted in his saddle, gripped his pommel closely. How he hated London! He had hated it as a child and his aversion had only grown with the years. London was a place where the sun never shone, a place where the vast sky of the moors was darkened in narrow streets by the leaning upper stories of the gilt and gabled houses of the merchants. Four times the size of York with its fifty-thousand inhabitants, it was a filthy, crowded place, filled with whirling wheels and clamour. Mercers, haberdashers, and customers argued in the streets while from the blacksmiths' shops the clanging of metal on metal mounted an assault on the ears. Turning into Butcher's Row, Richard averted his gaze. He had no desire to view the blood of freshly slaughtered animals in the gutters that reminded him of the carnage of a battlefield. There was no escape, however, from the rancid smell of urine from a nearby alley, so offensive it knocked the breath from him as surely as if a fist had reached out and punched him in the nose. The only aspect of the city he enjoyed was the churches. London had over a hundred. Their steeples could be seen everywhere and the city resounded with the eternal ringing of bells and the voices of singing clergy.

He clattered through Bishopsgate with his men, picking his way through muddy, unpaved streets to the river and holding his nose as he approached Fishmonger's Hall, releasing it when he reached Thames Street. Thames, which skirted the warehouses and wharves, was crowded with all manner of shops selling pitch, wax, thread, rope, fish, minerals, wines, and grains, but it was paved and afforded small glimpses of a wide blue curve of river, with swans and gilded barges.

A chorus of ravens announced an approaching funeral procession, led by a priest bearing a cross and a herald with a banner. Richard tensed. In dark robes with kerchiefs around their noses to ward off the stink of the rotting corpse, mourners followed the litter with lighted candles, swinging incense. The sour smell of death reminded him that he was responsible for the death of yet another Neville. While in Scotland, the Bastard of Fauconberg had experienced a change of heart, and had tried to join the Earl of Oxford, who was plundering English ships on the high seas and making raids on Calais. Caught aboard a ship he was attempting to commandeer, Fauconberg was executed on the spot. Richard had written to Anne about the incident and expressed deep sorrow at the step he'd been forced to take, but once again he feared her reaction, that she might blame him for yet another kinsman's death.

Blue twilight was falling and bells rang for Vespers as the high walls and battlements of his mother's London home, Baynard's Castle, came into view above the tiled roofs. The castle was a huge fortress on the banks of the River Thames, almost a city in itself, large enough to house much of his army. Since it was not the kind of place that turned one's thoughts to God, his mother came rarely to London, preferring her establishments in the North, usually at Fotheringhay or Berkhampsted, where she found the peaceful serenity of the countryside more amenable to her chosen life of prayer and contemplation.

After a hasty meal and bath, Richard donned a russet and silver doublet, threw a dark mantle over his shoulders, and took a barge to the Herber, Warwick's London house that now belonged to George. The night was chill but beautiful. Twinkling stars adorned the dark sky, and the black river, clear as a looking glass, reflected the brilliant moon and the torchlight from passing barges. The hour of Compline had chimed and a wind had risen by the time he reached George's residence. Only the sentries were about. No matter. He'd sent word ahead that he was coming and Anne was expecting him. His hand strayed to the letter he kept near his breast, inside his doublet. *If it takes forever, I will wait for thee.* He felt elated, yet dreadfully anxious.

George's guards were conversing among themselves on the ramparts and their voices floated out to the water from the house. The barge drew up to the water gate, the oars stilled, and the captain helped Richard onto the dock. A sharp voice called out, "Who goes there?"

Richard's squire gave an equally sharp rejoinder. "Richard of Gloucester!"

The first voice came again, "Pass then!" and the guards resumed their conversations.

Bidding his squire wait, Richard swung the postern gate open and entered the walled garden of the graceful London house that had belonged to Anne's father. He hadn't seen Anne in two years, and a lifetime had passed between. With his heart pounding in his ears and his lips as dry as tinder, he climbed the riverbank and crunched his way across the fallen leaves. He reached the sweeping outer staircase, looked up. And froze.

Framed by the torches flaring at the door, Anne stood at the top of the steps, her fair hair shimmering down to her waist, her violet gown fluttering around her lithe form. For Richard it was as though night had shattered and blazing sunlight flooded the world. Wild joy exploded in his breast. On her lips hovered the smile he'd remembered with such clarity, such aching and longing, these lonely, desperate years. Time hurtled backwards and he felt the earth warm, heard the laughter of those joyous days at Middleham. He held out his arms. She ran down the steps and stumbled into them with a sob. "Richard…"

"Anne…" he whispered into her hair, his heart hammering, his blood surging at the first shocking contact of her flesh with his. "Oh, Anne…" He crushed her soft red lips beneath his own and tasted wine. Ecstasy flamed through him. He drew back and stared down at her in rapturous wonder. "You're so beautiful, Anne… I'd forgotten how beautiful."

"I saw the barge from the window," she said in a breathless whisper. "I heard them call your name…"

He pressed her to him and laid his cheek against her silken hair. "Anne, Anne... How I love thee, Anne." Her name felt like a caress on his tongue and he couldn't keep from repeating it. "Anne... beloved Anne, how I missed thee... Marry me, Anne."

Anne looked up at him, eyes wide with joy. Then her expression clouded. "But the King..."

"My beloved lady, the King is grateful and has already granted permission!"

For Anne it seemed the ground on which she stood floated away, that the garden walls melted and a wind picked up the stars and twirled them about her. Then she remembered all that she had forgotten in her happiness. She jerked back from his arms. "But how can we marry? I have nothing to bring you."

Richard cupped his hand under her chin and tilted her face up to his. "You say you bring me nothing... Aye, 'tis so, if love be nothing."

She gazed at him, seeing dawn-grey eyes in a sun-bronzed face, and thick dark hair gleaming in the moonlight. He looked glowing and young, though the angles of his face were more sharply defined, the square jaw more firmly set than she remembered. The lines around his eyes and mouth were still there, but now they muted his youth with strength and didn't wrench her heart as they once had, for the fear was gone. He had changed. He was different from the young Richard she had known at Middleham. This Richard was a man, one who had proven himself with courage and will. But some things had not changed. He was still her rescuer, as he had been in their childish play on the green slopes behind the castle walls, and he still wished to wed her.

"Can this be?" she murmured, tears wetting her cheek. "Can such happiness truly be?"

"It can," he said, pushing stray tendrils of hair back from her brow. "It is, Flower-eyes." She was stealing a look at him in the way he loved: shyly, from below. He bent his lips to her mouth.

She lifted her arms to clasp his neck and Richard felt the cold jab of metal in his flesh. He drew away, seized her hand, looked down. "You still wear my ring."

"It never left my finger," she whispered as he covered her hands with kisses. "Not even when—not even, even..." She shut her eyes on a breath, and shivered.

Realising what she was trying to say, Richard winced. He gathered his cloak around her, pressed her to him and held her tight in his embrace. "Hush, my love, hush."

His arms warmed the chill in her heart. Her shivering ceased; the memories of Marguerite and Edouard fled. She opened her eyes and looked up at him. "Never leave me, Richard—the world is too harsh a place without you. Promise you'll never leave me."

"I swear it on my father's soul, beloved Anne."

She turned in his arms and they faced the river together. The wind had stilled. Fireflies glinted around them and the Thames flowed smoothly past, shimmering in the moonlight. A nightingale sang in the garden, matin bells chimed in the distance, and water lapped gently, bathing the night with calm and a beauty so profound that it caught at their throats. Neither spoke for fear of breaking the magical spell that bound them.

After a while, in a tone of wonder, Anne said, "What more could there be?"

Richard looked down with a soft expression, his grey eyes sparkling, his smile luminous. "But more there is, dearest Anne." He turned her to face him and took her hands into his own. "I've traded my lands and commands in Wales for the North. Edward's concerned about Percy. He doesn't trust him and has given me authority over him... He's also given me your father's estates of Sherriff Hutton, Penrith and..." He broke off, waited a moment, "Middleham." He heard her indrawn breath. "My love, we're going back to Middleham!"

A cry of joy escaped her lips. She flung herself against him and her heart streamed into his. He laid his cheek against hers and he felt her fragrant breath against his face. For one blessed, glowing moment, they stood locked together in each other's arms, and so piercing sweet was their joy that it seemed that Heaven itself reached out to caress them.

An ugly laugh shattered their enchantment.

"A pretty picture, indeed." George's voice.

The lovers separated, whirled around. George stood at the top of the staircase, his face shadowed by the torchlight flaring behind him, his fair curls shining brightly. As he strode down the steps, they saw that his features were twisted with fury. Anne instinctively clung to Richard.

"A fine sight and a fine thing when one's brother sneaks in by night to steal!"

Richard stared at him. "Sneak...? Steal...? What are you talking about, George?"

"You wish to marry Anne."

"Aye. And I will. What does that have to do with sneaking and stealing?"

"I've not given my permission."

"Your permission? All I need is Edward's permission and that he gave me in Coventry."

"She's not for you and you'll never marry her," George sputtered. "The affairs of the Nevilles are in my hands. I'm her guardian and I will never grant my permission!"

"We'll see about that!" Richard shouted. After all he had been through, to be treated thus by his own brother, a brother still fresh from his treasons both to his King and his father-in-law—it was too much to be borne. "You've gone mad, George. I shall marry Anne and there's nothing you can do about it. I'll appeal to Edward and we'll see which of us he favours."

"Aye, let's see which of us wins this contest." George spat the words.

Something in his manner struck a chill into Anne. George did not make idle threats. Aboard ship, he had sworn to make

Edward pay. And he had. Greed and jealousy were poisons in his blood, driving him ever closer to the dark edges of madness. No sane mind could anticipate his next move. She tightened her hold of Richard's arm.

"My dearest love," Richard said gently, "I fear you must obey for now, but know that I shall be back for you."

Sudden dread kept her frozen at Richard's side. When she made no move to follow, George grabbed her by the wrist and dragged her up the steps.

"Richard…" she cried, casting a long look back.

"I'll be back, Anne! Never fear, dear heart…"

The door slammed shut behind her. Its angry echo shattered the stillness of the night. Richard kicked the ground, and cursed.

CHAPTER THIRTY-EIGHT

"O brother… woe is me!
My madness all thy life has been… thy curse."

Through the halls and passageways of Westminster Palace crowded with boisterous, boasting Woodvilles, past the glittering, silently watchful Queen playing cards with her ladies, Richard made his way to the King's bedchamber the next morning. Magnificent in a green velvet doublet slashed and reversed with purple satin, his splendid legs encased in high black boots of fine Milan leather, Edward stood with a flask of wine in one hand, the other reaching for the skirts of a laughing chambermaid as she bent to smooth the bed. All the while the Keeper of the Wardrobe and his meinie struggled to measure the stately frame and to hold up bolts of gold and silver tissue, rich crimsons, and colourful silks and velvets for his inspection.

Edward said, "George was just here. He says you fought."

He took a gulp of wine.

"It seems we always do these days!" Richard exclaimed, betraying his frustration.

"What about this time?"

"I must speak with you in private, my lord," Richard replied in a formal manner. He had sensed the sudden interest of the servants in the room and already regretted his display of emotion.

Edward waved a hand and the room cleared instantly, with the exception of two men-at-arms by the door and the minstrel, whom Edward ordered back to his stool. The man began a lilting melody on his flute, but neither his cheery tune nor the fire crackling in the hearth, nor the opulence of the room with its bright tapestries and coloured tile floor, could brighten the dismal day. The chamber felt damp and cold, reflecting the gloom of the leaden skies and the rain-swept Thames.

Edward sank into a velvet chair, flask in hand, while Richard moved to the hearth and related his tale of the events of the previous night.

"George and his insatiable greed. I'm beginning to think he's a viper," sighed Edward. "He wants the Countess's lands and he fears that if you marry Anne, he'll have to share them with you."

"But the Countess's lands can't be confiscated—she had no part in Warwick's treason."

"I know, I know, but I fear I must give him what he wants, or he'll give me no peace."

It was an old tale. George had long ago figured out how to manage Edward and the years had taught him to hone the practice. Richard remembered one incident in particular and thought it strange that something so insignificant should linger in his mind after all the years.

They had just returned from exile in Burgundy after Edward had won the throne, and George was showing off his new clothes. "Purple and gold suit me best, don't you think, Dickon?"

he'd demanded. Richard had stepped into his grey gown without a reply, thinking that every day it was the same question, only a different colour. "You have but two gowns," continued George, "while I have twenty. Does that not bother you?"

Knowing George would persist until he received an answer, Richard said, "I don't wish to trouble Edward about such things when he has important matters on his mind."

George had regarded him thoughtfully. "I'll let you in on a secret, Dickon. You have to keep reminding Edward of what you want until you get it. He forgets, you see."

Nothing had changed, Richard thought now. The grown man was little different from the boy. He watched as Edward drained his flask and called for another. A server hurried over. Edward drank greedily.

"Clarence always wants something more than what he has," Edward said, wiping his mouth with the back of his hand. "To prove he's a better man than he is, I suppose. I know him, but I know not how to appease him. Once he has the Countess's lands, he'll turn his eyes back on the crown."

Richard noted Edward's new habit of referring to George by his title, as if to distance himself from their brother. Whether this was deliberate, he didn't know, but clearly, his affection for George had cooled and only on account of the blood bond did he tolerate him at all. But then, George had a way of wearing one down.

Edward pressed a hand to his brow. "George is in a foul and dangerous mood, Dickon. I must find a way to appease him. For the peace of the realm."

"Edward—you will not require me to give up Anne?"

Surprised by his tone, Edward regarded him a long moment. "George means to have her inheritance at any cost, Dickon, for the honours I have given you fester in his mind and he has a spiteful, jealous nature." He paused thoughtfully before he resumed. "As you know, I'm not one to seek a fight… But neither

275

do I shrink from one when my honour is at stake. Nay, Dickon, I won't ask such sacrifice of you a second time. I shall send to George not to interfere with your suit. You may have the girl, and I wish you both joy."

Richard's tense shoulders relaxed. He gave a deep bow. "With your permission, Edward…"

Edward nodded.

~*~

Armed with Edward's order, and with his retinue at his side, Richard galloped to George's house. Bidding them wait in the courtyard, he pushed George's servants aside when they tried to tell him Anne wasn't there and took the steps two by two to her chamber on the upper floor.

The room was empty.

His stomach clenched. The bed was made and the hearth swept. The stone-and-wood room had the cold air of a place untouched by human habitation. From the window he could see the bare branches of the trees stripped of their foliage, the thin lawn, and the muddy river flowing past, dark and threatening in the stinging rain. The startling difference from the night before filled him with dread. He turned quickly from the window.

George stood at the door, a thin smile on his lips. He wore a velvet doublet of purple and gold trimmed with miniver and he was studded with jewels from his fair curls to the points of his red shoes. "So, Dickon, you're back, I see."

Without a word Richard closed the distance between them and held out Edward's missive. George leaned against the stone embrasure of the doorway and broke open the royal seals.

"Where is she?" demanded Richard, when George had finished reading.

George let the royal letter flutter to the floor and folded his arms. "Since I hold no right of wardship over Anne, I'm not responsible for her whereabouts. Therefore, I neither know nor care."

For a moment Richard stared, dumbfounded. He realised suddenly that for him, as for Edward, the bond of brotherhood that had bound him tightly to George all his life had been so battered by years of wounding hurts and cruel demands that it had frayed into fine threads which would not hold much longer. He grabbed George by his fancy doublet and shoved him backwards into the room. "What have you done with her?" he demanded through clenched teeth.

George was seized with a moment's fear. He had never seen Richard this way, but he recovered quickly and shoved back. "She left of her own accord. I don't know where she went."

They circled one another warily like panthers. "There are ways to find out," Richard hissed. "Edward supports me in this. You'd best not push him too far, George." He landed a punch to George's left ear and his brother yelped. They hadn't fought since they were boys and it felt strange to Richard, brought back memories.

"He's always supported you!" cried George. "Always favoured you! I'm sick of it, I tell you! He's going to pay!" He let go with his fist, and missed Richard's jaw.

"You're mad!"

"You're going to pay, Dickon!"

"No, George. Get one thing very clear. You'll pay. If anything happens to Anne, I'll kill you."

George lunged at him then, a bold strike that came as unexpectedly as lightning out of a blue sky. The punch landed hard in his gut. Pain exploded in his side and flashed to his right shoulder, which had never mended properly after Barnet and sometimes ached, especially in damp weather. The breath went out of him. He doubled over, clutched his stomach, bit down hard on the bile that flooded his mouth and stumbled to the bed. He grabbed the bedpost to keep from falling. George's voice came in his ear. "Are you all right, Dickon?—Sit, Dickon, sit…" George eased him down on the bed.

Slowly the room stopped spinning and air returned to Richard's lungs. He looked up at George.

"I didn't mean to…" George swallowed, his misery in his eyes. "I didn't want to hurt you, Dickon."

Though breathing bruised his ribs, Richard gave him a wan smile. "You always… did win… our fights." With George's help, he struggled to his feet. After a moment's unsteadiness he found he could stand. Focusing his gaze on a rose carved into the stone above the doorway, he placed one foot in front of the other and forced his way forward. His stomach throbbed with burning pain, but he managed to reach the door. He inhaled deeply, turned around. "But this time, George, you won't win. I'll find her. And I'll marry her."

Standing as erect as he could, he exited the chamber. When he reached the staircase, he let out his breath and leaned his weight against the stone wall as he descended the steps. To his left three high arches opened into the great hall, where varlets scurried around with napkins, silver salt-cellars and trenchers, setting the tables for the noon meal. On the distant dais, ladies were rolling with laughter at the antics of a dwarf. A movement caught his eye deep in a corner by one of the arches. He halted.

Dressed in sombre black, her sparse hair hidden by a grey velvet hennig, Bella was barely visible in the shadows. She must have been waiting for him, for now she inched carefully out of her corner. He hadn't seen her since before she married George and he was shocked by the change in her. She had aged ten years in the short span of two, and she was paler, thinner, sadder than he remembered. He caught the surprise on her face and realised that she'd had the same thought about him.

Aye, she had buried a child, and he'd seen men die in battle. Life had marked them both.

She came out of the shadows. Their eyes met. Hers were red

with weeping. He stood quietly, appealing to her with his. For a long moment their gaze held each other. Then her mouth quivered, and she gave a nod. She would help him find Anne.

He acknowledged her consent with a barely perceptible nod and continued out the door silently so that no one would know they had met.

~*~

Christmas arrived. Windsor Castle filled with music, boughs of greenery, and much feasting, but little merriment. In the months since Anne's disappearance in September, George's bitter arguments with Richard had broken the peace and poisoned joy. George refused to tell where he had hidden Anne, and Bella, unable to discover her whereabouts, had sent no word. In the meantime, Richard's newly won offices and grants of Warwick's northern lands infuriated George, who wanted them all—every title, every scrap of land, every groat of income. "You can have Anne," George had shouted at Richard, "but you shall take her without a pence!"

Richard couldn't accept that. Middleham and Barnard meant as much to him as they did to Anne. He had promised to take her North to live and was determined to do so. To these demands, George, already the richest in the land beside the King himself, had added one other. He demanded to be given the Countess's lands, as if she were already dead. And the Countess had appealed to Richard for help. So the bickering continued, weighing down Richard's spirits and turning the season sour. The realm watched uneasily, mindful that disputes between royals often ended in bloodshed. Even Edward was despondent.

Returning to the great hall five days before Christmas with a letter he had received from the Countess, Richard halted at the entry, gripped with anxiety. *What ill tidings have come now?* he wondered, for silence hung over the crowded chamber like a shroud. So heavy was the mood that even the minstrels had laid down their instruments for fear of offending. Richard looked around for Edward. He stood alone by the window, deep in thought, clutching a book. He was surrounded by his lords, yet no one spoke to him. As Richard watched, Edward's oldest daughter, Elizabeth, approached her father. She was a beautiful child with hair of darkest gold, and Edward doted on her. Now he swung her up and sat her on a window ledge. Richard went over to join them but found himself reluctant to interrupt. He halted nearby, close enough to hear them speak.

"Why are you sad, my dear lord father?" Princess Elizabeth asked.

"This prophecy, dear child," Edward whispered, his voice cracking in a way that Richard had never heard. He showed her the book, for the child was well schooled. "Can you read?"

Elizabeth shook her head. "I am only six, my lord father," she said.

Edward almost smiled, then his face fell again. "It says, my dear child, that no son of mine shall be crowned king, but that you shall be queen and wear the crown in their stead."

"My lady mother likes being queen, so maybe I shall like it, too," the child replied, misunderstanding the reason for his sadness.

Gently, Edward stroked her hair.

So the book Edward held was on astrology. How strange that he should be so affected by a prophecy. He'd never shared the queen's interest in the occult or shown much patience for portents when they didn't accord with his wishes. He'd even had himself crowned on the ill-omened Holy Innocents' Day, the festival of Herod's massacre of the babes—a day on which even King Louis of France refused to conduct business—merely because he didn't wish to tarry in London any longer. Richard lifted his eyes to Edward's face, grim and battered by experience. The years had changed him much. He had moods now and one never knew what to expect. But one thing hadn't changed: he was still the same brother who had come every day to see him at his London lodgings when he was a small boy, alone and afraid during the civil war.

"Edward," Richard said gently.

Edward turned, aware of him for the first time.

"Prophecies don't always come true, Edward."

"I must be growing old, Dickon…" Edward sighed, dropping into a chair. "Looking back too much… No use looking back, Dickon, can't change anything…" Then in a burst of forced gaiety, he slapped his knees. "Welladay, is it pleasure or business that brings you here?" He was smiling, but his tone held anxiety.

Richard slipped the letter from the Countess behind his back. There would be time enough to speak of it later. She had written yet again, begging Richard to intercede for her with Edward, a heart-rending entreaty not to be sacrificed to George and left a pauper. "Pleasure, Edward," he said. Turning to the gallery, he gave the minstrels a signal and they struck up a merry tune.

CHAPTER THIRTY-NINE

"…thee, the flower of kitchendom."

A louver in the roof ventilated the cookhouse and let in the bitter cold air of March, yet the kitchen was unbearably hot. Bread baked in the brick oven and a boy on a stool turned a side of beef on the spit in the hearth, filling the room with smoke. The pleasant aroma of cooking, however, failed to drown the stench of animal entrails as chickens and starlings were gutted on a table in the middle of room, near the cellar alcove that stored wine and meat.

Anne's stomach recoiled. She who had nursed injured birds back to health could find no appetite in this mortuary. Mealtimes had become an ordeal as she forced herself to chew dark bread and swallow peas and a mouthful of boiled cabbage and potherbs. Weight had dissolved off her in the six months she had been in this place where George had hidden her, and she was now past slender to the point of being dangerously thin.

Her eyes stung with smoke and the seething steam from the cauldron of salt-beef she stirred at the fire. Sweat poured down her brow in a steady stream, clouding her sight, wetting her tangled hair, and soaking her gown, which stuck to her body and gave off an evil smell. She was filthy, had bathed only once in all these months, and itched from dirt and flea bites. In spite of all her scratching, her scalp burned beneath the thin cook-maid cap she wore. Her shoulders, already sore from carrying buckets of water from the well down the long flight of narrow stairs to the kitchen, ached with fatigue though it was only morning. Months of arduous labour had hardened the blisters on her hands into calluses and firmed her muscles but were depleting her energy. She had been prone to more colds and fevers than usual this winter, and she could feel her strength ebbing as her hope of rescue faded. Only last week that hope had been cruelly fanned.

A minstrel had come to sup with them. In a curious coincidence, he happened to speak at length about her father, the great Kingmaker, for whom he claimed to have once played. The Earl's eyes had been as blue as speedwells, he said, but everyone knew that. Afterwards, however, he proceeded to dazzle them with a description of the Kingmaker's banquet and the fragment of a song. It was the lament about love and death that Richard had sung on his eleventh birthday, *Call and I follow…*

Drawn from her lethargy, she had turned her eyes on him. At that instant, he spilt his soup. The help scurried to clean up the mess, and in the commotion that ensued, the minstrel had whispered, "Bella begs a token!" She'd slipped him all that remained of her past life, Richard's silver ring. Her heart pounding, she had lain awake every night expecting rescue. But nothing happened. The days passed. No one came for her.

She knew now that no one would come. It had been a hoax. She closed her eyes.

"Stir, wench, stir!" commanded the head cook. "How many times do I have to tell ye, this is not a charity house? Ye have to earn your keep here or ye'll be out on the streets, m'dear! And what then, I ask ye? What then?"

Anne stirred harder, not for fear of being put out, but to please the head cook. It was his favourite speech, no doubt because it was his own worst fear. Anne had heard it so many times, it echoed even in her sleep; but he meant well, the old man. His bray was worse than his nip and there was kindness in him. He had never taken the strap to any of the kitchen women, and when she was ailing he always sent her a bowl of soup and mead. He had shown kindness in other ways. The first time she'd been given the task of plucking out feathers and hacking at the bodies of little birds snared for dinner, she had swooned. She expected a whipping when she recovered, but the head cook merely shook his head and assigned her to other duties.

Because he treated her gently, she thought he knew her identity, then realised that wasn't so. To him she was merely Nan, an orphan with an unsound mind who gave herself airs and thought herself a lady, and whom the old couple who owned the house had taken in for pity's sake. That was what the help had been told, she'd learned; and it explained her differences aptly. She considered George clever to have thought of it.

Anne had suffered reversals of fortune in her sixteen years, but not since France had she felt so alone. They mocked her speech, these folk she barely understood, and her manners, which they took for affectation. At mealtimes they'd jab one another with their elbows and not let her forget how she had once asked for the salt reserved for the nobly born. When she worked the pulleys, raising and lowering heavy sacks of grain, and straightened to rub her aching back, they snickered, "A little harder than embroidery, isn't it, me lady?" Once, she'd inquired where the privy was. A young lass had led her up the kitchen stairs to a corner of a dirt courtyard, behind the dovecote. "Here's the 'privy,' mistress," she'd giggled with a mock curtsy. On her return, another girl had asked, "Find the 'privy' to y'er satisfaction, *mistress?*" It was her privy Anne missed most, with its wooden seat, window and curtains that ruffled in the breeze, and the little shelf where a candle always burned brightly and a jug of wildflowers stood in welcome. Even in winter, when the cold wind whistled through the narrow slits, it was a pleasant place.

Anne bore them no ill will, for she could dream of rescue, while they were trapped in this dread existence. And though her ways gave them cause for jest, their teasing evidenced more disbelief than cruelty. For the most part, they let her alone. The loneliness would have been acute were it not for the company of two dogs and three cats who shared the kitchen and generously offered their furry warmth in the chill of the night.

But Anne also learned things that kept her up at night, weeping. On his way home from work through the forest, the young brother of the kindly head cook had come upon an injured doe. Mortally wounded by an arrow, she'd moaned in agony while a fox feasted on her stomach. The boy had chased off the fox and put the doe out of her misery. But he was caught in the act. No one believed him, and the penalty for pouching was a merciless death.

Tears stung Anne's eyes as she stirred the salt-beef in the steaming cauldron. Life was hard, sometimes unbearable. For her it was devoid of hope now, devoid of regrets. Devoid of past and future and all that had once mattered. She was no longer Lady Anne Neville, Kingmaker's daughter, but a shadow worn down by fatigue, slipping deeper into oblivion. Sleep was all she wanted. The morning that had dawned too soon with carrying buckets of water from the well-pump would continue with the scrubbing of endless streams of tankards and greasy pots, the sweeping of floors, and the emptying of buckets of refuse until it all began anew for supper. Only sleep ended the hard pace of day.

Sleep, when she sank mercifully onto her pallet in the loft and covered herself with the hay that served as her blanket. Blessed, blessed sleep…

CHAPTER FORTY

"Here, by God's grace, is the one voice for me."

The March twilight softened the icy Thames with a touch of violet. The new year of 1472 had chimed, and soon it would be Easter, yet Anne was still missing. Patience had never been Richard's strength, and waiting for news was unbearable. The twilight hour was especially hard, since twilight with its magical reflections and tender beauty seemed made for lovers. Even so, Richard knew the night it ushered would be worse. Since Anne's disappearance he had slept fitfully and his dreams were troubled. Now the demon of his childhood had a face, and it was George. *You'll never find Anne!* George would sneer maliciously. *You're my brother; why are you doing this?* Richard would plead. Then George would throw his head back and laugh. *You're not my brother! You're no Plantagenet! The Duke of York was not thy father!*

Richard always awoke from these nightmares drenched in sweat. Once he might have reached for his lute but now music only served to underscore his pain, for life itself felt like a long dolorous melody, heavy with pounding chords. Dawn brought a measure of relief, but though he willed himself to concentrate on the work which filled his days, Anne was never far from his thoughts. She would intrude at odd moments, stop him in the middle of a task, halt him in mid-sentence.

As now.

He turned back to his scribe to resume dictation of a letter regarding the Earl of Oxford's estates, which Edward had recently conferred on him, but before he could finish, he was interrupted by a knock at the open door. It was Richard Ratcliffe, new in his service since Barnet. Ratcliffe had fought valiantly for Warwick, and Richard, who had affection for the men of the North, particularly those who had loved Warwick and John, had taken him under his protection. He was but a few years older, handsome, with broad shoulders and a nobly carved countenance, and he exuded a vigorous energy. Ratcliffe had lost no time winning Richard's trust, for he was a man of honour and intellect, and he had displayed that quality Richard valued above all else: Loyalty.

"A messenger, my lord. I told him you couldn't be disturbed. He said to give you this…" Ratcliffe presented Richard with a small ring.

Richard's hand shook as he took the silver circle of entwined laurel leaves. He couldn't breathe or think for the tumult in his head, and he stared at it incredulously, swept with both joy and fear. "Send him in. Make haste," he managed, unable to lift his voice above a whisper.

A moment later a ginger-haired lad of about fourteen tumbled in and fell at his feet. "Y'er Grace, my message's for ye alone."

Richard motioned with his hand and the room cleared. "Speak!"

"M'lord, I'm ordered to tell Y'er Grace this…" He paused to draw a deep breath. "The lady ye be seeking's in the kitchen o' a home in Cheapside." Clearly, the importance of his message

286

was not lost on him for he concentrated on the words as if he had been practising.

"Kitchen?"

"I'm ordered to tell Y'er Grace she's been disguised as a scullery-maid, M'lordship."

Richard stared at him, mouth agape.

"I know the house and can guide ye to it, Y'er Lord—I mean Me Grace—but I'm ordered to tell ye first some important things afore we go."

Richard swallowed hard. This was unbelievable! Impossible! Anne, a scullery-maid in someone's kitchen all these months? *Six months...*

Still on his knees, the youth had fallen silent, awaiting Richard's response. Forcing his attention back to the boy, Richard motioned him to rise and the boy clambered to his feet. "Go on!" he barked, horror of Anne's situation and concern for her safety making his tone harsh.

"The lady who sends ye this ring greets ye well, Y'er Lordship, and bids ye to follow her instructions so no one finds out who she be..."

As the lad spoke, Richard struggled to absorb what he said, but there was such a shaking in his chest that he could barely follow the words. His mind leapt from thought to thought: Bella had found Anne, God be thanked! But how could George be guilty of such a deed? His own brother, such a heinous, foul deed? Anne, so delicate and frail, toiling as a scullery maid! Well might such labour have killed her...

"Well might she have died!" he blurted out, surprising himself. He slammed a clenched fist into his hand and bit his lip to crush the thought that followed: George might have hoped for such an end! He cursed, and kicked at a table, which fell over with a crash, scattering nuts from a silver bowl over the tiled floor. George be damned to Hell! Fair George—whom he had loved, who had held his hand at Ludlow and urged him not to fear, who had proudly sworn to protect him from Marguerite's rampaging troops and comforted him in Bruges—how could that George have grown into such an evil, loathsome creature? Richard gave a bitter cry.

"M'lord, are ye all right?" the boy inquired in a frightened voice.

Unaware he had uttered any sound, Richard stared at him blankly.

"Ye said something, Y'er Lordship," the youth reminded him.

"How is she?" Richard shouted as though the boy were deaf. The lad looked at him in confusion. Richard grabbed him roughly by his jerkin. "Have you seen her?" he yelled in a panic. "Do you know how she is? Where's your tongue? Speak, boy!"

"Seen her, M'lordship?—I mean, Y'er Lordship…" Suddenly realising the Duke meant the lady who had been sent to the kitchens, and not the grand lady who had come to his father's cloth shop and hired him for the mission, he gulped, "My Grace, I've not seen her. There's been ne'er a word on her, save that she's alive."

Richard released his hold, went to the door, flung it open. "Miles, Ratcliffe, make haste! Don your harness, round up men! We ride to Cheapside!"

~*~

With a strong party of armed horsemen bearing torches, Richard galloped through the narrow London streets, his fierce expression serving as forcefully as his men's thundering hoofs to cut a wide swath through the rowdy crowds. The boy took them to Lombard Street and pointed to a high, narrow half-timbered house. "Here it be, Lordship!"

Richard dismounted. Ratcliffe pounded on the door. A wooden peephole opened and a frightened eye looked out. "Open in the name of the King!" cried Ratcliffe.

"That's not the King, he's not near tall enough," came

the answer.

"You shameless lackey—this is His Grace Richard, Duke of Gloucester, here on royal business! Open, or face the consequences!"

The door was cracked open. Richard slammed it back. His expression dark as a thundercloud, he pushed past the frightened servants into the main hall. It was empty and dim, lit by only a single torch. "Where is she?" he bellowed to no one, and everyone. A grey-haired man and a matronly woman in a wimple appeared from an adjacent parlour. The man looked at Richard's sumptuous clothes and the jewelled boar insignia on his velvet hat, blanched and gave an involuntary cry; the woman gasped and turned to flee.

"Seize them!" Richard cried. Two men at arms grabbed the man and wife, and twisting the man's elbow behind him, shoved him forward to Richard.

"Where is she?" he demanded. "Where are your kitchens?"

The woman began to cry. The man begged, "I pray ye, m'lord..."

"Save your prayers, old man! And your tears, woman! As Heaven is my witness, if you've hurt a hair on her head, you shall have need of them. Where are the kitchens?"

"M'lord Duke," the man cried, "We did'na have a say in the matter—we..."

Richard nodded to the man-at-arms and he gave the man's arm a jerk. "The kitchens," Richard repeated coldly. "I'll not ask again."

The woman cried out, "The kitchen be this-a-way, Y'er Grace, this-a-way..." She pointed to the back of the room. "I beg ye— dunna hurt us..." She hurried forward, fumbled a curtain aside, and unlatched a door. The courtyard was small and the ground fell sharply away at the back. On the edge of the incline protruded a low wooden structure with a louver in the roof and a door facing them. Taking a key from her belt, she unlocked

289

the door that was kept locked at night, and descended a flight of dark, narrow steps.

Richard followed, his men streaming behind him with their torches. The cellar was dank, the plastered wall damp with moisture, and instead of the pleasant aroma of foodstuffs came the odour of fish and boiled fat. A rat scurried over Richard's foot and disappeared into an opening between the steps. He shivered. Finally, he stepped into the kitchen. The room was so dark and quiet, at first he thought it empty. Then the straw in the loft began to move and several heads popped up, blinking in the torchlight.

A cry of joy broke the silence; there was a rustle of straw, and a young maiden stood up in a corner of the loft near the wood railing that overlooked the kitchen below. For a moment the world hung still and Richard's heart ceased its beating. "Anne," he whispered, almost to himself. He watched her descend the ladder and felt as if he were watching in a dream, so strangely slow and liquid seemed her movements. Then she was running into his arms. Richard swung her up, pressed her to him. The world flared, spun wildly. "My love," Richard murmured against her cheek, "my love…" But joy quickly turned to shock, for the girl he held in his arms felt as fragile as an ailing bird. He stiffened.

Anne suddenly realised how she must look, how she must smell. She pulled away, turned red as fire; a hand strayed to her hair and a few blades of straw floated to the greasy floor. She spread her palms over her soiled clothes to hide them as best she could, and retreated. "My lord," she said, trembling with shame, looking at him shyly from beneath her lashes, "You must not touch me. I have…"

She never finished the sentence. In a single stride, Richard had her in his arms. He crushed her mouth beneath his own, silencing her with his kiss. He released her, pushed back a tendril of her honey-gold hair. "Nay, Anne, nay, you misjudge me. Had

I the chance, I would have sent you a bolt of satin and a flask of rosewater..." He tilted up her chin and gazed steadily into her eyes, "...but for your sake only, my little bird. To me you are more beautiful at this moment, with straw in your hair and soot on your nose, than you ever looked in all your father's velvets and jewels."

Anne bit her lips and sank against him. Forgetting dirt, fleas, and odour, she sobbed violently against his chest. He slipped her a silken handkerchief and she blew her nose noisily, letting loose a flood of emotion that she had buried until now. He held her tight. Gently, very gently, he stroked her hair until the sobs eased.

She turned her tear-stained face up to him, and smiled. "It seems you must still be rescuing me, Richard, as you used to do when we played as children on the grassy slopes of Middleham."

Wordlessly Richard removed his cloak and placed it around her shoulders. With a protective arm holding her close, his gaze locked with hers, he led her up the stairs, out of her prison.

Had they been aware, they would have seen that many an eye in that kitchen watched softly, some with wonder, some with tears.

~*~

From the house on Lombard Street, Richard placed Anne in Sanctuary at St. Martin-le-Grand. He would have preferred something more luxurious after the deprivations she had experienced, but he wanted a refuge that would protect her from George without putting her under obligation to himself.

"I bid you keep her safe for me, my lady Abbess," he said. "Much evil has been done her and she has suffered greatly. Those who are responsible are still about."

"Fear not, my lord Duke. No power dares touch Lady Anne here, lest they imperil their immortal soul."

Richard took Anne's hands gently into his own. "I leave you

now, my heart, but I'll be back tomorrow, and every day, until we wed and are together forever."

Anne glanced around the chapter house with its gently flaming candles. Parting filled her with fear. There had been so many partings, and so many times she'd thought herself safe only to be rent asunder again and tossed about on stormy seas. She grabbed his velvet doublet.

Richard lifted her hand to his lips and pressed a kiss on her callused palm. "My dearest love, I swear to you, no one—and nothing—will part us ever again. We shall be married. But first I must deal with Clarence…" He stopped. Like Edward, his reference to George by his title was a slip of the tongue that denoted the distance that had come between them. The George of his childhood was gone, replaced by a glowering, spiteful, deranged stranger who meant to have Anne's inheritance at any cost. Edward had indeed met George's demands for the Countess's lands, yet that had bought no peace, only ugly recriminations and more demands. Richard compressed his mouth. He had loved his brother dearly once, but betrayals had soured that love, faded those memories, and put an irrevocable distance between them despite their bond of blood.

At the door of the cloistered hall, Richard looked back. Anne stood with the Abbess, watching him. Tears glistened on her cheeks and her eyes were luminous with fear.

CHAPTER FORTY-ONE

"O King, for thou hast driven the foe without,
See to the foe within."

Richard spent Christmas of 1472 at Windsor with Edward, and that meant with the Woodvilles, who had bred their numbers past the point where they could be counted with ease. In the meantime, Anne remained in Sanctuary. In February Edward called a council meeting to hear the case between George and Richard, but the council reached no decision, for while Richard had right on his side, George had an eloquent tongue that could paint wrong into right.

March arrived, bringing the promise of spring along with the snow. Feasting replaced the Lenten fast, but Richard had no joy. George was still glowering and implacable, still adamant that Richard could have Anne only if he surrendered all claims to any estates. It had become clear that there was but one way to end the impasse.

As the last snows melted and crocuses peeked through the hard earth, Richard journeyed to Shene from his mother's residence at Baynard Castle in London, where he had moved to be close to Anne and farther from Woodvilles. He strode into the royal apartments, seeking his brother, but found the room unoccupied. The castle itself seemed half empty. Edward must have gone for a hunt, and his servants had sought their leisure in the meanwhile. He was about to leave when a voice exclaimed, "'Tis not right. I will not have it! The blood of my father and my brother wets his hands." It came from behind the closed door of the bedchamber.

"Hush, *ma fille*," soothed a familiar voice with a French accent. "Calm yourself. We shall have our vengeance, but you must be patient. You are great with child again—maybe another son. *Alors*, we shall be rid of George, it is written in the stars, but all in good time, eh?"

So the queen and her mother, the witch Jacquetta, were plotting against George. Richard froze, hatred and anger coursing in his veins.

"George is not only our enemy, but also Edward's," cried the Queen angrily. "Yet Edward always gives in to him."

"What was it you have told me Edward said once...? Ah, I have it—about the earldom of Northumberland. Hastings asked of Edward why did he take it from a faithful friend and give it to Percy, who was against him always. Edward laughed and said—*ecoute bien, ma fille*—he said, 'One need not to placate a friend. One need to placate an enemy.' *Alors,* it is the reason he has not endowed much to his brother Richard. Richard will always be loyal, whether he be endowed or not, eh? But George must keep to be won over..."

"Richard!" the Queen snarled. "I care not for him either, with his glum, disapproving eyes always watching me. How dare he judge me!"

Jacquetta gave a deep-throated chuckle. "What a jest of nature these two are brothers... One so wanton, the other so holy... One taller than the gods, fair, and charming, the other dark, so much shorter, and very dull. 'Tis funny, no?"

Bess must have smiled, for Jacquetta said, "That is better, *ma fille*. Now when Edward returns, you will be calm and lovable, as he likes you to be."

The clatter of horses drew Richard's attention to the window. Edward and Hastings were riding into the cobbled court and Edward was laughing in response to something Hastings had said. Judging from his expression, something lewd, Richard thought with a frown. From the royal bedroom came Jacquetta's voice. "Ah, 'tis the King."

"Fresh from another woman's bed," retorted the Queen in an icy tone. "Which he has no doubt shared with wanton Hastings."

"What care you?" said Jacquetta, so softly now that Richard

had to strain to hear. "You have all you desire and it was never him, but what he could give you—if you be truthful with yourself, *mon bijou.*"

"But I do care, *Maman!* Hastings stole the Captaincy of Calais from Anthony and I shall pay him back for that one day. Indeed I shall…"

"*Eh bien,* that day is not now. Let us hurry and make you beautiful for your husband."

Voices from the stairwell slapped Richard alert. He made a speedy exit from the chamber, nearly colliding with the queen's brother, Lionel, Bishop of Salisbury, and the bishop's entourage. Without pause for greeting, Richard mumbled an apology and heard Lionel hiss under his breath. The bishop's arrogant glance followed him down the narrow stone passageway. Richard reached the bottom of the inner stairs as Edward stepped inside, leaning heavily on Hasting's shoulder. While Hastings looked on, Edward shouted a drunken greeting to Richard and gave him a clumsy embrace. "Brother, dear brother—just the man I need to see!"

Richard noted with distaste that Will Hastings's florid complexion glowed from the recent pleasures he had enjoyed. "See about what, my lord?" demanded Richard.

"France," Edward mumbled. Still leaning on Hastings's shoulder, he turned into a vaulted room, seeking privacy from the servants and men-at-arms who were about. "That damned Louis…" Edward's eye was caught by a passing maidservant. "Alice!" he exclaimed. Falling on the girl, he extracted a long kiss. Richard averted his gaze. Had Edward no shame? He suppressed the disloyal thought. Hastings was to blame. He was Edward's advisor, and while he was not as self-seeking and unscrupulous as the Woodvilles, neither was he the kind of man to teach Edward wisdom and lead him into the path of righteousness.

Edward released the girl. Smiling and blushing, she smoothed her hair. Edward grinned. "You were exceptional the other night, my sweet." She laughed as she left. Edward winked at Richard. "Women like to hear that, even when you pay. In any case, 'tis good statesmanship, eh, Hastings?"

Hastings guffawed. Edward staggered to a chair. "Wine!" he roared to a servant. "Louis's to blame for everything, Dickon. He's a pesky gnat buzzing about my ears. I must swat him once and for all."

"You mean war with France?" demanded Richard.

"Aye, aye! He's tried to destroy me for years. Now he's inciting Scotland and Denmark against us! I must make war on Louis— 'tis the only road to peace. What say you, brother?"

"You've threatened to invade France before. You even received a grant from parliament for the campaign. Nothing came of it," replied Richard dryly. Nay, nothing. The money Edward raised on pretext of war had been spent on lavish living.

Edward slammed a fist on his armrest, suddenly quite sober. "Because Scotland accepted ten thousand crowns from Louis to attack our borders, that's why! It was no time to leave England. Things are different now. You've brought James of Scotland to heel, brother, so now I can deal with Louis."

True enough. James of Scotland had honoured the truce Richard had made in '71 and the border had remained quiet ever since—to Richard's great relief.

Servants brought in platters of beef pasties and a tray with wine and cups. Edward stuffed his mouth with the meat and downed the wine as Hastings ate his patty thoughtfully. Richard refused both. "What about money, is that a problem?" Richard said.

Edward laughed. "When has it not been, brother?"

"So it's true. The exchequer is empty and parliament in no mood to grant money for a campaign." Richard cast Edward a sideways look. Having been fooled once, parliament no longer trusted him. "What will you do?"

"There's no way around it, is there? I shall have to go to the people and beg—like a pauper!" Edward threw his wine cup against the wall.

Richard waited for the clatter to subside before broaching the subject that had brought him to Shene. "Edward... about George. I've reached a decision that should settle our problem."

Edward looked at him expectantly.

"So he shall have everything," said Edward when Richard was done. "The Countess's properties, the earldoms of Warwick and Salisbury. You wish only Middleham, Barnard's Castle, and Penrith. All else goes to him. You also surrender to him the office of Great Chamberlain of England, which he has not demanded... Is that right?"

Richard nodded.

"'Tis a remarkably bad bargain, dear brother."

"Nevertheless, I am agreed."

"You must love her very much."

When Richard made no reply, Edward said, "A pity that such love must wait."

Richard's eyes widened, fixed on his face. A server entered, bearing a flask and another goblet for Edward. He ignored the goblet and grabbed the flask. He drank deep and wiped his mouth with the back of his hand. "Dear brother, have you forgotten? You and Anne are cousins. You may not marry without a papal dispensation, and the Pope grows greedier as he greys."

Richard's heart sank. He had been so consumed with appeasing George, he had overlooked the obstacle of the Church. Before he could gather his thoughts, a derisive laugh made him turn. George entered, grinning broadly, his entourage crowding around him.

"Ah, Dickon, my poor brother," he clucked. "You seem damned whichever way you turn. Why don't you just give up and face reality? God Himself is against you..."

In one stride, Richard had him by the collar. "Watch me,

George," he hissed in his face. "I will marry Anne, and nothing you can do is going to stop me. As for God…" He pushed him aside contemptuously. "Take care, George, take great care. God hates traitors, and the way you're going… Well, let's just say I wouldn't want to stand in your shoes. You're going to meet a bad end, George. Mark my words."

He strode to the door, turned back. "And I will marry Anne. I'll bet your life on it, George."

CHAPTER FORTY-TWO

"And Arthur said, 'Behold, thy doom is mine.
Let chance what will, I love thee to the death.'"

At the Sanctuary of Martin-le-Grand, in the Abbess's parlour, a nun kept her eyes discreetly averted as Richard held Anne close in his arms.

"My sweet heart, all is settled with George. Now 'tis the Pope whose price must be met," he said, unable to suppress a trace of bitterness.

Anne pushed out of his embrace. "It's no use, Richard. We're thwarted at every turn… I've prayed much this past year and I've come to believe I should take the veil."

"No, Anne, I'll not hear of it!" He seized her arm.

She shook his hand off. "Richard, there's no chance for us. Can't you see? Heaven is against our union."

Richard froze for an instant, hearing Anne echo George's thought. He dismissed his unease. "What reason could there be, Anne? What difference could our union make in God's grand design? How could it help the world if we are denied our happiness? 'Tis folly you speak! You must not think it. I'll not listen." He cupped her chin in his hand and tilted her face so that she looked into his eyes. "I love you, Anne. I don't remember a time when I didn't love you. Without you there is no sun above, no light in the world, and no hope anywhere. If you take the veil, you condemn me to a life of emptiness. Is that what you want?"

Tears clouded Anne's vision, rolled down her cheeks. She gave a cry and sagged against him. His strong arms enfolded her tightly and she clung to him, feeling safe and protected as only Richard could protect her. It was when they were apart, in the loneliness of her tiny room, that such notions filled her head. Aye, why should Fate be against them? Maybe she was the problem, not Fate. She and her irrational fears, premonitions, and prophetic dreams.

She drew back, looked up at him shyly. "I gave you my heart a long time ago, Richard. For me, there's only you, and when we're together, all is well with the world. I won't take the veil, not until I know you are lost to me. But what hope is there?"

"There is a way we can wed, my love," he whispered. As pious as Anne was, he almost dared not speak the words. His eyes flicked to the nun in the corner of the room and back. "Marriages are made daily without dispensations. We could marry, then get one." He added quickly, "That way we wouldn't have to wait. But…" He bit his lip nervously. "But people would talk… Some might say I coerced you into marriage, or that it wasn't a true marriage and I married you only to divorce you later for your lands."

"I'm in Sanctuary. You can't coerce me. And I have no lands."

"That would make no difference… I know not what else they would say, but they'd find something. People always do."

Anne's gaze went over Richard's shoulder, to the Cross glittering over the hearth, and in her mind's eye arose a vision of a French queen's cold black marble tomb in an abbey in Caen. *Without dispensation…* The cousins William and Mathilde had risked eternal damnation to wed without dispensation, chancing that God would forgive them their sin. Could she do the same?

With Edouard there had been dispensation, but no love. With Richard there would be love, but no dispensation. Which was more important? The popes were God's earthly representatives, but they had human failings and erred despite divine guidance. But love… Love was balm for life's wounds, God's most precious gift to man. Surely He would forgive them if they followed Mathilde and William's example and made atonement as they had done, by founding an abbey, or performing some great good work. And even if He did not, could she give up Richard now—and the chance to snatch some happiness after all the grief?

"Love is worth everything we have to pay, Richard."

"Oh, my Anne, I didn't dare hope…" He turned swiftly and called out to the nun sitting at the far end of the room. "Sister Beatrice, will you kindly fetch the Abbess? Lady Anne is leaving immediately! She will no longer be requiring Sanctuary."

~*~

They were married by Archbishop Neville at the chapel in his exotic manor of The Moor in Hertfordshire. Anne's reunion with her uncle was bittersweet. Though Richard had tried to prepare her, she was shocked at the change in him. She had not seen him since before Barnet and could not accept that his once erect and bouncing walk should have slowed to such a stooped and plodding gait, and that he should be so drawn and weathered, with all semblance of youth wiped from his face. Richard had ached for her as she gazed on him. Time and troubles had indeed done their work. The flesh was melted around chin and jaw, and beneath his drooping lids the Archbishop's faded blue eyes spoke of remorse. That much was no surprise, thought Richard. Betrayal of one's brother was a heavy burden to bear and guilt had taken its toll.

After a light meal in the great hall, they followed the Archbishop into his chapel, and the marriage ceremony began.

"You may kiss the bride," said the Archbishop when it was over. His mouth curved gently, and from the friends gathered together came smiles and sighs of relief, sending a rustle of garments and clink of armour through the chapel. Sunlight streamed through a coloured glass window, drenching the stone floor in jewelled beauty like a Saracen carpet, and doves cooed on the snowy windowsill. Fountains splashed in the garden, a peacock screeched, and a dog ran barking, but these sounds came to Richard dimly, as if muted by a vast distance. So swiftly had events unfolded that he was somewhat incredulous that Anne was finally his. He gathered her into his arms and crushed his mouth to hers for their first kiss as man and wife. Still in a daze, he walked her to the gatehouse and waited for the groomsmen to bring their horses. The Archbishop made the sign of the Cross over them, murmured a blessing, and embraced them in farewell. Richard helped Anne into the saddle of his bay destrier, and mounted behind her. They waved to her uncle till he disappeared from sight.

"Now we go north, Flower-eyes," Richard said, covering her with his heavy woollen cloak to protect her from the cold March wind. Anne laid her head against his shoulder and watched the birds wheel in the blue sky, their song more ravishing than any she had heard before.

~*~

They stopped at Barnet. Anne wept silently and laid snowdrops and jonquils on the field. Holding her close, Richard led her into Hadley Church, where they bought masses for the souls of her father and uncle. After a prayerful vigil at the altar, they took their leave.

"Don't look back, dear Anne. No one can go forward if they keep looking back. 'In last year's nest, there are no eggs,'" Richard said. "Your Uncle John told me that, God assoil his soul." Anne glanced up at his face and caught the pain that darkened his grey eyes. She tightened her hold of his hand.

Their first night was spent in a little inn on the edge of the forest in Epping. Richard looked around the rush-strewn room at the wood-beamed walls, trestle bed, and rough-hewn chair. A fire crackled in the hearth. "'Tis not what I had in mind, but at least it's warm and all about us are well-wishers." Suddenly nervous, he added awkwardly, "I shall leave you for a few moments."

A rush of pink stained Anne's cheeks. A maid entered. The woman washed her with rosewater, helped her change into a linen shift, and perfumed her body with lavender. Anne climbed into bed and dismissed her shyly. The last time she had waited for a husband was in Bayeux. She drew the sheet up to her neck and shut her eyes against the memory of her humiliation. "I'd be a fool to get you with child," Edouard had sneered, ripping her shift open and leering at her, "but I did wish to see what I was missing." With a snicker he'd added, "Nothing but a bag of puny bones." That was how it had begun. *But not how it ended, not what brought the pain…*

She bit down hard. A fierce trembling seized her and her teeth began to chatter. They were still chattering when Richard returned. He checked her brow for fever. "Beloved! What is it? Are you not well? I'll send for a potion…" He turned to call for the maid, but Anne restrained him.

"'T-t-tis nothing a potion can m-mend… H-hold me, Richard," she stammered. He sat down on the bed, enfolded her gently in his arms. "Never l-leave me, Richard," she whispered against his sleeve.

"I'll never leave you, Flower-eyes," he soothed, pulling back to look at her. "But why this fit, dear one, what can ail…" He broke off with sudden realisation. *Edouard.* Edouard must have done something vile! Marguerite had extracted a pledge from Louis that her son's marriage not be consummated until Warwick had won England for Henry, and though Warwick had driven

Edward out for eight months, he had failed to secure the land for Lancaster. Until now, Richard had not allowed the thought to cross his mind that Anne might have lain with Edouard.

"Dear Anne," he said roughly beneath his breath, "I know not what you have suffered, but if the marriage bed brings you such pain, I will wait as long as it takes, my love."

Anne burst into tears and, clinging to him, sobbed against his chest.

~*~

All the way from Epping to Barnard's Castle, Anne rode pillion behind Richard. They avoided as much as possible the big cities, choosing instead to spend their nights in small towns. The skies were blue as crystal, squirrels chased one another around the trees budding for spring, and when they were lucky, deer darted out from the forests into their path. Happiness felt like a strange new gift, as if a hand had suddenly opened and thrown them a bouquet of sunbeams.

The sun was a fiery orange when they arrived at Barnard's Castle and wound their way up the hill to its white turreted walls. The townsfolk had turned out in force to welcome them, throwing white iris and narcissus over their small procession, and the mayor presented them with a silver chalice. Richard noted how softly the man's eyes rested on Warwick's daughter. Aye, Anne was finally home. As the servants went to work unloading their belongings and preparing their rooms, Richard led her up the tower steps to the ramparts. Twilight had descended and the sky was like a faded rose. The river thundered past, shining a molten silver in the dusk, while the wind swept the trees with a loud rustling and birds shrilled in their ears with the din of a flock of minstrels.

"The music of the North," Richard whispered, drawing Anne close and breathing deep the freshness of the air.

"My lord?"

"I first noticed it as a boy when I came up to Middleham. The North sings, Anne. It has a melody all its own. A rejoicing, exultant melody…" He began to hum. "Here would come the tabors… and here the flute and harp… and here the clash of cymbals…" He tapped out the rhythm on the rampart. "Can you not hear it?"

"Aye," she smiled. "My heart hears it, my love."

"Someday I shall write down the notes. It will be a song for lovers to sing with the birds… No, our song, Anne, to remind us always of this perfect moment."

"This perfect twilight… Aye, whatever the future holds for us—come what may—we shall sing it together and remember this twilight. But a pity we shan't hear the birds and see the twilight here again."

"What do you mean?"

"The hall at Barnard has no window to the view."

"Then there's no way about it, Flower-eyes, is there? We shall have to climb the ramparts each evening." Now he knew what his wedding gift to Anne would be. In the gathering dimness, her huge eyes were dark as pansies, and her hair, no longer the buttercup of childhood, caught the last rays of the dying sun and gleamed a rich honey-gold. He brushed his lips against her forehead. There was so much he wanted to give her.

"I wonder, dear wife, how your lady mother would feel about leaving Sanctuary?"

Anne turned wide eyes on him. "But George has made her a pauper. Where would she go?"

"Middleham."

Anne didn't follow for a moment, then she gave an audible gasp. "With us, my sweet lord? Oh, Richard, oh—my beloved, dear heart…" She threw her arms around his neck, happy tears wetting her cheeks.

That night the sky was black as velvet and a great moon shone like spun gold. Fireflies glinted in the forest, turning

304

darkness into fairyland. They slept with the windows open and the bed curtains drawn back. Moonlight flooded the chamber and a cool breeze drifted in, laden with the scent of pine, the sound of rushing water, and birdsong.

"The winter seemed so long this year, I had forgotten that birds sang at night," Anne said, snuggling drowsily in Richard's arms.

Richard lay stiffly on his back, wide awake. There was a choking in his chest and a burning in his loins that cried out for the release that only Anne could give him. But he dared not touch her lest he lose control. These past few days in her bed had been agony for him, to lie so close and remain so apart. He would have to confine himself to his own chamber at nights from now on. There was no other way.

"Even then, 'tis rare," he managed. "Only on magical nights, when their hearts are filled to bursting, do they sing in the dark."

Softly humming the tune he had named the Song of the North, Anne turned and kissed him full on the mouth. His heart leapt in his chest. Her arms and legs went about him, silken ropes that would bind him to her forever, and he tightened his hold of her, like a drowning man in a surging tide. His breath caught, his mind reeled, and he was swept along on the tide, now sinking, now buoyant, into utter darkness and into blinding light. He soared up into that light and for a moment he felt himself embraced by the sun, then the brilliance faded, and the tide ebbed. Peaceful and whole at last, he floated back gently to Anne's arms and the moonlit room.

CHAPTER FORTY-THREE

"And thou, put on your worst and meanest dress
And ride with me."

Reluctant to leave Barnard's Castle, Richard and Anne stayed until the month of May. During these days, it seemed to them that time stood still and they lived in a golden moment. Richard had many duties to attend to from early morning until Vespers, but afterwards they listened to the songs of troubadours and readings of poetry, and strolled among the flowers in the castle garden, laughing at nothing and whispering together as lovers had done since the beginning of time. And after the merriment and the soft moments, Richard would lead her by the hand into their bedchamber, where they bestowed on one another ineffable joy. Then Anne would snuggle into the curve of his body, and entwined in one another's arms, they would fall asleep to dream.

One morning soon after May Day, in the darkness before dawn, they lay quietly together, savouring the fragrant summer air drifting in through the open windows. Richard nuzzled the back of Anne's soft neck. She turned over thoughtfully. "Richard…"

"Mmm…" he murmured, cupping a hand over her breast, which had become temptingly exposed.

"Richard, let's dress as pilgrims and run away!"

"You're mad, my love," he murmured between nibbles, his hand roving further down her smooth body to her thigh.

"Humour me, Richard—it would only be for a day and a night," pleaded Anne, rising so suddenly from bed that Richard found himself kissing a pillow. She went to the window and stood for a moment, gazing out at the moonlight. She turned and looked at him with her great violet eyes. "Soon we have to leave this beautiful place—the chance may not come again.

Think, Richard, to be alone together a whole night, to make love in the forest and beneath the stars. To have a whole day with no one to petition us, no councillors to wrangle you, no secretaries to bring you flocks of papers to sign! Oh, Richard—I've been dreaming of it for weeks—just once in our lives let's do it so we can always remember."

Richard sat up at last, realising she was serious. "But I have pressing matters to attend. There are appointments to be made, grievances to be heard, funds to be allocated, my sweet."

What he said was true. Unable to trust George, unwilling to trust Percy, Edward had saddled Richard with burdensome responsibilities. In addition to his offices as Admiral of the Sea and Warden of the West Marches, he was Warden and Justice of the forests north of the Trent, High Steward of the Duchy of Lancaster, and even constable of several castles. Anne felt a moment's guilt, but quickly banished it. Richard worked hard from dawn to dusk and denied himself all pleasure. He desperately needed respite from the gruelling pace he set himself.

"There's no end to your pressing matters, Richard, but there may never be a night like this again. See, the sky is not black, it's purple." She sat down beside him and trailed her fingers along the rough, curling hairs of his broad chest. She pushed back a stray lock from his brow, and cooed seductively, "I promise you, you won't regret it… beneath the stars… in the tall grass…"

Richard rose with a laugh. "My little dove, I can't deny you anything. I don't know why I even try."

"I shall wear a grey kirtle!" Anne exclaimed, breathless with excitement. "Take off your jewels…" She grabbed his rings, threw them into the jewel casket, and did the same with her own. She lit a candle and ran with it to a chest against the wall near the garderobe. She rummaged about. "Here," she said, throwing him a coarse brown sackcloth and a scrip covered with cockleshells. "Put this on—and this…" she threw him a pair of worn leather sandals.

"Where ever did you get these, Anne?" Richard asked in disbelief.

"I've been collecting them, for just such a day. I had no doubt you'd consent." She peeked at him over her shoulder and smiled.

They tiptoed over the sleeping servants, and those who awoke were sworn to secrecy. Quietly they stole across the gravelly court of the Keep, down the steep stone steps to the stables of the Middle Ward. Leaving their best horses behind, they mounted a dull brown mare. With Anne riding pillion behind him, Richard clucked the animal out to the sally port. "Open!" he commanded.

"Who goes there?" demanded the burly gatekeeper. Richard slipped his hood back and the man bent down, peered at his face. "My lord Duke!" he exclaimed with astonishment.

"Hush, fellow! Someone might hear you..." Behind him, Anne giggled.

"Aye, Your Grace!" the gatekeeper announced loudly, and immediately apologetic, whispered, "Aye, Your Grace."

"If anyone inquires, tell them we won't be back till the morrow."

"But Your Grace..." the man blustered, summoning his courage. "You are alone. 'Tis not safe."

"Safe enough," Richard replied.

Reluctantly the gatekeeper cranked open the portcullis. Richard dug his spurs into the mare's flank, perhaps too harshly, for she tore off at a gallop along the Tees Bridge, nearly dropping her royal load. Below thundered the river, swirling rapidly. Hair and cloak flying, bouncing wildly on the saddle as they raced across, Anne clung to Richard, half-laughing, half-crying.

Once across the bridge, they flew north along the deserted river bank, past the darkened houses of Startforth on their small plots of vegetable gardens and fowl-runs, past stone cottages, past a manor house, past open pastures and large arable tracts of barley and rye. Across the silent hills, a rooster announced himself. Soon this herald of the new day was joined by bells chiming for Prime and a chorus of bleating, barking, and braying from stirring farm animals. Darkness yielded to dawn, staining the sky fierce orange and crimson. Abandoning the road where they might encounter passers-by, they galloped across rolling green pastures and meadows covered with wildflowers, leaving behind the gentle river valleys for the rugged upland of the Pennines.

At the crest of a hill the lathered mare came to a halt. A flock of sparrows soared in the sky, black silhouettes against the rising sun. Richard and Anne sat quietly, listening to their cries and watching the fiery ball of fire melt into gold. Richard glanced back at Anne, and they smiled at one another. He tightened his hold of her hands locked around his waist, and she laid her head on his shoulder with a sigh. He felt her breath warm and moist against his neck, and caught the scent of her lavender fragrance. The ache in his loins kindled by her nearness surged into heat, and blood coursed through his veins like an awakened river, sending his heart hammering. He flung himself from the saddle, swung her off the mare, and swept her roughly down into the thick clover. "Is this what you had in mind?" he whispered, hoarse with desire.

"Not exactly," Anne said with a mischievous smile. Between slow, shivery kisses, she undressed him and cast his pilgrim's sackcloth aside until he lay naked in the dewy greenness. Her hand seared a path down to his legs. Richard undid her bodice with trembling fingers and let his hand move under her skirt to skim her hips and thighs. She quivered as her flaming body arched towards his and their legs entwined. He kissed her savagely and her perfume of lavender assailed his nostrils. A cloud of lavender lifted him up, hurled him headlong into a rushing wind, and there was naught in that wind but lavender, naught in that sky but lavender, naught but lavender in all the world. Lavender and an ecstasy that bore him to the fringes of Heaven.

Blissful with fulfillment, Richard lay on his back in the clover, cradling Anne's head on his shoulder. Her eyelashes fluttered against his cheek. He kissed her brow. Never could he have imagined such rapture, such complete harmony. He gazed at the emerald hills, curving one behind the other as far as the eye could see, and up at the sky, which was now liquid gold. There was a piercing sweetness in the song of the birds and an intoxicating perfume to the wildflowers. God's music bathed the world with blinding splendour.

Anne stirred in his arms. "Come what may, we'll always have this moment, Richard."

"Come what may, beloved, I shall love you till the day I die," said Richard.

~*~

Richard and Anne frolicked all afternoon. When they grew hungry they picked berries, and to quench their thirst they drank from babbling brooks with water that sparkled like crystals. Anne gathered wildflowers and made Richard a garland to hang around his neck, and they played Hoodman's Bluff, the prize any favour the winner might demand. Richard lost no time winning. He chased Anne into the woods where he staked his claim, and they made love in a clearing beneath an elm. The woods smelled of earth, fern, and wet stone, and the heavy summer air was full of molten light. He carved their initials into the trunk of an elm, and as the day was warm, and the sun at its highest, they lay down together and soon fell asleep beneath the boughs.

Hours later, they awoke. The skies had darkened, and the wind had risen. A storm was brewing in the east. In all haste they set out to find a village for the night, but before they could leave the woods, they were caught in a drenching downpour.

"We'll find refuge," said Richard to comfort Anne, but in

truth he was deeply concerned. She was clad only in a thin kirtle and a light cloak that afforded little protection against the weather. They were somewhat sheltered under an oak, yet she was already shivering. He shielded her with his body as they waited, but the deluge gave no sign of subsiding, and it was growing dark. If they didn't hurry, they'd have no hope of finding shelter before nightfall. Now he cursed himself for coming without escort. Besides the weather, there was the added danger of outlaws, and he was ill-prepared to defend Anne from either. How could he have given so little thought to this excursion? He, who prided himself on his meticulous planning of every venture he undertook, no matter how small or insignificant. He, who had been faulted for too much painstaking attention to detail.

He nudged the mare forward. They rode out of the woods and climbed a hill, but there was no smoke rising above the trees, no sign of a village or an abbey, not even a cottage.

They were lost.

CHAPTER FORTY-FOUR

"O friend, I seek a harbourage for the night."

Night fell. Richard and Anne were drenched, cold, hungry, and tired to exhaustion when they came upon the miracle of the cottage. Richard dug his spurs into the mare. For the last hours she had set herself a plodding gait that she refused to quicken, but now she broke into a gallop, as if she herself recognised food and shelter. Richard pounded on the door and was greeted by a hound's fierce barking. It was cracked open, emitting the smell of boiling cabbage and a welcome blast of smoky warmth from a fire burning in the centre of an earthen floor. Richard's stomach growled and he was so taken with the thought of food that at first he failed to see the man who stood at the door.

He was about thirty with a tanned, weathered face, and he was clad in a long belted tunic of coarse homespun and leggings, fawn-coloured like his tunic, which were heavily patched. The growling hound he held by the collar was fighting for its freedom and seemed about to get the better of the contest. Richard withdrew a step before its gnashing jaws and instinctively pushed Anne behind him. At that moment a woman appeared at the man's shoulder, her cheeks apple-red beneath the brown shawl. Her anxious expression vanished as soon as her eyes alighted on them, and she broke into a wide, gap-toothed smile. Pushing her husband out of the way, she thrust the door open wide.

"Coom, children, coom in! Piers won't hurt ye; in truth he's gentle as a kitten, aren't ye, Piers?" She tapped the hound lightly on the head and he lifted an apologetic paw. With a firm hand, the woman drew Richard and Anne out of the rain. The couple introduced themselves as the Brechers. In turn, Richard gave Anne's name as Joan Peymarsh, who had been his nurse at Fotheringhay, and his own as Richard Peymarsh, her husband.

"O poor child…" the good wife clucked as she removed Anne's sopping cloak and laid it to dry by the fire. "Cock's bones, but y'er wet as a drowned kitten, ye are." She mopped Anne off as best she could with a piece of coarse linen and draped her shoulders with a patched wool blanket. "Now, my sweeting, that's better, nay? You'll be hungry, too, I warrant." She squeezed the towel out over the fire, which sizzled and sputtered a moment. "Here, sit ye down, children," she commanded, patting a pallet on the beaten earth floor. To her husband, she said, "Get their horse to shelter and give her some oats, and nay be slow about it, Brecher."

It was a two-room cottage with a timber frame, stone walls, and a thatched roof. A poultry perch was attached to one side

312

of the dwelling, and beyond that lay a horse's stall, from whence came an occasional braying. For the first time Richard and Anne noticed three sheep and a piglet curled up in a far shadowy corner on a bed of hay, watching them carefully. Richard noted with interest that the family had a trestle table and two coffers. Their possessions and the stone walls meant they were not poor peasants, but of some means. Freeholders, no doubt. A ladder led to the second floor, where two small sons slept, so the good wife informed them. In a bucket tucked in a corner was tossed woman's work: reeds for plaiting horse collars, a sheep-skin saddle, half stitched, and a few rushes waiting to be peeled for candles.

The door opened, admitting a sharp blast of rain and wind as the yeoman returned from caring for the mare. "Our thanks to you," murmured Anne gratefully. He nodded, took his place across from them. Sitting by the fire, warm and comfortable, a hot mug of ale in her hands, Anne began to relax. The good wife ladled cabbage soup into wooden bowls and passed it to them with bread. Anne ate slowly, sipping delicately, but Richard tore into his meal and soon accepted the offer of more.

"Lost are ye?" the goodwife said when they had eaten. "Where are ye from? Where are ye going? Mayhap we can help ye find yer way home."

Anne blushed. Richard replied, "We're pilgrims from Raby, on our way to Walsingham, and we prepared ill for weather. We're much indebted to you for your hospitality."

"Nay, nay," muttered the good woman. "'Tis naught, and you'll be welcome to it, such as it is. No doubt ye could use some mutton, to put meat on those little bones of yours, lass, but it'll be three more days before we'll be having flesh in this house again."

"I never touch flesh," Anne smiled, stroking the hound, who had abandoned his master's side for her. The hound turned over and offered his belly, which she scratched. Richard tickled his ears.

Suddenly there was a squeal and the piglet bounded over to them from the corner and lodged herself jealously in Anne's lap. She laughed. The man, who had been watching them as suspiciously as his sheep, softened his gaze and spoke for the first time. "Piers has never taken to strangers before, nor has Bessy. Ye must be good people." He leaned forward, addressed Richard. "Son, what think you of your new lord? He's married a Neville from your parts, so you must know more of him than us here. What can we expect?"

To the man's annoyance, it was his wife who answered. "Gloucester's a good lad, wants to set things right, so they say."

"If that be true, he has his work cut out for him," the man replied testily.

"How so?" inquired Richard.

"God's blood, fell off the moon, have ye?" the man exclaimed. "Ye've but to look around to see the corruption everywhere. All manner of thievery thrives, while honest men starve."

"We live alone and keep to ourselves, my wife and I," Richard replied. "We've managed to get by without trouble so far."

Anne almost burst out laughing at the enormity of the lie.

"Then ye be the only ones in Yorkshire. Take me, for example. I've had naught but trouble. 'Tis why I'm here, far from kin, and not in the West Country, where I belong."

"Why is that?" inquired Richard.

The sorry tale lost no time in the telling. The man had been married before, to one of two sisters, and in giving birth to a son, his young wife had died. Her father followed her to the grave soon thereafter, leaving a small inheritance of a farm and some sheep. By law the inheritance should have been split between the two sisters in the absence of a male heir, but law notwithstanding, the other sister's husband claimed the whole property. Brecher found no redress in court, for the husband had taken care to bribe the jurors.

"But that's not fair!" exclaimed Richard heatedly. The tale had struck too close to home.

"Son, life's not fair," the yeoman replied, regarding him indulgently. "Innocent men are imprisoned or hanged for crimes they didna' commit. Judges are corrupt and men perjure themselves for gain. Sometimes greed is nay what drives them, but desperation. We live in hard times. If a man owes money, and owns nothing, what is he to do?"

"Why didn't you seek higher justice?" demanded Richard, not to be put off.

Brecher gave a laugh. "Who from? The Marquess of Dorset?" Richard was silenced. "In truth, I did try," the man admitted after a pause. "I left my sheep many a time for Dorset's halls, but they were filled with the likes of me, and he was never there.

"You should have gone to the King."

"Simple, you are, friend. Don't ye know it costs money to petition the King? And who am I to get justice when my betters can't get it for themselves?"

"But king's justice is for everyone, like God's justice," said Richard, not about to give up.

"Bah! Words. God's justice never made much sense to me, and king's justice less. The world's a hard place, son, and there's no noble who cares more for us than for filling his own purse!"

His wife interrupted, "That's enough, Brecher. Don't ye see, he's just a young un'? No use spoilin' it for him. If he doesn't know now, he'll know soon enough. Forget yer troubles and drink. Things are nay so bad. We still have a roof over our heads and food to offer guests, don't we?"

Anne stole a long look at Richard over the rim of her mug. Richard's eyes held a faraway look, but when he caught her stare, he nodded imperceptibly and winked. They would make it up to these good people.

It was time for bed. The yeoman Brecher brought out some hemp-spun sheets, laid out hay, and put a few more twigs on the glowing fire before retiring upstairs to sleep.

Morning broke clear with the song of the birds, and Brecher pointed them the way south, to the river.

CHAPTER FORTY-FIVE

"Live pure, speak true, right wrong, follow the King—
Else wherefore born?"

In the middle of May, soon after Richard and Anne moved to Middleham, the Countess of Warwick arrived to a joyous reunion with her daughter. Richard had spared no expense on the Countess's apartment. The walls had been hung with damask, the floors tiled and decorated with carpets, and now the chamber afforded more light and a view of the surrounding hills through a lovely mullioned window.

The Countess had aged much, Richard thought as they embraced.

"Thank you, Your Grace," she said.

Richard noted her use of formal address. Was she unsure of his affection after all that had happened, or just showing deference to a superior lord? Aye, there was a strange irony in their changed circumstances that was not lost on him. Years ago he had come to Middleham fearful of the powerful Nevilles, bewildered and hurting, having lost a father; much as she came now, having lost a husband. The Wheel of Fortune had spun again.

"I am still Richard, my dear lady, and you are welcome," he said gently. "It would please me if I can make you as happy here as you once made me."

The Countess's eyes grew moist with emotion and she whispered softly, "My dear Lord Richard, your reward must come from God, for only He can grant the bounty that your kindness has surely earned you."

There followed many a picnic on the riverbanks and happy evenings in the great hall, with readings of poetry by the fireplace as in days gone by. Sometimes Richard would see the Countess glance to where her husband used to sit and dry a tear at the corner of her eye. Then he himself would remember the great Warwick and his valiant brother John, and would whisper a silent prayer for them in his heart.

During these months, Richard spent much of his time on matters concerning the Scots, where he had inherited John's mantle. Of all his offices, his most demanding was the wardenship of the West Marches. Despite the truce the border was often troubled by hostilities and raids. He worked hard to ensure that the frontier garrisons were properly manned, repaired, and victualled, and he spent much time conducting conferences on breaches of the truce. As steward of the duchy of Lancaster, he held official residence at Pontefract Castle, so he was often gone from Middleham to attend matters there. He missed Anne during these long absences, but he took comfort in performing his duty. A variety of business affairs were also brought to him at his castle of Sherriff Hutton, which lay close both to York and to the principal manors of Henry Percy, the Earl of Northumberland. Mindful of Percy's absence from Barnet, Edward had given Richard jurisdiction over him. Nevertheless, Richard took great pains not to offend the prickly lord, and consulted him often.

Such were the duties given him by Edward, and though he laboured hard to do his best for his king, it was not where his heart lay. It lay in dispensing justice to the poor. From that ride into the Durham dales was born an idea.

"It isn't fair, Anne," he said as they lay in bed together one night. The bed curtains were drawn back and the windows stood open so they could listen to the wind caress the trees, as was their custom.

Anne stirred in his arms. "What, Richard?"

"The Brechers, people like them. Justice should be for all, even the poor... I know we sent them enough gold to buy back the farm they lost in Dorset, but what troubles me is the larger issue—the evil that drove them from their land in the first place. There's no remedy for the poor when others abuse their authority. I must do what I can to right such wrongs." He felt her smile in the darkness.

"Like King Arthur, Richard?"

"Like my father, Anne," he corrected. "I have the power to do here in the North what my father did in Ireland." He turned on his side and propped his head on an elbow. He gazed at her face, faint in the moonlight. "I want people to live in peace, to enjoy their property, to know that no one—no matter how powerful he be—can rob or hurt them with impunity. I want them to know that if they get no justice in the courts, they can come to me, and I shall hear them, and right their wrongs."

As he spoke, Anne remembered the poor wretches who had worked with her in the kitchen on Lombard Street. She'd fled that nightmare because Richard had chosen to champion her. The poor had no champion, nothing, not even hope. *Until now.* "Richard," she murmured, taking his hand in the darkness and drawing close. "Richard, my love..."

~*~

At first it was only the helpless and the poor who came seeking Richard's justice, yeomen and peasants at the mercy of the baronage, or greedy landlords who found ways around the law. But as time passed, men of all classes sought his aid. His council developed from a court of appeal for the poor into a great judicial body called the Council of the North. Among the councillors who assisted him on his court of equity were other lords who shared his passion for justice: Francis Lovell, and the Lords

Greystoke and Scrope of Bolton, who had fought for Warwick against Edward but were now devoted to Richard. The Council of the North placed increased demands on Richard's time, leaving him little to spare, but during the tranquil autumn he managed to find three days for an important personal mission.

The countryside sparkled in its rich attire of wines and golds as Richard took Anne to Barnard's Castle to see her wedding gift, which was finally completed and ready to be unveiled. He made Anne close her eyes while he led her into the great hall and placed her in position. "Look, and tell me what you see," he said.

She opened her eyes and a gasp of awe escaped her lips. Stone, seven feet thick, had been chiselled away to make space for a magnificent, soaring oriel window. Situated directly in the centre of the great hall, it projected out to the cliff and overlooked the thundering River Tees and rich forests of larch and pine. An intricate boar insignia was carved into the stone below the window seat and sunshine poured through a border of coloured glass that displayed the Plantagenet and Neville coats of arms, spilling rainbows at her feet. From where she stood, she could see a sweeping panorama. Far in the distance, nestled in brilliant autumn colours, glimmered the arched stone footbridge that dated from Alfred's time, and beyond stretched orchards of glistening pears, and beyond even that, the undulating hills covered in heather. Over all this beauty hung the vast sky, splashed with vivid blue and white like a painter's palette.

As she stood spellbound, Richard flung open the windows. The sound of rushing water and the call of wild peacocks, wagtails, and wood pigeons burst into the room like song. Entranced, she moved to the window and inhaled deeply. The wind felt cool on her cheek, and the air was fresh and moist with the fragrance of fern, for there had been a rain shower earlier.

"Here we can sit in comfort, watch the twilight, and sing the Song of the North," Richard said as he smiled.

"Oh, Richard, my dear lord," she whispered. "And here, in the sunshine, I can sit and sew, amidst this beauty—why, 'tis like being by our chestnut in the woods..." She pushed away from the window and moved tenderly into his arms. "Tonight," she murmured with shining eyes, "you shall know my thanks."

~*~

During these months regular missives arrived from Edward, recounting the news from court. In May came news that Lord Howard had been made a Knight of the Garter on St. George's day, that the queen had given birth to another daughter in April, and that Bess's mother Jacquetta, the old Duchess of Bedford, had died. There was also news that the Earl of Oxford was making raids on Calais with the help of the Hansards and the backing of France, but that did not trouble Edward, who was devoting much of his leisure time to the chase, Archbishop Neville being a frequent companion in these royal hunting parties. This pleased the Countess, who smiled over her embroidery.

Only days later came news that was shocking and unpleasant. Late in April the Archbishop had been removed to the Tower, placed aboard a ship the next day, and sent to Calais. From there he had gone into imprisonment in the fortress of Hammes Castle, there to remain at the will of the King. Edward had seized his bishopric, made a crown out of the gems in his mitre, and given the Archbishop's other jewels to his son Edward, the Prince of Wales.

The Countess caught her breath, half-rose from her chair on trembling legs. "Of what is the Lord Archbishop accused?" she whispered.

"Of communication with the Earl of Oxford, my lady," said Richard.

"But Oxford is our brother-in-law!" exclaimed the Countess.

"He's also a bur in Edward's saddle. He's sworn to bring down the House of York and is financed by Louis and the Hansards to make raids on Calais."

"A crown out of a mitre—I see the queen's hand in this. Lord Richard, I beg you to help him. Hammes Castle, 'tis a harsh place—he cannot survive!"

Richard took her hand. "My lady, you know I'll do all I can."

~*~

At the King's call, Richard arrayed a small force in Yorkshire and led them south. The Earl of Oxford was a serious threat and Edward wished to be prepared. As he reached London, Oxford seized St. Michael's Mount and was seeking to rouse Cornwall against Edward. Richard found Edward in a foul temper at Westminster and in no mood to listen to entreaties on Archbishop Neville's behalf.

"Brother, I am done pardoning him! If I could put him to death, I would—Hammes shall do it for me, and good riddance to him. He has been a traitor and now he's a spy. He's fed Oxford information to help France. That infernal Louis has been using Oxford and the Hansards to make trouble for England, and Neville is in the thick of it all! As if that's not enough, he's been stirring George against me."

"George needs no stirring, Edward."

"True, true. But in any case Oxford now has one ally less without Neville. George is enough, by God! Oxford's seizure of St. Michael's Mount has encouraged him to array his men—against you, he claims—but I'm not deceived. 'Tis the crown he wants. He calls me bastard behind my back and gives out that I'm the son of an archer and he's rightfully king!" Edward up-ended a table, and a bowl clattered to the ground, sending a load of apples bobbing across the tiled floor. He threw himself into a chair, and bowed his head in his hands.

Richard rested a hand on his shoulder.

But Edward was fortunate. Neither Cornwall nor Louis responded to Oxford's call—Cornwall, because the people had had their fill of dying in battles, and Louis, because he was facing the threat of war from the Duke of Brittany. George, unwilling to commit himself to a lost cause, decided to wait matters out with his small force. Soon Oxford was forced to surrender for pardon of his life only. Edward sent him to Hammes Castle.

In the antechamber of his bedroom, Edward gave a laugh. "Let Oxford keep his friend the Archbishop company. Maybe they'll kill each other and save me much trouble!" He toasted Richard with a cup of wine and plopped a handful of green grapes into his mouth from a gilded bowl. He wiped his mouth with the back of his hand and grinned. "At least I'm not alone in my misery. Louis has his share of problems. Francis of Brittany claims Louis poisoned his brother Guienne and he threatens war." He chuckled, gave Richard a hearty slap on the back, and lowered his voice to a conspiratorial whisper. "'Tis my turn to have fun at Louis's expense—I shall send archers to help Brittany. Now, about George…" He took Richard by the shoulders. "He wishes the question of the division of lands to be reopened between you. This time shall be the last, I swear it, brother! This time I'll have Parliament ratify the agreement."

Richard closed his eyes. Was there no end to this strife? "I shall never give up Middleham," he said. Middleham was not merely his home; it was his refuge in this battering world of dissension and greed.

"You shall have more than Middleham, by God! That viper shall not seize all from you. I give you my word."

"Edward…"

"Aye, brother?"

"Archbishop Neville… will you release him into my keeping?"

"Your request," Edward said after a long pause, "will

be considered."

With that to comfort him, Richard returned to Middleham. And there, with Anne and the Countess, he spent a blessed Christmas.

Decorated with greenery, bouquets of dried flowers, pine-scented rushes, and hundreds of candles and tall burning tapers, Middleham Castle had never shone so festive and bright, not even in the days of Warwick the Kingmaker. For in those days there were still war troubles to touch them; now there was only George, and he seemed very far away this Christmas. Feasting, carols, mummery, and dancing filled the halls from snowy mornings to dark nights, and laughter rang louder than church bells. Richard and Anne were always together, hands clasped, for there was much joy to celebrate.

Anne was with child.

CHAPTER FORTY-SIX

*"The birds made
Melody on branch and melody in mid-air."*

All during the blessed months of her pregnancy, life unfolded for Anne like an heirloom tapestry lovingly stitched in jewel colours, detailing joyous intimacies and many a tender mercy. Friends came visiting bearing gifts and laughter. There was Francis, who journeyed from Minster Lovell, his home in Oxfordshire, and there were the lords Scrope of Bolton and Scrope of Masham, and Greystoke, who lived nearby and dropped in frequently. There was Richard's sister Liza, Duchess of Suffolk, and her ten-year-old son Johnnie, Earl of Lincoln, whom Richard nicknamed Jack and grilled fondly on poetry, for in Jack's veins ran the blood of Geoffrey Chaucer. On one occasion when young Jack gave the correct answer, Richard rewarded him with the prize of a hound, born to a litter sired by Percival, who had passed the years of strife safely within the walls of Middleham and now had reached the venerable age of ten.

There was one who came and brought a special joy: John's wife Isobel, Lady Montagu. She arrived hand-in-hand with her seven-year-old son George Neville, the little Duke of Bedford, and her eyes never left the boy. She had married again, as widows are obliged to do unless they take the veil, and had borne two more children in the intervening three years. Anne thought she looked too thin and a trifle weary, though Isobel assured her she was well enough.

But there was one who came not.

Anne had not seen Bella since that terrible night George had deposited Anne in the kitchen of the house on Lombard Street, and she felt her sister's continued absence keenly, like a rip in a perfect tapestry.

Sitting in the window of her solar in the early evening as she embroidered a blanket for her baby, Anne's needle hovered in the middle of a stitch. She missed Bella, especially now. There was so much to share. The blanket, which bore her baby's coat of arms of the Neville saltires and Richard's fleur-de-lis, could as well have been designed for Bella's son, two-year-old George, whom she'd never met. He, too, was half Neville and half Plantagenet, like her own unborn child. She swallowed on the knot that came to her throat and drove her needle and its load of scarlet through the velvet. The minstrel in the corner began a lullaby on his flute, and a tiny voice spoke in her head: *Don't let sorry thoughts blight your happiness—who knows what the future brings?* Servants appeared to light the tapers and brightness flooded the chamber. She cut the thread and knotted it firmly. "How do you like the blanket, my lord?" She glanced at Richard, poring over papers at his desk, and held it up for his inspection.

Richard lifted his head. Griffins and crosses, lilies and leopards, danced brightly across the white velvet in silvers, golds, and shades of reds and blues. Below Anne had embroidered his motto, *Loyaulte Me Lie*, Loyalty binds me, and the motto of the Nevilles, *Ne Vile Velis*. Wish nothing base.

"Splendid, my love."

"Can you not come and sit beside me?" Anne patted the wine silk cushion where she sat. She wished Richard didn't drive himself so hard. "The sunset is lovely."

"I must finish, dearest... To think tomorrow is the first of May—how time does pass! It seems we were only yesterday celebrating Christmas."

"And such a lovely Christmas it was. I never would have guessed there was so much happiness in the world."

Richard laid down his quill pen with a sigh. "If only there were not so much work."

"You've been up past Matins these three days. What's so important?"

Richard heaved a sigh and sank back in his chair. "Percy."

"I thought your troubles with him were over when you formed the Council of the North... He swore to recognise your superior authority, and I know you've been considerate with him. 'Tis not in your nature to be otherwise. So what can the matter be?"

"I try not to offend him, but there's still friction between us. He resents me. On occasion I've had to step in and reverse a decision he has made. As I am doing now..." His voice faded away wearily.

"Tell me," Anne pressed.

"The city of York discharged one of their clerks, and the man went to Percy, who reinstated him. The city appealed to me. I looked into the matter, and I had Edward's own lawyers examine the case as well. The man was abusive and incompetent. York was perfectly within its rights to dismiss him. I shall have to rule against Percy. Once again."

"Why would he resent it when the King's officers found for the city? Surely he does not intend to be unjust?"

"The Percys have been all-powerful in the North for a hundred years and don't take kindly to others clipping their wings, whether for right or not. Besides, justice is not to him what it is to me."

Anne laid down her needlework. Richard's qualms over Percy had touched her, but the pride she took in him had stirred her more deeply. She gazed at her husband, finding him better looking than ever before. Gone was the diffidence of childhood and the fear she used to see in his eyes. Gone the sad set of his mouth. His grey eyes had the sheen of purpose, and his skin, bronzed by wind and sun, no longer contrasted starkly with his dark hair. He had gained weight, so that his nose did not dominate his otherwise well-proportioned face, and the lines about his mouth and eyes, which had once etched his face with care, now served to mute his youth with strength. He exuded energy and princely authority in his red and gold doublet, and in spite of his present mood, there was a new contentment to him.

"I hope our babe is a boy, and is as handsome as you, and as clever, and as generous, and as brave, and as princely, and as good," she mused dreamily.

"I hope so, too," replied Richard. She stared at him in astonishment. Arrogance was unlike him. Then she saw his smile and they both burst into laughter. She pushed from her window seat with effort and waddled over to him slowly, for she was nine months with child. Standing behind his chair, she clasped her hands around his neck and laid her cheek to his.

"'Tis no mystery why I love you, Richard," she said, giving him a kiss on the cheek. "'Tis for all those virtues, and one in particular…" She gave him another on the tip of his nose. "You care for the poor and wretched who have no one to speak for them." As always when recounting Richard's virtues, she remembered George, who was as different from Richard as Cain from Abel. How Richard had turned out so opposite was a mystery she couldn't fathom, any more than she could count the drops of water in a well. "Of all the nobles, you're the only one willing to champion them, though they can offer you nothing in return. I know what they suffer. I've walked in their shoes, but you have not... So how is it you are as you are?"

Richard slid her carefully onto his lap. Though her body had become too unwieldy for comfort, her face was radiant in its beauty. Pregnancy had heightened her colour, and her cheeks, which had always been a touch pale, reflecting her frail health, now blushed with rose like a May morning. Her lips were the colour of berries, and her violet eyes shone with joy and blessed expectation. He placed an arm around her shoulder, the other on her stomach, where he might feel the baby kick.

"When I was a boy, I saw an innocent man hung..." He blinked to banish the painful memory that rose before him. "So when it falls in my power to help, I cannot turn away. Besides," he added on a brighter note, "I learned from your father, and John."

"If my uncle John were earl of Northumberland, you'd not be troubled so."

"He was a true knight."

"Much like you, Richard. You might have been born brothers."

Richard winced. "In many ways, we were."

"I never thanked you for what you did for his Isobel."

A silence fell. Richard stared into the blue twilight, his mind tumbling back to the first time he'd seen Lady Montagu after John's death. It was in August, nearly three years earlier, that Lady Montagu and John's squire had come to him in Bamborough on the Scots border. Richard had received his visitors in a tent and had been so swept with memory he had been unable to say much. The squire had knelt at his feet, and Lady Montagu had given Richard the ring he'd once given John. Her eyes were red with weeping, and emotion so threatened her composure the squire had to speak for her.

"My Lord Duke," George Gower had said, "on the eve of the battle of Barnet, my master gave me this ring and said I should take it to my lady if anything... if anything happened to him. He told me to have my lady bring you the ring... for you would understand."

In the light of the high lancet window, the sapphire had shone with the colour of John's eyes: deep and calm as the sea on a gentle day. Richard had a sudden vision of John sitting with him on the rocky cliff at Barnard's Castle, hugging his knees and smiling, his tawny-gold hair whipping in the wind, and again he'd heard him say, *"We younger sons... have no say in weighty matters..."*

"Dear lady," he had replied, "ask, and it shall be granted."

Richard came back to the present abruptly. He smoothed the folds of Anne's silk chamber gown around her swollen stomach and felt a small movement that might have been the baby. All Lady Montagu had requested was the wardship of her four-year-old son George. Now that his father was dead, the boy would have been granted to someone else for the few pounds of income he held in his own right. He took Anne's hand into his own. "Is your lady aunt happy in her new marriage?"

"Happy? Nay, my lord, she loved my lord uncle too much to be happy again, but Sir William Norris is a good man and kind to her. In that much, she is happy."

"At least she has made a splendid marriage for her daughter Lizzie. Lord Scrope of Masham is a fine man, and a wealthy one."

"He must have loved Lizzie very much, for he married her though she was penniless." Anne smiled meaningfully and moved to kiss him, and froze. A gasp of pain escaped her lips.

With Anne's weight in his arms and fear at his heart, Richard struggled up from the chair. "Is it time, my dearest?"

A hand to her back, Anne looked at him with frightened eyes. "It is, my lord."

CHAPTER FORTY-SEVEN

"And tho' she lay dark in the pool she knew
That all was bright, that all about were birds
Of sunny plume in gilded trellis-work."

Richard strode down the hall, creaked the door open, and went down the circular staircase and into the dark garden without realising he had moved. A light shone in Anne's room high in the round tower. He stared at the window, wondered why he was outside, turned on his heel, and went back.

In the torch-lit antechamber, the physician, a greyfriar with a silver and crystal rosary dangling from his waist, waited outside the birthing chamber, ready to advise the midwife. Through the door came screams so terrible Richard could scarcely bear the sound. His eyes flew to the friar's face.

The physician said kindly, "My Lord Duke, 'tis normal."

"But it has been hours!"

"'Tis always so. I pray you retire to the hall, my lord. We will send word when it's time."

Richard left reluctantly, with many a backward glance as he went down the passageway, and hesitated when he caught sight of the Countess's weary face leaving Anne's room. Anne wasn't visible but he glimpsed a tiring woman carrying away a basin of dark liquid that he knew was blood. The door closed. He slipped around a corner, sagged against the wall, and loosened his collar. He took a deep breath. Battle had not affected him so, when men stood with their bowels hanging out of their bellies, yet this…

The Countess did not see him as she passed. He leaned out and grabbed her arm. "How is my lady?"

She looked at him and bit her lip. Taking his elbow, she led him back around the corner. "The birth is difficult, my lord. She suffers much. I fear for her. She is delicate, as you know." She avoided his eyes. "The midwife says..."

"Aye?" Richard managed. "Aye?"

"The midwife says..." Her voice cracked. "She says she may not be able to save both child and mother... You will have to choose."

Richard felt as if a black wave rolled over him. "I—I—Anne..." he cried through parched lips, stumbling out towards Anne's room. The Countess seized his arm. "My dear lord, you cannot go in there!"

He turned wild, bewildered eyes on her. "Anne..."

"Anne is frail, and childbirth difficult. We must pray for her and the child. 'Tis all we can do."

He laid his forehead against the cold stone. The Countess rested a hand on his shoulder. "All unfolds according to His will," she said softly. "Therein must lay our strength." She pushed her crumpled handkerchief back into her sleeve and lifted her chin. "Now come, my lord, and take some rest. You have a decision to make."

~*~

Richard did not take long to give the Countess an answer. Anne must live. Without Anne, there was no light, no air, no warmth in the world. Without Anne, he could not go on. The night passed. Richard did not sleep. Day broke; rain fell; nothing changed. The hours passed in wretched anguish for Anne and the babe who would not be born. He rose from the altar in the chapel where he had knelt all afternoon and went to the window. A storm had blown in and rain pelted from the dark skies, drenching the castle grounds. Lightning struck nearby, and a moment later, the crash of thunder rattled the windowpanes. Church bells tolled: he counted five. Almost a full day had passed since the evening in the solar. It seemed so long ago. He wandered through the passageways of the Keep and took the bridge to the birthing chamber in the Round Tower.

Cries still drifted from the room, though weaker than before, and the greyfriar still waited, though now he drooped on a stool. The lady-in-waiting was the first to notice Richard. She curtsied. The physician rose. "My lord, I have instructed root of peony be crushed and mixed with oil of roses. The mixture applied to my lady's stomach eases pain," he explained gravely.

"How much longer?" demanded Richard.

The physician shook his head. "There is no knowing. Sometimes the birthing takes days."

"Days?"

The greyfriar omitted to add that in such cases where the birth dragged on for more than thirty hours, the babe was born dead. Longer than that, and infection was bound to set in and claim the mother. He looked at the Duke with pity, for many a beloved wife had faded out of this world with her babe just so, and physician though he was, and learned in the ways of medicines, potions, unguents, and the stars, often he had naught to do but sit outside their room until it was time to grant extreme unction.

"I must do something!" Richard cried.

"There is prayer, my lord," the friar replied.

As if to mark his words, church bells clanged nearby and were echoed across the distance. Aye, all over the North prayers were being said. All that could be done was being done.

"My Lord Duke, if it be solace, I have consulted the stars and they are not ill-omened. Saturn is in dangerous alignment, but Jupiter is favourable to her moon."

Richard inclined his head in a gesture of thanks. Anne had said that Heaven was against them. She was wrong. That, at least, was comfort.

~*~

Richard spent much of the evening in Anne's chamber, on his knees at her prie-dieu. At last sleep stole on his bleary eyes. He fell into bed and tossed by the dimness of a candle, seized by dreams that sent him bolt upright in his sleep. There was Ludlow, lit by burning crosses and grinning fiends who danced in their flames… There was George, his blue eyes contemptuous, tossing his flaxen curls, sneering, *Thou art not our father's son; thou art the son of an archer*… And there was the pale doomed face of Henry VI, holding up his silver crucifix, which grew until it blotted out all light behind it, while Henry smiled a secret smile. *Darkness will fall upon thee; I shall be avenged.*

"No!" Richard panted, twisting his head from side to side. "No!"

"My lord, my lord…"

Someone was shaking him. Richard opened his eyes and sat up dizzily. His gaze focused slowly. The face that bent over him was blurred and he could not tell whose it was.

"My lord," said his new squire, John Nesfield. "The Countess has sent me for you. 'Tis time."

Richard leapt from the bed, his heart in his throat. "What hour is it?" he mumbled thickly, pushing his hair back from his brow. He must have slept more soundly than he realised; he had heard no church bells.

"Almost daybreak, my lord," Nesfield replied.

Richard panicked. "My lady…?"

Nesfield shook his head. "I know nothing, my lord. A maidservant sent by the Countess bade me make haste and fetch you."

Richard leaned over the silver ewer on the sideboard. Nesfield picked up a pitcher of water and poured. The frigid water stung. Richard grabbed the towel Nesfield offered and briskly dried his head and neck. He felt much better, except for his legs, which refused to carry him and moved as unsteadily as a drunkard's. He grabbed Nesfield's shoulder, indicated he should lead the way, and stumbled after him. They reached the anteroom of Anne's birthing chamber. Her mother was waiting. Richard let go of Nesfield's shoulder and practically fell on the Countess. He searched her face, his heart in his throat.

"My lord Richard," she said. And smiled.

Joy exploded in his breast. "Anne!" He seized the Countess by the shoulders. "Anne will live!"

"It looks well for them. For them both..." Her smile widened, then slowly dimmed. "Only..."

Richard's heart began the fearful pounding again.

"She will be unable to bear more children, my lord."

So that was all! Richard's face split into a smile from ear to ear. "What more need I, when I have Anne and the babe?"

Beaming, the Countess thrust open the chamber door. Richard's eyes flew to Anne. She lay propped on a pile of satin pillows, a smile on her pale lips, a bundle of white cloth in her arms. "Anne!" He ran to her. Though she was pale and wan, she was smiling and her violet eyes looked up at him, wide and clear.

"Richard, behold your son," she whispered with pride. He followed the movement of her hand to the bundle in her arms.

He stood staring. Anne spoke again, but he barely heard her words, so awe-struck was he with the child. The babe made little sleeping movements with its tiny, crinkly red face. It had dark hair. He reached out and touched it gently, oh so gently, with the tip of a finger. It opened its eyes. They were dark, but whether blue or grey, he could not tell. The eyes stared at him with an unfocused sleepy depth in them. He fell to his knees and threw his arms across the two treasures of his life, feeling as though he floated in a golden light.

And indeed he did, for the sun had come up at that moment to fill the new day with glittering dawn. Doves, which had flown up from the dovecote, sat on the windowsill, cooing gently amid the ivy, and through the window thrown open to the garden drifted the fragrant scent of roses. Aware, yet unaware, Richard felt their touch, each and every one. As the notes of lute, lyre, harp, and rebec in the hands of genius combine into music of a nearly celestial order, so the notes of the morning fell on his heart, which was swept with almost holy bliss. Doubts, uncertainties, foul dreams fled, banished by love; a love augmented, holding twice its promise, flinging open its doors ever wider into a world blazing with hope and joy. Ignorant and blind sinner that he was, somehow he had managed to lose the darkness of the past and stumble into radiant light.

Anne's words filtered into his consciousness at last. *There won't be any more babes. Forgive me, my dearest love...* Richard gazed at her tenderly. "We may have only one child, but we will give him the love of ten, beloved Anne."

Anne turned to gaze at the babe in her arms, and as she did so, a flutter on the windowsill drew her attention to the departure of the doves. A raven stood on the sill they had abandoned, staring at her with hard yellow eyes, his ebony bulk blotting out the light. As abruptly as he had appeared, he flew off with a flap of his large black wings. A shadow passed across the room.

Her arms tightened around the infant she held. "And we shall keep him safe, Richard, won't we?" she whispered.

"With God's help," Richard replied, "we shall keep him safe."

— End of Book One —

AUTHOR'S NOTE

Much has been written about Richard III, and many readers are familiar with Shakespeare's portrayal of him as England's most reviled and villainous monarch. What is not as widely known is that Richard III gave us a body of laws that forms the foundation of modern Western society. His legacy includes bail, the presumption of innocence, protections in the jury system against bribery and tainted verdicts, and "Blind Justice"—the concept that all men should be seen as equal in the eyes of the law. He was the first king to proclaim his laws in English so that poor men could know their rights, and the first to raise a Jew to England's knighthood.

Such ideas were revolutionary in the fifteenth century. They alienated many in the nobility and the Church and played no small part in Richard's ultimate fate. Two hundred years later, when it was safe to do so, men questioned the traditional view of Richard bequeathed to them by the Tudors and found themselves unable to reconcile the justician with the villain, the man with the myth.

Two of Richard's most well known modern-day critics, Alison Weir and Desmond Seward, subscribe to Shakespeare's depiction of him as a hunchbacked serial killer. In his book *Royal Blood: Richard III and the Mystery of the Princes,* Bertram Fields, a prominent U.S. attorney and author, examines the school of thought represented by Weir and exposes the inconsistencies and deficiencies of the traditional view.

Richard III caught my imagination when I saw his portrait at the National Gallery, London. Then I read Josephine Tey's *The Daughter of Time.* This compelling mystery inspired me to consume whatever I could find on Richard and to make several research trips to England in search of the true Richard. It was in Paul Murray Kendall's *Richard the Third* that I finally found him.

Kendall, a professor of English Literature and Shakespearean scholar, provides a most convincing and illuminating portrayal of Richard and his times, and it is his interpretation of events that is reflected in this book.

While Shakespeare was a great dramatist, he never claimed to be an historian. In an age of torture and beheadings, he wrote to please the Tudors. The authority Shakespeare drew on was Sir Thomas More's *History of King Richard III*, a derisive account that More never finished, of the last Plantagenet king. An enduring mystery is why More broke off in mid-sentence and mid-dialogue to hide his manuscript. Fifteen years after his death, it was found by his nephew, translated from the Latin, and published. Had Sir Thomas More discovered the dangerous truth that the true villain was not Richard III but the first of the Tudors, Henry VII?

The question remains, and the debate continues.

For those who wish to know more about Richard's story as I have presented it, here are some brief notes.

It may come as a surprise to many readers that there were, indeed, vegetarians in the fifteenth century. This fact is documented by John Stowe in *Stowe's Survey of London,* which has been regarded as the prime authority on the history of London from its initial publication in 1598.[1] Richard's deformity appears to be a Tudor invention since history makes no mention of a hump, but does record that the Countess of Desmond, who danced with Richard at a banquet, commented on his good looks.

The window that Richard installed and embossed with his Boar insignia still stands at Barnard's Castle, gazing out over the magnificent view that may have changed little since Richard's day. Anne did disappear during the family feud between Richard and George, and she was disguised as a kitchen maid, although in whose kitchen has not been recorded. It is my cherished theory that perhaps this most romantic episode in their lives inspired Charles Perrault's *Cinderella* centuries later.

While it is commonly thought that Richard wed Anne in the Hall of Rufus, in view of the strained relationship with George and the fact that they were married without a papal dispensation, a formal state wedding seems unlikely. For that reason, I have taken Swallow's suggestion that they were married by Archbishop Neville in his manor.[2] No information exists, however, on the identity of the woman, or women, who might have borne Richard's two illegitimate children, and I have taken Rosemary Horrox's suggestion that it was Katherine Haute.[3]

The reader may also be interested to know that Senor de Gruthuyse's palace has survived in Bruges and is now a museum, and that the celebrations that marked Margaret of York's wedding to Charles the Bold in 1468 are re-enacted every summer between April and October in that charming medieval city.

John Neville's letter of farewell to his wife written on the eve of battle draws heavily from an actual letter written on July 14th, 1861 during the American Civil War by Major Sullivan Ballou to his wife Sarah. Major Ballou was killed at the first battle of Bull Run.

In closing, I wish to acknowledge that Francis Lovell is not known to have had a club foot, but several clues seem to suggest a disability of some kind. Here I beg the reader's indulgence, since a full explanation of my thesis cannot be provided until the third and last book of this series, *The Rose of York: Fall From Grace.*

Endnotes

1. *Stowe's Survey of London*, (Introduction by H.E. Wheatley); Everyman's Library, Dutton, New York; p. 415

2. Henry Swallow, *The House of Neville*, p.221. According to Swallow, Archbishop Neville officiated at the marriage of Anne to Richard. Had the marriage been a state wedding held in the Hall of Rufus, the Archbishop of Canterbury would have officiated.

3. Rosemary Horrox, *Richard III: A Study of Service*; Cambridge University Press, 1989; p.81